CYANIDE GAMES

ABOUT THE AUTHOR

Richard Beasley grew up in Adelaide, before moving to Sydney where he has worked as a barrister since 1997.

He is the author of three previous novels: *Hell Has Harbour Views* (which was adapted for ABC Television in 2005), *The Ambulance Chaser*, and *Me and Rory Macbeath*. The second Peter Tanner novel *The Burden of Lies* will be published in 2017.

RICHARD BEASLEY

CYANIDE GAMES

London · New York · Sydney · Toronto · New Delhi
A CBS COMPANY

CYANIDE GAMES: A PETER TANNER THRILLER
First published in Australia in 2016 by
Simon & Schuster (Australia) Pty Limited
Suite 19A, Level 1, Building C, 450 Miller Street, Cammeray, NSW 2062
This edition published in 2017

10 9 8 7 6 5 4 3 2 1

A CBS Company
Sydney New York London Toronto New Delhi
Visit our website at www.simonandschuster.com.au

National Library of Australia Cataloguing-in-Publication entry
Creator: Beasley, Richard, 1964-, author.
Title: Cyanide games: a Peter Tanner novel/Richard Beasley.
ISBN: 9781925368130 (paperback)
9781925368147 (ebook)
Subjects: Crime – Australia – Fiction.
Corporations – Corrupt practices – Australia – Fiction.
Dewey Number: A823.4

Cover design: Lewis Csizmazia
Cover image: Kiszou Pascal/Getty Images
Typeset by Midland Typesetters, Australia
Printed and bound in Australia by Griffin Press

The paper this book is printed on is certified against the Forest Stewardship Council® Standards. Griffin Press holds FSC chain of custody certification SGS-COC-005088. FSC promotes environmentally responsible, socially beneficial and economically viable management of the world's forests.

For Trish, Nic and James

PROLOGUE

She assumed the jet was company owned. Citadel Resources was in the top twenty of the *Fortune* Global 500 list of the world's largest companies; it owned mining and exploration projects in twenty-eight countries. And probably many jets.

Anne Warren knew Citadel's environmental and human rights record mirrored that of its competitors and was murky at best, but she had found ways of letting herself off what she knew was a moral hook – her work helped companies like Citadel at least mitigate their impact. She helped them be as 'green' as they could be.

The document she was given when she boarded the jet was headed *Confidentiality Agreement*. It had her name on it, her work address, and described her as a 'water consultant'. The counterparty was Citadel Resources. She read it quickly. Citadel sought to forbid her from discussing anything to do with the reasons for her travel to Tovosevu Island, or from saying anything about what work she might perform there. She was not allowed to reveal, unless compelled by law, that she'd even been to the island.

According to the next clause, she was to be forbidden from revealing the details of any work she'd performed for the company. It was as though she was to expunge Citadel Resources from her life.

The final section of the document was headed 'Penalties'. Should she breach any of her 'Confidentiality Obligations', she would be liable for liquidated damages of five hundred thousand dollars per breach, even if Citadel was unable to establish such damage in a court. Beyond that she had to indemnify Citadel for *any loss it suffers as a result, directly or indirectly, of any breach of the confidentiality obligations outlined above.*

'Would you mind signing that now?'

Warren's mind was still scrambling when the man standing next to her spoke, his soft voice deadened by the sound of the jet's engines being started. She looked up and saw an Asian man, perhaps late thirties, smiling faintly at her.

'Here,' he said, holding out a pen. She took it instinctively.

'I can't,' she said. She looked at the paper in her hands, then back at him.

The jet started to taxi, and the man placed his hand momentarily on the back of her seat to steady himself. 'Sorry,' he said. 'My name's Joe Cheung. I'm a lawyer for the company. You're . . . ?'

'Anne,' she said quickly. 'There's a problem with this. It has to be changed. I can't –'

'Anne,' he said, 'I'm not sure there's scope for negotiation.'

'You don't understand. I'm nearing the end of my PhD. Some of my research has been at Citadel mines.' She looked up at him, waiting for him to acknowledge he was following. 'Surely it can't be meant to cover –'

'It's okay,' he said, nodding like he understood. 'I'm sure it's only meant to cover what you're about to do, and where we're going now.'

'But that's not what it says. I need to speak to Martin. My boss, from GreenDay? Martin O'Brien? He's sitting at the back.'

The lawyer crouched down. 'Mr O'Brien has already signed one of these. I'm sure it will be okay. It's not my understanding that it's meant to cover what you're talking about.'

'That's not what it says,' she repeated. 'It covers everything.'

'Is there some problem?'

Anne looked at O'Brien as he joined them. 'Martin, this document,' she began, 'it's too wide. It –'

Joe Cheung held up a hand. 'Anne was just explaining about her PhD thesis,' Cheung said. 'I'll talk to Citadel.'

'I have to be able to –'

'Calm down, Anne,' O'Brien said. 'Think about it. If this was enforced strictly, we wouldn't be able to lodge an EIS with the government for Citadel. Don't get so literal with every–'

'I still don't think I should –'

'Anne, this isn't the place for –'

'– be forced to sign a document like this.'

'Anne,' the lawyer said calmly, 'I'm sure for your thesis, Citadel will give you a specific release from the obligations in this agreement.'

'Can't we just cut that clause out, then?'

'I've been told we can't take off unless everyone signs,' O'Brien said.

Cheung laughed slightly, and shook his head. 'That's a bit dramatic, Martin.' He turned back to Anne. 'Look, I'll sit down with one of the guys and talk to them. I'm sure I can sort something out to give you comfort. Hang on to it for now. I'll come back once we've taken off.'

He smiled at her and she nodded. O'Brien sighed, shook his head, and went back to his seat at the rear of the jet.

When he returned thirty minutes after take-off, Cheung said, 'I've spoken to one of the guys. There shouldn't be any problem with what you've done so far on your thesis.'

'Who are "the guys"?' He made them sound like a pop group.

Cheung smiled. 'They might need to check what you intend to cover. This thing though,' he said, pointing to the confidentiality agreement she still held in her hands, 'isn't intended to stop you using the work you've done on their other mines for your thesis. You'll just need permission.' He paused to look at her over the top of his glasses. She nodded slightly. 'Just sign it for now. When your thesis is done, Martin will get the all clear from Citadel. I'm sure there won't be a problem.' He smiled the kind of smile she assumed a lawyer gives when he's expecting a yes.

'So why then – ?'

'When your thesis is done,' Cheung said, 'Martin can call me. I'll liaise with Citadel for you.'

He handed her a card. Black embossed lettering. *Joseph Cheung. Bloomberg Butler Kelly. Partner, Mergers & Acquisitions/ Energy & Resources.* Her instincts still told her not to sign the document.

'If there's not going to be a problem about what I've done other than whatever it is on Tovosevu, can't we just cross out – ?'

'Anne, they aren't going to negotiate with you.'

'And if I don't sign it?'

'They're not anticipating that.'

'But . . . what would happen? Hypothetically?'

Cheung squatted. 'Can I give you the benefit of my experience?' he said softly. 'They're not that well acquainted with people saying no to them. Do you understand?'

She shook her head slowly. 'Actually, I don't.' There was anxiety in her voice, but also defiance.

'You really have to sign this.' His tone was calm, but firm.

She sighed and ran her hand through her short hair. 'I should have my own lawyer look at this.'

'Do you have a lawyer, Anne?'

The wry grin he gave her almost made her smile. 'I guess you guys would be out of my league, price-wise?'

He smiled. 'This is about Tovosevu, Anne. They're just being cautious. Sign it for now, then have Martin call me when your thesis is done.'

She didn't trust Citadel, though she felt she could trust this man, for no particularly rational reason other than he seemed trustworthy. He spoke like he was on her side. She wondered if it was an act, some lawyer's trick. He was, after all, Citadel's lawyer, not hers. But she needed her job. Making an enemy of Citadel wouldn't help her prospects.

She signed the document quickly.

'We'll mail you a copy,' Cheung said.

When they disembarked at the island's airstrip, they were driven to the mine site, and allocated worker's huts. Warren was shown to hers by a man dressed in khaki shorts and work boots, his shirt wet with sweat. 'Someone will get you soon,' he said.

She looked out of the window, and saw a square-shaped area about the size of two football fields, that had been cleared of trees. About two dozen army tents had been set up on the cut native grass. In the background, over the crest of a hill covered in shrubs through which a dirt road had been carved, was the mine she'd seen as they flew in to land. From above, it sat like a giant grey wound on the jungle floor. An enormous open cut pit, and the entrance to the underground workings.

Fifteen minutes later another worker knocked on her door. 'Miss Warren?'

'Anne.'

'I'm Greg,' he replied. An Australian accent, a touch of sunburn on his nose, a waspish blond beard. He looked not much more than twenty. 'Ready?'

'For what?'

'To go.'

'Where?'

He looked confused. 'To the river,' he then said.

There were four others in the jeep. Greg was the driver. In the passenger seat was an older man, in Citadel khaki attire, and a green floppy hat. He said his name was Ivan, and that he was the deputy mine manager. His neck glistened with sweat, and its thick band of fat swelled and rolled like the tide with the movements of his head. O'Brien sat next to her, looking tense, saying nothing. It was humid, thirty-two degrees Celsius. Someone had told her it was always thirty-two degrees on Tovosevu. Sometimes it rained, sometimes it didn't.

As they drove towards the gate of the workers' compound, a truck overtook them on the dirt road, swerving close as it went past. It was carrying twelve men in the back, sitting six a side on two benches, shaded by a canvas tarpaulin. The men had rifles. The truck pulled away from them on the unsealed road, a cloud of dust in its wake.

'Who are they?' Warren asked. No one answered. Ivan had put his window down when the truck went past, and the jeep's diesel engine was loud, so she wondered if she'd been heard.

'Who are – ?'

'Just security,' Ivan said.

'Security for what?'

'For the mine,' he replied.

'What does the mine need protection from?'

Again Ivan was slow to answer. 'Every mine in the world we have has security,' he eventually said.

'Where are they going?'

'Routine patrol.'

Tovosevu Island had five villages, and about three thousand native inhabitants. She knew that from the internet search she'd done. She wondered how dangerous they must be for such security. Citadel had a lease from the PNG government over the whole island. The terms of the lease were effectively a grant of sovereignty. Citadel controlled communications, who arrived and who left. As a condition of its mine approval, it had to fund a school and a medical centre. Almost everyone on the island worked for the company.

'The rifles,' she said. 'They look –'

Ivan laughed. 'They're private security, miss. They wouldn't be security without being armed.'

Because the window was down, she knew what had happened before they stopped. Greg pulled the vehicle as far off the unsealed road as he could. When the engine cut, she could hear the river, somewhere down at the bottom of a ravine to her right.

'We'll go down here,' Ivan said as he opened his door. He and Greg got out of the jeep.

'You can't smell that?' Warren said, looking at O'Brien. He shook his head. 'Anything now?' she said when they got out.

'Jungle,' O'Brien said. She saw him sniff though, and something registered on his face.

'Now?' she asked.

'Something burnt?'

'Something bitter,' she said, correcting him. 'Can you smell almonds?'

He looked down the green ravine. 'Perhaps,' he said.

'It's not almonds,' she said. 'It's cyanide.'

The affinity of gold for cyanide was the kind of chemical paradox that amused Anne Warren – the bond between wealth and death. Down the green slope, at the edge of the riverbank, there was death. Several fish had washed up near them, she saw others floating down stream. The smell was strong near the water; the spill recent. The toxic plume was still spreading down the river from somewhere.

'We had a breach of the main tailings dam,' Ivan said.

'A breach?'

'A wall collapse. Incredible rains the last few months – even into what's meant to be the dry months. No one could have predicted it.'

'What was the capacity?'

'We think maybe two hundred million litres,' he said.

'And the dam has been built near this river?'

'We need water to mine, miss.'

'How much tailing slurry has flowed into it?' she asked.

He shook his head, turned up his palms. 'The wall collapsed at night,' he said. 'Assume most of it.'

'Have any of the villagers been – ?'

'We're taking care of that.'

'They've been warned though, right? The cyanide is lethal. You'll need to truck in water or –'

'We're taking care of that, miss.'

She wanted to tell him to stop calling her 'miss'. 'I'm just saying –'

'There's going to be a thorough clean up,' Ivan said. 'We're doing it right now.'

Whatever part of the river the cyanide plume flowed through, the fish that swam in it would have died within minutes. But cyanide degrades quickly and she knew already what her test kits and lab results would reveal. Arsenic. Cadmium. Copper. Lead. In concentrations lethal to complex life. All much harder to remove than cyanide.

'You need to clean up the dead fish,' she said. 'If anyone or anything eats them –'

'As we understand it,' Ivan said, 'the cyanide will break down in –'

'The cyanide isn't the only problem. I assume you're taking steps to stop any flow into tributaries or aquifers? You're going to need to dredge a lot of the river, especially closest to the dam. Do you – I mean, this is a massive task, and in the meantime none of the villagers who use this river should be –'

'Miss, miss,' Ivan said, smiling. 'We have a lot of people working on all that. You have to focus on your tasks. We've picked out some spots for you to test the water and sediments.'

'I'll decide where I need to test.'

He gave her a crooked smile, and used his index finger to wipe some sweat from his moustache. 'Let's get started, then.'

It was forty hours since the spill. She tested the water, and took samples of the river sediment using a small boat, two hundred metres from where the tailings dam water had first flowed into the river, and at five hundred metre intervals downstream.

Warren knew that three of the island's five villages were on the river, downstream of where the contaminated water had flowed into it. She'd expected to be taken into the affected villages, to test the waters the people used, take samples of the nearby sediments, make sure that warnings were being given. She was told they could not go in.

'I need to test there,' she protested. 'It's crucial that I –'

'Things are sensitive,' Ivan said. 'We're trucking in water.'

'But if you explain we're only helping,' she said. 'I need to know –'

'We cannot go into any village,' Ivan said, closing the subject.

Warren surveyed the food carefully before selecting her meal. One of the cooks noticed her examining the fillets of barbecued fish that lay in tins on a trestle table with the other food.

'Mahi,' he said. 'Salt water, not from the river.' He smiled. Electric white teeth. She chose lamb.

She sat on a table on her own, before O'Brien and the lawyer joined her with their meals.

'Any particular reason you had to come here?' she asked Cheung after he sat down.

'What do you mean?'

'We could have signed the confidentiality forms at the airport, not midair.'

He smiled, but said nothing.

'What else are you doing?'

'Taking briefings,' he said.

'About what?'

'About what happened.'

'What's happening in the villages?'

'Anne,' O'Brien said curtly.

Cheung smiled. 'It's okay,' he said. 'I can't discuss that with you, Anne. You know, client privilege?'

'Seriously?'

He nodded. 'Seriously.'

'Did anyone die?' she asked, looking right at Cheung.

'Anne,' O'Brien said, anger in his whispered voice. 'No one has died.'

'How do you know?'

'The villagers were alerted straight away. There's water being –'

'Alerted in the middle of the night when no one knew what had happened?'

O'Brien stood up and put both hands on the trestle table, leaning towards her. 'No one died, Anne,' he said again.

'This is my fault,' Cheung said, looking at Warren. 'It all seems a bit cloak and dagger, with the confidentiality deed, and saying I can't answer your questions.' He paused for a moment. 'I've been assured that cleaning up is the number one priority, not gold or copper production.'

She noticed how cool he looked. She could feel wetness under her arms, and down the back of her legs. 'Joe,' she said, 'is this mine still meant to be using cyanide for extracting gold?'

'Yes,' he said casually.

'Is there a treatment plant?'

'There is.'

She nodded. 'When I got back from the river this afternoon,' she said slowly, 'I wanted to check something on the internet. I asked someone if I could use the wifi, but I was told I needed permission for the password. Can you give me that, or do I need to speak to someone from Citadel?'

'What did you want to look up?' Cheung asked.

'A map.'

'Of what?'

'The island.'

'Why?'

'There's a tributary of the river not far from the tailings dam. I saw it when we flew in.'

'That's not where the wall failed,' Cheung said.

'I saw a fence along both sides of it,' she said. 'Has the dam ever spilt into it?'

'I have no idea,' he said. 'This place is run in accordance with the government conditions imposed on it. That's always been my experience with this client.'

'Do the villagers have to sign a confidentiality deed too?'

Cheung laughed, shook his head. 'No one will be silenced, Anne.'

'Apart from us, you mean.'

'That's a temporary precaution. There's a report to prepare.'

'A temporary precaution?'

'Very normal in the circumstances.'

'This is normal? A cyanide spill?'

'That's not what I meant,' Cheung said. 'The way this event is being handled is normal.'

Warren laughed. 'This event?' she said. 'Are you a lawyer, or a PR consultant?'

He smiled. 'When your main clients are mining companies, you get to be a little of both.'

'Do the villagers have a lawyer?'

'For fuck's sake, Anne,' O'Brien said. Cheung said nothing.

'Have you been elsewhere for Citadel, Joe?' she asked. 'I mean, when there've been other "events"?' She made quote marks in the air.

Cheung picked up his glass and examined the precipitation on its surface. 'This is my first one,' he said.

In the report she drafted after she was flown back to Australia, she documented where each sample of river water and sediment had been taken. She prepared a chart outlining the heavy metal readings, comparing them to WHO guidelines. Cyanide readings were recorded separately. She'd been able to estimate where the plume had been most concentrated, mainly washing down the river's right bank, where the current appeared strongest.

She made recommendations for ongoing testing. Human testing was also required – blood tests for all, but especially for children, given what lead can do to development. Audits ought to be made of the gold extraction processes, and of the dam repairs under the Cyanide Management Code.

She emailed the draft report to O'Brien, to pass on to Citadel.

It was nearly eleven when her phone rang.

'I'm sorry to call late,' Joe Cheung said after giving his name.

'You've got my report already?'

'My client's confused,' he said. 'No one asked GreenDay for a written report.'

'It's what scientists do when we've been in the field.'

'It wasn't part of your brief.'

'How else – I don't understand. Unless there's a report – it's prepared to help them. So they know –'

'I'm not an expert on scientific protocols, Anne. I've been asked to remind you of your legal obligations.'

'I'm aware of them.'

'Have you discussed it with anyone beyond Martin?'

She hesitated. 'No.'

'Not even someone at GreenDay?'

'No.'

'Who typed it?'

She laughed. 'I did, Joe. We're not a big law firm. I don't have an assistant. When's this going to be made public, anyway?'

'I've only been asked to make sure you're abiding by your agreement.'

'I did some online searches about the mine,' she said. 'When Citadel bought it, the PNG government approved an expansion. They promised to build a new tailings dam and to stop using cyanide to extract the gold. That was five years ago.'

Cheung paused. 'You're mistaken. There's nothing in the conditions of mine approval that legally required that.'

Warren laughed sarcastically. 'Seriously? These things are optional?'

'I doubt Citadel see it as any of your concern.'

'Citadel has some applications for mine approvals here,' she said. 'We're doing some work on them. This delay with the report about what happened on –'

'Anne? Those aren't things I can discuss with you.' His tone was colder, final.

'Can I ask something else, then?' He didn't respond. 'You invited me to contact you,' she said. 'About my thesis. Do you remember?'

'Yes,' he said flatly.

She hesitated for a moment. She'd rehearsed raising this with him, but now struggled for the right form of words. 'When Citadel makes all this public, I'd like to include the work I've just done. Would you talk to them about that? I want to discuss the kind of readings you get in a watercourse from a spill like this. You know, the levels of heavy metals, how far they travel, how far the cyanide plume travelled. All in the context of a dam of that size.' She knew she'd started to talk too quickly, and paused to slow down. 'I'd like to do more testing later, to check the recovery rate of the river, and the effect of the rehab measures. I know I've got to wait until Citadel announces whatever it is –'

'Anne,' Cheung said, stopping her again, 'Citadel hasn't finalised the announcement it's going to make. It would be counter-productive for me to speak to anyone yet. It's not the right time for me to speak to anyone at Citadel for you. I'm making myself clear, aren't I?'

'Any idea when – ?'

'No, Anne, I don't,' he said. He sighed. 'I'm sure it won't be long.'

Anne Warren's second flight to Tovosevu, a week after Joe Cheung had called her, was not by Citadel jet – she was booked onto a commercial airline from Sydney to Port Moresby. From there, she flew by light aircraft to the island.

Dredging was under way near where the contamination had first flowed into the river. Engineers were working on a rebuild of the dam wall. The river no longer smelt like it had four weeks before.

'Well,' Ivan said, as she silently looked at a plastic vial full of water.

'Negative,' she said. It was what she'd expected. Natural degradation and evaporation had rid the waters of cyanides. The heavy metals would be another matter.

When her second round of tests were complete, she was flown

back to Port Moresby late in the afternoon. It was dusk when the plane landed. She wasn't flying back to Sydney until the following day, and Citadel had reserved her a room at the Grand Papua Hotel for the night.

A driver was waiting for her in the baggage hall of the terminal. He held a sign against his chest, a whiteboard with her name in black. He was shorter than her, a local man, with a black beard. He wore a baseball cap, faded red with old sweat stains at the front.

As she approached him, she said hello, and introduced herself. 'You're taking me to my hotel?'

He nodded, and walked off, leading her out of the terminal building. It was almost dark, and the car park was sparsely lit. It was half full, and under a small tree a group of women had set up some tables where they were selling trinkets – wooden bowls, scarves and other touristy offerings. Two of the women called out to her as they walked past. She waved shyly, said, 'No, thanks.'

Her driver had an ancient Honda, that had once been royal blue. The car smelt clean. There were hints of bleach. The man started the car, and music came on immediately, too loud until he turned it down. He revved the car, looking over his left shoulder and behind her to reverse. His eyes were black, the whites bloodshot. A stuffed toy caught her eye – a small yellow dog, wearing a red vest, hanging from the rear-vision mirror.

'Grand Papua,' the man said softly.

'Yes,' she replied.

They drove past a hotel two minutes from the car park. She wondered why Citadel hadn't booked her a room there.

The streetlights were on down the highway, some white, some smoky yellow. There were people walking along either side of the road, and a few children on bikes. She had a headache, and her left forearm itched. She'd scratched it on the fronds of a plant walking to the river the morning before. She put her fingers and thumbs in the sockets of her eyes and rubbed, trying to push the headache away.

They turned off the highway and drove down a road that was

less well lit, and turned off that onto another road, which had no streetlights or buildings. Soon after they made another turn, and the road was no longer sealed and there was dense greenery on either side. She'd never been to Port Moresby, and had no idea where the city was from the airport, and at first she thought he must have known some quicker route.

The taxi started to slow. 'I don't have any kina,' she said, for a reason she didn't fully understand. 'Just Aussie dollars.'

The driver didn't respond, but looked briefly in the rear-vision mirror. The headlights of the taxi flashed once. Up ahead, the headlights of another car, parked by the side of the road, flashed twice.

'Is this near the hotel?' she said. She knew it was not, but made herself ask. Her heart was beating hard, her stomach hollow, like it had vanished, leaving a void. She thought she would be sick.

The driver said nothing. He pulled the taxi over to the side of the road, in front of the other car. He turned the motor off, opened his door, got out and walked away. In the gloom she saw four figures approaching her.

They did not speak to her either.

PART ONE

1

Alejandro Alvares was standing outside courtroom 13A when Peter Tanner walked out of the lift. Alvares acknowledged Tanner with no more than the slightest raise of an eyebrow. He gave a flick of his dark brown hair, then sauntered to the far end of the corridor while talking softly into his mobile phone.

Tanner was appearing in the matter of *Director of Public Prosecutions (Commonwealth) v Tomas Alvares*, the Federal Prosecutor's appeal against a sentence that was said to be inadequate. Tomas Alvares was Alejandro's nephew. Eight months before, Tomas had copped a plea to a charge of possessing a large commercial quantity of an unlawfully imported controlled drug: he'd been apprehended with forty kilos of cocaine, which had a purity approaching seventy per cent, and a wholesale value of about eight million. On the streets, it could fetch over thirty million.

Tanner had appeared for the accused in the District Court, and had made submissions on sentence. He had taken the unusual step of calling Tomas to give evidence at his sentencing. He'd done this after the prosecutor had refused to agree to stipulate to facts that Tanner said his client should be judged on. Tomas's version of events was that finding forty kilos of coke was a complete surprise. Yes, he was a drug addict. And on the night of his arrest he was in need of a hit, which was what he thought he'd be getting. He told the judge that he had no idea who his dealer was. They met in public places, and the guy went by the name of Barry. Barry told him to go to the depot that night, bring a package of drugs to him, and he'd deal some out. It was just a favour. Tomas was expecting to collect a few hundred grams from the dude who worked at the depot, nothing like the amount they found.

Calling Tomas was high risk, high reward. The kid, though, was rat cunning. The police had no phone taps or evidence to prove him a liar. The sentencing judge gave him the benefit of the doubt on the underlying facts. He accepted Tomas wasn't a willing courier; he'd gone to collect more than a fix, but not forty kilos more. He gave Tomas a six year and six month sentence, with four years, four months non-parole. That was five years less than the prosecutor was willing to stomach.

For the sentencing hearing, Tanner had charged fifteen grand. When he still hadn't been paid two months later, he cancelled his invoice, and issued a new one for thirty. Two days later he got a cheque for the original fifteen.

When the appeal brief came and he sent it back, he got a phone call from Alejandro Alvares's personal assistant, asking why he was refusing to appear.

'Because you owe me fifteen thousand,' Tanner said.

'But the invoice for thirty was just a tactic, wasn't it?'

'Tactics are for the courtroom. Tell your boss he's fifteen short.'

'But you originally charged fifteen?'

'Then I didn't get paid for two months. And then I was driving in Maroubra, and I saw one of the monstrosities Alejandro has just built. There are probably a dozen young people living in that block of flats who are doing drugs he's imported into the country. And I decided then that my fee was thirty grand, not fifteen.'

There was a long pause on the other end of the line. 'Do you expect me to tell him that?'

For the appeal, Tanner said he wanted cash, paid up front.

When Alvares finished his phone call, he walked back from the far end of the corridor and handed Tanner a thick envelope.

'Is that all of it?' Tanner asked.

'Hello, Peter,' Alvares said. 'Nice to see you.'

'Is it?' Tanner had quoted twenty grand to do the appeal. It wasn't about the money. It was about Alvares not ripping him off.

'There's ten there. The balance is for after.'

Tanner threw the envelope in his barrister's bag, and looked at Alvares. 'Do I look like a banker to you?'

'Is this a trick question?'

'I don't look like your banker, Alejandro, because I'm not your fucking banker.'

'I'm aware of that, Peter.'

'I'm not in the business of lending money. Not to people as wealthy as you.'

'I just handed you ten thousand –'

'I'm not going to wait two months for the rest.'

'Peter, you seem to regard everything about my nephew's situation as coming down to money.' Alvares had a rich voice, his place of birth lurking at the back of it, along with a hint of menace when required.

Tanner nearly laughed. 'Alejandro,' he said, 'when I act for people like your nephew, trust me, it's *only* about the money.'

After the prosecutor finished his submissions, Tanner focused his on what the police didn't have.

'There's no evidence that Tomas Alvares contacted anyone about bringing the drugs into the country. The Commonwealth has nothing but unsubstantiated suspicion to suggest it wasn't as the judge below found it to be. That is, Mr Alvares had no idea on the night he was apprehended that he was potentially about to facilitate the distribution of a large quantity of cocaine.'

'I can't help but feel that's unlikely, Mr Tanner,' one of the judges said. 'As you say though, that mightn't be enough?'

'Your Honour's right – it's not enough. If this court has no more than doubts, then that doesn't entitle it to interfere with the sentencing judge's findings. The prosecutor complains about them but hasn't once made out anything that amounts to legal error.'

'It's a very lenient sentence, though, Mr Tanner, given the maximum is life imprisonment?'

'I wasn't aiming for the maximum, your Honour. And I don't accept "very". The sentencing judge took account both of the maximum penalty, and the street value of the drug. A lenient sentence shouldn't be increased on appeal unless some legal error is identified. The Commonwealth has to demonstrate the sentence is manifestly inadequate, not that another judge – or even your Honours – would have given a longer sentence.'

It took the court only twenty minutes' deliberation to dismiss the appeal. The sentence was light, but appealable error hadn't been made out. If he made parole, Tomas Alvares would be out in three and a half years.

When it was over, Alvares invited Tanner to join the family for a drink at his home. Making sure the devil got due process was the job; dancing afterwards wasn't. He said no, but Alvares insisted he at least give him a lift home.

Alvares had parked his Series 7 BMW illegally in Phillip Street outside the court complex. As they reached the car, he plucked off a parking ticket that had been attached to a wiper, then screwed it up and threw it in the gutter.

When Tanner sank into the passenger's seat of the BMW, he felt something hard jab into the base of his spine. He retrieved the largest hairbrush he'd ever seen. Thick black bristles amid white polymer pins on a mahogany frame embedded with jewels of some kind.

'Do you own a dressage horse, Alejandro?' Tanner asked.

Alvares looked at the brush, then pointed to the glove box. 'Put that in there,' he said. 'You were wrong, Peter,' he continued as the car pulled away from the kerb.

'Wrong about what?'

'You said they'd increase Tomas's sentence.'

'I said they could, not that they would.'

'You agree with the prosecutor? The sentence wasn't long enough?'

Tanner looked at Alvares. 'He got less than a year for every ten kilos. That's light.'

Alvares nodded. 'People are sick of lenient judges.'

'Really?' Tanner said flatly. 'Which people?'

'Everyone.'

'"Everyone" could be stretching the truth.'

'Decent people,' Alvares said. 'Civilised people.'

Tanner laughed. Tomas was the third drug case he'd been involved in that had a link to Alejandro Alvares. If even drug barons believed judges were too lenient, the shock jocks were doing a better job on 'law and order' than Tanner thought.

'Who are the civilised people losing sleep about lenient judges?'

'Most judges know nothing about the real world,' Alvares said. 'That's why they fall for sob stories.'

'You mean like Tomas's story?'

Alvares let out a long breath, then smiled. 'You think he was collecting those drugs for me, don't you?'

Tanner shook his head. 'It doesn't matter what I think.'

'I can assure you he was not.'

'That's very reassuring.'

'He's learnt a big lesson.'

'Four years in jail should teach you something.'

Alvares shook his head, and turned to look at Tanner as they stopped at a traffic light. 'He will never go behind my back again.'

'Behind your back?'

'That deceitful shit borrowed money from his father. My idiot brother dotes on the boy. Treated him like a prince from the day he was born.'

'What are you talking about?'

'You don't really think Tomas thought he was collecting a couple of hits that night, do you? This was a play into the game.' Alvares shook his head. 'He didn't get anywhere near long enough.'

Tanner glared at Alvares. 'Pull the car over.'

'What?'

'Pull the car over.'

'What's wrong?'

'Pull the fucking car over.'

They were next to St Mary's Cathedral on the way to William Street.

'Peter, I'm sure I don't know why you're –'

'Can I tell you something about the criminal justice system, Alejandro?' Tanner said.

'You're going to no matter what my wishes.'

'Occasionally it screws things up. Like giving your nephew less than five years when he should have got ten. But I don't want to be a knowing party to screwing the system myself. Do you get that?'

'You should calm down, Peter.'

'I told that judge last year that Tomas had no idea he'd be getting so much coke.'

'Keep your voice down, Peter.'

'And I told Tomas at the time, and I told you, that I found his story very hard to believe. But I ran with it, because he swore it was true. And you insisted it was too, Alejandro. Remember?'

'Well –'

'I know a lot of my clients are a pack of liars, Alejandro, but I don't need you confirming it.'

'You should get out, Peter.'

'If you're going to make me a vehicle for perjury Alejandro, don't fucking tell me about it after. Given that it's not fanciful to think the drug squad or the Feds might be bugging your car, can we agree on that?'

'What I was telling you –'

'The reason I'm getting out of your car, Alejandro,' Tanner said, opening the glove box and taking out the hairbrush, 'is that if I stay here, and you say one more word about lenient judges, or about how clever your nephew was in getting half the sentence he should have, I'll take this fucking hairbrush and hit you with it. Do you understand?'

Alvares gave him a patrician look of deep offence. Then it slipped from his face and was replaced by something darker. 'I would not recommend you doing that,' he said slowly.

Tanner smashed the hairbrush into the dashboard of the car. The brush cracked down the middle and three or four decorations flew off in various directions.

Tanner got out of the car carrying the brush. He threw it into the first bin he saw, like he was ridding himself of a murder weapon.

2

Tanner walked in his front door just after four. School was finished, and his son was home. Maria, their part-time housekeeper, was too. The house smelt of garlic. It always smelt of garlic. They went through three litres of milk a week and, it sometimes seemed, four litres of olive oil. The olive oil was from Andalusia. He suspected Maria was frugal satisfying her own needs, but not those of his son.

He found Dan in his bedroom, sitting in a red chair that folded out as a single bed for when he had a friend home for a sleep over. He was shoeless, in shorts and a T-shirt. His school clothes were littered around the room. Tanner often told Dan to put his clothes in the laundry basket. The boy would say yes, then wait for Maria to do it for him. Tanner would tell Maria not to pick up the clothes. She too would say '*Si*, yes, *si*.' Later, she would pick them up. The cycle would repeat.

Dan had his laptop open, resting on his thighs, and headphones on. Tanner walked over to the boy and pulled the headphones gently from his ears.

'Hi.'

'Hi, Dad.' Cool, but friendly enough.

'How was school?'

'Good.'

'Anything interesting happen?'

'Not really.'

'What did you do today?'

'The usual stuff.'

'How did you go?'

'Normal.'

He looked down at the boy, who was staring again at his screen, punching keys. 'Done your homework?'

'Most.'

'Walked the dog?'

'Later.'

'What are you doing on that thing?'

'Mathletics.'

'Looks like a game.'

'It is.'

'Finish your homework.'

'Sure,' the boy said, not listening. He looked up. 'Been in court?'

'Yeah.'

'Murder?'

Tanner smiled. 'People who retain me for murder don't usually plead guilty.'

'They expect you to get them off.'

'It's what I'm paid for.'

The boy nodded, and went back to his mathletics.

'I came close to needing my own lawyer this afternoon.'

'Why?'

'I considered killing my client's uncle.'

The boy looked up again, narrowed his eyes.

'I'm serious.'

'Why?'

'I wasn't told the truth, so neither was the court.'

'Can't you just dob them in?'

'That's not great for business.'

'How were you going to do it?'

'What?'

'Kill the guy?'

'With a hairbrush.'

'Dad.'

'I was going to beat him to death with it.'

'Sure.'

He had a strong desire to protect the boy's innocence, keep him young for as long as possible. He wondered sometimes why this was, and whether it meant anything. What was he clinging to himself, in wanting the boy to cling to his own youth, to defy puberty, adolescence, manhood? He wondered if it was something to do with Karen, her early death when Dan was just six. He didn't know, thought he should, but guessed such precision about himself was beyond him. He knew that other boys in Dan's class were allowed to watch MA movies, and play MA games on PlayStation or Xbox. They shot people, with terrifying guns. They blew them up. Tanner saw enough of the end results of real violence in court. When Dan was an adult, he could play those games, if that's how he caught his tricks.

He turned to leave the room.

'Why'd you let him live?'

Tanner shrugged. 'He's a good source of work.'

Tanner lay across his couch, a glass of red wine in one hand. He was thinking about the ways he could measure his ageing. His face had resisted most of the usual signs of reaching forty. The nervous energy he spent defending felons had stymied middle-aged spread. There was the odd grey hair now though amongst the dark, and some fine lines around his eyes. And he was becoming more and more conscious of the increasing speed of time.

The wine was a pinot. Karen had liked shiraz.

He had a small cellar under his kitchen full of shiraz that would never be drunk.

She'd been getting headaches for weeks. She had some nausea one morning, and the next. He was in the middle of a trial, and had paid little attention to her complaints. Then she told him, from a hospital bed, that she'd been looking at a patient's MRI earlier that day and had realised she didn't know what she was looking at, or looking for. She no longer knew what the differing shapes or contrasts meant. And, they told her later, that's when she'd had her first seizure.

The strangest thing, she'd told him, was that when she saw her own MRI, only hours after the seizure, she knew *exactly* what she was looking at. Glioblastoma multiforme. Left parietal lobe, almost certainly inoperable.

In the middle of their first discussion with her neurosurgeon, about radiotherapy and chemo, about time and its limits, about all the years that would not be left, Tanner's phone rang. He looked at the Caller ID. It was his clerk, no doubt ringing to check his availability for a trial for another malefactor who was proclaiming his innocence. He put the phone on silent.

'I hope you use earphones,' the surgeon said.

'What?'

'Electromagnetic radiation.'

'I didn't think there was any proof about a link,' Tanner said.

The surgeon shook his head. 'Trust me,' he said, 'heavy mobile phone use and brain tumours. Always on the side that the patient uses their phone. One day you guys are going to have a field day with a class action against the telecoms and phone makers.'

'I'm not that kind of lawyer.'

The surgeon nodded. 'What do you do?'

Tanner started to answer, stopped, looked at his wife. 'I help keep people out of government accommodation,' he said. 'For a fee.'

The surgeon smiled. 'Sounds lucrative.'

'Sometimes,' Tanner said. 'It's called capitalism. I think the medical profession understands how it works.' He felt his wife squeeze his hand. 'What caused Karen's cancer?'

The surgeon shook his head. 'I'd like to be able to tell you, but I can't.'

When the consultation was over, and they got back in their car, he read a text he'd been sent.

Can you do a bail application tomorrow week?

'What is it?' Karen asked.

'Nothing.'

'It's not nothing.'

'Nothing important,' he said.

She smiled at him softly. 'You're not going to be able to do that forever.'

'Do what?'

'Treat nothing as important unless it's my tumour.'

He pushed the ignition button. Karen turned the volume of the radio down, and kept looking at him.

'It's – I see now that it's not important,' he said.

She held her hand to his mouth, put her fingers over his lips. She was so damn calm. 'It could come quickly, Pete,' she said.

Before he could say anything, a horn sounded behind them. The car park was full, and someone was waiting for the space. The male driver looked ready to explode, his female passenger embarrassed. He opened his mouth to say something, then stopped himself.

'Don't get angry,' she said.

He looked at her, took a deep breath.

It did come quickly.

Another tumour grew. It was removed, but she developed an infection in her blood. It had to be treated intravenously in hospital, and her mind and body started to fail simultaneously. In the final week, the hospital staff put a foldaway bed in her room for him, but he often felt that part of him wasn't there. In the day, her room was full of people – family, friends, colleagues, old high school and med school classmates. Some were even strangers to him. Her sister put photos of Karen's life around the room. And most of the day, Tanner rarely spoke. He sat in a chair, or stood in a corner, like he was a ghost, removed from the others, watching the scene but not within it. Some of the time he felt numb, paralysed. Then he'd feel something like pity, but wasn't sure whom he was feeling it most for.

And when he wasn't feeling pity, or numb, his other state, which came in brief, occasional waves, was anger – rage so intense that he had to clench his jaws, grind his teeth to suppress it.

On the night before Karen died, Joe Cheung and his wife Melissa were among the last visitors to leave. Tanner and Cheung were the same age, and had been friends since law school. 'I'm not going to get to tell her I'm sorry,' Tanner whispered to his friend that night in the corridor outside Karen's room.

She'd had to forgive the way his mind wandered from their lives to clients, to the next trial, the next verdict. She'd had to forgive the way that he, the alpha lawyer, wore her down with clever argument, cut across her at dinner parties, finished her sentences, completed her stories, restricted her world to what she could see on an MRI or CT scan. He was so sorry for all that.

'Go back in the room, Pete, and hold her hand,' Joe Cheung had said. 'Tell her you're sorry now.'

At about midday on the day she died, Tanner's father came to the hospital. He was reluctant to go in her room first, and Tanner was reminded of his mother's death several years before. His father had loitered in the hospital corridor that day too, leaning against a wall, looking down at his feet. His parents had been divorced for many years, and rarely spoke.

'You can go in,' he said. 'Standing out here doesn't – just go in.'

He didn't stay long. Brief hellos to Karen's parents, short words of sympathy. He stood by the bed for a minute or two, and ran his hand lightly up and down Karen's forearm, before retreating again to the corridor.

'If you need a hand with Dan,' he said to Tanner when he joined him. 'Any time.'

Tanner nodded. 'Thanks,' he said softly.

'What about you?' his father said.

'What about me?'

His father looked at him, but didn't say more.

'I'm okay,' Tanner said.

Three days after Karen died, he opened a wardrobe door in their bedroom, and was almost shocked to see it was full of her clothes.

3

As he considered whether to have another glass of wine, Tanner's phone began to vibrate. He didn't look at the screen. A late call sometimes meant another lawyer hoping to get him to go to a police station for some very important client whose son had just been caught selling the latest party pill, or who was beginning to regret some alcohol-fuelled act of violence. But when it rang again he looked at the screen, and then answered quickly.

'Melissa?'

'Pete. I'm so sorry to call this late – I don't know who else to call.' She was fighting back tears, swallowing words.

Tanner sat up and put his wine glass on the coffee table. 'Take a deep breath,' he said. 'What's happened?'

In the silence as she composed herself, he wondered how long it had been since he'd seen her. Three months? Cheung was busy, or away half the time.

Tanner and Joe Cheung had met in law school. Cheung's parents were Chinese-Malaysian migrants. He and his father liked to gamble, and Tanner discovered he had that in common with them. They spent a lot of study time at racetracks and various betting parlours. Cheung still got first-class honours, and the University Medal. As a law student, Tanner was a handicapper, but Cheung was a Derby winner.

Cheung had similar success once he joined the firm that would soon become part of the Bloomberg Butler Kelly global network. He was a prodigious worker in a firm of workaholics. In his second year, he worked so hard on one transaction that he collapsed at his desk and spent the night in a ward in a public hospital. By then Tanner had started at the criminal bar. He visited Cheung the next morning after a mutual friend had told him what had happened. 'Having associates die from overwork is something all these big firms want to tell their clients,' were the first words Tanner said to him. 'I'm all for it, but I'd prefer it not to be you.'

They kept in touch throughout their careers, and after they married, although they moved in vastly different legal worlds. As the years passed, the demands of work and young children meant the times they caught up had gradually widened. When Karen became ill, Melissa brought around food she'd cooked for him and Dan. Eventually she helped Tanner's sister-in-law take care of Karen's clothes.

'It's Joe,' Melissa said, when she was composed enough to talk again. 'He's in China. He should have been back four days ago.'

'He's missing?'

'The consulate in Shanghai called me today.'

'And told you what?'

'They said he'd been detained. That's what they said they were told. I don't – we went to the airport to collect him. All of us – It's Tom's birthday. Joe was meant to be back for his birthday.' She started to cry, and Tanner waited while she regained control.

'What do you mean "detained"?'

'They said he's in custody. They're investigating him.'

'About what?'

'They don't know.'

'Where is he?'

'They don't know – somewhere in Shanghai. The Chinese won't tell them.'

'Melissa, stop for a moment,' he said. 'I'm going to ask you some questions, Okay? Because this sounds crazy.' He paused to collect his own thoughts as much as to allow her to compose herself. Joe Cheung getting caught up in any kind of trouble seemed insane. A mistake must have been made; some misunderstanding had to have occurred. 'When did he leave?' he asked.

'A week ago.'

'Why?'

'For work.'

'What work?'

'I don't know. We didn't discuss it.'

'He must have said something about why he was going?'

'I don't know the details, Pete. He said he had to explain something – a client was being difficult. They wanted to meet face to face, something like that.'

'A Chinese client?'

'Yes.'

'What does this client do? Did he say?'

'I really don't know. I didn't . . .'

Tanner thought quickly about the conversations they'd had about Cheung's work. When they talked shop it was usually about one of Tanner's trials, which Cheung said sounded far more interesting than his boring corporate work.

'Most of his clients are banks or mining companies, right?'

'I think so.'

'Was he there for one of them?'

'I don't know,' she insisted.

'When did you last talk to him?'

'Wednesday. He called before the kids went to bed.'

'In Shanghai?'

'Yes. It should have been his last night there. He was going to the office on Thursday, flying home Thursday evening. We were all at the airport to meet him Friday morning. I was going to drop the boys at school after we'd surprised him. He didn't come through customs. He hadn't rung me.'

'Go back to when he last called. Did he sound all right?'

'Fine.'

'Did he say he was in any trouble?'

'No.'

'Did he say anything unusual had happened?'

'No,' she said. 'Most of the call was talking to the kids anyway. I got about thirty seconds. He was in a taxi going back to his hotel. He'd been shopping.'

'Does he usually call before he catches a long flight?'

'Yes.'

'And he didn't this time?'

'No.'

'Did you try and get him?'

'I got voicemail, then nothing.'

'And when he didn't come out of customs at the airport?'

'I wondered if I'd made a mistake, or he was delayed – you know, had to take a different flight or fly with a different carrier.'

'Did you try calling him again?'

'Yes, yes,' she said. 'I got nothing.'

'Did you call his work?'

'I called his hotel first. They told me he'd checked out.'

'When?'

'The morning before. Which was what he told me he was going to do. Then I called Jen – she's Joe's new assistant. She didn't know what was happening. She said she'd call the Shanghai office as soon as it was eleven here. That's eight there.'

'Did she?'

'I don't know. Dennis called me.'

'Dennis?'

'Dennis Jackson,' she said. 'He's BBK's CEO.'

'What did he say?'

'He said he didn't know Joe had even gone,' she said, starting to cry again. 'He said don't worry, there had to be a simple explanation. He told me he'd call the Shanghai office too, and he'd call me back when he had some news.'

'Did he?'

'Yes, later that afternoon. He said Joe had been in the Shanghai office on Wednesday, but didn't show up Thursday, and didn't make his flight. That's all they knew.'

'Did – he must have said they would do something?'

'He told me to call Joe's parents and his brother and sister, and see if they'd heard from him. I wondered – Christ, he asked me – I'd been thinking it – he asked me if it was possible Joe could be with someone.'

'A woman?'

There was a long pause before she could answer. 'I told him no, that Joe – I told him no.'

'Did you call his parents?'

'I didn't want to alarm them. I just asked if they'd heard from Joe. They hadn't. And I forgot Dennis . . . Dennis said they'd call the consulate, and he'd get someone to contact the police. Then I got a call from the consulate.'

'Who called you?'

'His name's Jon.'

'What's his last – ?'

'I'm looking it up on my notes. Clarkson. Jonathan Clarkson.'

'What did he say?'

'He said they'd liaise with local officials, and the police.'

'And since then?'

'I keep ringing the firm, trying to get Dennis. His assistant called me back and said there was no news. The police had no information – the consular guy, Jon, he said the same thing at first. I kept saying a person can't just disappear into thin air. Then today.'

'Who called today?'

'Jon. He said the police had contacted them. They said Joe had been detained.'

'For what?'

'They won't say yet.'

'There had to be some reason given?'

'They haven't, Pete,' she said, raising her voice. 'Jon said for some offences, some investigations, they don't give reasons.

I don't know what it could be.' She burst into tears again, and was unable to talk for the moment.

'Did he tell you anything else?' Tanner asked when Melissa's sobs had subsided a little.

'He said he hoped there'd be some clarification in a few days.'

'That's it?'

'Yes.'

'But Joe . . . he hasn't been charged with anything, right?'

'They said he's under investigation. I kept telling Jon they must have given a reason, but they haven't. It has to be some kind of mistake, Pete. It has to be.'

She cried again, and Tanner waited until she was able to compose herself. 'And the consulate doesn't know where they're holding him?' he asked.

'Jon said it's likely to be a detention centre in Shanghai. He said he'd call as soon as they know.'

'Have you spoken to the firm since?'

'Dennis rang me tonight,' she said. 'I told him it has to be a mistake, Joe wouldn't deliberately do anything wrong. I asked what he was doing there, but he said he couldn't say.'

'Are they arranging a lawyer?'

'I don't – I should have asked that. He said they're trying to find out themselves why Joe's been detained.'

'I'll call him,' Tanner said. 'As soon as I hang up. I'll go see him tomorrow.'

'Would you? Please?'

'What about the consulate? When are you next due to speak to them?'

'Jon said he'd call me as soon as they're told something. I got upset . . . I know he's doing all he can. I told him – I don't know – I think I just started crying. It's killing me. That's why I called you.'

'Let me ring BBK for you. I'll call you in the morning.'

'Please . . . can you call me back tonight?' She gave Tanner Dennis Jackson's mobile number.

'If you don't hear from me, I haven't been able to reach him. What time does the consulate open our time?'

'Eleven thirty here. Will you ring Jon for me?'

'You ring him first, tell him I'm your lawyer.'

When he ended the call, Tanner got up from his couch and poured the rest of his wine down the sink. He dialled Jackson's number, but got voicemail. He left a message saying who he was, and asking to be called back no matter how late.

He went to bed well after midnight, and fell asleep at about two, without his call being returned.

4

Hendrik Richter sat behind the desk of his office and studied the press release. He held it in the fingers of his left hand. The hand had now seen many summers, and his skin was blemished and thin. He checked the time on his watch, like he had somewhere to go. His wrist was narrow, and appeared fragile, like the rest of him. That was an illusion, of sorts.

He looked to the man standing with his back to him, gazing out the window. 'Are you satisfied with this, Andre?' Richter asked. He spoke in a clipped, precise English. He'd lived in London for ten years before moving to Australia. The move to London had been made before Mandela was released.

Andre Visser turned his head. He nodded slightly, then returned his gaze to the water. Like Richter, Visser was from the Western Cape. A few years younger than the man who'd founded the company, Visser had been with Citadel Resources from the beginning, since the days of Richter & Co. Over the years, mines had been bought in the Americas, Australia, PNG, Indonesia, Mongolia, and in several African countries. Copper mines. Gold mines. Nickel. Silver. Alumina. Iron ore. Coal. The company had listed on the New York Stock Exchange, with a secondary listing in Hong Kong. Annual revenue had now reached more than two hundred and fifty billion. Market capitalisation was more than a hundred billion. Visser had stood down as CEO a few years ago, but remained on the board. He was still the right-hand man of the king.

'And the Chinese will be saying something soon, you say?'

Visser didn't turn this time. Out on the street forty floors below them, it was already thirty degrees, even though it was still early spring. It was going to be a hot summer. 'Hard to know for sure with them,' he said slowly. 'We think so.'

'This'll be released after that,' John Richter said. He had thick, dark brown hair that was combed back from the front, chiselled features, and big brown eyes, which occasionally gave him a slightly startled look. His suit and shoes were bespoke. He was deeply tanned. Everything about him screamed wealth.

Not for the first time, his father and Visser ignored what he said.

'When they make their statement,' Visser said, talking to the window, 'we'll put that out the following day.'

Hendrik Richter scanned the draft press release again, found the word he wanted, picked up his pen, and circled it. In the margin he put a large cross. 'How much do we pay our – what exactly are they? The PR people?' He didn't really want to know the answer, and no one responded. 'They wrote T, H, E, I, R,' he said, '"their have been no charges".' He dropped the paper onto his desk in front of him. 'Did you read it, Andre?'

Visser didn't turn his gaze from the blue water, but he smiled slightly. 'That's why I brought it to you, Hendrik,' he said. 'To fix the typographical errors.'

Hendrik looked again at his old confidant. 'It's not a typographical error,' he said. 'It's illiteracy. Thirty years ago, my mother would have made me fire the person who drafted this.'

'We'd be down seventy thousand employees under those standards.'

'I don't expect a mine worker to have mastered Strunk & White,' Richter said, 'just the people who draft our corporate literature. Surely they . . .' He gave a flick of his hand, but didn't bother to end the sentence.

Visser stifled a laugh. 'Literature might be a grand term for the work product of our message people.'

Richter looked at his son. 'You didn't draft this, did you, John?'

The younger Richter slowly shook his head.

For much of his life, Richter had called his son Jack; through prep school in the UK, and even through his senior years at an exclusive school on Sydney's North Shore. Then there was a party when his son was finishing university, some fancy-dress thing. Jack had gone wearing a toga. He was a Roman emperor. He took along his girlfriend, half a case of Krug, and thirty grams of cocaine. There was a misunderstanding over a dance the girlfriend had with another young man.

Even at school, John Richter had a reputation for violent outbursts. Once drugs and alcohol entered the scene, young John, heir to a billionaire, became known as someone not to cross. The week following the party, it cost Hendrik Richter a sizeable sum to resolve the misunderstanding. It was then that Andre Visser told his friend about his son's nickname: 'Jack the Richter'.

Hendrik Richter began calling his son John after that.

Richter was seventy-one, and in no hurry to retire. The new CEO they'd brought in would get five, maybe seven years at most. That was as long as anyone should be CEO of such a huge business, Richter believed. Maybe John would have matured by then.

Richter's daughter, Isla, had no interest in running the company. Mining wasn't sexy, only the vast fortune it provided. She was sharper than John, but her obsessions were Instagram and plastic surgery. He forgave her the latter; only the boy had inherited the best of both parents. Isla was, in truth, a pleasant-looking woman, but moved in circles where only drop-dead gorgeous would do.

Five to seven years, Richter thought. Then John might be ready.

'When are we lodging the development applications?' Richter asked. His son opened his document holder. Visser beat him to the answer.

'Close to Christmas,' he said. 'A day or two before.'

'Here and Queensland?'

'Yes.'

'How long for approval?'

Visser smiled softly, and finally turned to face his old boss. 'If it's only months, we'll all be happy. Within a year.'

'And the – ?'

'Every wheel that we can grease,' Visser said, 'is being greased.'

Richter nodded. 'And the gold mine here? Bageeyn River? I don't need to emphasise its importance to anyone, do I? With coal the way it is?'

Visser shrugged. 'You left that one with John, Hendrik.'

Richter turned his gaze to his son. 'Well?'

John Richter smiled. 'Every wheel that can be greased,' he said, 'is being greased.'

5

Bloomberg Butler Kelly's reception hall had a white tiled floor, white leather chairs and couches, and a white marble front desk. As he walked out of the lift, Tanner saw floor-to-ceiling windows, through which Sydney Harbour lurked between the buildings. To his left was a giant TV. Under it, built into the wall, was an enormous fish tank, containing tropical fish from the Barrier Reef. To his right was the receptionist. By some dystopian directive she too was in all white, her red lipstick vibrant against white skin. On the wall behind her, in lettering an optometrist could have used, was a list of all the firm's offices.

'Can I help you?' she asked.

'My name's Tanner,' he said. 'I'm here to see Dennis Jackson.'

For a short moment she looked surprised. 'Please take a seat,' she said, picking up the phone.

He walked over to the wall of glass instead and looked out. He'd never been able to conceive of a career in a place like BBK; he'd only ever seen himself in a courtroom. A few minutes later someone approached. He turned around, and saw a woman somewhere in her thirties, on the tallish side in the heels, wearing a blue skirt. She had on a matching jacket, from which the frills of her white blouse spilled like cream from a bun.

'Mr Tanner? I'm Helen Bishop, Mr Jackson's executive assistant.'

'I need to speak to him urgently,' he said. 'He knows why it's important.'

'He's very busy today,' she replied, 'but he's able –'

'We're all busy,' he said quickly. 'I called last night and again this morning. I'm surprised to have been ignored, given the circumstances.'

'What I was about to say is that Mr Jackson can give you ten minutes.'

He looked at her for a moment. 'That's very kind of him.'

She nodded. 'Mr Jackson's office is this way.' She walked to a door behind reception and used the security tag clipped to her waist to open it. 'After you.'

They walked down the corridor, past fishbowl offices on one side and cubicles on the other, to the north-west corner office, a fifty-square-metre glass box. The CEO was standing behind his desk, a phone to his ear. He didn't look at Tanner, just held up his hand to indicate no one was to enter yet.

Tanner looked at the nameplate on the door. DENNIS JACKSON, CEO, AUSTRALIA. 'Are any of you confused about who has this office?' he said.

'Everyone has a nameplate.'

He nodded and looked through the glass at Jackson, who'd now turned his back.

'I guess he doesn't want me to lip read what he's saying?'

'Can you?'

'It's handy to know what appellate judges are whispering to each other.'

She smiled.

'Everything looks new.'

'We've only been here a year.'

'Interesting building.'

'It's a Lund.'

'A Lund?'

'He's the architect. He's quite well known.'

'I'm sure.'

'The building is ultra-green.'

'What does that mean?'

'We have geothermal wells underneath us. They help with the heating in winter.'

'What self-respecting law firm doesn't have a geothermal well?'

She smiled again. 'The lifts are solar-power enhanced,' she said. 'That's what they tell us, anyway.'

'Do they get this high on a cloudy day?'

'Always,' she said.

'An ultra-green office tower full of the lawyers and bankers of the world's great polluters,' he said. 'Now that's ironic.'

She glared at him for a long moment. 'Mr Jackson is ready to see you now,' she then said.

Tanner's eyes shifted from Helen Bishop to Dennis Jackson, who made a slight gesture, ready to grant an audience.

'I understand you're a friend of Joe Cheung's,' Jackson said, holding out his hand. Tanner shook it and nodded. Jackson's grip was modest, his fingers almost unnaturally long. He was as tall as Tanner. A personal trainer was involved in the lean frame. 'I'm sorry I haven't been able to get back to you yet.'

'I'm a friend of Joe and Melissa's,' Tanner said. He noticed a bike leaning against the far wall in the left of the office.

Jackson smiled. 'Got it last week,' he said. 'I had a Cervélo before.'

'Did you,' Tanner said flatly.

'It's an American brand. They're more technologically advanced than the European bikes these days.'

Tanner looked at the bike again. He saw an upmarket pushbike, not something that could fly to the moon.

'A group of us here cycle three or four times a week.' Jackson walked over to his bike. He touched the handlebars as though Christ had ridden it. 'Cost me an arm and a leg. Carbon frame, Shimano brakes, the wheels are –'

'Dennis,' Tanner said, 'I'm not here to talk about the specifications of your bike.'

Jackson stopped smiling. 'You seemed interested.'

'I'm not. I'm here to talk about Joe Cheung, and I'm told you don't have much time.'

'That's right.'

'Then tell me what's happened.'

Jackson sat down behind his desk. The desktop was frosted glass, nothing on it but a computer screen, a keypad, and a solitary silver fountain pen. 'If you've spoken to Melissa,' he said, 'then I probably know less than you.'

'That surprises me.'

Jackson narrowed his eyes. They were dark, and too small for Tanner's liking. 'Who are you representing, exactly?' he asked. 'Joe?'

'Why not?'

'He hasn't retained a lawyer yet, as far as we know.'

'He's in a Chinese detention centre. They don't appear to be rushing to give him his phone call. I'm acting for Melissa.'

'I've told her what we know.'

'Tell me.'

'We've been told very little. Generalisations, no specifics.'

Tanner leant forwards. 'Whatever has happened,' he said, 'whatever is alleged, this is an almighty fuck up.'

Jackson shrugged barely perceptibly, but didn't respond.

'Dennis?'

'From what we've been told, it doesn't sound like they think they've made a mistake.'

'Who are "we" and "they"?'

'This firm. The Chinese. The state security bureau.'

'Is there a Chinese equivalent of Inspector Clouseau? Who have you been speaking to?'

'People in our Shanghai office.'

'Who in those offices?'

'We have contacts in the government. I can't –'

'And what have the people with contacts in the government been told about Joe?'

'There have been no charges laid yet.'

'I didn't ask that. They're obviously interrogating him about something. What?'

'They suspect corrupt conduct. That's what we've been told.'

'Joe's not corrupt,' Tanner snapped. He looked at Jackson for a long moment.

Jackson shrugged. 'It's what we've been told.'

'Corruption in relation to what?'

'I don't know.'

'What was he doing in Shanghai?'

'I can't tell you that.'

'Why?'

'It's privileged.'

'Jesus,' Tanner said, raising his voice. 'Is that what you expect me to tell Melissa?'

Jackson squeezed his chin with his thumb and forefinger, some kind of nervous tic. 'This doesn't leave this room.'

Tanner shook his head. 'I have to be able to speak to Melissa about what we discuss. I'm not going to tell anyone else.'

'I know how Melissa must be feeling, but I can't –'

'You haven't got a clue how she's feeling.'

'This involves a client, Peter. A global client. It's sensitive. It could be extremely damaging.'

'She's not going to start spreading rumours about her husband's alleged corruption.'

Jackson poured himself a glass of water from the platinum jug on the edge of his desk, but offered Tanner nothing. 'It involves an exploration licence.'

'For what?'

'Coal and CSG.'

'Whose licence?'

'A client's.'

'Which client?'

Jackson laughed sarcastically. 'You know I can't tell you that.'

'There aren't that many global mining clients. Which one?'

Jackson stared at Tanner and shook his head slowly.

'What corruption?'

Jackson took a deep breath, and then sighed. 'It's being said that Joe tried to sell information about what our client would bid for this licence when the government put it up for tender.'

'Who did he try and sell this information to?'

'Another Chinese company, we think.'

'When was this meant to have happened?'

'When the government put the licence up for tender. About three years ago.'

Tanner paused. 'Joe would not do that,' he said firmly.

Jackson leant back in his chair. He looked at Tanner like he was a child. 'How well do you know Joe Cheung, Peter?'

'What the fuck does that mean?'

'I'm only –'

'I've known him since law school,' Tanner said. 'He wouldn't do that.'

'I'm only repeating an allegation.'

'Where's the licence area?' Tanner asked.

'This state.'

'This firm acted on the bid?'

Jackson shook his head. 'I can't discuss client business with you.'

'It was a public tender?'

'I think a few of the bigger mining companies were invited by the government to tender.'

'How is this only coming to light now after three years?'

'I've said more than I should.' Jackson took another sip of water and put the glass down firmly. 'I've got another meeting, Peter.'

'How much does Joe earn?'

'What?'

'He's a full-equity partner, right? What does that mean in a place like this? One point five mil? More?'

'You think that makes him incorruptible?'

'He's not a criminal,' Tanner said sharply.

Jackson stood and retrieved his jacket from a cupboard in the corner of the room. He put it on, then tugged aggressively at each French cuff of his shirt to make things perfect. The guy was anal. He wouldn't like mess. Joe Cheung had somehow made one. He put his hand on the door. 'Helen will walk you out.'

'What are you doing to help him?'

'There's not much we can do at the moment. Not until we know more. The embassy and consulate are –'

'How about finding out where he is? Talk to the consulate, find out when you can see him, and when his family can. This firm has powerful contacts in China, doesn't it? Find out what evidence they're holding him on. And I assume you're getting him a lawyer?'

Jackson dropped his hand from the door handle. 'Peter, you're being a bit naive for a criminal lawyer. This is China. They do things differently. We'll be told where he is and why he's there when they want to tell us. And if you listened to what I've told you about what we're hearing, this firm could find itself in a very embarrassing position. One that creates a big conflict with taking care of Joe's interests.'

'What conflict?'

'The conflict you get between a big client and one of your partners who's alleged to have committed a crime that could have harmed that client enormously.'

'He's your partner, Dennis,' Tanner said. 'It's people like Joe who help pay your mortgage. And for that fucking bike over there. What are you proposing to do to help him?'

'When we find out exactly what –'

'Dennis, you're obliged to provide assistance to him. You need to get him a local lawyer. A good one.'

'If you let me finish. When we find out –'

'You can't leave him high and dry because of some crazy allegation –'

'An allegation made concerning a major client of ours.'

Tanner stood up, put his own hand on the door handle and opened it. 'You need to help him.'

'We need to find out what we're dealing with first.'

'I'm sure there are some lawyers here who aren't entirely honest, Dennis,' Tanner said. 'Joe isn't one of them.'

As he walked into the lobby, Tanner rang BBK's reception from his mobile phone.

'I need to speak to Nadine Jenkins, please,' he said when the switch operator answered.

There was a pause. 'Do you mean Nadine Bellouard?'

Tanner thought for a moment. 'I guess I do.'

A few moments later a familiar voice answered the phone. 'Mr Gault's office.'

'Nadine?''

'Yes.'

'It's Pete Tanner.'

There was a slight pause before she spoke. 'Pete . . . is this about – ?'

'What do you know?' he asked.

'Nothing. I mean – there's all kinds of rumours. What's happened?'

'I'm heading to the coffee shop in the lower level of your building. Can you get away for a few minutes?'

'Give me five,' she said, and hung up.

She looked older than when he'd last seen her. Maybe it was the shorter hair. It occurred to him how few times he'd actually seen her, despite the many times they'd spoken. She looked anxious, on the verge of tears. He was going to shake her hand, but she grabbed him and hugged him. She smelt of flowers, potpourri.

'Do you want a coffee?' he asked as they sat.

She tried to smile. 'Just water please.' Tanner mouthed the order to a waitress behind the counter.

'What are people saying?'

She looked at him for a moment. 'Joe was meant to be back at work days ago,' she said. 'Melissa rang Jenny from the airport – no one knew where he was . . . I rang Melissa. She told me –'

'When did you ring Melissa?'

'This morning. She told me that Joe's been arrested for some reason.'

'What reason?'

She shook her head. 'No one knows. Or if they do, they're not telling staff.'

'You know as much as me then,' Tanner said. 'I just came from a meeting with Dennis Jackson.'

'Doesn't he know?'

Tanner shook his head, thinking it best not to pass on everything Jackson had said. 'Not yet.'

'Joe wouldn't have done anything illegal.'

'I know.'

'When are we going to know more? They can't just – they can't just keep him, can they?'

'It's China,' he said. 'Melissa told me the consulate is trying to find out.'

Nadine nodded, and took a sip of her water.

'Do you know why he was in China?' he asked.

'Not really,' she said.

'Not really?'

'He had a meeting. That's all we know.'

'When you say "we", you mean . . . ?'

'Jenny – his new admin. She doesn't know all the details. He had a meeting in Shanghai with someone. He didn't tell her who. The trip was being billed to Citadel, though.'

'Citadel Resources?'

She nodded. 'He emailed audio files of his time while he was away.'

Nadine had been Cheung's assistant for many years. Most times Tanner had called Joe's direct line, she'd answered the phone. She was French-Mauritian – her name was Nadine Bellouard when she'd started with Joe before her marriage. She had a lively sense of humour, and a loud laugh. Occasionally, before everyone was married, she came with Joe if he met Tanner and others for a drink after work. She and Joe were close. Joe went to her wedding; she came to his. Then she had kids, and was off work for several years. When she came back part time, Joe had a new assistant, and she was allocated to another partner.

'How long has Jenny worked for Joe?' Tanner asked.

She paused. 'Months. Maybe six. Claire's on maternity leave.'

'She'd know the sort of work he was doing for them, right?'

'Of course.'

'Could you ask her?'

She looked confused. 'Didn't you ask Jackson?'

'Dennis is – he's a bit anal about privilege.'

She nodded. 'I'll let you know what I can.'

'Thanks.'

'This all . . . it has to be some kind of mistake, doesn't it, Pete?'

'Sure.'

They sat for a moment, looking at each other, thinking about Joe.

'I haven't asked you how you are,' he said, breaking the silence.

She smiled faintly. 'Okay.'

'I used Jenkins when I asked for you.'

She nodded. 'We're getting divorced. That's why I'm back full time.'

He nodded slowly. 'I'm sorry to hear that.'

'It's a relief.'

'How old are your kids?'

'Will is eight,' she said. 'Lizzy's nearly five.'

'Joe didn't tell me.'

She shrugged. 'I only told him about three months ago,' she said. 'I wasn't ready before. How's Dan, anyway?'

'High school next year.'

'Wow.'

'Yeah.'

'You seeing anyone?' she asked, smiling again.

'Not really.'

'What's that mean?'

'It's the lawyer's version of "no".'

She smiled, and looked at her watch. 'I'd better get back.'

'If you can speak to Jenny more,' he said, 'if she remembers something about what he was doing there . . . let me know.'

She nodded. 'If you hear something – if Jackson finds out what's –'

'I'll let you know.'

'It has to be –'

'It'll be okay,' he said. 'You're right. It's some terrible mistake.'

6

Melissa Cheung's front doorbell rang just as she was about to call Tanner. Two men in dark suits stood before her when she opened the door.

'Mrs Cheung?'

'Yes.'

'My name's Jordan Irwin. This is Steve Marshall. We're colleagues of your husband's. From BBK?'

Her heart started pounding, and her stomach dropped. 'Has something happened? Is Joe – ?'

Jordan Irwin smiled and held up his hand. 'Nothing's happened, Mrs Cheung. We're just –'

'Has the firm heard anything? Do you know where he is?'

The man put his hand up again as a signal for her to stay calm. 'We don't mean to alarm you, Mrs Cheung. I was assured you'd been told we were coming.'

Melissa paused, and took a deep breath. 'Why are you here?'

'Nothing to do with any bad news about Joe. I –' Irwin's eye's drifted from Melissa to the corridor behind her. Lily Cheung was standing unsteadily in a doorway, and had started to cry. 'Obviously doesn't like the look of lawyers,' he said, smiling.

Melissa turned around and picked up the child. 'She's just teething.'

'Look, Mrs Cheung –'

'Melissa.'

'Thanks. Can we come in for a moment? I'd like to talk about one of the things we're doing to help Joe.'

'Of course,' she said. She led the men down the hallway to the back of the house, where there was an open-plan kitchen and a dining table. She offered them seats. 'Can I make you some tea? Water?'

'We're fine,' Irwin said, speaking for both of them. 'We don't want to take up more of your time than we need to.'

'It's okay,' she said. 'If it's to help Joe, I don't care how long it takes.'

Melissa sat at the head of the table, her back to the kitchen. She had Lily on her lap. Irwin sat next to her, but the second man, who was maybe six foot five, and built like a rugby forward, sat at the other end of the table.

'One of the things we're trying to do,' Irwin began, 'is put together a chronology of what Joe was doing on this trip to China.'

'You mean what work he was doing?'

'Precisely,' he said. 'We don't know why the Chinese have detained Joe. You probably know from the consulate, we're having to guess until they give us something specific. They have a very different way of doing things to us as far as arrest procedure and rights are concerned.' His eyes widened slightly as he took in her Chinese face. 'I'm sorry, I didn't mean –'

'It's okay,' she said.

'We want to put a document together that outlines exactly what work Joe did in Shanghai, who he met, that kind of thing. Do you understand?'

'I think so.'

'We'll give this document to the relevant authorities. So they have something official from us – from BBK – that says, look, Joe Cheung was in China on firm business, here's what he did, here's when he did it. We don't know if it'll clear things up, but it's a start.'

'Sure.'

'One difficulty we've got, though, is that we don't have Joe's laptop. We assume it's been confiscated.'

'I'm sure he took it with him.'

Irwin nodded, and leant forwards. 'I know this is an intrusion, Melissa, but what we'd like to do is look at Joe's home computer. Just to check if there's anything on it that might help us put this document together.'

'Joe usually used his laptop,' she said. 'He didn't often use our home computer.'

'Okay,' Irwin said, nodding. 'Like I said, I'm really sorry for the intrusion, but could I take a look anyway? Just to see if there's any work-related material that could help us. We want to be as thorough as we can. We're sure Joe was only engaged in legitimate BBK client work in China, and we want to produce something that backs that up.'

'Joe would never do anything he shouldn't have. He – it's absurd.'

Irwin nodded vigorously. 'I know,' he said. 'We're all astonished about this. We think it has to be some mistake, some –'

'It is,' she said quickly, her voice catching slightly.

Irwin nodded again. 'Of course,' he said. 'Anyway, it'll just take a few moments. Can I check your computer?'

The other man remained at the kitchen table while Melissa took Irwin into the study. 'The computer's actually mine,' she said, turning it on. 'It's got a lot of home stuff on it. You know, photos, our music, our –'

'I won't be looking at any of that.'

'I'm just – it's also got some records from my own work. I'm a GP. Not patient details, just –'

'I'm only going to look for things that are obviously BBK related,' he said. 'It shouldn't take long.'

She paused, then nodded slightly, and left the room.

Less than five minutes later, Irwin walked back into the kitchen. 'Can I ask a favour?' he said. 'I know it's an inconvenience, but would you mind if we took the computer with us just to check some things? We really won't have –'

'Take it with you?'

'Do you have your own laptop?'

'I've got one at work, but – why do you need to take it? I don't think that's a good –'

'I'll be honest with you, Melissa,' he said, 'there's material on the computer that belongs to BBK.'

'What do you mean?'

'There are some documents relating to work Joe was doing. That's BBK's proprietary material. The work product belongs to our clients. Do you see what I mean?'

'No,' she said firmly. 'I don't. The computer is mine. It's got family photos of –'

'And we'll be very sensitive about that. But given Joe's predicament, we can't leave material our clients own on your computer. We need to retrieve it, and that could take a while to check thoroughly.'

'What material?' she said. 'Can you show me, please?'

'I can't do that. We can't breach client privilege like that. I can assure you, though, that we'll only take from the hard drive what's ours or our clients', and we'll get it straight back to you.'

'I still don't think –' Melissa stopped talking as Irwin nodded to the other man, who rose and walked out of the kitchen towards the study. Irwin stepped closer to Melissa, only a metre away. Lily stood unsteadily next to her mother, holding her dress with an arm.

'The last thing I want is to have to tell work I don't have your computer, but it's got some of our files on it,' Irwin said, his voice down a notch. 'I really don't want someone coming back here this afternoon with a court order.'

'A court order?'

'That's our clients' property on the hard drive, Melissa. I'm sure Joe would hate it if BBK had to get a court order to retrieve it from your computer. We'll have it back to you in no time.'

She looked at him, still uncertain. In the doorway she saw the other man, who was already carrying her iMac. 'Let me call my lawyer,' she said. 'Can you talk to him?'

'I'm not authorised to talk to your lawyer,' Irwin said. 'We'd have to get our own lawyers to talk to him.' His tone had remained friendly until then. Now it was colder, final.

'It will only –'

'This can't wait, Melissa.'

'Just let me call Peter Tanner. He's my lawyer. I just want to –'

'We can't leave our clients' property here, Melissa.'

She started to dial Tanner's number, but the men were already walking down the corridor to the front door.

'Wait, please, just let me call Peter.'

The door shut before Tanner answered the phone.

7

It was a ten-minute walk from BBK's offices to the building where Tanner shared chambers with forty other criminal lawyers. The building was Art Deco; the lifts were not glass boxes that glided effortlessly up a sky-high atrium. They had mass that struggled to defy gravity; their doors could hold out armies.

As he said good morning to the receptionist, he felt his mobile phone vibrating in his jacket pocket.

Melissa was hysterical. When she managed to tell him what had happened, he told her to write it all down, and that he'd be there in fifteen minutes.

When he arrived, Melissa had managed to compose herself. She had Lily sitting in a high chair in the kitchen, eating macaroni cheese straight off the chair's plastic table.

'Sorry, this looks so disgusting,' Melissa said.

'I see worse at chambers lunches.'

She made tea, and took him through what had happened, using the note she'd made.

'This man Irwin,' Tanner said when she was done, 'did he say he was a partner at BBK?'

'He said he was one of Joe's colleagues.'

'Has Joe ever mentioned him?'

She shook her head.

'And the other guy?'

'He said nothing,' she said. 'I can't recall his name. He didn't look like –' she paused.

'What?'

'I don't think he was a lawyer.'

Tanner nodded. 'And you didn't say they could take the computer?'

'They just took it,' she said, starting to lose composure again. 'I wanted to ring you. I asked them to wait.'

'Listen to me. Did you say no?'

'They said they could get a court order. I didn't –' She started crying again.

'I'll go and see Jackson again,' he said. 'I'll get it back. Okay? Melissa?'

'Okay.'

He told her not to worry, but it didn't seem like BBK's motive was to help Joe Cheung. They'd be putting their own interests first, the clients' second. Joe would be a long last.

When she composed herself, Melissa told him she'd called the consulate that morning, but there was no further news. 'Tell me what Dennis Jackson said,' she asked. 'He must know something?'

'This trip to China. Did Joe say it was for Citadel Resources?'

'I know the name. Joe doesn't talk much about work.' She shook her head, a look of frustration on her face. 'Half the time I'm not listening, Pete. You know, if he comes home early, the kids are making noise, talking to me, talking to him, yelling . . . it's that time of the day. If he comes home late, I'm often asleep. He had to go for a meeting with a client he said was being difficult. He was – I don't know if this is to do with anything, but he was worried about something recently.'

'Worried about what?'

'It was more – I've been thinking about this – something was bothering him for a while now, but when I asked him, he said it was nothing. It was worse recently. Since he came back from New Guinea.'

'New Guinea?'

She nodded. 'About six weeks ago. There was some kind of meeting at a mine site with the owners or operators. Some government approval had to be sorted out. That's all he told me.'

'Was this also to do with going to China?'

She shrugged. 'I don't know.'

'Where's the mine?'

'They had to fly to a small island.'

'Do you know its name?'

She sighed, and smiled lightly. 'I'd remember it if you said it.'

'We'll check later. I'll get someone to do a search.'

'I remember he couldn't call us. I mean, not on his phone. The mobile communications were down. He had to use a phone that was in an office building.'

'How long was he there?'

'Three days.'

'You must have talked to him about it when he got back?'

'He said that he'd had his meetings, and it all went okay.'

'Meetings with who?'

'I don't recall, Pete,' she said. 'If Joe was dealing with a particular bank, he'd just call it "the bank". Same with mining companies. They were usually just "the mining company".'

'Did he go with anyone else from BBK?'

She shook her head. 'I know it sounds vague, but we only had general discussions about these things. It was urgent, though. He only got about twenty-four hours' notice.'

Tanner nodded.

'You're not telling me what Dennis Jackson said, Pete,' she said.

Tanner leant forwards in his chair. 'Nothing is confirmed.'

'What did he say?'

'A client of BBK's won a tender for an exploration licence from the government a few years back. That's a licence given to a mining company to explore for minerals in an area, you understand?'

'Yes.'

'These licences are expensive if it's already known that minerals are in a particular area. They're often bought in a public tender. The miners submit confidential bids to the government. The bids can be pretty high, because if they're confident mining will be viable, almost always the company granted the licence will be granted an approval to build a mine. Jackson suggested Joe's part of an investigation about whether someone tried to sell his client's tender bid to another company.'

Melissa straightened in her chair and looked at Tanner coldly. 'Joe would never, ever do that.'

Tanner nodded. 'That's what I told Jackson.'

'Jesus, Pete. He's the most honest man I've ever met. It drives me nuts sometimes he's so – shit.' She'd sounded firm while defending her husband, but now her voice cracked again, and she started to cry.

Tanner pushed her glass of water closer to her, and waited while she drank.

'Sorry,' she said.

'All my clients cry the first time I see them.'

She sniffed back a small laugh. 'Really?'

'Both corrupt politicians cried like babies.'

She smiled and took a deep breath. 'He wouldn't do that, Pete. This has to be some misunderstanding, some . . . I don't know.' She stood and walked to the sink and poured herself another glass of water. She sipped it, then sat down, trying to calm herself. 'When will I be able to see him?'

'I'll speak to the consulate for you.'

'Will BBK get him a lawyer?'

'I'm hopeful they'll sort that out.'

'You're hopeful?'

'Yes.'

'How can they just – ?'

'The client involved is obviously a big one. Jackson said they're going to need to find out more information first. I understand their position about wanting to know the facts.'

'Do you?'

Tanner hesitated. He wanted her to think – for the time being, at least – that BBK hadn't just hung her husband out to dry. 'I'm sure Jackson will get him a lawyer, Mel. What they'll do beyond that, I don't know. It'll depend on what's alleged.'

'Jesus.'

'I'll do everything I can to help.'

'They can't just abandon him. I know he hasn't done anything wrong. They can't just –' She broke down again.

'I'm sure –'

'If he's convicted, Pete –' she said through tears. 'It's China, for Christ's sake. It will be years. The children won't have a father. They won't even be able to see him.'

'It's a long way from –'

'He would not have done anything wrong,' she said, her eyes gleaming, tears streaming down her check.

She cried for a long time. Tanner hesitated to touch her, but in the end took her hand, while she wiped her wrecked face with the other. She went to the bathroom. When she came back she was flushed, her eyes puffy, but the tears had gone.

'Keep calling the consulate,' he said when she sat down. 'Every morning, every afternoon. I'll call too. And I'll get your computer back, okay?'

'Thank you,' she said softly.

He called a taxi to take him back to the city. When it arrived, she stood in the doorway, watching him leave.

He turned to her when he reached the front gate. 'If they won't get him a good lawyer,' he called out, 'then I will.'

8

Nikki Richter paused in the apartment's entry hall before putting her handbag on the console. She held her breath for a moment and listened. Six hundred square metres of space with just her to fill it. 'Resort living in the heart of the city,' Jack had said of the residential tower he'd built next to Hyde Park. The seed money had been his father's. It had been Jack's first business venture away from the mining empire.

'Jack?' Silence. 'Are you there, Jack?'

In the seven weeks since they'd separated, she was certain he hadn't returned to the apartment, except once to collect his belongings. That time he'd been supervised. She still felt a sense of dread that he might be there, though. On the last night that he'd lived with her, his hands had been around her neck, squeezing hard to stop her breathing. She had felt, for a moment, the unbearable fear that he might crush her throat. The power in his hands had been terrifying. 'I could kill you easily,' he'd said. 'And I'd get away with it just as easily.' Apart from some vulgarities, those were the last words he'd said to her that night.

She waited a moment longer, heard nothing, then walked to the kitchen.

She poured herself a glass of water, and drank it quickly. For the last two hours she'd been at a Paddington salon. Some error in bookings meant the usual cutter was late. When it was at last her turn, the cutter sang out a flippant apology before asking (emphasising, *darling*, that he didn't want to pry) whether the gossip columns about her and JR were correct. She was more annoyed by the half-arsed apology than by the question, and for being made to wait. But she knew the wives of millionaires were highly valued by the salon's owner. She was sure that would apply to the soon-to-be ex-wife of an heir to a billionaire.

'None of it's true,' she told her cutter. 'Except for the part that I'm keeping the apartment, and we're getting divorced.'

She'd been a client at the salon for fifteen years, sent there by her agent when she was a few weeks short of her seventeenth birthday. Her modelling career had involved mainly swimwear; she was a rung below supermodel. It was enough to win Nikki Perovic the attention of John Richter, but it was not a suitable pursuit for Mrs Nikki Richter. The first time he'd been rough with her, they'd only just started dating. He took her to a friend's party, and got drunk. He started dancing with an old girlfriend. Their bodies entwined, his hands were everywhere. They were almost having sex on the dance floor.

Nikki called a cab, and was waiting for it on the footpath outside the the house when he reached her. He wanted to know what she thought she was doing.

'I'm leaving,' she said. She was flushed with humiliation. She could feel an intense heat on her cheeks.

'Come back inside.'

She turned and started to walk off. He grabbed the collar of her dress and yanked it back. She heard the fabric tear, and then she was on the ground. She felt a sharp pain as her elbows hit the footpath. He pulled her to her feet. He looked as shocked as she felt – as though, for a moment, he'd been stunned by the ferocity of his rage, incredulous that it wasn't something he could control. She ran down the street and met the taxi at the bottom of the hill. That should have been it.

Every time they'd fought, Jack found a way of blaming her. Now, looking back, she blamed herself too – she should have known. She understood some of his anger, the idea that he was not a chip off the old block. Sometimes she'd just want to say to him, 'You have *so* much money. Can't you just be happy?' And who'd want to be like Hendrik? Who'd want to be like that cold bastard, with that voice that frayed her hair?

She opened a door of the double-sided fridge and took out a bottle of wine. It was from somewhere called Meursault. Jack's wine was bought for him by a broker, but he bought his cocaine from his lawyer.

She was going out later, the thirtieth birthday of her personal trainer's fiancé, at a private club in Bondi. One of the haunts Jack liked to go when he wasn't sleazing around at his own club. She found a bottle opener and poured herself a glass. She was supposed to be detoxing, but felt the need to loosen up. She took a sip, and tried to remember if she'd told her trainer to leave the name Perovic at the door. She was going back to Nikki Perovic.

After she was married, no longer working, there was a lot of time to fill. Jack wanted to go out every night. He could get in anywhere. He had a key to every room in every city where the young and the rich met. They fitted that billing. They were young, beautiful and obscenely rich. She got bored. Not straight away, but quickly enough that it surprised her. And there were times when he looked bored too. Alcohol was not enough. Not even coke. 'Jack loves smack,' he'd say to his dealers. The Jack loves smack period lasted nearly two years.

It wasn't long before she worked out he was fucking other women. He flirted with them in front of her at clubs, half fucked them in booths and on dance floors. He wanted threesomes. He wanted her to watch. He wanted to watch her. On candy and H, she went along. She was now a rich, rich girl, wife of the heir, doing what his fantasies demanded, taking drugs to cover the sadness. She thought she was pathetic.

One night in a bar, after a few lines of coke, she called him Jack the Richter. He slapped her hard across the face. When she got outside, she threw her engagement ring across the street. She went into rehab. Jack claimed seven hundred and fifty K from an insurer for the 'stolen' ring.

She came out of rehab for the second time on Valentine's Day; they were going to dinner. He rang in the afternoon and said he had to work late. They were buying a stake in a mine in South America. 'The deal isn't going to be placed on hold for fucking Valentine's Day,' he'd said when she complained. She knew he was lying. He didn't come home that night. The mine deal fell through.

She hired someone after that. She felt stupid about it, but wanted to be sure. He used an apartment she didn't know he owned. He took women there three or four times a week.

She went to a lawyer, who told her to get anything that might loosen the strict terms of her pre-nup. So when they went out to nightclubs or to parties, she would sometimes pretend to make a phone call to friends. She filmed him doing lines of coke, and talking about how good it was, how pure. Heroin was no longer chic, he said one night. It was for the plebs. Like he'd fucking know.

She got into his computer at home, and his laptop. His password was 'black gold'. He'd told her that once, never thinking it would matter. She read stuff about Citadel she thought she could leverage against him later. She was not going to be fobbed off with seven million – she was taking more than that. She'd give half to charity. All those starving kids in Africa. It was their minerals that had made the Richters rich.

When she told him she knew about the other girls, and that she wanted a divorce, he'd laughed, but soon flew into a rage. She'd got her timing wrong. He was agitated and aggressive with coke. He must have been doing lines in the office with that weasel of a lawyer.

He'd slapped her across the face as hard as he ever had, but wasn't satisfied with that. Not when she screamed that she'd seen a lawyer, and told him how many zeros the cheque would need to have. He'd grabbed her hair and dragged her into the bedroom. That's when he'd started to strangle her. He must have thought better about what he'd do then, because he stopped. 'Pack your fucking clothes,' he'd said. 'Or I'll throw you in the street.'

She'd contemplated calling the police, but then called her lawyer. She sent a text to her father-in-law. *Your son just assaulted me*, it said. *I'm calling the police.* She took a selfie of a reddening eye, which she sent to *Lady* Richter as well. *My lawyer has these*, she said in another text. She took more photos of the marks around her neck.

It seemed like only twenty minutes before the men arrived. There were two of them. Jack knew them. He buzzed them up. The older one took Jack into his wine cellar, and shut the door. When they came out, Jack left with the younger man.

The older man walked over to where she was standing in the doorway of the bedroom. 'He did this,' she said, pointing to the left side of her face, which was blotched pink and white, and to her neck, his fingerprints almost glowing on it.

The man nodded. He said his name was Steve. He was in a blue suit. She knew it was expensive. A white shirt, a white kerchief in the breast pocket. He had a shaved head, a goatee in a mix of rust and grey. He looked kind, she thought. He had sad eyes.

'Mr Richter asked me to tell you this is your home,' he said. It was one of those accents you could have two or three guesses at and still be wrong. 'There's no need for the police.'

She said nothing.

He stood there, looking at her, smiling faintly. 'Ma'am? There's no need for the police?'

She nodded. 'Yes,' she said softly. He had the kind of face that made you say yes.

Jack called her the next day. It took her thirty seconds to realise it was one of his versions of an apology. She hung up. Then he rang the day after her lawyers wrote their first letter. 'Don't think you've fucking won, you cheap bitch,' were the first words she heard. He sounded drunk.

She explained briefly why she'd win. The things she knew that made the pre-nup not worth taking out of his lawyer's safe. His drug habit. His hands on her throat. And things she knew about Citadel. The mighty fucking Citadel. This time, he hung up.

In the weeks since, she'd come to realise that one thing she didn't want was the apartment. It made her feel like she was in the most lavishly appointed prison in the world. She didn't say this to anyone. It didn't seem right to say she hated an apartment that was worth $18 million. She'd decided to sell it once the property settlement was finalised. More than one Chinese billionaire would be very happy with it. Probably one in the same game as the Richters, digging up shit, killing the planet.

Nikki kicked her shoes off in the lounge room, and told herself to shake off the memories of her marriage and its failure. She walked into the bedroom, then into the bathroom. She started a bath. The tub was made of stone the colour of Bondi sand, and shaped like half a dinosaur egg. The window faced east. The lights had now come on in the houses and apartment buildings of Elizabeth Bay and Double Bay, and the big spreads of Point Piper. She could see the Richter family mansion. There were yachts still sailing in the harbour, even in the fading light. Hendrik might be on one, for all she knew. He and Jack did the Sydney to Hobart every year. Was it wrong to hope their fucking boat sank in next year's race?

She stood and stretched, and went back to the bedroom to get undressed. She threw her dress on the bed, put her hands on her hips, stood still. The room was dark, lit only by the light coming from the bathroom. She thought about what she'd wear to the party.

She felt a chill before he grabbed her. A gloved hand went over her mouth, the other on top of her head, tilting it towards the ceiling. She thought at first it had to be Jack – no one else could get in. Only a split second after the hands were on her, someone else took hold of her wrists, and then her feet and legs were quickly lifted.

'Don't struggle,' a man said in her ear, his voice a harsh whisper. 'You won't get hurt if you don't struggle.'

Her heart slapped against her chest. They were strong, without hurting her. She could not flay her arms and legs. She knew she could not get out of their grip.

There was a fire in her arm. Fear drained away a moment later, euphoria followed. She felt safe. They were here to protect her. They wouldn't hurt her. He'd made a promise. She was warm. She was tired. She wanted to fall asleep in their arms, in the arms of the man who'd whispered in her ear like a lover. Her mouth felt dry, but her body was in water. She wondered if she was breathing. She didn't think she was breathing. She was dreaming. It was all a dream.

The water was still warm when her heart stopped.

9

Tanner tried to speak with Dennis Jackson the following morning without success. He had a trial on, and tried again over the lunch break, but still couldn't reach him.

When court finished for the day, he had two missed calls from Melissa Cheung. He hurried back to chambers to ring her from there, but his chambers phone rang before he could. He was told Dennis Jackson was on the line.

'What the hell are you doing stealing my client's computer?' Tanner said as soon as Jackson was put through.

There was a pause. 'The computer wasn't stolen,' Jackson said. 'There was work product owned by this firm on it. Melissa understood, and consented to us taking it.'

'You sent goons to the home of a woman whose husband is in custody in China. She didn't consent to anything.'

'We don't employ "goons". I'm going to hang up if –'

'Who's Jordan Irwin? I can't find him on your website.'

'Head of cyber security for this region.'

'Jesus Christ. You have a head of cyber security? What the fuck do you want from Melissa's computer?'

'Material this firm owns.'

'What material?'

'We explained it to her. I'm sure she's told you.'

'Send it back now.'

'She'll have it soon. Talk to our lawyers if you want to make any more allegations.'

'Have you got Joe a lawyer yet?'

'That's complicated.'

'How is getting him a lawyer complex?'

A slight pause, an exhalation of breath. 'We think a statement about Joe is about to be released. That's why I'm calling.'

This was what Melissa must have tried to reach him about. 'Released by whom?'

'The Chinese authorities.'

'Saying what?'

'We think Joe is about to be charged with attempting to sell state secrets.'

'What? What state secrets?'

'Citadel won the exploration licence tender I spoke to you about previously. They're in a joint venture with a Chinese company, and paid two hundred and fifty million for the licence.'

Tanner was momentarily stunned by the size of the figure. 'What's Joe alleged to have done?'

'It's in line with our previous intelligence: we think the charge will relate to Joe seeking to sell Citadel's bid price to another mining company – so that they'd know they'd have to go higher than two-fifty if they wanted the licence.'

Tanner was silent for a few moments.

'Peter?'

'How much was he seeking to sell this information for?'

'Fifteen million – that's what one of our Shanghai people was told.'

'Who told you this?'

'Some information has come from the consulate. Some to our Shanghai office.'

'Do we know where he is yet?'

'No. I spoke to the consul general myself. She was hopeful that –'

'What's her name?'

'Michelle Barrett. If you let me finish, she told me she hopes they'll be able to see him within a week. She says they're working towards a deal.'

Tanner tried to absorb the enormity of Joe being charged. 'I take it BBK's position is that you don't think Joe would do this, right?'

'I don't know.'

Tanner closed his eyes and held the phone away from his mouth. 'You need to arrange a lawyer for him now,' he said. 'Your people in Shanghai should be working with the consulate to help get visitation rights.'

'Peter, I'm the Australian CEO. Citadel is a global client. So is its joint venture partner. Every one of our offices around the world has a stake in this. I can't –'

'Joe's your partner.'

'I can't make a unilateral decision to help a man who's alleged to have tried to damage a client of this firm in relation to what is potentially a multibillion-dollar mining project.'

'Did you hear what you just said, Dennis? You said "alleged".'

'Be real for a moment.'

'Since when did your law firm get to reverse the presumption of innocence?'

'This isn't about presumptions. We have a partner who looks like he's about to be charged with doing something that could've had a devastating economic impact on a client.'

'Does it occur to you as relevant that it didn't have such an impact? Citadel got its EL, didn't it? Joe couldn't have done a very good job of corrupting someone in a country where that's usually not that difficult.'

'You're not listening.'

'Just get your China people to give us a heads up on a decent lawyer.'

'The consulate is in just as good a position to recommend a lawyer as we are.'

'Fuck you, Dennis. You have lawyers in your office there who must know who the good criminal lawyers are, right?'

'It's not my call.'

'Didn't you like Joe? Do you – ?'

'Liking Joe is not the issue.'

'You said you were the Australian CEO, Dennis. Act like it. He's one of yours.'

There was a snort of derision down the line. 'You know, Peter, there are no such concepts as presumption of innocence or beyond reasonable doubt in China. You mightn't have such success for your clients if you had to practise under their rules. Evidence of guilt only has to be sufficient and reliable. Do you think they'd be laying a charge without that?'

'Joe would not have done what they're saying.'

'I'm only telling you what the burden of proof is.'

'He has three children, Dennis. The oldest is eight. Can you consider that for a moment? You can't abandon him on the back of an allegation.'

There was no response from Jackson, and Tanner wondered if he'd hung up.

'Dennis?'

'Peter . . . it's not . . . it's not my call.'

On the same day that Nikki Richter's body was found, the Minister for Foreign Affairs and the Australian Consulate General in Shanghai released brief statements concerning the detention in China of Joseph Cheung, a partner in the firm of Bloomberg Butler Kelly. The consul general confirmed that on the morning of 12 September, Mr Cheung had been detained by officers of the Chinese Ministry of State Security. He was being held on suspicion of stealing state secrets, and of seeking a bribe in relation to the grant by the New South Wales Government of an exploration licence to Citadel Resources three years ago. Australian consular officials were presently being denied access to him, but were hopeful of establishing visitation rights soon. The minister's statement echoed that of the consulate.

BBK put out a statement immediately after, jointly signed by local CEO, Dennis Jackson, and global chairman, Sir James Parr. It confirmed that Joe Cheung was a partner of the firm, that he had been detained, but it offered no information as to the precise circumstances surrounding his detention. The firm was cooperating fully with Chinese officials, including making attempts to meet with Mr Cheung, and expressed 'surprise' at what had occurred.

After BBK, it was Citadel's turn. It was 'alarmed' by the detention of Mr Cheung, one of the external legal advisors to the company. It would take 'a keen interest in the outcome of the investigations into Mr Cheung's conduct by the Chinese Authorities', but noted that no charges had been laid. The statement was signed by Citadel CEO, Jacques Proctor, and board chairman and founder, Hendrik Richter.

Four days later, the Australian Government released a further statement, saying that it had now been informed that Mr Cheung had been charged with seeking a secret payment from a Chinese commercial 'entity' in exchange for the sale of a state secret. No further details were provided. Consular officials had now, however, been granted a date to visit Mr Cheung in custody.

10

John Richter came out of the lift first. He walked down a corridor towards a brilliant white door. Next to the door was a security pad, and an intercom. There was also a box with a glass face. Underneath the box were the words RETINAL SCANNER.

The security pad was real. He inserted a red card into it, and then punched in a passcode. The door clicked, and he pushed it open. He and his friend walked into one of the city's most exclusive clubs, Pantheon. It was on the top floor of a six-storey redevelopment called Olympus in the north of the CBD, not far from Circular Quay. Ordinarily the red card he'd used to gain entry to the club would cost its owner ten thousand a year. Membership was by invitation only. It included your first five thousand in drinks, but there was an expectation that in any calendar year you'd be paying for your drinks by Good Friday. If you weren't, you shouldn't expect a renewal. Every year there were a couple of new bright young things or high flyers in the corporate world suitable to take the place of absent friends.

Richter sat on the committee that decided who would be invited to join the club, and whose membership would not be renewed for another year. That was part of what he got for his twenty-five per cent investment in the entertainment complex that was crowned by the private club.

In the nine days since his wife's death, Richter had kept out of the public eye, apart from the afternoon he'd attended her funeral. His family had earlier put out a statement expressing their deep sadness and profound sense of loss. The people who minded him had told him to lie low – no nightclubs, no parties.

He'd followed the advice, but the funeral was over. He was entitled to get out for a quiet meal. Even so, Richter's driver took them to the rear of the building and they'd been shown in via the kitchen. After dinner, he'd suggested the private club upstairs. It didn't offer anonymity, but it was an oasis away from any paparazzi, or just from some idiot with a smart phone.

A hostess greeted them as they walked in, and escorted them to a corner booth that had been reserved in an elevated part of the huge main lounge area. Like the other women working there, she was in a black dress. The neckline was almost profoundly low. The man with Richter was an old school friend. Justin Matheson now worked at Stott Ackerman, the global investment bank. He specialised in raising finance for gaming and hospitality developments and resorts. He and Richter hadn't been especially close at school, but they'd fallen in together after Matheson moved to Stott Ackerman, not long after a stint with another investment bank in New York.

Richter hadn't liked Matheson at school: Matheson had been captain of the cricket team, and the school swimming champion. Back then, he'd often wanted to rearrange those perfect white teeth. The same teeth that were smiling now at the blonde hostess. The hostess who'd waited on Richter the last two times he'd been to the club.

Hendrik Richter dug holes in the ground and brought minerals to the earth's surface. Those simple acts had made him a billionaire. John Richter wanted to do something other than look for more carbon. He wanted lights, cameras, Vegas. Justin Matheson knew his stuff – he was in Nevada, Singapore, Atlantic City, Macau, five or six times a year. He wanted to do deals about casinos and luxury resorts. Richter wanted to own them. They were each valuable to the other.

'What can we get you to drink?' The blonde hostess was joined by a brunette. She had an accent. Her skin was deeply tanned, her hair darker. Richter's eyes flitted from her chest to her lips, which were a warm topaz.

'Is there a cocktail special?' he asked.

'There is. It's –'

'No, no,' he said, smiling. 'We'd like to be surprised.'

'Of course.'

'Just make sure there's whisky in it. A good one.'

The hostess looked confused. 'But that – that won't be the special then.'

'Tell the barman we'd like our own special.'

'Certainly,' she said, walking off.

'I'll be right back,' the blonde said to Matheson. She'd been whispering in his ear and giggling while the drink order was taken.

'What are we drinking?' Matheson asked.

'The special.'

'Which is?'

'A surprise,' Richter said. 'What were you discussing with the blonde? Do you like her?'

Matheson smiled. 'Her name is Klaudia,' he said. 'With a K.'

Richter nodded. 'And your wife's name is Sarah. With an S.'

Matheson glared at him, but said nothing.

'Which part of England is Klaudia with a K from?'

'London,' Matheson said, 'but her folks are Polish.'

'Jesus, the life story. You didn't answer my question. You like?'

Matheson sat back in the leather booth, and shrugged. 'She seems friendly.'

'She's paid to be friendly.'

'Careful, the barman said these are powerful,' Klaudia with a K said, placing their drinks in front of them.

'What is it?' Richter asked.

'It's a rol and rye,' the brunette answered. 'Whisky, Aperol, soda and orange.'

'Arancia,' Matheson said.

'Yes,' she replied.

'Aperol is Italian, isn't it?' he asked. '*Sei Italiana?* I'm right, aren't I?'

'*Si.*'

'*Di dove sei*?'

'Rimini.'

'On the coast? The Adriatic?'

The girl smiled and nodded.

'So, you're what? Travelling at the moment?'

'I'm studying here.'

'*Che cosi studi*?'

'English literature.'

'Wow,' Matheson said. 'I'm impressed. And your name again?'

'Elena.'

'*Piacere*,' he said. 'I'm Justin.' He picked up his glass. '*Salute*.' He took a sip. '*Perfetto*.'

'*Prego*.'

'Something else, gents?' Klaudia with a K said. 'Something to eat?'

'Maybe later,' Richter said. 'So Justin,' he said when their hostesses had left to attend another table, 'who are you making a play for here, Klaudia with a K or the Italian babe? Or are you getting greedy on me?'

'I don't know, Jack,' Matheson said. 'They're both gorgeous. Which one do you like?'

Richter took a long sip of his cocktail. 'I didn't know you spoke Italian.'

'I don't.'

'What was all that, then?'

Matheson smiled and leant over the table. 'That, Jack, is the basics you pick up after your first day's skiing in Cortina.'

'Is that right?' Richter got up and straightened his jacket. 'The blonde or the Italian, Justin?' He left the booth and headed for the bathrooms.

John Richter looked up from washing his hands as another man entered the men's room. The man nodded briefly at him, then walked, a little unsteadily, to one of the urinals. Richter picked up one of the folded hand towels.

'Sorry about your wife, mate,' the man at the urinal said.

Richter turned and looked at the back of the man's head, then threw the hand towel into a basket next to the marble sink. 'What?'

The man at the urinal turned his head as far as he could. 'Sorry about your wife,' he repeated, more softly this time.

'Is that some kind of joke?'

'No,' the man said. 'I –'

'What the *fuck* is it to you?'

The man finished what he was doing and zipped himself up. He turned around slowly. Richter stood between him and the hand basins. 'Nothing,' he said. 'I was just –'

'Keep your fucking mouth shut.' Richter's nostrils flared. His right hand, resting against his thigh, had formed into a fist. 'Are you a member?' he asked.

'I'm . . . I'm a guest.' The man would have to pass him to leave the bathroom.

Richter was half a foot taller. He leant over the man, who moved back, nearly to the urinal behind him. 'You even look at me again,' he said, 'and I'll throw the whole fucking lot of you out.'

The man nodded, said nothing. He waited until John had left the bathroom before leaving himself.

Klaudia and Elena were thinking about sharing a flat together, a few streets from Bondi Beach. The men found this out on their fourth round of rol and ryes.

'I suppose you're studying English lit as well?' Richter said to Klaudia.

She shook her head. She was seated on Justin Matheson's lap. It was after three am. The club was winding down, only a handful of members and guests left. Elena sat next to Richter.

'We met at our modelling agency.'

'Models too? Which agency?'

'Jade,' Klaudia said. 'Do you know it?'

Richter froze for a moment, and Matheson looked at him. Jade had been the agency Nikki Richter had been with, when she'd still been Nikki Perovic.

'By reputation,' he said.

'What kind of modelling do you do?' Matheson asked.

The girls looked at each other. 'The usual,' Klaudia said. 'It was a gothic-glam shoot today, though.' She grabbed hold of one of Elena's hands, held it up and laughed. The Italian girl had ultra-long black fingernails.

'Wow,' Matheson said.

'The usual has to include swimsuit, surely?' Richer asked.

Klaudia put her mouth next to Matheson's ear. 'Sometimes,' she said.

Matheson looked at Elena. 'So, you're studying English literature, you work here part time, and you pick up more spare cash as a swimsuit model?'

She shrugged heavily, and smiled. Matheson picked up his drink and sipped while looking at Richter. He grinned, a bit lopsidedly. He was starting to slur his words. He'd been drinking since the start of a business lunch earlier that day, and the rol and ryes were taking their toll.

'That's always been your ultimate fantasy, hasn't it, Jack?' he said. 'Beauty *and* brains?'

At three thirty am, Richter sent a text to his driver. A few words with the manager of Pantheon, and the hostesses had accepted a chauffeur-driven ride back to the Richter estate at Point Piper.

Richter opened a bottle of champagne after they arrived. They were in the guesthouse his father had built next to the main house. He'd put John in it after he'd finished school. It had two palatial bedrooms, a huge lounge area, and a home theatre that seated ten in reclining chairs. They called it the Retreat.

He put the champagne on a coffee table in the living room where he'd seated his guests. Matheson was on one lounge, Klaudia with a K on his lap. She was whispering in his ear again, but he looked in danger of falling asleep. Richter went back to the kitchen and opened half the cupboards. He cursed, and took another bottle from the fridge.

'No champagne glasses,' he said when he returned. 'They're . . . gone.' He was about to say that they were still with fucking Nikki, but caught himself. He handed a bottle to Matheson, slammed his own hard into it, and they both took swigs. Klaudia laughed. Richter handed his bottle to Elena. 'I'll be right back,' he said.

When he returned, he threw the packet of powder on the coffee table. 'Party time.'

When he'd first started buying from his in-house lawyer, he was paying over four hundred dollars a gram. This annoyed him, because in the States or London he could buy it for half that price, although the quality varied. He asked the lawyer how much he was paying his dealer. The lawyer assured him no margin was involved. Richter asked for the dealer's number. The lawyer though, with Citadel's best interests in mind – and that of the heir to the throne – suggested it was safer for Richter to only come into contact with the product once it had been safely purchased. Richter agreed, but still baulked at the price. They settled on three fifty a gram, which reflected a compromise between the wholesale and street prices of the product. Richter told the lawyer later that negotiating the per-tonne price of iron ore with the Chinese was easier than dealing with him. And, unlike ore, the price of coke rarely dropped.

Justin Matheson ran his hand through his hair and straightened up. 'Is this still the most expensive blow in Sydney?'

'I've negotiated a drop in price,' Richter said, as he started cutting lines with his Pantheon member's card. He bent and snorted. 'But not in quality,' he said when he'd finished.

The coke didn't prove the instant hit he expected. Matheson made a token attempt at doing a thin line. He'd had a bad reaction on two previous occasions, and wasn't up for swollen nasal cavities again; he went back to intermittent swigs of the Krug, and laughing and giggling with Klaudia. She had a line too, but Elena required coaxing. 'I like the champagne,' she kept saying.

'This is *the* stuff,' Richter said. He was sitting next to her, putting his fingers in her hair. 'Very pure.'

Klaudia jumped off Matheson's lap momentarily and picked up Richter's red card. She cut a fine, short line, right in front of Elena. 'Just this much for you, baby,' she said. She leant towards Elena, and kissed her hard on the lips. She smiled, then put her lips to Elena's ear. 'It's *perfetto*,' she whispered.

Another bottle of Krug was opened. Matheson took it in one hand, and led Klaudia away with the other. Richter watched them walk towards the corridor that ran down the back of the Retreat. He heard Klaudia shriek. Then he heard laughter. A door was shut firmly.

'Music?'

'No,' Elena said.

'I'd like you to dance.'

'I'm tired.'

'On coke?'

She smiled. 'It is many hours in the club today.'

Richter ran his fingers through Elena's long hair. He took a swig of champagne. The bottle was a third full, but the intensity of the bubbles had gone. He did another line of coke. It gave him a rush, but he was still waiting to feel like Superman; it was taking more and more to get there. He wanted to feel like he had once, the first time he'd taken it. Like the ruler of the world. He had the money to rule the world. He wanted to *feel* it.

'How long have you been with Jade?'

'Only my time in Australia.'

'How long is that?'

'Nearly one year.'

He moved his fingers from her hair to her face, running his index finger over her lips. She recoiled by just the barest amount.

Next to the couch, on a table with a lamp that was designed like a spotlight outside an old movie theatre, was his iPad. He picked it up, then turned his body away from her, so she couldn't see the screen. In less than a minute he had what he was looking for.

'There you are,' he said. He held her face up to her. Then he scrolled down the screen. 'And here,' he said, holding the screen up again, 'is Klaudia with a K.'

She smiled, said nothing, and shifted in her seat.

'Let's have a look,' he said. He touched her face on the screen, and thumbnail photos of her portfolio came up. On the left of the screen, her unadorned details. *Five foot ten. Bust 33. Waist 26. Hips 35. Dress: 8. Shoes: 8. Hair: Brown. Eyes: Brown.*

'You're in imperials,' he said. 'They don't do you justice.' He flicked along the photos. 'Amazing how you can look like an entirely different person,' he said, 'depending how your hair and make-up is done.'

She said nothing.

He magnified a photo of her in a black bikini. The top was tied together in a bow. 'Nice,' he said. He slowly ran a finger along her breasts on the screen. Some fashion shoots followed, all casual clothes. He kept flicking. 'Whoa,' he said, leaning towards her, raising his eyebrows. 'This is more like it.' He was looking at a series of photos taken for a line of lingerie. He used his fingers to enlarge the shot, and held it up to her. 'Justin was wrong,' he said. 'This is my fantasy.'

Elena stood up. 'I'm not enjoying this.'

He threw his iPad to the other couch and stood too. He reached out and grabbed her hand. 'C'mon,' he said. 'This way.'

He took a step towards his bedroom. She went with him briefly only because of his momentum and strength. Then she resisted, and pulled her hand from his grip.

'I should go,' she said.

'C'mon.'

'I'm very tired.'

He smiled, and took her hand again. 'Don't be silly,' he said. He moved forwards to kiss her.

She stepped away.

'What's wrong?'

'I'm tired. I'd like to go.'

'Sleep here,' he said. He tried to take her other hand as well, but she pulled away from his grasp.

'What's the matter with you?'

'Please. I am really tired.'

'There are no cabs around here.'

'It's okay,' she said. 'I'll find one.'

'Don't be an idiot.' He spoke more loudly now, anger at the back of his voice.

'I want to go,' she said. She picked up her bag, and threw it over her shoulder.

'What the fuck are you doing?'

She walked past him, heading for the door. As she did, the bag hit his arm and dragged across his chest.

He only meant to grab the bag. He was going to snatch it from her, and throw it against the door. Fucking tease. If she wanted to go, she could go. That was all he meant to do.

The website for Jade Modelling Agency had her measurements. It did not have her weight. Had they divulged that, the Jade people would have said she was one hundred and seven pounds.

He'd only meant to grab the bag. When he tore at it with all his force, though, she came with it.

There was a loud bang as her head hit the coffee table. What was left of the cocaine he'd taken from the packet flew upwards in a small, precious cloud of dust.

He thought at first that she was looking at him, that she would get up. She would be angry or scared. She might fly at him, or run. Then he saw that her lids were open, but her eyeballs were flickering. It was as though they were being controlled by rubber bands stretched to breaking point, straining to pull her eyes to the back of her head. Her left arm was held upwards and bent, like she was fending him off with her forearm. It was in spasm. Her body twitched twice, the second time so violently that he stepped backwards.

He'd only meant to grab her bag.

Slowly he leant down next to her, not sure whether to touch her. 'Oh fuck,' he whispered.

He saw blood. A dark crimson stain on the beige carpet, coming from the back of her head. She made strange sounds from deep in her throat. A gargling noise.

'Fuck,' he said again. 'Oh fuck.'

She twitched once more. Her head moved upwards slightly. He nearly jumped in fright.

'Elena?' he said. 'Elena?'

He saw blood in one of her ears. Her right arm was still gripping her bag. Her left arm lowered slowly. The noise in her throat stopped.

'Oh Jesus,' he said.

He sat down on the couch, and started rocking back and forth. He kept willing her to get up, to get out of his house. The bloodstain grew larger.

He went to the kitchen. He picked up his phone, and then quickly put it down. He opened a drawer, and took out a set of keys. He went out the front door and walked through the garden. The wind had picked up. Leaves blew past him and into the pool. He walked to the main house and unlocked the French doors that led into his father's study. Next to the wall, he punched a keypad to turn off the alarm. He closed the door carefully.

He sat down behind the antique desk and picked up one of the three phones – the one he knew was secure. He checked his own mobile for the number. It was four fifty am. A man answered on the fourth ring.

'What?'

'It's me.'

'What?'

'There's been – um . . . I need your help.'

A long pause. 'What is it?'

'There's . . . a girl. I'm – I'm pretty sure she's not breathing.' He didn't cry often. Not even when he was told Nikki had OD'd. When he said these words, though, he thought he might.

There was another pause. 'Fuck,' the man said, sounding exhausted. Then, 'Where are you?'

'Home.'

'Your father's house?'

'I'm – yeah, I'm calling from there. But –'

'Where's the girl?'

'Next door. Where I'm staying.'

The man sighed. 'Is this something I can handle on my own?'

John Richter tried to think. He rocked back and forth in the chair. 'Um, you know, I don't think so . . . there's . . .'

'Are there drugs involved?'

'Um, not much, yeah.'

'What?'

'Coke.'

'What else.'

'Just coke.'

'Your coke, John?'

There was a pause. 'Yes.'

'Anyone else there?'

'A friend of mine. And another girl.'

'Christ,' the man said slowly. 'Where are they?'

'In a bedroom. I think.'

'You think?'

'They're in a bedroom.'

'Where's the girl?'

'She's in the lounge.'

'And how long has she not been breathing?'

'Just now. Five minutes.'

'Why is she not breathing?'

Now John Richter paused. 'She – it was an accident. She fell.'

'Fuck you, John,' the man said, his voice deep and hoarse. 'Where is the coke?'

'What do you mean?'

'Is it in a fucking plastic bag, is it – ?'

'Yes. There's some on the table, and the floor. The rest is in a plastic bag.'

'Go back to the house. Don't touch anything. Don't touch her. Don't call me from there.'

'What do I do?'

'Wait.'

11

On the plane to Shanghai, before he tried to sleep, Tanner thought back over the years he'd known Joe Cheung. He would have been amazed if Joe even once mildly exaggerated his time for a bill. The idea that he'd seek a bribe seemed ridiculous.

Something Dennis Jackson had said had stuck with him, though. *How well do you really know him?* Tanner remembered Joe once telling him that was the strange thing about working in a big law firm: you could be partners with someone for years, yet never get to know them. You saw them under stress, or when they were too busy, or not busy enough. You were there when they were worried about a case or a file, or when they were fretting over some real or imagined mistake. Judging lawyers is fraught with danger; many want to do the right thing, but the game won't let them.

If there was a way of making a fortune quickly, even a dishonest way, would Cheung take it? The money was good for a partner at a big law firm, but it was no way to instant wealth. It was a long, hard grind.

In his own practice, Tanner had many clients who were recalcitrant. Some seemed programmed to be violent; others had it beaten into them. Some wrecked their lives with a single moment of madness. There were others who had never appeared remotely capable of committing a crime until the day they did.

Then you could look at the same life all over again, and see how the whole catastrophe was always inevitable.

Their flight touched down in Shanghai just after six am.

'Why are you coming to China?' the customs official asked Tanner.

'To see a prisoner in one of your jails seemed provocative. 'On business,' he said, which was more or less the truth.

The drive from the airport to the Grand Hyatt took nearly an hour. Tanner had at first booked a different hotel, but Melissa said she wanted to stay where Joe had been when the police came for him. 'I just do,' was all she'd said when he'd asked why.

Their bags were put in storage until their rooms were ready later in the day. They weren't due at the consulate until eight forty-five, so they took a table at the Grand Café in the hotel's lobby near one of the huge windows. Melissa ordered tea, and Tanner coffee. They were silent for a few minutes, both anxious in their own way about what the day would reveal.

'Joe called me from here,' she said, looking out of the window. They were fifty-four floors up, and the other skyscrapers of Pudong were barely visible through the misty air.

'When?'

'The day he got here. He must've arrived at the same time as us. I'd just come back from dropping the boys at school.' She took a sip of tea, and looked at him.

'How did he sound?'

'Tired. He told me he didn't sleep on the plane. He said he was looking over Shanghai from the window. It must have been clearer than today.' She smiled. 'He said his coffee was too weak.'

Tanner nodded. 'I'll stick to tea from now on.'

'We've got a new machine at home,' she said. 'It takes him about an hour to make a cappuccino with it. He grinds the beans, makes sure the temperature of the milk is –' She picked up her napkin, and dabbed at her eyes, looking at her reflection in the window. She shook her head and tried to smile. 'Joe makes really good coffee, Peter.'

It was a twenty-minute taxi ride across the Huangpu to the Australian Consulate. Before flying to Shanghai, Tanner had contacted some lawyers he knew who worked at firms with offices in China. He'd asked them to help find someone to act for Cheung. One recommended a lawyer called Yinshi Li, who was on a list provided by the consulate. Li agreed to be retained, and the plan was to meet at his office at eleven, after meeting with the consular officials. When they arrived at the consulate, though, they were told Li had just called to cancel the meeting.

'Did he give a reason?' Tanner asked when the woman on the reception desk gave him the news.

'He said he was very sorry, but something urgent had come up. He said he'd call later to arrange another time.'

Tanner looked at the woman, knowing she was just passing on the message. *And this isn't important?* he thought.

The Consul General came out to reception to greet them. Michelle Barrett was in a dress suit, which was cut to just below her knee. If Tanner had been asked to describe its colour, then based on his location he would have said it was Communist red. Next to her was Jonathon Clarkson, the official who'd first spoken with Melissa when Joe had disappeared. They were led into a meeting room, where they were offered tea.

'As you know,' Michelle Barrett began after they'd taken their seats, 'Jon and I are seeing Joe tomorrow at the detention centre. We'll make sure he's doing okay, check that he's been treated properly and that sort of thing. Then his lawyer will see him the day after.'

'When can I see him?' Melissa said.

'In a few days,' Barrett said. 'We're just waiting on confirmation.'

'Why can't I see him tomorrow too?'

'They won't allow more than one visitor a day – and usually no more than one visitation a week,' Clarkson said.

'We've impressed on them that Joe has a young family in Sydney, and you have limited time. They know you're here, and that you have to fly back soon.'

'So I don't have a confirmed time to see him yet?' Melissa said, her voice cracking a fraction.

'We're sure we will soon, Melissa,' Barrett said, 'but we're at their mercy.'

Melissa sat back in her chair and looked at the ceiling. She let out a deep breath, and nodded. Tanner thought she was trying hard not to scream.

'Do you know why Li cancelled?' he asked.

'I'm sorry, I'm not aware of that,' Barrett said. She turned to Clarkson. 'Jon?'

Clarkson shook his head. 'I don't –'

'We had an appointment to meet him later this morning,' Tanner said. 'We've just been told he's had to cancel.'

'I wasn't aware of that,' Clarkson said, 'but he sent us this yesterday.' He opened a manila folder and took out a two-page document. 'It's what I think you would call the indictment – or at least the edited version that's publicly released. It was served yesterday by the Supreme People's Procuratorate.'

'That's the prosecutor?'

Clarkson nodded. 'He's given us a copy for our records.'

Tanner looked at the document. 'Can you get it translated?'

'We'll organise that,' Barrett said.

'What does "edited version" mean?'

'I know you know this,' Barrett said, 'but just so we're totally clear: one thing we can't do is give legal advice.'

'I'm just trying to get information,' Tanner said.

Barrett gave a reserved smile. 'Sometimes we find the line between information and advice can get a bit blurry.'

Tanner looked at the strange characters on the document. 'My Chinese is blurry,' he said. 'What does this say?'

'It's consistent with what we've been told,' Clarkson said. 'Three years ago Citadel Resources put in a tender for an exploration licence in an area of land in northern New South Wales.'

'It's called Red Gum Basin,' Tanner said.

'You know about it?'

Tanner's assistant had got him the publicly available details from the internet. The government had granted Citadel a five-year exploration licence to explore for coal and coal-seam gas. The grant was made by the relevant minister following a tender process. Citadel's own website also had details of the EL, and was publishing updates about the results from its exploration program so far.

'A massive coal and coal-seam gas reserve,' Tanner said. 'Citadel was a bit late getting its share of the resources pie in Australia, but they've been making up for it in the last few years.'

'So you know about the tender?'

'I know what's on the public record. The government was offering an EL over a 450-square-kilometre area in the far north-east of the state. It's full of coal and CSG. Citadel put in a bid of two hundred and fifty million, which was the winning bid. The price of coal was still high at the time. They own an adjoining EL to the north, and a mine just over the Queensland border. This Red Gum EL would give them the chance to make a super mine up there. Economies of scale, that sort of thing.'

Clarkson nodded. 'And you know they're in a joint venture with a Chinese company?'

'North Shanxi Resources,' Tanner said. 'I don't know much about them, other than they're in some other joint ventures with Citadel, and they've got mines in Mongolia and Africa, as well as here.'

'The joint venture is why the Chinese consider Citadel's bid price was a state secret,' Clarkson said. 'North Shanxi is a state-owned enterprise.'

'Does the indictment state who Joe's meant to have sought a bribe from?'

'Another Chinese state-owned company. It's called XinCoal.'

'Did they put in a tender for Red Gum?'

'The indictment says they were considering it.'

'Considering it? What's that mean?'

Clarkson shrugged. 'There's no detail about that – they won't put in full particulars about the charge in what they release publicly in a state secrets case.'

Tanner shook his head. 'It must say something about what Joe supposedly did?'

'It says he tried to corrupt one of XinCoal's officials. He'd tell them Citadel's bid price, and in exchange they'd pay him.'

'Where's he meant to have done this?'

'It doesn't say.'

'Does it say when?'

'No precise date – it gives a three month range covering the period the tender was open.'

'How did he meet the person he's meant to have tried to bribe?'

'It says XinCoal tried to retain Joe – or at least BBK – to act for it if they went ahead with a tender. That's how Joe knew they had an interest in the EL.'

'You look frustrated, Peter,' Michelle Barrett said.

'The people I've spoken to at BBK haven't mentioned anything about XinCoal.'

Barrett nodded. 'Jonathon?'

'That's it, but for the bribe amount sought.'

'Which is?'

'Fifteen million.'

'I assume that's a reference to dollars, not to Yuan?'

'US dollars,' Clarkson said. 'Five up front, another ten if XinCoal got the EL.'

Melissa put her tea cup down heavily on the table. 'That is – it's crazy. Fifteen million? Why not fifty? Joe wouldn't do this.' She breathed out slowly, fighting to stay composed.

'Who's the person from XinCoal Joe's meant to have sought the bribe from?'

'It doesn't say.'

'How are they described in the indictment?'

'It just says a senior – the literal translation would be "senior official of XinCoal".'

'So not the mail-room clerk?'

'Not the mail-room clerk.'

'Is that normal here? Not naming in the indictment the person who's meant to be the target of the bribe?'

Clarkson made a gesture to indicate he didn't know.

'That's really something you'd need to ask Joe's lawyer,' Barrett said.

'If he was here, I would,' Tanner said. 'And this unnamed person just happens to wait nearly three years before deciding to go to the police or the security bureau?'

'We don't know what happened, Peter. He may have gone to his superiors first. The indictment doesn't provide an explanation for the delay, or even when the allegation was first made to the authorities.'

'I'm sorry, I just don't understand a lot of this,' Melissa said. 'How is what Joe can tell them worth fifteen million?'

'I'm afraid I can't answer that, Melissa,' Clarkson said.

'If you were a mining company and you really wanted this EL,' Tanner said, 'knowing what Citadel was going to bid in a secret tender would be very valuable. The highest bid wins, and because of its other ELs in the area, there was a fair chance a crowd as ambitious as Citadel was most likely to go highest. If you thought that in the long run you'd end up with a multi-billion-dollar mine, I can understand why you'd be willing to pay big dollars for that information. Knowing what your likely nearest competitor was going to bid also allows you to outbid them, but not overdo it.'

Clarkson nodded. 'Anyway,' he said, 'there's nothing about that in the indictment.'

'Can you help me understand something?' Tanner asked. 'Joe's alleged to have approached some unnamed official of XinCoal, correct?' Clarkson nodded. 'And XinCoal is a state-owned company?'

'A state-owned enterprise,' Clarkson said.

'So the Chinese Government owns it?'

'It's more complex than that,' Clarkson said slowly. 'That's a bit broad these days. In a general sense –'

'Just bear with me,' Tanner interrupted. 'So, Joe approaches this person from XinCoal, and says, "Give me fifteen million dollars, and I'll tell you what Citadel is going to bid for this EL"? That's what it says in the indictment?'

'Yes.'

'And the reason it's a state secret he'd be giving away is that Citadel's in a joint venture with North Shanxi Resources, right?'

'Yes.'

'Which is another of these state-owned enterprises?'

Clarkson nodded.

'So Joe is alleged to be trying to get a bribe from the Chinese government, in order to sell what in part is a commercial secret of another part of the Chinese Government?' Tanner paused and looked at both Clarkson and Barrett. 'Do you see my confusion?'

Clarkson started to answer, but the Consul General cut him off. 'I think we can help you here,' she said. She stood and offered more tea to Tanner and Melissa. 'Chinese state-owned enterprises aren't all as state owned as they used to be,' she began. 'Now that China has a more market-based economy, things have changed dramatically. First, there are privately run companies. Secondly, there's been a lot of quasi-privatisation of SOEs. The government still has a stake, but private investment is allowed also.'

'Private investment from within China?'

'Foreign companies can have investments in SOEs too.'

'So how are they managed?'

'The more diversified the ownership of a SOE, the more likely it is that it might have management and governance from private sources, whether they're domestic or foreign.'

'And North Shanxi and XinCoal? They have foreign investors?'

Barrett shook her head. 'That we can't help you with. You'd need to investigate yourself, if you think it's relevant.'

Tanner nodded slowly. 'It's possible, though, these companies might be part owned by private investors in China, or by foreign investors?'

'Yes, but – and again speaking generally – there's now real competition between SOEs that operate in the same markets.'

Tanner nodded. 'So North Shanxi and XinCoal, even if they're state owned wholly or in part, they'd still regard each other as competitors?'

'Vigorous competitors,' Clarkson said.

'You mean something beyond the general ruthlessness of big corporations in capitalist markets?'

Clarkson shrugged. 'I mean . . . North Shanxi is, as you said, involved in joint ventures with Citadel for a variety of minerals. XinCoal is the coal arm of Xin Resources Co of China. They're big companies competing for a dwindling supply of resources.'

Tanner nodded. 'So when I said it was confusing that Joe's alleged to have been seeking to sell the government its own secret, I was being naive?'

'Well . . . the ownership structure of these companies – that's something you might want to find out. SOEs enjoy a privileged status. They have access to state loan funds if needed, they return profits to the state, they're a means of China bringing in foreign expertise but still keeping its ownership share in vital industries.'

'They're still the long arm of the Chinese state?'

'You could say that.'

'I guess that's what Joe's found out,' Tanner said.

Clarkson raised his eyebrows and shrugged, but didn't respond.

'And so – tomorrow?' Tanner said.

'We're seeing Joe at ten,' Barrett said.

'How long have you got with him?'

'Technically thirty minutes, but they're usually flexible with consular or embassy staff. We'll probably get a little longer.'

'Thirty minutes?' Melissa said. 'How can he tell you – it's not long enough, Michelle.'

Barrett nodded. 'We're only there to check how he is. He can tell us what he wants about the charges, but that's not the primary purpose of our visit.'

'Is there any chance you can talk them into letting me see him tomorrow?'

Barrett shook her head. 'I don't want to raise that yet. After we've seen Joe, I'll make calls to sort out your visit.'

Melissa was about to say something more, but Barrett beat her to it.

'I know how anxious you must be to see Joe. We'll do everything we can to confirm your visit as soon as possible.'

Melissa nodded a reluctant agreement.

'You'll call us after you've seen him?' Tanner asked.

'Of course,' Barrett said.

Before they left, Melissa excused herself to use the bathroom. The Consul General said her goodbyes, but Clarkson waited with Tanner in the foyer by the lifts.

'One thing I did check,' Tanner said, 'not long after I'd heard about Joe, was acquittal rates for people who end up charged with a crime here.'

Clarkson raised his eyebrows knowingly. 'It's the same throughout Asia. If you're charged, they consider the evidence to be overwhelming.'

'I'd almost consider being a prosecutor here. I like winning.'

'Chinese defence lawyers' lives are fraught with danger. If a prosecutor considers you've brought forward untruthful evidence, they can and will charge you.'

'I'd be doing life in prison,' Tanner said. 'Do you know how long it might be before a court hearing?'

'A trial? Within about twelve months, I'd expect. Perhaps a bit longer. Less if Joe . . .'

Tanner nodded. 'He didn't do it,' he said. 'For what it's worth. I've known him a long time. Something has gone really wrong here. This is a not a guy who seeks a bribe.'

Clarkson nodded, but said nothing.

'The half-percent acquittal rate – how's that hold up for offences like this? If the charge is to do with the interests of the Chinese state?'

Clarkson sighed. 'You'll have to ask Li.'

'Have you ever heard of an acquittal?'

Clarkson was prevented from answering by Melissa's approach.

As Tanner pushed the button for the lift, Clarkson shook his head slowly.

12

'I only meant to grab her bag.'

It was the second time John Richter had said this. He spoke more loudly this time, as his words had already gone unacknowledged.

'Keep your voice down,' Stefan Fehrmann said. He was kneeling over Elena's body.

'She's dead, isn't she?'

Fehrmann looked away from the dead girl's face and up at Richter, who was standing next to the couch, smoking a cigarette. 'Don't talk again unless I ask you a question,' he said.

Stefan Fehrmann had spent nearly forty years cleaning up messes. For Hendrik Richter, he didn't mind. Empires have to grow, and need defending. Sweeping up after the idiot son was something else. Fehrmann had moved up quickly around the mines, keeping workers in check. The security company that employed him was now one of the largest in the world. Then he'd joined Citadel, and made it all the way to head of security. He'd fixed bigger problems than John Richter could make – negotiating with greedy and corrupt governments, cajoling local militia and law enforcement, handling issues concerning native landholders – always sensitively at first; with force when required. He worked out who needed to be bribed or blackmailed, and who needed to be squeezed, and how hard.

He liked Australia, and moved to Sydney ten years ago, when Citadel was cranking up its investments down under. He was now an Australian citizen. He was still called head of security, but only for the Sydney office. He did 'special projects' if Hendrik Richter or Andre Visser called him. An ongoing special project was looking after Hendrik's children.

Fehrmann stood and told the two men he'd brought with him to stay in the lounge room with the body. He'd woken them up after Richter had called. They were two of Hendrik's bodyguards, and were meant to be on call 24/7, even if the boss was out of town. 'Try not to fall asleep,' he said.

He pointed to a door that led to a study off the lounge room. He walked in with Richter, and shut the door. It was Richter's home office, and he went to sit behind the desk, but Fehrmann pointed to one of the chairs in front of it.

'Sit there.'

Fehrmann sat in the chair behind the desk. He took off the spectacles he was wearing, and rubbed at the dents they'd left in either side of his nose with his gloved fingers. Then he sighed loudly, and stared at Richter. He put his hand inside the jacket he was wearing, took out a gun, and put it on the desk. A Glock 26. A baby gun, easily concealed. His weapon of choice since moving into semiretirement.

John Richter moved his eyes from Fehrmann to the weapon. 'Why do you have that?'

Fehrmann glared at him for a full five seconds. 'To shoot you.'

'What?'

'Your father told me to shoot you.'

Richter narrowed his eyes and bit his lip. 'I rang you, Stefan. I didn't want to involve my –'

'He told me to shoot you the moment you fail to cooperate.' Fehrmann's voice was deep and precise.

'If you've spoken to –'

'Shut up.' He paused, making sure he was not going to be interrupted. 'Where have you been before here?'

'I went out with friends.'

'Answer the question. Where have you been before here?'

'Four of us went to a restaurant. At Olympus.'

'Which one?'

'Andiamo.'

'Who saw you?'

'What do you mean? The restaurant was –'

'Did you see or speak to anyone you know?'

'Um . . . not customers. The staff. I know the waiter, the front of house.'

'How did you get there?'

'Mario took me.'

'What time did you get to the restaurant?'

'About nine.'

'What time did you leave?'

'About eleven thirty?'

'How much did you drink there?'

'I don't fucking know.'

'How much?'

'A few beers. Maybe three bottles of wine between the four of us.'

'Did you all drink the same?'

'I wasn't measuring, Stefan.'

Ferhmann picked up the gun, and ran his fingers down the barrel, felt its weight in his left hand. 'Did you all drink the same?'

Richter rolled his eyes. 'Yes.'

'And after the restaurant?'

'Justin – the guy who's still here – he and I went upstairs to the club.'

'Was anyone there that you knew?'

'A couple of hostesses. People may have recognised me. It was quite busy.'

'Who recognised you?'

'I don't know. No one I know.'

'What time did you leave?'

Richter breathed out, tried to calm himself. 'Around three thirty.'

'Were people there when you left?'

'Just a few, and some of the staff.'

'And you left with the girl out there?'

Richter nodded.

'And Justin and . . . ?'

'Klaudia,' he said. 'Her name's Klaudia.'

'She's with Justin now?'

Richter nodded again.

'And Mario drove you here?'

'Yes.'

'Where did he pick you up from?'

'Out the front.'

'Had you met . . . the girl lying here. Had you met her before?'

'No. She hasn't been at the club long.'

'What about the other girl . . . Klaudia?'

'A few times.'

'What was happening at the club with these girls?'

'What do you mean "what was happening"? They served us drinks all night.'

'Use your fucking imagination, John. Were you fooling around with them at the club?'

'A little,' he said. 'Especially Klaudia and Justin.'

Ferhmann nodded. 'What happened here?'

'I told you,' Richter said, his voice urgent. 'I only meant to grab her bag.'

'What happened when you got here before you took her bag from her, John?'

'We had a few drinks.'

'How many is a few?'

Richter shook his head like an annoyed child. 'A few bottles of champagne.'

Ferhmann glared at Richter. He imagined shooting him. He wanted to see the surprised look in his eyes as the bullet went between them and blew a hole out the back of his head. But then he'd have another mess to clean up.

'You buried your young wife three days ago,' he said, 'and tonight you're drinking champagne?'

'I –' Richter started to say something, then stopped.

'How much coke did you have?'

'A few lines.'

'And the others?'

'Justin barely sampled it. Klaudia did a line. More like half. The other one less.' The final words were almost a whisper.

'What happened after that?'

'Justin and Kaudia went off together. They were pretty wasted. He's smashed.'

'How long ago was that?'

'An hour maybe. A bit longer now.'

'Did you touch this other girl in any way,' Fehrmann said, 'other than "grabbing her bag"?' He used his hands to put quotation marks around his words.

'No. And I was only trying –'

'Did she touch you?'

'What do you – ?'

'Was there any form of fight?'

'No.'

'Did she scratch you?'

'No.'

'Are you sure?'

'Yes, I'm sure.'

'How much coke is here?'

'I've got most of a thirty-gram bag left out there. I've got another in my bedroom.'

Fehrmann stood up, and motioned for Richter to do the same. 'Let's go and get it.'

Richter stayed seated. 'Don't you want to hear what happened? To Elena? I was just –'

'I already know.'

'But I haven't –'

'She wanted to leave,' Fehrmann said. 'You wanted to fuck her. Now she's dead.'

'I only meant to grab her bag.'

Fehrmann shook his head. 'Go and do what I told you to do,' he said.

John Richter walked back into the lounge from his bedroom carrying a bag of cocaine, and gave it to Ferhmann. 'What are you going to do with it?'

'Go back to the study, and shut the door,' Fehrmann said. 'Don't come out until I tell you to.'

Once Richter had gone, Fehrmann went to the kitchen. He put some of Richter's cocaine in a glass, and mixed it with water. He took two syringes from his bag. One was full of just enough alcohol. The other he filled with what would be a lethal dose of coke. When he was done he returned to the lounge and the other men.

'If he's still out of it,' he said, 'it's plan A.' The men nodded. He pointed at the shorter man, who was shaped like a body builder, rocks shoved under the skin of his arms and shoulders. Christ only knew how many steroids he took. 'You take the girl. Get her out to the car and keep her there. Don't hurt her, but encourage her not to make noise. You follow?' The man nodded.

Klaudia woke as she was lifted off the bed. The bodybuilder put a hand over her mouth when she started to thrash and tried to scream. She succumbed to his strength soon enough and he carried her out of the room.

Justin Matheson was wasted. Fehrmann went with plan A.

The needle went in the vein. Just a gentle push was necessary. Bypassing the work of the stomach and intestines, the alcohol would make him unrousable for a while yet, and still very drunk for hours.

Fehrmann and the second man carried Matheson out to the lounge room and laid his body next to Elena's. Fehrmann picked up the dead girl's hand and ran her long black nails across Matheson's face and chest. His breathing changed slightly, but that was all. The other man went back to the bedroom for Matheson's clothes. They put his briefs and trousers back on him, threw his jacket and shirt over a couch, and left his shoes and socks under the coffee table.

Fehrmann took the bag of coke he'd been given, and put it in another small plastic bag he'd brought with him. He took Matheson's left hand and squeezed his fingers around the bag lightly. He repeated this a few times, then did the same with the right. Then he put the bag in one of the pockets of Matheson's jacket. While he was doing that, the second man returned carrying the sheets and pillowcases he'd stripped from the bed.

'Take them to the car,' Fehrmann said. 'Make sure everything's all right with the girl.' When the man left, Fehrmann walked into Richter's study.

He found him sitting behind the desk, staring at the ceiling.

'You've got linen here?' Fehrmann asked.

'What?'

'Do you have clean linen here?'

'Why are you – ?'

'I know it's a long time since you made a bed, John, but as soon as we're gone, put some clean sheets in that bedroom.'

'Why?'

'Just do it. Then wait another ten minutes, and ring an ambulance.'

'An ambulance? But –'

'You're going to tell them there's an injured girl here, and you don't think she's breathing. There's a man lying in the same room, so drunk he can barely talk. If they ask whether drugs are involved, you're going to say yes, and what kind.'

'I will get –'

'Ask for the police too.'

Richter shook his head violently. 'No, Stefan, I'm not –'

'When they arrive, you're going to tell them what happened.'

'What?'

'You went to your club. You're depressed. You had too much to drink.'

'Stefan, I can't –'

Fehrmann moved swiftly to the desk and grabbed Richter by the throat. He pushed his head back against the chair. 'Listen to me. You came back here with your friend Justin and the two girls. Justin was very drunk. Are you following me, John? Please tell me you're following?'

Richter clenched his jaw, but nodded as much as he could. Fehrmann released his grip, but put his face closer to that of his boss's son.

'If the police ask you whether you've taken any drugs last night, what are you going to say?' He glared at Richter, who said nothing. Stefan Fehrmann hit the heir to the Citadel throne across the top of his head with an open palm as hard as anyone had ever dared. He grabbed him by the face, his thumb pressing on the right side of Richter's jaw, his fingers on the left. 'What are you going to say, John?' Fehrmann said slowly.

'Yes,' Richter said, barely audibly.

'And who gave you the cocaine?'

Richter looked at Fehrmann helplessly.

Fehrmann released his grip, straightened and smiled. 'Why, Justin gave it to you, John, don't you remember?'

Richter cautiously touched his jaw, and nodded. 'I could get –'

'You were very upset about the death of your wife. You made some errors of judgement tonight because of grief, and a great deal of alcohol.'

Richter sighed, then nodded.

'After Justin brought out the coke, you went into your study with the girl who miraculously is still alive after coming here.'

'With Klaudia?'

'With Klaudia. You two went to your study to talk, and you left the dead girl and Justin out in your lounge room. Okay?' He waited.

'Okay,' Richter said.

'You took her back to her house, and Mario drove you both. Then when you got back, you found the other girl bleeding in your lounge room, and Justin paralytically drunk. You called the ambulance, you called the police, and you're so sorry this has all happened.'

Richter glared at the ground for a moment, thinking. 'Wait. Justin? Is he – ?'

'Justin and Elena must have had some kind of argument. He wanted to fuck her, and she said no. Sound familiar? There was a terrible accident, Elena hit her head on your coffee table, and now she's dead.'

Richter shook his head. 'But – but Justin, he's going to say –'

'Who cares what Justin says?'

Richter stood and shook his head, smiling in frustration. 'Justin is going to say he was with Klaudia. He's going to say I was with Elena. How is that – ?'

'He's going to say that, John. But Klaudia isn't. She's going to say she was with you, and that you took her home. I'm going to have to make it worth her while to say that. I'm going to have to convince her that's the only option she has. Do you know how much work that will take? Do you know how much it will cost?'

Richter ran his hand across his eyes and forehead, then through his hair. He stared at a spot on the ground. 'Can't – can't Elena just . . . disappear?'

Fehrmann had to stifle a laugh. 'Disappear?'

'Yes,' Richter said. 'Disappear.'

Fehrmann walked up to Richter, who took a step back. Fehrmann placed his hands softly on his shoulders, though, and shook them gently. 'Where did you go tonight, John?' he said.

'I told you.'

Fehrmann nodded, and frowned thoughtfully. 'And how many CCTV cameras will have caught you with this missing girl? How many do you think are running at any one time inside and outside of – what's it called? Pantheon?'

'Could – ?'

'What are you going to tell the police when they start investigating this girl's disappearance? What about Justin? Does he disappear too? And Klaudia? Does that sound like a good plan?'

Richter shook his head and pushed Fehrmann's arms away from him. 'I'm stressed. I'm not thinking straight.'

'Klaudia will say what we tell her to say. She does not disappear. You need her.'

Richter nodded. 'So why'd she leave then? Why did Klaudia leave so soon. Before . . . you know . . .'

'She wanted to go home, John. Or you can say you decided not to try to fuck her, if that makes you feel better. You're such a good little boy. So cut up over your wife's death. You took Klaudia home, then came back to a mess.'

'I don't want to say –'

'After you've called the ambulance, you call your father. He'll arrange a lawyer to get here for you.'

'My father will –' Richter said, but couldn't complete the sentence.

Stefan Fehrmann laughed, a deep, real laugh, which stopped as sharply as it began. 'John, if I was your father,' he said, 'I would be digging a grave for you next to that girl out there.'

13

The cab ride to Qingpu took just over an hour. The prison was surrounded by gardens, and Tanner thought he'd been taken to the wrong place at first.

Five days before, he'd been with Melissa when Michelle Barrett, the Consul General, had called. She'd just returned from visiting Cheung. They'd been expecting to see him in the detention centre, but the police rang Clarkson that morning and said he'd been moved to Qingpu. They didn't know why – the prison was usually for people who'd already had their trials and been convicted, not for prisoners on remand.

Cheung was physically well, Barrett said, although his mood was subdued, which was understandable. Barrett said he understood what charges had been made against him, and what was in the indictment. He hadn't wanted to discuss any of that with them.

Three days later, Melissa was granted an access visit. They'd let her stay for an hour. When Tanner met her in the hotel café after, he could see she'd been crying. He'd pressed her on what they'd talked about, but it seemed she was in shock, almost unable to speak.

'He must have told you something, Melissa. Does he have any idea what's happened?'

'He told me he could only speak to his lawyer about it.'

'You're okay with that? You must have –'

'I'm not okay with any of this!' Her cry had brought a temporary hush across most of the café. Then she'd burst into tears. He'd tried to talk to her about it again that night at dinner, but she shook her head, and refused to say more about her visit.

He'd called the offices of the lawyer Yinshi Li after lunch with Melissa, and again the next morning. Both times he was told Mr Li would call him back, but no call had come. He'd given up on being able to see Joe, and their flight back to Sydney was booked for the next day. Then the consulate called him, and said he'd be allowed a visit too. He was surprised, but hopeful.

In the main building a large number of prisoners, all dressed in blue, were seeing loved ones or friends. There was a drone of voices in the hall, and to his untrained ear it sounded to Tanner like a dozen or more arguments were breaking out. The smell was no different to the other prisons he had visited. Aggressive fumes from ammonia and chlorine, beyond which human waste lurked. For some reason, the smell made Tanner think of death. He wondered if this was his imagination. He'd been told as a young lawyer this was how prisons smelt. The sense of death though, that was completely real.

Tanner scanned the tables, and saw Cheung in a far corner. Cheung raised his hand in a gesture of hello when he saw Tanner approach. At the table next to Cheung, a prisoner was nursing a young child.

Joe Cheung shook Tanner's hand, then gestured to the chair in front of him.

'Unusual place for BBK to open a new office,' Tanner said.

'We're always opening a new office somewhere,' Cheung said. He smiled faintly. He had dark rings under his eyes.

Tanner looked around the large hall. 'The fit-out's not up to your Sydney office standards.'

'Everyone's worried about overheads these days.'

'I've always wanted to come to China.'

'What do you think?'

'It's a long drive to the Great Wall. The least you could have done was get arrested in Beijing.'

'The Pudong skyline's pretty spectacular, though, don't you think? You're at the Hyatt, right?'

Tanner nodded. 'They must think I work at BBK. They keep asking me to fix up your bill from when you were last there.'

'I left in a hurry.'

'You've lost weight. How's the food in this place?'

Cheung shrugged. 'I'd kill for some Peking duck.'

'I should have brought you some.'

'Have you had it here?'

'I'm guessing it's better in Beijing.'

Cheung smiled. 'Unless you know where to go, it's actually better in Sydney.'

'How are you doing, Joe?'

Cheung looked at the prisoner to his left, who was stroking the plump, rosy cheeks of his child. He turned back to Tanner and shook his head.

'You've seen the lawyer?' Tanner asked.

Cheung nodded.

'He doesn't seem to want to return my calls. How have you found him?'

'He knows what he's doing.'

'And what is he doing?'

Cheung paused, then let out a long breath. 'He's representing my interests,' he said.

'Does that mean he's preparing a defence?'

'He's representing my interests, Pete. We're in China.'

'Has he represented people charged with state offences?'

'He has.'

Tanner narrowed his eyes and leant forwards. 'Joe,' he said softly, 'can you please tell me why you're here?'

'Why do you think I'm here?' It wasn't sarcasm in his voice, it was something deader. Like it didn't matter what the answer was.

'It's never been you to answer a question with a question, Joe.'

Cheung looked down at the table, then slowly up at Tanner. 'It must be the Chinese in me coming out.'

'I don't think you got in here by seeking a bribe from some mysterious man from XinCoal. Did you?'

'Why else would I be here?'

Tanner exhaled and examined the face of the man sitting in front of him as though he was meeting him for the first time. Cheung looked back with a blank expression.

'Is that some kind of joke?' Tanner said.

Cheung's smile was that of a beaten man. 'This doesn't seem like a place for jokes, does it?'

Tanner glared at him. 'I've come a long way to visit you,' he said. 'Can you tell me why the hell you're here?'

'It doesn't matter why.'

'It doesn't matter?'

Cheung put his elbows on the desk, his hands clasped together, chin resting on his interlocked fingers. 'Do you know the acquittal rate for people charged with serious offences in China?'

'That's not –'

'It's effectively zero.'

Tanner hesitated, stumbling over thoughts and words in his head. 'I want to help somehow. I want to understand, at least. Tell me –'

'I'll get ten years less if I plead guilty,' Cheung said.

'Ten years less than what? Is that Li's advice? Give up?'

'I'm not giving up.'

'What are you doing, then?'

'I'm telling you I'm guilty. I feel guilty.'

'You *feel* guilty? What does that mean?'

Cheung shook his head. 'It doesn't matter.'

'It matters to me. It might matter to your family too. Think of them.'

'I am.' Cheung looked across to the table on his left. The prisoner was now standing up, saying goodbye to his wife and baby. He was allowed to kiss them both. 'Do you know how old my children will be if I force a trial?'

'You'd rather they think you're a crook?'

'I can explain it to them.'

'Explain it to me. Whatever evidence the prosecutors serve, I'd like to see it. I'd like to see the witness statement of this mystery man who seems to have waited three years to report that you tried to bribe him with Citadel's tender bid.'

Cheung sat back in his chair and shook his head. 'You think you can appear for me, Pete? Are you going to knock out the evidence on some technicality, or sway a jury with some oration about reasonable doubt? Do you think it works like that here?'

'What you just said, Joe,' Tanner said, 'is the first time I can remember you really annoying me. I know the system is different.'

'The system here is simple. If you're charged with the crimes I'm charged with, you're guilty.'

'You can't give up yet, for Christ's sake. Let me look at the evidence. Tell me what you know, what you think has happened. If it can't be beaten in court, then . . . I don't know – if it looks like a weak case I can discuss it with the consulate or the ambassador. Maybe the government can make representations behind the scenes. If this is some kind of mistake or . . . setup, something I don't understand yet, there may be a way of helping you outside of the courtroom.'

'You think you're that good?' Cheung said flatly. 'You and whoever else you enlist for me?'

'I don't know what you mean by that.'

'The Chinese Government says I tried to sell their commercial secrets. Do you think you or anyone else can talk them out of it?'

'I don't know what it is I can or can't do yet. If there's some representation that can be made on your behalf, let someone make it. But I need to hear your story first.'

'I appreciate your offer of help, Pete, I really do. I appreciate you being here. I'll forever be grateful for the support you've given Melissa. I've always –' For a moment the deadened expression dropped, and Cheung appeared close to tears before he recovered. 'I need you to stop.'

'Stop what?'

'I'm pleading guilty, Peter. You can't help me. We're not home.'

'This is crazy, just –'

'It will be much better for me if I plead guilty.'

'What were you doing in Shanghai? What have you been doing for Citadel?'

Cheung gave a sad smile. 'You know the law of privilege, Peter.'

'Joe, give me the name of the person saying you sought a bribe. Explain to me why he took so long to come forward. It doesn't make sense.'

Cheung stood, raised his hand, and called out to a guard, who moved to the table quickly. Cheung said something in Chinese. The guard looked at Tanner and motioned for him to move towards the exit. Cheung held out his hand to Tanner, who slowly stood. The men shook hands.

'Thank you for everything, Peter,' Cheung said. 'Please do as I ask.'

'Joe, I –'

'Do you want to be my lawyer, Pete?'

'Yes.'

'Then do nothing further. Those are my instructions.'

It was five pm when Tanner arrived back at the hotel. In the taxi he'd played out in his mind why Joe Cheung would shut him out. He understood a guilty plea. China was no different to most places in the world when it came to that: save the state a trial, and shave off a quarter or so of the sentence you'd get if you went with not guilty and lost. And when the odds of acquittal are nearly non-existent, even the innocent will cop a plea. Maybe only the insane wouldn't.

Pleading guilty was an endgame, though. Joe Cheung wasn't at that point yet. Why not take a look at the evidence first, and see if the case has weaknesses, inconsistencies, or is purely based on the word of one man? Why not find out more about that man?

Tanner went straight to Melissa's room. When she opened the door, she was wearing only her hotel robe. Her eyes were red, the skin underneath them puffy from crying.

'Want me to give you a moment to get changed?' he said.

She sighed, but held the door open further. 'No,' she said. 'Come in.'

She walked past the bed and sat on an apricot lounge in the corner of the room. Tanner wheeled over the chair that was behind the desk. He looked out the window, the neon lights of the skyscrapers beginning to glow through the gloomy mist.

'Are you seeing him before you go back?' he asked.

She nodded.

'When?'

'Sunday. I'll fly home Sunday night.' She looked out the window. 'Are you still leaving tomorrow?'

He waited for her to look back at him before he spoke. 'Why didn't you tell me, Melissa?'

She shook her head. 'He wanted to.'

'Why?'

'I don't know.'

'He's acting prematurely.'

'Please, Peter. He says it's for the best. He says he has to.'

'Is he guilty? Did he try and sell his client's bid price?'

'No,' she said. 'I don't know.'

'You don't know?'

'I don't – he's doing the best thing, Pete. I have to trust that.'

'Did his lawyer recommend this?'

'That's not what he said.'

'Not what Joe said?'

'Not what Li said.'

'You've spoken to him?'

She took a deep breath and looked out the window again. 'I've seen him.'

Tanner shook his head, trying to keep his anger under control. 'When?'

'Today. At his office.'

'Why didn't you tell me about this?'

'Because Joe told me not to,' she snapped.

'Why?'

She closed her eyes, and took a deep breath. 'He wanted me to see Li first. That's all.'

'And what did Li tell you?'

'He explained what would happen. When Joe might be in court, that kind of thing. He said Joe would get twenty years if he fought and lost. Doing it this way . . . he said the prosecutors would tell the judge to be lenient. He was hoping for no more than ten years.'

'And you're okay with that? Whether he's guilty or not?'

'Twenty years is a lifetime, Peter.'

'Why not wait until we know what the evidence is? Let's look at the documents, a witness statement, whatever is handed over. He shouldn't throw away even the slimmest chance of trying to convince the prosecutors their witness might be the one lying. Tell me he's guilty, Melissa. Tell me he's guilty like you mean it, and I'll shut up.'

Tanner stood and walked to the windows, then turned back. 'I only want to have to ask this once,' he said. 'What aren't you telling me? Tell me what Joe won't.'

Her eyes welled with tears, and her chin dimpled and quivered. She could only say one more word: 'Don't.'

Half an hour after Tanner got back to his room, his phone rang. It was Jonathon Clarkson from the consulate.

'When are you next seeing Joe?' Tanner asked after they'd exchanged greetings.

'In about a month. Just to keep updated about his health, make sure he's been treated fairly, that kind of thing. How did your meeting go today?'

Tanner paused. He decided to treat Cheung's decision to plead guilty as privileged for the time being. 'Nothing he said changed my mind about his innocence,' he said. 'Is that why you called?'

'No,' Clarkson said. 'I'm calling about Mr Li.'

'What about him?'

'He's just called me. He asked me to tell you that he can meet you tomorrow night.'

'What?'

'Seven thirty. At your hotel.'

'I'm on a flight back home at seven thirty-five tomorrow.'

Clarkson hesitated. 'Oh. Well, I'm just passing on a message.'

'Why'd he speak to you, rather than call me?'

'That I don't know.'

'Can't he just see me at his offices tomorrow morning, before I fly back?'

'You can try and call him, but he said it was the only time he had. He said he'd see you at seven thirty tomorrow night at Cloud 9. That's the bar –'

'I know where the bar is,' Tanner said, before ending the call.

14

Cloud 9 was busy, but just before seven thirty Tanner was taken from his stool at the long bar, to a table on the mezzanine level. He was scanning the wine list when he felt the presence of someone by his side. He glanced up, and looked into the face of what appeared to be a schoolboy. The only thing that gave away that Yinshi Li was over twenty-one was the wispy black hair on the top of his round head, and the tailored suit from Hong Kong.

'You're Mr Tanner,' Li said confidently. His was the smile of the cheekiest boy in the classroom.

'I am.' Tanner stood and took Li's hand. A soft handshake. He towered over the Chinese lawyer.

Li gestured to a bank of windows before he sat down. 'Nearly the best bar for views in Asia,' he said. There was that grin again, and a gentle laugh. His English was good.

'What's the best?'

'The Peninsula in Kowloon, perhaps?'

'Is that the other bar where you see your clients?'

Li laughed. 'You're not a client, Mr Tanner.'

'Call me Peter. Can I get you a glass of wine?'

'Yes, please. And just call me Li.'

'White or red?'

'White, please.'

'There's a pinot grigio on the list.'

Li nodded. 'I like many Italian things.'

'It's from my part of the world. It'll be drinkable, though.'

Li nodded, but his smile became uncertain, and Tanner wondered if something had become lost in translation. He signalled to a waiter and ordered the wine.

'I thought you'd be older.'

'You were expecting Rumpole?'

Tanner smiled at the reference. 'You're a Rumpole fan?'

Li nodded. 'I like many TV shows about lawyers.'

'Rumpole started as a book.'

'I watched him on DVD. I also watched crime shows for many years. Mainly American.'

'Are they the reason you became a criminal lawyer?'

Li laughed again. 'I mainly watched to learn my English.'

'Seriously?'

'Yes.'

Tanner smiled. 'Stick with Rumpole.'

Their drinks arrived. Tanner picked his glass up and held it towards Li. 'How's it go again? *Gan bei*?'

'*Gan bei*,' Li said, smiling.

Tanner asked him how long he'd been a criminal lawyer. Li recited his whole legal history. For a number of years he'd worked for a large Chinese firm doing corporate work. He'd been working as a criminal defence lawyer for more than ten years now, although he still regularly consulted to his previous firm.

'Is it a foreign firm?'

Li shook his head. 'Oh, no,' he said. 'A Shanghai firm.'

'Why criminal work?'

'That is a very long story, Peter.'

'Got an edited version?'

'My father's best friend was executed twenty years ago for a crime he did not commit.'

Tanner paused, waiting for Li to say more, but that appeared to be it. 'That does sound like the short version of a much longer story.'

Li nodded. 'I will tell you another day. You have your own friend to worry about.'

'Why still do the consulting for your old firm?'

Li patted his belly. 'I need to eat, Peter.'

Tanner smiled. 'Paying clients hard to come by?'

'Very rare.'

'Why here, Li? Why didn't we meet in your office?'

'My office is bugged.'

'Bugged? By the police?'

'By them. By the security bureau.'

'Because of Joe?'

Li laughed again, the entirety of his small plump body jiggling. 'My office is bugged all the time.'

'You're okay with that?'

'It's – your saying is "occupational hazard".'

'For a defence lawyer?'

'Yes.'

'How do you know it's bugged? You've got some security guy who's swept it?'

Li laughed again. 'The police have told me, Peter.'

'I'm assuming that's against the law? All of it, I mean. The bugging, and then the telling you about it?'

Li shrugged.

'How do you have conferences with clients?'

'Most clients are in prison before I become involved.'

'But if they're not. How can people speak freely in your office?'

'I have careful conversations.'

Tanner nodded. 'I see.'

'Of course, it can be a very dangerous occupation in China to be a defence lawyer who defends the guilty.'

'So all your clients are innocent, Li?'

'Very few, Peter.'

'What about Joe Cheung. Is he innocent?'

Li paused. 'I am sure that there is a very long story that might answer that question. The short one is "no".'

'No?'

'Mr Cheung has instructed me that he will be pleading guilty to the charges the state has made against him in the indictment.'

'Has Joe even seen the evidence against him? Have you?'

'It would please me greatly to be able to discuss that with you. I cannot.'

'Why?'

'This is a case involving state commercial secrets,' he said. 'No one other than me will be able to see the evidence. No one other than me will be allowed in the courtroom for Joe. Even consular officials won't be able to observe. It will not be a public hearing.'

Tanner sighed. 'You could ask the prosecutors to let me look at the evidence as well, couldn't you? As Joe's Australian lawyer? I'd sign whatever confidentiality document they wanted me to.'

Li shook his head. 'The evidence must be kept confidential. There are no exceptions.'

Tanner took a sip of his wine and leant forwards. 'Joe's got three young kids, Li. If he pleads guilty, how long will he be in Qingpu?'

'I hope to achieve no more than ten years.'

'Ten years is a long time. Especially so far from home. That's why I want to look at the evidence. I want to talk to our consular officials if it looks weak. We all know about the odds of acquittal, but I don't want him to give up without at least seeing what we're up against.'

Li smiled fractionally, but didn't speak for a few moments. 'What Joe is up against, Peter, is China.'

'I want to see the evidence,' Tanner said firmly. 'I want to know something about this person from XinCoal Joe is supposed to have tried to corrupt.'

Li smiled again, but the friendliness dropped from his face. 'And I would go to jail for as long as Joe if I showed it to you.'

'If you thought the case was weak – if that was the view you came to – could you discuss it with our consulate? Surely you can do that?'

'I cannot.'

Tanner glared at him for a long moment.

'I can see you're frustrated, Peter,' Li said. 'Our legal system is really not so different to yours. There are rules of procedure, and admissibility, and fairness. This is a state security crime, though. The rules become different. Like they do under your terrorism laws.'

Tanner shook his head. 'Have you seen all the evidence? Will you advise Joe to plead guilty even if the case seems weak?'

'I can't answer either question.'

'Why the hell not, Li?'

'Joe is my client, Peter. We are in my country. He did not authorise me to breach his confidence, and I cannot discuss the evidence with you in a case like this.'

'What's the point of this meeting, then?'

Li looked at Tanner for a long moment. 'Joe told me to ask you to trust him,' he said. 'He also wants you to trust me.'

'Trust you? I don't know a thing about you.'

'This is what I have been asked to say to you.'

Tanner sighed, and drained the last of his wine. 'Another?'

Li gestured towards his glass, which was still half full. Tanner ordered two more anyway.

'Have the prosecutors served their evidence yet?'

'Some. I expect to have the balance soon.'

Tanner nodded. 'When you get the whole case, will you . . . if the case seems thin . . . Would you tell Joe not to plead guilty then? Will you at least try and point out to the prosecutors that their witness might be a liar, or just plain mistaken?'

Li shook his head slowly. 'Joe intends to plead guilty. If he changes his mind, I'm sure you'll be told. For now, though, it appears that my job will be to attempt to persuade the court to minimise his sentence.'

'Forget his instructions,' Tanner said, anger in his voice. 'If the case looked weak, what would your advice be?'

'Joe's instructions are clear, Peter. I cannot say it any other way.'

'Is the case based on the word of one witness? A witness who's appeared out of nowhere after three years? Does it come down to that?'

'You know that I must not say.'

Tanner leant back in the chair and shook his head. He looked out the windows for a few moments, before turning back to face Li. 'I'm going to ask our consulate to seek permission from your government to let me look at the evidence against Joe. I'll sign a confidentiality undertaking, or whatever they want me to. Please, can you have him wait until I've at least made that request?'

Li paused again, before nodding slowly. 'Joe's case will not be before the court for some months yet. I can ask him if he wants to delay indicating that he will plead guilty until all the evidence is provided.'

Tanner leant forwards in his chair again. 'I'd really like to talk to you about that evidence, Li. I'd like the name of the man who said Joe offered to sell his client's secrets.'

Li sat impassively.

'We're not being listened to here, are we?'

Li said something in Chinese.

'What does that mean?'

Li smiled. 'It means the wine is very good'

PART TWO

15

Her name was Lisa Ilves.

He recognised her from a photo on her firm's website. Her dark hair was pulled back, lifting her cheekbones with it. She had feline features. She was wearing a black jacket, and leather jeans suitable for riding a Harley. She was thin and tall. When she sat and crossed her legs on the bar stool, there were angles everywhere.

'Where's your name from? Ilves?' Tanner asked after he'd been given a drinks list. They were in a wine bar he'd suggested in Hunter Street, near where she worked.

'My grandfather's Latvian,' she said. 'He came out to help build the Snowy dam.'

Tanner nodded. 'My father's from Sweden.'

'Wine?'

'Red.'

'Any preference?'

'Shiraz.'

'There's a Margaret River shiraz on the list that's said to have hints of blackberry and leather. How's that for a combination?'

She shrugged. 'Don't ask the sommelier on my account.'

'I can see you like leather,' he said, looking at her legs.

'I got them online last week.'

'Your generation is killing retail.'

'I don't think that's restricted to people my age.'

'Maybe,' he said. 'My divorced colleagues get their new spouses online.'

She smiled. 'That's how I met my last boyfriend.'

'I hope you buy books in stores,' he said, and then turned to order the wine. He looked in the mirror behind the bar, and saw that she was watching him.

'I was here about a month ago,' she said. 'Almost the same seats.'

'Did you meet him online?'

She shook her head. 'He spent most of lunch looking at himself.'

'Couldn't have been a member of the criminal bar then.'

'A political advisor.'

Tanner turned to her. 'Even with all that online choice?'

She shrugged.

'The last date I went on was with a prosecutor,' he said. 'That didn't work out either.'

When the wine came he picked up the menu. 'I'm starving,' he said. 'Do you want to eat?'

'Something quick.'

He gave her the menu.

'I'll have a burger.'

'You're divorced?' she asked, after he'd ordered two burgers. 'Assuming the prosecutor isn't your wife?'

'She died six years ago.'

Lisa paused. 'I'm sorry.'

'It was a logical question.'

She took off her jacket. She was wearing a black sleeveless T-shirt, and on her right shoulder were two red circles, each with the letter O in the middle. They sat on either side of a larger black circle, which had her skin as letter C in the middle. Drawn over the top of the whole thing was a giant X.

'What's that?'

She smiled. 'The enemy.'

'The enemy?'

'Of the planet.'

'You've got a CO_2 molecule tattooed on your shoulder?'

She nodded.

'When did you get it?'

'About three years ago,' she said. 'A thirtieth birthday present.'

'Who from?'

'Myself.'

'Is it your only tattoo?'

'I have others.'

'Do you disclose that in your online dating profile?'

'No.'

'Are the other tattoos greenhouse gas molecules?'

'No.'

'Where are they?'

She sighed. 'Do you want to talk about my tattoos, Peter, or do you want to talk about Citadel Resources?'

Lisa Ilves was a new partner at a law firm called Corcorans. They were class action specialists. For several years she'd been acting for various community groups who were opposed to the grant of mine approvals around the state.

When he returned from Shanghai, Tanner did some more research on the exploration licence granted to Citadel that had Joe Cheung in prison. He found a community action group opposed to mining in that region. On their website the group listed Corcorans as their legal advisors. He also found an article in a legal journal and some newspaper pieces about Corcorans advising other action groups who opposed mine approvals in other parts of the state, including two others involving Citadel. Corcorans couldn't provide Tanner with the answer as to why Cheung was in prison, but they might at least have more information about where the projects were at, and what work Joe might have been doing for them.

Within a year, Lisa told him, the government was expected to grant development approval to Citadel for three new mines. It was seeking approval for what would be one of the world's largest gold mines about halfway between the towns of Cowra and Orange in western New South Wales. There was also a proposed new coal mine in the Upper Hunter Valley. In the far north of the state, not far from the Queensland border, Citadel had paid two hundred and fifty million dollars for a vast exploration licence for coal and CSG – the same EL that Joe Cheung was accussed of seeking a bribe over.

'So if the government grants approval for these mines, your action group will take it and Citadel to court?' Tanner asked.

'We lobby the government not to approve the mines in the first instance. We just think that's a battle we can't win.'

'Too much money at stake?'

'For Citadel, and for the government in royalties.'

'Do these groups pay you for lobbying?'

She shook her head. 'We believe in the cause. It's why I'm at a place like Corcorans. And there's a long-term strategy as well. These mines are bound to end up causing irreparable damage of some kind – either to the environment, or to human health, or maybe both.'

'You want to be on the ground floor for any class actions?'

'We'll earn the right for that.'

When the burgers arrived, Lisa picked hers up and took an enormous bite. The mayo and meat juice ran down her chin. 'Sorry,' she said.

Tanner offered her his napkin. 'Good?'

'Excellent.'

'What's your pleading look like?' he asked. 'Say if this Hunter coal mine is approved?'

'We'll argue that the approval shouldn't have been made on its merits, and that it's legally invalid as well.'

'Different concepts, right?'

'We'd argue an approval has no merit on the facts. Invalidity would require us to prove some error of law in the decision-making process. Either way we win, although it's better to win the first way.'

'Because the legal error can be cured, and the government just grants approval again?'

She nodded. 'If a court finds on the facts that the mine shouldn't have been approved – say for a human health or environmental reason – it's much harder for a government to justify approving it at a later time.'

'And why shouldn't the mine be approved on the merits?'

'I can give you twenty reasons, but one will do: dust.'

'Dust?' He waited as she chewed another large bite from her burger.

'The whole area is full of particle pollution,' she finally said.

'Because of the other coal mines there?'

She nodded. 'We're talking cumulative impacts. A new mine will add coal-dust pollution to air that's already over-saturated with particles.'

'The straw that breaks the camel's back.'

'The camel was flattened years ago.'

'What about this proposed gold mine?'

'It'll have to be the edited version,' she said, looking at the time on her phone. 'I've got to be somewhere in half an hour.'

'Did you meet him online?'

She rolled her eyes.

'Another wine?'

'You go ahead.'

Tanner caught the bartender's attention, who refilled his glass.

'It'll be one of the biggest gold and copper mines in the world,' she said. 'Underground workings, and a huge open pit as well.'

'That means how big?'

'Maybe two million ounces of gold per year, and nearly a hundred million tonnes of copper. They want approval to mine for forty years.'

'And the edited version of what's wrong with that is what?'

'Water,' she said. 'There's a river running right through the proposed mining lease area called the Bageeyn.'

'Hence the Bageeyn River Action Group. I read about them when I came across your firm.'

She nodded. 'The mine will kill it. It'll also take out most of the aquifers that farmers use in the area.'

'How does a mine kill a river?'

'The Bageeyn's vulnerable. It's becoming almost intermittent. Some years it has a constant flow down its entire length, but occasionally now it nearly dries up in some sections. There's always a subterranean flow, though. This mine will kill the river, and all the wildlife that depends on it.'

'How?'

'You don't know much about gold mines, do you?'

'You're about to tell me a lot of water's involved.'

'Sixty to seventy million litres a day. They're saying it will be half that, but they're lying. They're also saying the river will survive, and the drawdown the mine will cause on local aquifers will recover, but they're lying about all of that too.'

'Who's lying?'

'Citadel. Its experts. The government's expert.'

'Lying is a strong word.'

'Citadel's experts are guns for hire. They're like insurance doctors in personal injury cases. Nothing's ever wrong with the plaintiff.'

'Surely the government uses –'

'You think they can't be paid off?'

Tanner shook his head, and smiled a bemused smile. 'I'm assuming you can prove that allegation?'

'No.'

'That won't help your court case.'

'Citadel knows the mine will kill the river.'

'They know it?'

She looked at him. 'I'm not sure I can say any more.'

'Why?'

'I've got client confidences to respect. Privilege?'

'We could consider this a conference. I'm a lawyer, after all.'

She smiled faintly. 'You're not retained by our clients to give advice, Peter. This is beyond the public record.'

'Could what you're about to say have something to do with Joe Cheung?'

Now she paused. 'I don't know,' she finally said. 'I've only been thinking about that since you called.'

'The corruption they've accused him of –' Tanner said, shaking his head, '– there is no way Joe would do it. He's looking at ten to twenty years. Please. I promise you, anything you say to me, I'll keep between us. I'd consider myself bound like you were one of my clients.'

She drained the last of what was left in her glass, and put it back on the bar. 'Citadel had a report for their environmental assessment that told them the mine would kill the river.'

'What do you mean, "had"?'

'It went missing.'

'What?'

'It, and the hydrogeologist who prepared it.'

'Is this a conspiracy theory, Lisa, or do – ?'

'This gold mine is vital to them.'

'Why?'

'They're not making the money from coal they once were. A gold and copper mine is a different story. It's very important to Citadel's future bottom line.'

'And how do you know this report went missing?'

She hesitated for a few moments before answering. 'We had an informant. Two of them.'

He paused and looked at her. 'People at Citadel?'

'A hydrogeologist who worked at a firm that was engaged by them.'

'And this whistleblower and his report have – what, vanished?'

'It was a woman. And yes, she's left.'

'Where?'

'I don't know.'

'Do you have a copy of the report?'

'No.'

'Okay,' he said, taking another sip of wine. 'You said you had two informants?'

She nodded. 'There was another scientist who knew about it, but she wasn't working directly on it.'

'And has she vanished?'

'She's dead.'

'Dead?'

'She was killed in Port Moresby.'

He leant towards her. 'I saw – was this on the news a few months back? Some gang attack?'

'Yes.'

'Was she working in PNG?'

'I don't know. Citadel have mines there.'

When Melissa had told him that Cheung had been to a PNG island not long before his arrest, Tanner did some research on what mines Citadel owned there. Several came up, including a gold mine on Tovosevu Island. 'Do you know anything about a mine called Tovosevu?' he asked. 'It's on a PNG island.'

She shook her head. 'No. Why?'

'What kind of scientist was the woman who was killed?'

'An ecotoxicologist.'

'Meaning?'

'She checks water around mines for pollution, among other things.'

'This report,' he said, 'the one that went missing about the river – would someone like Joe have seen it?'

'I don't know.'

'Would he – ?'

'Peter?' she said. 'You can't talk to anyone about this. When the informants spoke to me, we were probably all breaking the law.' She looked at him and he nodded.

'Is there anything else about this gold mine case you can tell me?' he said.

She put her jacket back on. 'Maybe,' she said softly, 'but I have to go now.'

'You haven't said anything about the CSG mine yet.'

'You've heard of fracking?'

'Sure.'

'Do some reading, if you're interested. Have a look at how much water is needed, and what kind of substances can end up in aquifers. While you're at it, do some research about Citadel.'

'Why?'

She got off her stool and stood next to him. 'It's not just about coal dust and water. I don't – I don't know what your friend has seen or heard, or why he was arrested, or what he's done. His client, though, is an organised criminal. They're the mafia of the corporate world.'

'I'm going to need you to explain that more fully to me.'

'Citadel shouldn't be allowed to operate here. Our governments know they pollute in other countries on a catastrophic scale. They lost the moral right to mine any of our resources years ago.' She shook her head slightly. 'When I said that a hydrogeologist and her report had gone missing, and that I thought another expert had been corrupted, you looked at me like I was crazy. Ask your friend in prison in China if I'm crazy. They kill people, Peter. Native landholders, union leaders in poor countries – people who stand in their way. Lying about water tests is small time for these guys.' She put out her hand to say goodbye.

'You're going to need a barrister eventually, aren't you?' he said. 'If any of these cases get to court?'

She stared at him. 'We don't pay the money you'd be used to.'

'I'm in our profession for love.'

She grabbed her bag and looked at him for a long moment. 'I know you're a heavyweight in your area, Peter, but you're not a planning lawyer. You don't do environmental cases, or class actions. How would I tell the clients we should use someone who specialises in crime?'

He smiled. 'Haven't you just been telling me that's what these cases are all about?'

16

The next night, Tanner took his son to dinner at an Italian restaurant just out of the city that they'd been going to since Dan was a small child. He'd been working late for the last fortnight, away in China for a week before that. He wanted some time with his son away from the distractions of the house and TV.

It had been six years, but when they were taken to their table for two it still felt like there was an empty place where Karen should be. She'd died when Dan was in kindergarten; he was now weeks away from finishing primary school. Those years had swept by him. When the pain stopped, Tanner didn't feel connected to the world. Part of him had become uncoupled, and watched the remainder go through the motions of life. He wasn't sure if he was heading away from the catastrophe, or still caught within it. Life only seemed real when he talked to his son. The rest felt like a kind of dream. And on fleeting moments, he wondered if this was how he coped with the job of defending the guilty. Perhaps not just the guilty. Those who were both guilty and depraved. Was it by making his life a play, part of him standing outside it, that allowed him to be the spokesman for evil?

This was the excuse now. He no longer remembered what he'd told himself before Karen had died.

'Mrs Bussell spoke to me,' Tanner said after they'd ordered drinks. 'She rang me at work.'

Dan nodded, but said nothing.

'Do you know her daughter? Is it Kate?'

'She's in my class.'

'She said Kate might give us a call. She might ask you to a movie.'

The boy looked shocked at first, then hid whatever it was he was feeling. 'Do I have to?'

'It'd be mean to say no, don't you think?'

Dan looked at him blankly.

'You should be pleased there's a girl who likes you.'

'She doesn't like me.'

Tanner smiled. 'Is she nice?'

'I don't know.'

'Do you like the – do you think she looks okay?'

'Normal.'

'You're going to want a girlfriend soon. Trust me.'

'When are you going to get one?'

The question had become more frequent. The first time Dan had asked was about three years earlier. This year he'd asked more than once.

'You know how busy I am.'

'Last time you told me all the women you liked are in prison.'

'You thought I was joking?'

'You said they had to be innocent, but in prison.'

'That's a limited market.'

The waitress came to take their food orders. Dan looked at his father. 'Can we have the *bistecca*?'

Tanner paused for a moment. 'It's a kilo of steak.'

'I'm hungry.'

'Will it be enough, then?'

'Maybe.'

'Medium-rare okay?'

'You say there's no other way.'

When the waitress left, Tanner leant forwards in his seat and spoke conspiratorially to the boy. 'If I was younger, and I was looking for a girlfriend, I'd like our waitress.'

Dan turned and looked quickly at the woman, who was now talking at the next table.

'Why don't *you* ask *her* to a movie, Dad?'

'She looks twenty.'

'Too young?'

'If I was mid-sixties, she'd be perfect.'

'Are you talking garbage again?'

'I'll tell you in twenty-five years.'

Over gelati, the boy quizzed him about whether anything more had happened with Joe Cheung.

'I'm trying to find some things out,' Tanner said.

'He's still not telling you much?'

Tanner shrugged. 'It's hard for him to tell me anything when I'm here.'

'You think you can get him off?'

'His Chinese lawyer will have to do that.'

'Will they?'

'I'm not sure.'

'You told me he's not guilty.'

'He isn't.'

'Why not, then?'

'It's a different system to ours. Apparently his lawyer gets sent to jail too if he pleads not guilty and loses.'

Dan looked up from his gelato, a puzzled expression on his face. 'I don't get that.'

'The Chinese have a well-developed sense of humour when it comes to criminal defence lawyers. Or maybe it's a more developed sense of justice.'

'I don't get that either.'

Tanner looked at his watch. 'Finish up,' he said. 'I've got work to do after you're in bed.'

'Murder?'

Tanner picked up his coffee cup. 'Yeah.'

Tanner first heard about Elena Mancini's death while in China, checking the front-page news back home on his iPad.

What most attracted his attention was where the victim had been found – on the estate of Hendrik Richter, the founder of mining giant Citadel Resources. Richter's son John lived where the girl had been killed, but another man had been arrested and charged – Justin Matheson, an investment banker from Stott Ackerman.

Ten days after Tanner's flight from Shanghai had touched down at Sydney Airport, his clerk gave him a message to call Charles Porter of Sharrop & Prentice regarding Justin Matheson. Sharrop & Prentice were one of the country's top-tier law firms, and he'd acted for one of their clients the previous year, a company director who'd had a lucky escape on an insider trading charge. Tanner guessed that, as the Mathesons had money, they'd gone to the big end of town, bypassing the more boutique-sized criminal firms. It would be a no-expense-spared defence. Tanner and a few of his colleagues at the criminal bar called them 'no budget' matters.

It was no great surprise that Porter had called him – Tanner guessed his name may have come up when Porter discussed who to use with his partners. There wasn't a long list of defence counsel who got briefed in high-profile murder cases. For a wealthy defendant like Justin Matheson, five or six names at most would have been considered.

'You may have heard you weren't the Mathesons' first choice,' Porter said after a brief exchange of pleasantries when Tanner returned his call.

'Was I second?'

'Justin's parents wanted Trevor Jennings.'

'Justin's parents? He's the one in custody, isn't he?'

'They're the ones who'll be paying the legal fees.'

'Your client's the accused, not his mum and dad.'

'They want to meet before we formally retain you.'

'I don't do beauty parades.'

'You come highly recommended by –'

'Justin was denied bail, wasn't he? I read that in the paper. Who appeared for him then?'

'Jennings.'

'So he's already been sacked?'

'Bill and Judith didn't –'

'Relax, Charles,' Tanner said. 'That decision just increased Justin's chances of acquittal. And don't get me wrong, it's a good idea to do some due diligence on who to use as counsel. Contact Silverwater and make a date for us to go and see the client. Then put together all the material you've got so far, and get it to me today.'

'First we'd like to –'

'Once you've done that, then I'll do your screen test.'

Tanner was introduced to William and Judith Matheson in a Sharrop & Prentice conference room. Judith was perhaps sixty, painfully thin, still beautiful, and impeccably groomed, though the carefully applied make-up couldn't conceal the ravaged look of someone who hadn't slept in weeks. Dr William Matheson looked just as Tanner expected of a Macquarie Street obstetrician: old-school hair product holding perfectly combed greying locks; a golf club tie with a Windsor knot. The suit had to be ten years old, and didn't fit properly. It was either off the rack, or more likely from an overrated hustler from Hong Kong, who'd been supplying Dr Matheson and his colleagues with suits that didn't quite fit for thirty years.

Tanner sat on the far side of the conference table, his back to the windows, leaving the harbour view to the Mathesons – they were the ones paying for it. When Porter sat down, he was with another lawyer. He introduced him to Tanner, who failed to catch the name. He wore a sharp suit, a two-hundred-dollar haircut, and a look of supreme self-confidence.

Porter started the meeting by telling Tanner what arrangements had been made to meet with Matheson at the Silverwater Correctional Facility the following morning.

'Who's going to be my junior counsel?' Tanner asked, looking at Porter.

'We thought – and Bill and Judith are comfortable with this – that Henry could fulfill that role, rather than –'

'Who's Henry?'

There was a slight pause, then the lawyer next to Porter put up his hand.

Not every lawyer should appear in court. Tanner felt that included half the independent bar. 'No,' he said.

Porter shuffled in his seat, and his eyes moved quickly to Bill Matheson, then back to Tanner. 'Peter –'

'No.'

Porter smiled tightly, and lifted both hands, palms towards Tanner, as if to politely tell him to shut up. 'As I said, Peter, Bill and Judith are comfortable with –'

'I'm not,' Tanner said. 'I don't mean any disrespect to anyone, including to – I'm sorry . . .'

'Henry.'

'. . . but my assisting counsel will come from the criminal defence bar.' Tanner then wrote three names in his notebook. He tore the sheet off, folded it, and handed it to Porter. 'In order of preference,' he said.

Porter smiled a forced smile. 'You don't seem to be leaving scope for negotiation.'

'I'm not. Let's move on.'

Porter nodded, and scribbled something on his pad. He then started to say something, but Bill Matheson cut him off.

'Mr Tanner,' Matheson began, 'our son shouldn't be in jail.' He hesitated over his words, like a man who'd rehearsed a speech, but who'd suddenly forgotten, if not the notion behind it, then the means of putting it together. 'He shouldn't be there,' he said forcefully. 'This whole thing is . . . wrong. You must win this case.'

Must? Tanner paused before he responded. This was a man torn up by anger and worry, but also by shame. Nothing remotely like this had ever happened to the Matheson family. He was probably still in shock, still expecting at some stage to be told his son's arrest was some awful mistake. Bill Matheson also sounded like a man used to getting his own way. A man whose commands had been followed all of his adult life.

'Dr Matheson,' Tanner said, 'I know you and your wife believe your son is innocent. If Justin tells me tomorrow he didn't commit this crime, I'll do everything I can to secure an acquittal.'

'He should've been granted bail,' Bill Matheson said.

'I can't change the law, Dr Matheson. Justin's charged with murder. I'm sure you already know from his bail application that if you're on a murder charge there's no presumption in favour of bail. Just the reverse – you have to show cause why detention isn't justified.'

'Is innocence a reason for bail?' Judith Matheson said, almost pleadingly. She ran her fingers nervously over a strand of white pearls that hung around her neck. 'Our son couldn't have done this. He wasn't with that girl. John Richter was.'

'I've read Justin's statement, Mrs Matheson. And I've read the police interviews.'

'We know he was drunk. We know he shouldn't have been there. He – he could not have done this.'

'The prosecutors are going to say that people do all kinds of things when they've had too much to drink.'

'Justin would never –'

'And just to finish that thought, I'm sure Charles has discussed with you that Justin has some options here. Intoxication isn't a defence to manslaughter, but it is to a crime of specific intent like murder. If he – If he was to instruct us that maybe he was involved with how this girl died, then I could base a defence to the murder charge on how drunk he was. I think the prosecutor would probably take a pass on murder and accept a plea to manslaughter.'

'He doesn't need some technical defence, Mr Tanner,' Bill Matheson said loudly, anger in his voice. 'Justin didn't hurt this girl. And John Richter got him drunk, and it was his cocaine too.'

'That's not what Richter says, and it's not what the other woman . . . Klaudia . . .?'

'Klaudia Dabrowska,' Porter said.

'. . . that's not what she told the police. She's told them she was with Richter.'

'She's –' Bill Matheson's voice was full of choking rage. 'Do you know how much money the Richter family has? This girl was with Justin. He didn't touch the other girl.'

Tanner nodded slowly. 'His DNA was found under her nails. We're going to have to deal with that.'

Matheson took his eyes off Tanner and glared at a spot on the conference table, like he was trying to burn a hole in it. The muscles on either side of his jaw tightened. 'Justin did not do this . . . John Richter . . . these boys were at school together. He was a violent teenager. On the rugby field –' For a moment, Dr Bill Matheson's voice almost cracked. He straightened in his chair, and breathed out slowly.

'Justin was at Richter's house when this girl died,' Tanner said. 'He was drunk, and he'd taken cocaine. John Richter called the police, and the ambulance. The other girl says Justin was with Elena. She says Justin gave them the coke. The police found the same coke in Justin's jacket. Justin's DNA is on the dead girl. That's why Justin didn't get bail, and that's why the case against him is strong.'

Tanner paused to see if either of the Mathesons wanted to respond, but neither spoke. Judith looked on the verge of tears again.

'I'm noticing Justin's wife isn't here,' Tanner said. 'I can imagine a few reasons she's not pleased with him at the moment. Is she going to support him at trial?'

'That's a work in progress,' Porter said. 'Because of the cocaine, the police got a warrant to search Justin's home. The children were there when they came. They're five and two and a half, I think . . .' He looked to Bill Matheson for confirmation, who nodded. 'You can imagine the scene?'

Tanner nodded. 'I'd like to go and prepare more for meeting Justin tomorrow.' He stood and looked at Porter, and pointed to the sheet of paper with the three names. 'That's the first call you make once I leave here.'

'Mr Tanner,' Judith Matheson said, still struggling to stay composed. He sat back down.

'Call me Peter.'

'I'm sorry. Peter. It's – it's very important to Bill and I that you believe our son is innocent. I'm sure – I'm sure you're very good at what you do. Our son's not a killer. We need to know that whoever is representing him believes that like we do.'

Tanner tried to formulate the right words, ones that would not seem too distant or harsh. The truth was it didn't matter what he thought. People have trouble understanding that. Even he did at first.

'I wasn't at the Richters' house the night Elena died, Judith. If Justin tells me what he's told you, I'll defend him with every effort I have.'

'But we –'

'I'll defend him to the best of my abilities, Judith. That's the most I can offer.'

17

Hendrik Richter took off his sunglasses and put them on the dining table of his outdoor terrace. He placed his fingers gently on his eyelids and rubbed slowly.

He'd been working hard for over forty years. Once he'd answered only to a few; now he had to worry about shareholders, investors, fund managers, joint-venture partners. The price of commodities was volatile. Coal in particular had headed south, and he now had the climate change industry ceaselessly yapping at his heels. Life had once been one new find, one new acquisition, after the other. But the world no longer sat still so he could gobble it up.

He picked up his sunglasses with one hand, and pushed the bowl of his half-finished lunch away with the other. The cook had given him a quinoa and baby spinach salad with low-fat ricotta. It had been dressed with far too little oil. He wondered who set the menu. It was probably his board – they wanted him to live forever.

'Apologies for the tasteless salad,' he said.

'That's quite all right, Hendrik,' Andre Visser said. He was busy punching out emails on his phone.

'So, this other boy, Matheson,' Richter then said. 'He's going to blame John? Based on what was said at his bail hearing?'

'Hardly unexpected,' Visser said.

'How concerned should we be?' Richter asked. 'Beyond the obvious?'

'None of it enhances John's reputation,' Visser said softly, putting his phone into the pocket of his jacket, and turning his gaze onto the still waters of the pool below the terrace. 'Measures are in place, though.'

'The girl's gone?'

Visser nodded.

Richter slowly cleaned the lenses of his sunglasses with his napkin, then put them back on. He picked up his glass, drank the final sip, and then looked at Visser. 'You obviously suggested this meeting for a reason, Andre?' he said.

Visser took a piece of paper out of the inside pocket of his jacket and slowly unfolded it. He handed it to Richter. 'We've drafted this.'

Richter took off his glasses and examined the document. 'What is it?'

'A press release. Regarding what was implied in the bail hearing. Just refuting the idea that John might have had anything to do with this girl's death.'

Richter looked up from the paper. 'She was found dead in his lounge room,' he said softly, almost to himself.

'It reminds people who called the police and the ambulance,' Visser said. 'And whose skin was found under the girl's nails.'

'Do we need to correct it for any grammatical errors?'

'No, Hendrik,' Visser said.

Richter dropped the paper on the table, then looked at Visser. 'I'm sure you wanted to discuss more than this?'

Visser's mouth tightened, into something between a smile and a grimace. 'I've had some calls over the last few weeks. From the board.'

'Anyone in particular?'

'I'd call it a unanimous front.'

'Aren't *we* on the board?'

'I've also had some discussions with our investors.'

'Who might they be?'

'Some fund managers. And others.'

'Are the others Chinese?'

Visser nodded. 'People who speak for them.'

'Any government people, by chance?'

'Well . . .'

'Let me guess, people who speak for them?'

'Something like that.'

'John's name came up in these discussions?' Richter searched Visser's face for a clue. 'This hesitancy isn't like you, Andre.'

'There's a view,' Visser said, 'that we can't really have John touching the gold mine at Bageeyn River. Or any other projects of environmental or political sensitivity.'

'Really?'

'Yes, Hendrik. Really.'

'This a strong view?'

Visser turned and gazed towards the distant boats on the harbour, breathing out deeply. 'An extremely strong view.'

'I see,' Richter said. 'Is it a view you share?'

Visser looked back at the man for whom he had worked for more than thirty years. 'I do.'

Richter nodded slowly. 'I can't say I'm surprised.'

'I didn't think you would be.'

'Tell me, Andre,' Richter said, 'is there anything he *can* fucking touch?'

'Not without damaging it, Hendrik.'

'Perhaps I should send him overseas?'

'Perhaps when this trial is over . . .'

'We'll be mining Mars before John's ready to take charge.' Richter pushed his chair back and stood. 'You're right, of course. John can't run any of our projects. Not in this country.' He walked to the railing of his long terrace, and looked out over the harbour. 'Is this wrong, Andre?'

Visser turned to look at Richter, but he was still facing the other way. 'Is what wrong?'

Richter shook his head. 'I don't care,' he said. 'I'm his father, but there's no part of me that really cares at all.'

18

The wind rushed through Tanner's hair as his solicitor accelerated. It was a clear morning and the roof of the Mercedes convertible was up. The Silverwater Metropolitan Remand and Reception Centre was a twenty-kilometre drive west of the CBD. Justin Matheson had been there for twenty-five days. In that time, he'd been visited three times by his parents, once by a group of three friends, and twice by Charles Porter and his previous barrister immediately before his first shot at bail. His wife Sarah had not yet made the trip.

'We're going to stick out a bit at Silverwater in this,' Tanner said.

'How I'd look in a prison car park wasn't foremost in my mind when I bought this car,' Porter replied.

'Any update on Stott Ackerman?'

'The head of Justin's group made it clear that his position was now untenable. They sent him a letter of termination at Silverwater yesterday while we were meeting.'

'Don't investment bankers believe in the presumption of innocence?'

'He said he'd spoken to his US head. Gaming requires you to be squeaky clean. The drug charge is almost worse than the murder charge.'

In the brief was a recent photo of Matheson from a publicity brochure for Stott Ackerman: sitting on the corner of a desk, one leg on the ground, the other up slightly, the city skyline in the background. He had on a dark business suit, a white shirt with no tie. There was the faintest smile on his face that was hard to define. It wasn't quite arrogance, it was more the self-assured look of someone who'd never known any kind of failure.

When Matheson was walked into the legal interview room where Tanner and Porter were waiting, prison greens and four weeks in a cell had wiped away that look.

'I'm not asking you for the sake of it, Justin,' Tanner said after Porter had introduced them. 'How are you doing in here?'

Matheson shook his head slowly. 'It's not exactly an Aman Resort.'

Tanner nodded. 'Are you having any trouble with anyone?'

Matheson paused. 'I'm not making life-long friends.'

'I hope you don't have to.'

Matheson leant forwards in his seat. 'Mr Tanner,' he said, 'I didn't do this.'

'It's Peter.'

'I didn't hurt this girl.'

'We'll get to that.'

'You have to get me out of here. I swear, I didn't do this.'

Tanner held up a hand as a gesture for Matheson to relax. 'Charles told me your employer sent you a Dear John letter yesterday?'

Matheson smiled crookedly. 'They couldn't work out how to pitch my new status as accused murderer to the clients.'

'Really? I didn't think you could get a job in investment banking unless you were a violent cokehead?'

Matheson straightened in his chair, and raised an eyebrow.

'You'll get used to my sense of humour, Justin,' Tanner said.

'My parents won't.'

'I'll be more delicate with them. You want to tell me what happened that night?'

Matheson told Tanner the events that had led to him sitting in a booth at Pantheon on the night of Elena Mancini's death.

'You're a member of this club?'

'Yes.'

'How often do you go there?'

'Maybe once a month,' he said. 'It's more a place to take clients, you know, interstate or overseas clients if they're in town.'

'Did you know either of these girls?'

'No.'

'Never seen them before?'

'Klaudia had only been working there for a few months. She obviously didn't work the times I'd gone. Elena was new.'

'Did Elena and you talk much at the club?'

'She was quieter. I had a short chat with her in Italian. Just basic stuff.'

'Were you flirting with her?'

'Not really.'

Tanner raised an eyebrow and glared at him.

'Define flirting.'

'No,' Tanner said. 'Answer the question.'

'A little.'

'Did other people hear you talk to Elena?'

'No. I don't know.'

'That's two answers, Justin. I want one truthful answer to my questions. Did anyone hear you to your knowledge?'

'I don't know.'

'Klaudia sat on your lap at some stage?'

'Off and on, all night.'

'She's from England, right?'

'Her parents are Polish, but yeah.'

'Did you talk to her in Polish, Justin, or English?'

Matheson paused and glared at Tanner. 'In English, Peter.'

'What about?'

'I don't know.'

'She was on your lap all night, mate. What did you talk about?'

Matheson sighed, and shook his head. 'Where she was from, her accent. What kind of modelling she did, how long she'd been living in Australia . . . um, her mum had died a few years back, her dad sold clothes . . .'

'Don't tell me you don't know something again, when you do.'

'My memory of that night is pretty blurry. I –'

'Then how do you know you didn't kill Elena?'

Matheson sat bolt upright in his chair. 'I didn't hurt that girl,' he said loudly.

'Calm down, Justin. What about John? Did he know Klaudia?'

'Yes.'

'You drank at dinner?'

'Maybe three bottles of wine between four of us. A couple of beers too.'

'And at the club?'

'Maybe five rounds of whisky cocktails.'

'Did you know anyone else in the club that night?'

'I didn't see anyone I knew.'

Tanner told Porter to issue a subpoena to the company that owned Olympus for the names of the people who used their card to access the club that night, or who used a credit card in Pantheon, and another for the names of the staff who were working. He also wanted the CCTV footage taken inside and outside the complex, which the police were likely to already have.

'Whose idea was it to go back to John's place?'

'His.'

'How many people were in the club when you left?'

'Not many.'

'Is not many fifty, or five?'

'A couple of tables.'

'Did they see you leave?'

'I don't know.'

'Who did see you leave?'

'How am I supposed to know that?'

'C'mon, Justin. Security at the doors? Any staff you might know?'

'The guys on the door of the club, I guess.'

'What happened when you got back to Richter's place?'

Matheson shook his head. 'It's like I told the police. And Charles.'

'Tell me.'

'Jack opened some champagne.'

'The drink of choice after you've just buried your first wife. One bottle?'

'At first. We had more.'

'Then what?'

'Then he went to his bedroom, and came back with a packet of coke.'

'How much?'

'I didn't weigh it.'

'Have a guess.'

'A smallish bag.'

'Then what?'

'I didn't have much. I was pretty wasted already.'

'How drunk were you?'

'Slurring . . . I – you know, when you know you've had way too much?'

'How much coke did the others have?'

'John had a couple of lines. Maybe Klaudia too.'

'What about Elena?'

'They coaxed her into having a thin line.'

'Then what?'

'Then I went to the bedroom with Klaudia.'

'Whose idea was that?'

'I don't know.'

'What do you mean you don't know?'

'I may have said, "Let's be alone." She had her tongue in my ear half the time, she was rubbing me . . . you know . . . rubbing my groin.'

'You can say it, Justin. We're big boys.'

'She was rubbing her hand up and down my dick.'

'What were John and Elena doing?'

'I wasn't paying much attention.'

'Did you see any intimacy between them? Were they touching each other?'

'I don't think so.'

'So you went to the bedroom with Klaudia. Then what?'

'It's what I told the police.'

'What happened?'

'We got undressed. Can't you just read about this in the police report?'

'I'm not getting aroused, Justin. If you think it's awkward telling us this here, wait until you're in front of a judge and a packed gallery. Don't expect a standing ovation from a jury either. You had sex, right? That's what you told the police.'

'God knows how. I remember the room spinning after, and thinking I might throw up.'

'You romantic.'

'Dude, your bedside manner is –'

'Your wife and children are at home when you're with Klaudia, Justin, so let's not discuss bedside manners. A jury is going to like mine more than yours. So, what are you telling me? You passed out after sex?'

'The next thing I remember is waking up with the cops there. And seeing Elena.'

'Nothing else?'

'A dream.'

'A dream?'

'Yeah, I had an intense dream.'

'Don't tell me you were killing a young woman in it?'

'For fuck's sake, no,' Matheson said, his voice rising. 'I was fighting people off me. Not even real people. Like zombies.'

'I'll make a note to use an insanity defence as a last resort. Okay. The DNA.'

'I have no idea how –'

'The scratches, and your skin under her nails – that's a mystery to you?'

'He must have done it.'

'Who?'

'John.'

'How?'

'I don't know.'

'It's a big problem for us, you get that?'

'She didn't scratch me. I didn't hurt her. I've been set up. It wasn't my coke and I didn't hurt her.'

'Never had a fight when you've been drunk?'

'No. John has though.'

'So?'

'He broke a girl's skull with a champagne bottle.'

Tanner studied Matheson's face. Then he glanced at Porter. 'When?'

'Ten, twelve years ago. Maybe a bit more. We were finishing university.'

'And he just ran amok with a bottle?'

'He was – I don't know what provoked it – his girl was dancing with this guy. She and John came as some Roman emperor and empress. She had on a pretty revealing toga.'

'And?'

'John smashed the bottle on her head, then left the party.'

Tanner looked up from his notepad, and shook his head. 'What about the police? Was he charged?'

'No.'

Tanner nodded slowly. 'Let me guess, the girl with the fractured skull came into some money?'

'That's the rumour.'

'What's this woman's – ?'

'She won't help.'

'How do you know?'

'Someone told me she had to sign some kind of confidentiality deed.'

'Who told you?'

'I can't remember. It was years ago. The girl's name was Felicity Horton. I haven't seen her in ages.'

'Who witnessed this assault?'

Matheson shook his head. 'No one.'

'No one?'

'John – someone told me John dragged her off the dance floor into a bedroom. He was walking around with a champagne bottle. Next thing he's gone, and someone finds her unconscious on the ground in the room.'

Tanner shook his head. 'Someone must've called an ambulance?'

'No,' Matheson said. 'The guy whose parents owned the house freaked. There were drugs at the party and he was worried about cops. The party was in Darling Point. Her friends got in a car and rushed her to St Vincent's.'

'We need names of all these people.'

Matheson smiled a crooked, bitter smile. 'No one is going to verify this. I don't know who took her to the hospital.'

Tanner looked at Porter. 'You need to start looking into this,' he said. 'I've got an investigator I use. I'll email you his details.' Tanner made a note on his pad, and then checked his watch. 'We'll go over all of this again, Justin,' he then said. 'So many times, you'll hate me for it.'

Matheson nodded.

'Just one more very important thing before we go. You understand that you're charged with manslaughter in the alternative to murder as well?'

'Of course I know.'

Tanner nodded. 'If it was an accident, Justin – just some accident how Elena got hurt – now would be the time to tell us. Now would be the time we could get the best deal for you, if that's what happened?'

'That's not what happened,' Matheson said firmly.

'You were rotten drunk, Justin,' Tanner said. 'If you don't remember what happened that night, then we may well have at least a good defence to murder based on intoxication. I'd be surprised if the prosecutor wouldn't look favourably on a plea to manslaughter based on how drunk you were. An early plea might mean a sentence as low as maybe five years.'

Matheson looked at Tanner for a long moment. 'I'm not pleading guilty, Peter. I didn't do this,' he said. 'You've got to get me out of here.'

19

Tanner collected the gifts from behind the reception desk, then took the lift downstairs to catch a taxi. It was just over two weeks until Christmas, and the city was crowded with shoppers. The north-west summer wind was hot and dry, and it took him ten minutes to find a free cab. By the time he did, perspiration was running down both sides of his face. He loosened his tie and told the driver to head to Queens Park.

He knocked on the Cheungs' front door, and Melissa soon appeared. She smiled. 'Come and put them under the tree,' she said, looking at the gift-wrapped boxes.

'Wow,' he said when they walked into her lounge room. In the corner was a tree nearly as tall as the roof, covered in baubles and decorations and tinsel of all colours. Underneath it were at least two dozen presents. 'I'm feeling guilty,' he said. 'We haven't even put ours up.' Karen always made putting up the Christmas tree a big deal, especially after Dan was born. When Dan was old enough, they spent an hour together, weighing the branches down with countless coloured balls and Christmas trinkets. After she died, he hadn't been able to put the tree up, and fell out of the habit.

'Peter? You okay?'

'Sure. Just put these with the rest of them?'

She nodded. 'Nothing for me, I hope.'

'Just something small.'

She sighed. 'Now I feel guilty.'

'Don't be silly.'

'Can I offer you a drink?' she said. 'Wine or tea?'

'Do you have something open?'

She smiled. 'It's nearly Christmas. Let's have a glass of wine.'

They went to the kitchen and he sat at the table as Melissa took a bottle of white wine from the fridge.

'After the last time we spoke I saw in the paper you've been briefed to defend Bill Matheson's son,' she said. 'Will that be in court soon?'

'The committal's early next year. A trial six or so months after that. Do you know his father?'

'By reputation.'

He nodded, and took a small sip of wine. 'You know who John Richter is, of course? Citadel?'

'I know who he is.'

Tanner turned his glass back and forth by the stem. 'When did you last speak to Joe?'

'He's allowed to call home once a week.'

'How are the kids coping?'

She looked at the table for a few moments before speaking. 'A boy at Tom's school – they're just children, I know – he told Tom his dad was in jail because he'd stolen something. I don't –'

'What are you telling him now?'

'I'm saying it's a mistake that people in China have made, and that his father will be home soon once that's sorted out.'

Tanner nodded. 'When's he next in court?'

'April,' she said. 'The twenty-ninth, I think.'

'And there's been no change to his plan?'

'No change.'

'Is that date proposed for plea only, or sentencing as well?'

'I think it's to let the court know what Joe intends to do.'

'That's what Li told you?'

'Yes.'

'Has Li been served with all the prosecution evidence now?'

'I think so.'

'I still don't understand the decision.'

She shook her head, and pushed her glass to the centre of the table. 'You don't get the difference between twenty years and ten?'

'I understand the choice may become stark eventually. In the meantime, though, if Joe is innocent there'll be a weakness –'

'Joe says he'll be convicted no matter what weaknesses there might be,' she interrupted, her voice cracking slightly. 'The only issue is how long he stays in prison.'

'What was he doing there, Melissa? He must have told you now.'

She shook her head, and looked down.

Tanner sighed. 'I'm not trying to upset you,' he said. 'How are you, anyway, financially, are you . . . ? I'm not trying to pry . . .'

'BBK are still paying Joe's partnership drawings.'

'That's going to change if he pleads guilty.'

She nodded, but said nothing.

'When I asked about your finances, I was really meaning what will they look like once his drawings stop?'

'My salary won't cover the mortgage, so . . .' She shrugged, and picked up her glass again.

'Joe's parents?'

'They don't have that kind of money.'

'Have you heard from BBK? Since you got the computer back?'

She shook her head.

'Have Li or Joe told Dennis of his plans to plead?'

'I think they know,' she said.

'When did you last speak with them?'

'They've stopped calling me.' Her eyes welled and tears ran down either side of her face. As they did, he heard a door open, and a series of footsteps. Oliver, the middle child, waking from his afternoon nap. He was unsteady on his feet when he appeared, his hair damp and plastered to one side of his forehead.

'Have you been crying, Mummy?' he said.

'No, no,' she said, standing to walk over and hug him, wiping her tears away. 'Mummy's got a cold.'

'Did this man make you cry?'

'No, sweetheart, he didn't. You remember Peter, don't you? He brought presents.'

'For me?'

'Yes, for you. Say thank you.'

'Thank you. Can I open it?'

'Sure,' Tanner said.

'Let's wait until Christmas,' Melissa said. 'We'll open all the presents on Christmas Day. That's what we agreed. Remember?'

The child nodded slightly, acknowledging the memory, not his agreement.

Tanner kissed her goodbye. 'I'm sorry,' he said. 'I'd better go.'

She smiled. 'It's okay.'

'Say hi to Joe for me when he calls next. And . . . tell him what I said about the evidence again. For what it's worth.'

She nodded. 'Thanks for the presents.'

Tanner checked his emails as he waited for a cab outside the Cheungs' home, and found one sent a few minutes before from his clerk.

Please ring Sally Cook from Sally Cook & Associates Family Lawyers re private matter.

He'd never heard of Sally Cook & Associates. When his cab arrived, he returned the call. By 'private matter' he thought either Sally Cook herself, or someone close to her, was in the kind of trouble that required help from a member of the criminal bar. The number he'd been given looked to be a switchboard number, but on the third ring the principal answered.

'Sally Cook.'

'Sally? It's Peter Tanner. I have a message from my clerk to call you.'

'Oh,' she said. 'That was quick.' She sounded nervous; caught off-guard.

'Is there something I can help you with?'

'It might be the other way around,' she said.

'I'm not sure I follow.'

'I'm sorry to sound so . . . vague. I've been tossing up calling you for a while.'

'Do you have a client in trouble, Sally?' he asked. 'Or are you calling about something concerning yourself?'

'I had a client in trouble.'

'I don't understand.'

'You're defending Justin Matheson? The man charged with that – that girl's murder?'

'Yes.' There was a long pause, and Tanner thought the line had dropped out. 'Sally?'

'I'm guessing he's no longer a friend of John Richter's.'

'I think the relationship is unlikely to survive the trial,' Tanner said. 'Why do you ask?'

'This conversation has to remain strictly confidential.'

'Of course,' he said. There was again silence. 'What's this about, Sally?'

'It's about John Richter's late wife.'

'You knew her?'

Sally Cook sighed. 'I'm a divorce lawyer, Peter.'

'She was your client?'

'She was.'

'Do you know something that could help my client?'

'Perhaps we should meet?'

20

Sally Cook was halfway through a glass of wine when he arrived.

They'd arranged to meet at seven the following night at a wine bar in Surry Hills. It had a long communal table, and she was sitting at the far end, looking at her phone.

'Sorry,' he said, when he sat down. 'I had a client I couldn't push out the door.'

'I was about to leave.' She was somewhere in her forties, attractive, and immaculately groomed.

'I like your suit,' he said. It was charcoal grey, with a deep purple stipe. Underneath the jacket, she had on a matching purple shirt.

'You wouldn't believe what I have to spend on my appearance now,' she said.

'You do high-end divorces, I take it?'

'The only kind worth doing.'

He smiled, and looked at her nearly empty wine glass. 'Same again?'

'I might try a red.'

'Anything in particular?'

'Something earthy, but not too heavy. They'll know what to recommend.'

When he returned from the crowded bar he was carrying two large glasses of a red wine with a brown tinge. 'It's nebbiolo from Piedmont,' he said. 'Tannins not too heavy. Pepper and savoury characteristics. I forget what else he said.'

'Sounds perfect.'

Sally sipped her drink, then ran a hand up to her face to catch a loose strand of hair, which she tucked behind her ear. 'I was married to one of your colleagues,' she said. 'Tom Hunt?'

Tanner shook his head. 'I don't know him.'

'He's at the commercial bar.'

'Then I hope you took all his money.'

She smiled. 'The hardest part was keeping mine.'

'Divorced long?'

'Five years.'

'You have kids?'

She shook her head quickly, and looked down at her wine glass. 'What about you?'

'I was married.'

'What happened?'

'She died.'

She looked uncomfortable for a moment, and was about to say something, but he put up his hand in a calming gesture. 'It was a while ago now,' he said. 'Some days it even feels like that.'

'My divorce doesn't.'

'I'm sorry to hear that.'

She took a long sip of wine and then smiled.

'So,' he said. 'Nikki Richter. And her husband, John.'

She nodded. 'We can't be having this meeting.'

'What meeting?'

She picked up her phone and retrieved an email, opening the photo attachment. She handed it to Tanner. He saw the face of Nikki Richter. There was a red swelling above her left eye, bruising to the throat.

'John Richter did this?' he said softly.

'She sent me several of these.' She took the phone back, found what she wanted, then handed it to him again. Another photo, to similar effect. In the email itself, a message from her then client, describing an assault.

'How much of this is there?'

She picked up her wine and took a long sip. 'She first instructed me over a year ago.'

'About a divorce?'

She nodded. 'The pre-nup was the main thing she was worried about. On top of the way he treated her.'

'No exclusions for violent conduct?'

'No,' she said. 'She'd done seven years with him. She got nothing up to five. Between five to ten years she'd get a million per year – fifteen if there was a child.'

'She felt ripped off?'

'He was constantly unfaithful,' she said. 'That's why she first saw me. I'd acted for one of her girlfriend's mothers. At first we just organised surveillance. We filmed him leaving clubs with other women, checking into hotels with them, or going to some apartment he owned.'

'The surveillance was for what? Blackmail?'

She put her glass down firmly on the table. 'For property settlement negotiations,' she said, raising an eyebrow, speaking slowly and loudly, 'not blackmail.'

'Sorry.'

'There was no way around the pre-nup contractually. We were looking for another way. Nikki wanted to do better.'

'Surely she didn't want all the Citadel mines?'

She shook her head. 'She was angry. She told me he got her hooked on heroin. She was lonely. He cheated on her from almost day one of the marriage. She felt like he'd stolen seven years of her life. She thought she was owed.'

'How far down the track were you when she died?'

'I told Richter's laywers we'd get an AVO if he came back to the apartment. We'd told them we were going to file divorce papers ahead of schedule.'

'Ahead of schedule?'

'Technically, they'd only been separated for six weeks. We were going to argue that in truth they'd been separated for years, that the marriage had become a pretence.'

'These photos, Sally,' Tanner said. 'My client says he didn't hurt the girl he's alleged to have killed. He says it had to be John.'

'Why do you think I've been agonising over contacting you?'

A plate of antipasto he'd ordered with the wine was put in front of them.

'Thank god,' she said. 'I'm starving.'

'I could really go after Richter with this at trial.'

She took an olive pit out of her mouth, and put it in a small bowl. 'It's one of the reasons I decided to call you.'

'One of them?'

She picked up her glass and sighed, looking over to the bar, then back. 'Her death,' she said. 'I don't buy it.'

'You don't buy it?'

'No.'

'Don't tell me Richter killed her too?'

'I don't know much about heroin addicts,' she said. 'And she told me she'd been one. She was very together every time she spoke to me, though. Every conference we had, every phone call. I'm not saying she was a genius, but she wasn't a stupid woman either. She had a plan; she had a goal in mind. She didn't strike me as someone who was on heroin.'

'They found a needle in her arm and heroin in the apartment, didn't they? She had a track record.'

Sally shook her head, and picked up another olive. 'I'm giving you my gut feel, Peter. Of course I don't know for sure.'

'Can I have those photos?'

'There's a problem.'

He looked at her, waiting for her to explain.

'Privilege. It survives her death.'

'Can I speak to – ?'

'Let me finish telling you why I called first.'

'Okay.'

'She also said she had something up her sleeve with John.'

'Beyond the photos and surveillance?'

'She'd seen something,' she said. 'Something about his work.'

'What?'

'She wouldn't tell me.'

'How do you know it was about his work?'

She picked up a piece of frittata, bit into it, and lost half of it in her lap. 'She said that much, but wouldn't give me details. She wanted to see how far we could go with the surveillance and the threats to go public over the violence. It was a last resort for her. She said she'd tell me if she had to.'

'Did she keep some kind of evidence about this?'

'I don't know.'

'All of this, if you could –'

She grabbed his arm gently and held it. 'Peter, privilege.'

'Can we speak to – it's her estate isn't it? They could waive privilege, couldn't they?'

Sally smiled, and nodded. 'The executor could.'

'She had a will?'

'Yes.'

'So we could speak to the executor and ask him – is it a man? Is there more than one?'

'Just one. It's a man.'

'Can you – it would be better at first if you spoke to them. They could then contact me.'

'I could, but it won't help.'

He looked at her, then leant back in his chair and looked up at the ceiling. Now it was his turn to swear. 'John Richter is her executor.' He ran his hand through his hair, picked up his glass, and finished his wine. 'We made a mistake, Sally.'

'What?'

'We should have ordered a bottle.'

She stood and looked towards the wine list on the blackboard behind the bar. 'Allow me.'

21

The decorations were wrapped in tissue paper and sealed inside a plastic storage box. The box had *Christmas Decorations* written on it in permanent black marker; he could remember watching Karen write the words. She had a singlet on, and shorts. The weather must have been hot.

'Dad?' Dan's voice had an edge of frustration. 'I said, I can't reach any higher.' He was standing next to the tree, which was about seven feet high, holding a green bauble.

Tanner got up from the couch and took the decoration from his son. He held it up near one of the top branches. 'Here?'

The boy nodded. 'You'll have to do the rest.'

Tanner looked inside the plastic box, now full of crinkled tissue paper. He fished around for what decorations were left, and hung them randomly near the top of the tree. When he finished, he sat on the couch next to Dan.

'Is it okay?'

The boy shrugged.

Tanner looked at his father, who was also sitting on the couch, drinking a beer.

'It'll look better when it's dark and the lights are on,' Karl said.

Tanner took in the tree. It didn't look the way Karen used to do it. Some lack of balance; shapes and colours in the wrong spots. 'I guess it's not my area of expertise,' he said.

'It'll look better when the lights are on,' Karl said again.

Tanner walked over to the wall. He flicked the switch and a hundred or more fairy lights came on. The effect was underwhelming.

'You have to wait until it's dark, Peter,' his father said.

'I was checking if they were working.'

Karl Tanner nodded, but said nothing further.

After dinner, Tanner let Dan stay up later than usual to watch television, while he sat with his father at the kitchen table. He was drinking red wine, but his father was still on light beer; Karl had found that he'd lost the taste for wine when he came out of jail. They hadn't spoken much since Dan had left the table and, when they had, it had been safe topics: sports, politics, the decline of fairness in the country. They were on the same page.

'Do you have a girlfriend yet?' Karl said suddenly, sounding uninterested in the answer.

Tanner looked at his father. The man was in his early seventies now. He looked it, and he didn't. He had deep lines in his fair skin, and long and widely spaced white hairs on the top of his head. His face was thin, and his eyes still electric blue.

'You have someone in mind for me?'

Karl wrapped his fingers around his beer bottle, and brought it to his mouth. He put the bottle down and looked at his son. 'No.'

'Let me know when you do.'

'What happened with the lawyer? She was a prosecutor, I think you said.'

Tanner swirled his wine. 'Not compatible.'

His father ran a hand over his mouth. 'What is it?'

'What's what?'

'It's more than five years.'

'There's a statute of limitation?'

Karl Tanner shook his head. 'That's a silly thing to say.'

For a moment Tanner bristled. The man who'd got himself sent to jail for seven years – seven years when he was still needed as a father – was lecturing him on 'silly'. He took a deep breath to let the feeling subside. 'There's always Maria,' he said, trying to lighten the mood.

Karl looked at him, a grim stare, unamused.

Tanner leant back in his chair and closed his eyes for a moment. 'She's still here,' he said softly.

'What?'

'In my head. In my dreams sometimes,' Tanner said. 'Karen's still – she's still there.' And she was. Her possessions and clothes were long gone, but he still sometimes dreamed she was alive.

'Dreams aren't real,' Karl said. He leant across the table. 'Enough time, Peter. Get a girlfriend.' There was authority in his voice. A paternal order.

Tanner smiled tightly. 'Just like that?'

'Go online if you have to.'

'What?'

His father shrugged. 'Why not? I have.'

Tanner put his glass down, and shook his head. 'Jesus Christ.'

'Nothing permanent has come of it yet.'

Tanner stifled a laugh. 'Why not?'

'My seven years in government housing isn't universally respected.'

'I'm sure you'll find someone who's turned on by that,' Tanner said.

Karl pointed to the wall of the adjoining room where Dan was watching TV. 'You're not alone, Peter,' he said. 'Get a girlfriend.'

Tanner laughed, almost to himself, and stood and picked up the dishes, as a means of closing the subject.

His father got the message. 'What's happening with that Chinese lawyer?'

'He's an Australian, Karl.'

'Who is?'

'The Chinese lawyer. He was born here. We've been friends since law school. You know that.'

'My apologies. Have you been able to help him?'

'Not from here.'

'He has a lawyer there?'

Tanner nodded.

'What will happen, do you think?'

'He's pleading guilty.'

His father frowned. 'How long will he get?'

Tanner shrugged. 'At least as long as you. You want another beer?'

Karl Tanner said nothing for a few moments. 'And the other one – Matheson, is it? What's he doing?'

'He's pleaded not guilty.'

'Is he?'

'I don't know.'

'Do you care?'

'Not at all.'

'I've always found that –' he paused, searching for the right word, '– remarkable.'

'Me caring won't bring the girl back to life.'

'There should still be justice for her,' Karl said, 'and for the living who did this to her.'

'There wasn't much justice for you, Karl,' Tanner said, almost under his breath.

Karl Tanner glared at him for a long moment. 'You at least care about justice, then?'

Tanner looked at his father and nearly smiled. 'I do.'

Karl Tanner had received justice.

He'd been an insurance broker for the first half of his working life. He and a partner then set up a boutique financial planning business. Within a few years, the partner was not only selling financial products, he was giving investment advice. Clients' money was littered around the stock market, often without express instructions. Then the market suddenly 'corrected', and the money disappeared.

Karl tried to clean up the mess, though. Doing nothing meant exposure; financial ruin. He made some bad decisions gambling with other clients' money to try and get it all back.

When the securities commission people came knocking, Karl's partner had the better lawyer. He squealed first and loudest. He did four years. Karl Tanner did seven.

When the plates were packed away, Tanner's father said it was time for him to go. They walked quietly into the next room. Dan had fallen asleep on the couch. The room was lit only by the glow of the TV, and the lights of the Christmas tree.

'You were right,' Tanner said softly.

'What about?'

'The tree. It does look better now.'

When his father had left, and Dan had gone to bed, Tanner poured another glass of wine and sat at the kitchen table. At the top of the page on a yellow legal pad he wrote *Joe Cheung.*

He made a summary of all he knew. In the end the whole prosecution – the entirety of Cheung's alleged corruption – depended on one man's word. Tanner had no way of even finding out who this man was.

Next he wrote *Bageeyn River & Tovosevu.* Cheung would have advised Citadel on its application for the gold mine out west. A water report had been buried, and its author had gone missing. Cheung had been sent to the island. Another woman who'd gone there had been killed.

He finished with several short sentences that he wrote in capitals.

WHAT DID JC KNOW ABOUT BAGEEYN RIVER?
WHERE IS THE HYDROGEOLOGIST?
WHO IS NORTH SHANXI?
WHO IS THE MAN FROM XINCOAL?
WHY DID JC GO TO TOVOSEVU?

He pushed the pad away, picked up his glass, and turned his thoughts to Justin Matheson. What about him? Cheung said he was guilty. Tanner knew he was not. Matheson said he was innocent. The DNA didn't lie – his client's was under the dead girl's nails. For his client to be innocent, it wasn't only John Richter who was lying: so was Klaudia Dabrowska. Richter had a reason to lie. What reason would Dabrowska have? He wrote those words on another page of his pad.

The ultimate truth – what had happened to Elena Mancini the night she died – didn't matter. An acquittal was what mattered.

He sat for a moment longer to think about that. The truth did not matter for Justin Matheson. It was different for Joe Cheung.

22

Nadine Bellouard agreed to have dinner with Tanner a few days after he arrived home from summer holidays with Dan. It was early in the new year, and he was about to return to work.

It was a warm and still evening, and Woolloomooloo Wharf was busy with people by the time she arrived at the restaurant. She'd added some auburn highlights to her hair since he last saw her and her arms and shoulders had a deep tan.

'Been away?' he said.

'Yes.'

'By a beach?'

'Maui,' she said. 'A new resort there.'

'Sounds expensive.'

'I think it is.'

'How long were you there?'

'Just over a week.'

Two glasses of champagne arrived, along with the menus.

'Known him long?'

She shrugged. 'Long enough to let him take me.'

Tanner nodded. 'Good for you,' he said. 'You like this guy?'

She smiled, faintly. 'He's nice with the kids.'

He looked at the condensation around his glass, then picked it up. 'My father told me to get a girlfriend when we had dinner at Christmas.'

She picked up her glass and clinked his. 'You should listen.'

He nodded, and studied the menu for a few moments. A waitress came to take their order, but Tanner asked for a few more minutes.

'We're here to talk about Joe?' Nadine said.

'Have you spoken to Melissa lately?'

She nodded slowly.

'Has she told you Joe's plans? What do you think?'

'I don't know, Pete. We all – we all think there's been some misunderstanding with something Joe said . . . I just don't know.'

'A fifteen-million-dollar misunderstanding?'

'No one can work it out.'

Tanner nodded slowly. 'What's being said around the firm? Do people know he's going to plead guilty?'

'No one is saying anything. Maybe the partners know, but none of the staff have officially been told anything.'

'Who do you work for now?'

'Simon Gault,' she said. 'He's an M&A partner.'

'Have you spoken to him about Joe?'

She nearly laughed. 'He would never talk to me about anything like that.'

'Does Joe seem to you like the kind of guy who would sell a client's secret?'

'Of course not,' she said.

'Do you think he'd ask for a bribe?'

'Pete, why are you asking me this?'

'I need to know what work he was doing before he was arrested.'

'He was there to meet Citadel's Chinese partners, wasn't he? That's what –'

Tanner shook his head. 'No. I mean the precise details of what he was doing.'

'He was doing the kind of work he always does. He was working for Citadel on its acquisitions and mine applications . . . the one he's been arrested about was part of that. His AA doesn't know anything . . .'

'I want to know the details of all of that.'

'Can't you ask – ?'

'I don't want anyone at BBK to know I'm interested,' he said.

She looked at him for a long moment. 'Except me?'

'I need to know more than what he was working on. I want to know who he was dealing with, what documents he read, all that kind of thing.'

Nadine narrowed her eyes. 'You want me to help with this?'

'It's why I asked you to dinner.'

'Pete, it sounds like – I can't take files from the office for you.'

'I'm not going to ask you to do anything high risk,' he said.

She raised an eyebrow at him.

'Joe's files – our computer system for files requires a passcode to get into. I won't have that. Even if I got it, there'd be a record of me accessing the file. Other partners have taken over Joe's work. Even getting to look at hardcopy documents would be –'

'I don't want you to do any of that,' he said. 'You've known Joe since he started as a junior lawyer. We both know he's an honest man.'

The waitress came back and asked if they were now ready to order. Tanner asked for another five minutes, but told her to decant a bottle of Barolo from the wine list.

'You're trying to bribe me to do what you want with an expensive wine?' Nadine said.

'No,' he said. 'I want the wine anyway. For you, I only need to use guilt – Joe's not just your old boss, Nadine. He's an old friend. He has three young children. His eight-year-old will be a man by the time he gets home.'

She stared at him for a few moments. 'I don't know what you're looking for,' she finally said, 'but how's it going to help Joe, anyway? What's your plan?'

'My plan is a work in progess,' he said. 'It's unlikely I can help him. I'd like to try, though. To do that I need more answers than I have.'

She picked up her glass, and drained the last of her champagne. 'I can't lose my job,' she said. 'Even for – with my separation, I need my –'

'You won't lose your job, Nadine,' he said. 'This won't leave a trail. There will be minimal risk.'

She sighed. 'It won't be legal, though, will it?'

He shrugged. 'There won't be any innocent victims.'

The waitress returned with the bottle of Barolo to check that it was the one Tanner wanted. He nodded. 'Nadine will taste it.'

The waitress took the cork out of the bottle, and poured a small amount into Nadine Bellouard's wine glass. She took a sip.

'Is it okay?'

'It's lovely,' Nadine said, 'but not good enough to commit a crime over.'

The waitress gave them a confused smile, then filled their glasses.

'And if I do get into trouble?' Nadine said when the waitress left. 'What then?'

'I'll defend you at your trial,' he said. 'And for a greatly reduced fee.'

23

They'd left from the city at nine. By eleven, the temperature was in the mid-thirties. The road ahead shimmered in the distance with the heat. In the background, the eucalypt-covered hills looked smoky blue, while the valley itself was lush with greenery, the rows of vines dense with grapes.

He'd spoken to Lisa Ilves three times on the phone since they'd met for a drink. In his call a week before, he'd told her he was sure he could help her clients. She said he'd have to meet them first; he had to prove a commitment beyond that he had for Joe Cheung.

'Nearly harvest time,' Tanner said as they drove between the fields of grape vines. Lisa nodded, said nothing.

She drove on, climbing up into the hills forested with gums, before the car turned around a steep curve near the top, where she pulled over to the side of the road.

She opened her door. 'C'mon.'

He walked around the back of the car and stood next to her. Below them was a bleak, uneven crater, gouged out of the earth. It ran for kilometres in either direction, an enormous ashen scab that was itself scarred with grey arteries upon which the coal trucks rumbled in the distance. It could have been the surface of the moon.

'That's what an open-cut mine looks like,' she said.

'It's huge.'

'It's eight kilometres long. They're digging more than ten million tonnes of coal out a year. And it's far from being the only big mine here. Now Citadel wants approval to dig a hole that will eventually be bigger than this.'

'I get it. Enough's enough.'

'The people who live here are under assault. The air they breathe is overloaded with coal dust. They run their coal trains all night. Their draglines run twenty-four-seven.'

'Why the speech?'

She looked towards the vast grey scar below them. 'Should anyone have the right to do that? Just for money?'

Tanner looked at the mine for a moment longer, then back to Lisa. 'We're talking a lot of money, right?'

'What happens when the coal runs out, or no one will buy it anymore?' she said. 'What do you do with a place like this? What will the mine workers do? What will their kids do?'

'I don't know.'

She shook her head. 'Thanks for coming to meet June, but to be involved I need to know that you're committed.'

'Committed to what?'

'To my clients' causes. To help us do everything we can to stop the mines being approved.'

'The best trial lawyers are detached from their client's causes and prejudices.'

'Concern for the environment isn't a prejudice, Pete, it's a necessity.' She was wearing a black singlet, and her CO_2 tattoo was fully visible on her shoulder.

He nodded, then smiled. 'My level of commitment. It doesn't extend to having to get one of those, does it?'

She shook her head. 'Get in the car,' she said. 'We're late.'

They arrived at the home of a woman called June Martin, who lived a few kilometres north of Singleton in the Hunter Valley. She owned a cottage on a couple of hectares of land, with an immaculately maintained rose garden out the front that was in late summer bloom. Martin was the president of the Save the Upper Hunter Action Group. Save the Hunter had three main objects in its constitution: to lodge court challenges to any government approval of new mines, to seek to have most of the existing mines in the valley closed, and to educate people about the environmental and health risks of coal mining.

When the front door opened, Tanner saw a small, thin woman in denim jeans and a white T-shirt, wearing a pair of shoes made for comfort, not elegance. She was perhaps mid-sixties, with shoulder-length salt and pepper hair, held up by a clip at the back.

June Martin kissed Lisa hello, then looked Tanner up and down. 'You're here to see if I like you?'

'How am I doing so far?'

She shrugged. 'Good enough to come in and take a seat.'

They went to the kitchen and she put a kettle on. The kitchen smelt of something that had been freshly baked. Cake, or scones. 'Lisa's passed on good things about you to our group,' Martin said as she sat down.

'I haven't done anything yet,' Tanner said.

'You must have a good reputation, then.'

'Among the nefarious, I do.'

'Isn't that a good thing, in your game?'

'Not every member of the community shares that view.'

'Somebody has to defend the sinners, don't they?'

'That's a mature and responsible view, June.'

'I'm a mature woman,' she said. 'But not very responsible.' She smiled, demonstrating every crease in her sun-touched face. She had generous teeth, which looked like they'd sampled more than a few vintages of Hunter Shiraz.

'How did you end up president of your action group?' Tanner asked.

'I've lived here a while.'

'How long is that?'

'Is sixty-three years long enough?'

'I don't believe it. Do you work?'

'High-school teacher. Closing in on retirement.'

He nodded. 'The action group, then. What drove you to join it?'

'I didn't,' she said. 'I started it.'

'Why?'

The kettle whistled, and she got up to pour tea. 'We live in a rural community, Peter. We don't want our land or wildlife destroyed by more mining. We pay taxes. We ought to be able to breathe the air and not worry about it.'

'Life-long passion?'

'I'll throw myself under a bulldozer to stop this mine.'

'I'd do my best to make sure you don't have to.'

Martin nodded. 'Your best's all we ask for. We don't expect miracles.'

'What a strange client you'd make.'

She smiled. 'You'll help us with Rob?'

'Who's Rob?'

'I haven't told Peter about Rob yet,' Lisa said. 'You told me not to.'

Martin looked at Lisa and raised her eyebrows.

'What am I missing?' Tanner asked.

Lisa poured milk in her tea from a small jug Martin had put on the table. 'Rob's how you prove your commitment to June's group, Peter,' she said.

'And how do I do that?'

'You'd better tell him quick,' Martin said, 'he'll be here in a minute.'

'Rob's a member of our group. He's in trouble with the police.'

'What kind of trouble?'

'An assault charge.'

'We're wondering if you'll act for him,' Lisa said.

Tanner looked at her for a long moment. 'Apart from you springing this on me, is there some reason why I wouldn't?'

She shrugged. 'He can't afford you.'

'I hate those words,' he said. 'Was the victim injured?'

'No.'

'I tend to do cases where the charge is more serious.'

'You only help murderers, Peter?' Martin said.

'If they can afford it.'

'Rob hit a neighbour.'

'Is adultery involved?'

'The neighbour had just received a large cheque.'

'I'd prefer it if Rob had,' Tanner said. 'Then he could pay me.'

'The cheque was from Citadel,' Lisa said.

Tanner shook his head, and then smiled. 'Start at the beginning.'

When Citadel was granted a new exploration licence for coal in the Hunter two years ago, June Martin's action group set out to be as disruptive as possible. They encouraged landowners not to willingly grant access to their properties for exploratory drilling. If a court ordered that access be granted, they organised blockades of properties.

'Tim Byrne objected to one of our blockades,' Martin said.

'He's the alleged victim?'

'Nothing alleged about it. I saw Rob belt him.'

'Then I won't call you as a witness. Why did he hit this guy?'

'When Citadel was granted its EL,' Lisa explained, 'it asked three of the owners of the ten properties on Lovelock Lane to give it access to carry out drilling on their land as part of their exploration program.'

'And Byrne said yes?'

'He said yes for his parents.'

'His parents?'

'For thirty thousand dollars,' June Martin said.

'What happened?'

'Byrne's parents own one of the properties. He lives in Sydney. The other owners are members of the action group,' she said. 'We set up a blockade.'

'How do you do that?'

'People power. We roster people on and off. We feed them, set up tents for sleeping. We use cars and trucks and tractors to stop Citadel's vehicles. All other traffic we let through.'

'What's the aim?'

'We're trying to stop another great, big, dirty, open-cut coal mine in our backyards. That's the aim.'

'But this is just exploration.'

'The exploration program inevitably leads to a mine approval,' Lisa said. 'The aim is to disrupt that for as long as possible.'

'So what happened between Rob and Mr Byrne?'

'We've got high rates of respiratory problems,' Martin said. 'Bronchitis, asthma. It's chronic because of the coal dust. The Health Department would shut most mines down if they had their way.'

'How did that make Rob throw a punch?'

'He'd just come from the hospital,' she said. 'His son had an asthma attack. Rob's boy – he's only nine – has always suffered from breathing problems. He came to the blockade after leaving the hospital.'

'Did Byrne say something to provoke him?'

'He was arguing with me when Rob turned up. He said we were stressing his parents, and that they were too old for that. I told him to calm down, that this was a friendly protest, and that I'd spoken with his parents, who'd told me they didn't give too hoots about our blockade.'

'And?'

'Rob was very upset, emotional, you know? He said something to Tim about forcing his parents to take their thirty thousand pieces of silver from the coal company, and … well, Tim called him naive and stupid, then – bang. It's awful. Tim's parents are lovely. They just didn't want a fight with the coal company.'

Tanner glanced at Lisa, then turned back to Martin. 'Is this what you told the police?'

'I haven't said a word to the police yet.'

'Has Rob?'

'No,' Lisa said. 'As soon as it happened, June rang me. I told Rob not to say anything. He was charged on the back of what Byrne told the police.'

'Anyone else see what happened?'

'We had about fifteen people at the blockade,' Martin said. 'Amazingly, none of them saw Rob throw a punch.'

'Incredible,' Tanner said.

'Rob works for the Department of Family and Community Services. If he gets a criminal conviction, he could lose his job. He's got young kids, a mortgage –' As she spoke, there was a knock on the front door. 'That's Rob now.'

'Are you letting my client in, June,' Tanner said, 'or am I?'

Rob MacQuaid was late thirties but looked younger, and he wasn't carrying any unnecessary kilos. He wore a NO MORE MINES FOR THE HUNTER T-shirt.

'I haven't thrown a punch since I was a kid,' he said after they'd taken their seats around June Martin's kitchen table. 'Lisa and June have probably told you – if I get a conviction for an assault, I could lose my job.'

'We've discussed that.'

'Not that – The main thing is stopping the mine.'

'Rob,' Tanner said, 'you're not going to stop a mine in the Singleton Local Court criminal list, okay?'

MacQuaid looked at Lisa, then back to Tanner.

'Tell me what happened at the blockade.'

MacQuaid sighed. 'Brock had a bad asthma attack. I'd been at the hospital all night. They –'

'When did you arrive at the blockade?'

'Maybe nine thirty.'

'Why did you go?'

'Jan – my wife – was taking Brock home. He was fine by morning. I was meant to be on shift that afternoon. It was a Saturday, so I just went early.'

'What happened when you got there?'

'Byrne was yelling at June and some others when I arrived.'

'Yelling about what?'

'He was telling them to get the cars and trucks off the lane. He said the blockade wouldn't work, that it was just a waste of time.'

'Do you know him well?'

'No. He's an accountant in the city. I really only knew his parents.'

'Did you say something to him?'

'I called him Judas.'

'Nice.'

'I was upset.'

'Then?'

'He got angry. He poked me in the chest and told me not to speak to him like that.'

'What else?'

'I don't remember much else.'

'What do you remember?'

'Just – I just swung at him. I was so angry when he poked me . . . I just . . . I didn't even think about it. I shocked myself as much as anything.'

'How hard did you hit him?'

'All I've got.'

'So, not much then?'

MacQuaid gave a slightly embarrassed shrug.

'How did he react?'

'He looked like he'd kill me. He moved towards me to square up, but Bill was too quick.'

'Who's Bill?'

'Bill Sanders. He's a regular on the blockades. He's got a dairy farm near here. He wrapped Byrne up in a bear hug from behind. Pulled him away, tried to calm him down.'

'Did he?'

'Well, he was still yelling, said he was going to call the police.'

'Did you see Byrne again that day?'

'No. Yes.'

'It can't be both, Rob.'

'He's nervous,' Lisa said.

'That's not a defence. Did you see him? Yes or no?'

'Maybe an hour later in his car, going to the police station, I assume. They came to my house later that day, and told me he'd made a complaint.'

'Did the police tell you he was injured?'

'He told them I'd punched him.'

'Listen to me,' Tanner said slowly. 'Did they say he was injured?'

'No.'

'Okay.' Tanner made some notes. 'Did you tell the police he'd hit you?'

Rob MacQuaid looked at Lisa, before looking back at Tanner. 'What do you mean?'

'You told me he poked you in the chest.'

'With his finger,' MacQuaid said softly.

Tanner nodded. 'How tall are you, Rob?'

'What?'

'Your height?'

'One metre seventy-four.'

'Weight.'

'About seventy kilos, I think.'

Tanner stared at him. 'Wringing wet,' he said. 'What about Tim Byrne?'

'He's taller.'

'Much taller?'

MacQuaid nodded slowly. 'Yes.'

'He's much heavier, too?'

MacQuaid nodded.

'And when he struck you, because he's so big, you were scared, right?'

'I don't –' Rob MacQuaid shook his head, a pained smile on his face. 'Can I – I'm just not clear about this. Are you asking me to lie?'

Tanner lifted his eyes from his notes, put his pen down, and glared at his client. 'I am not asking you to lie,' he said. 'Is that clear?'

MacQuaid shook his head. 'Not completely.'

Tanner rubbed his chin with his hand and smiled. 'Let me make it clear, then, Rob. Under no circumstances do I want you to lie. Do you follow?'

'Yes.'

'It's a fact Mr Byrne is much taller and heavier than you, correct?'

'Yes.'

'And he was yelling in the face of a small woman who's a friend of yours?'

'Yes.'

'Who touched who first?'

'He touched me.'

'Do you really know how hard he hit you?'

'I –'

'It hurt a bit, didn't it?'

'I –'

'Were you worried he might strike June? Don't answer me. Just think about it, okay? And I want you to think about whether you were scared or not, Rob. Because I would've been. A big bloke like that, screaming at people, making contact with you – I would've been scared. I'd have been in self-defence mode.'

MacQuaid motioned like he was about to say something, but stopped himself.

'Any questions?'

MacQuaid glanced at Lisa. 'So what now?'

'I'm going to write to the police prosecutor and get the charge dropped.'

MacQuaid looked at Tanner for a long moment. 'You're going to argue self-defence?'

'You had a lunatic screaming at June and jabbing you in the chest, Rob. A lunatic from the city. You were defending June, and defending yourself.'

MacQuaid shook his head. 'June's not scared of anyone.'

Tanner stood, to signal the conference was over. 'June's very scared of you losing your job, Rob,' he said. 'So I think we can count on her being terrified of Mr Byrne.'

24

They had dinner when they got back to Sydney that night. They dropped Lisa's car at her place in Leichhardt, then walked to a nearby restaurant in Norton Street.

When they'd finished eating, Tanner picked up his satchel from under his seat, took a thick document from it, and put it on the table. 'I was going to show you this after we'd met June,' he said. 'I got sidetracked by Rob.'

She smiled. 'Sorry to spring that on you,' she said. 'It was June's idea to do it that way. What's this?'

'When we first met, you told me that a report Citadel had for its Bageeyn River gold mine went missing.'

'Yes.'

'A hydrogeologist's report? And the author has disappeared?'

'I can't find her.'

He paused for a moment. 'Her name is Gabriella Campbell, right?'

She stared at him, a puzzled look on her face. 'How do you know that?'

'She was employed by GreenDay Environmental Consultants? You knew her?'

'I met with her. How do you – ?'

'Who organised the meeting?'

'Anne Warren.'

'The woman who was killed?'

She nodded.

'How did you know her?'

'She contacted us. Pete, how do you know all this?'

'You wanted commitment, Lisa. I'm giving it to you. Who is "us"?'

She sat back in her chair and glared at him. 'Someone in the Bageeyn River Action Group set up to stop the gold mine,' she said. 'Anne and Gaby were co-workers. Anne contacted them on Gaby's behalf. She was put on to me.'

'Who did Anne talk to?'

She shook her head. 'That doesn't matter. Anne was given my number as the group's lawyer. I told her she could trust me, that what she said would remain between us. Anne – she was angry about what was happening to Gaby. She told me Gaby was under huge pressure over a draft report she'd done on the Bageeyn River.'

'Warren told you this, or Campbell?'

'Both.'

'What pressure was she getting?'

'We set up a meeting. I went to Anne's house, and Gaby was there. She told me what work she'd done on the proposed mine plan and production rates, and that she'd estimated how much water would be needed. Because it was so much, she'd then spoken to other experts: an ecologist, a riparian expert; those sort of people. Her conclusion with their input was that taking the amount of water from the river system that she thought would be needed would kill it. The ecosystems would fail. When she told Citadel, they said she was wrong.'

'The people at Citadel who said she was wrong – were they experts of some kind?'

'I don't know.'

'Did you tell anyone in your firm about talking to Warren or Campbell?'

She shook her head. 'No. It's – I know I've broken the law, or at least some ethical obligations. I just –'

'Who else knows?'

'No one. I'm not sure yet how to use what I know. Even with the hydro expert we've engaged for the action group.'

Tanner finished what was left in his wine glass. 'When you met Campbell at Anne Warren's house, did she have her report?'

'She had a draft.'

'Do you have a copy?'

She shook her head. 'We looked at it on her laptop. She wouldn't give me a copy.'

'Why?'

'She wasn't sure what was happening. She was trying to convince them she was right.'

'What were the highlights of the report? If you were trying to kill a gold mine approval and not a river.'

'Just what I've said. Gaby was convinced they'd need more water than Citadel was saying it would,' she said. 'Among other things, she thought a mine of that size would deplete the base flows of the river enough to kill it.'

'"Among other things"?'

'The aquifers under the mining lease area would be depressurised. The water table drops, people can't get water out of bores. Gaby thought it would be a massive drop, and last for hundreds of years – maybe forever.'

'Did anyone else see this report?'

'She discussed it with the government's expert. She told him what was in her calculations, how she'd approached it.'

'And the government expert didn't agree with her?'

'Worse. He rang someone he knew at Citadel and told him she'd called him.'

'That's what got her into more trouble?'

She looked at him like he was a fool. 'Pete, it's their report. It's confidential. She couldn't just start discussing it with someone without their consent. They make you sign confidentiality deeds when you're working on big projects. Citadel told GreenDay to use another hydro, and dump Gaby.'

'And since then?'

She shook her head. 'The last time we talked, Gaby was being hauled in for a meeting – I haven't heard from her since.'

'Did they fire her?'

'I don't know. I rang GreenDay when I couldn't reach her, and was told she'd resigned. They didn't have any contact details, and the mobile number I had was disconnected. Then – then Anne got killed . . . and . . .' She closed her eyes, took a deep breath.

'Are you okay?'

She looked at him. 'She died two weeks after I asked her again for a copy of Gaby's report. I needed it. It had calculations – it was based on computer modelling I didn't have.'

He thought for a moment. 'What was your plan? If Campbell had given you her report.'

Lisa gave a rueful smile. 'I didn't think any of it through. I knew Gaby's draft report was commercial-in-confidence at least. They were burying it, though. I thought maybe I could leak it to someone – I don't know.'

Tanner smiled. 'Have it fall off the back of a truck?'

She shrugged and put her hands over her face.

'What is it?'

'I encouraged those women – I – with Gaby, I really pressured her to do something. She called the government expert because of me. I would really like to know what's happened to her.'

She turned away from him, and he gave her a moment. Then he picked up the document he'd taken from his satchel.

'The hydrogeologist briefed by the government. What's his name?'

'Shields. Why?'

'How did he get involved?'

'They knew water would be a controversial issue. The government department probably didn't want to solely rely on the GreenDay report in Citadel's environmental assessment.'

'So, it's like some kind of peer review?'

She nodded.

'And his report supports the GreenDay report, and is silent about Gaby's views?'

'Yes.'

'Phillip Shields, is it?'

She nodded. 'You've looked online?'

'Online?'

'The department has to put the EA on its website so the public can read it. Shields' report is on it.'

'Shields isn't the only one to see Gaby's report. Nor are you.'

'How do you know?'

'Joe Cheung read it.'

She leant forwards in her chair. 'He told you this?'

'No,' he said.

'Someone else at BBK?'

He handed the document to her. 'That's a printout of all the bills BBK has sent to Citadel on the file for this proposed gold mine, starting at January last year, right up to the end of December.'

She looked at the pile of paper, then back at him. 'How did you get this?'

He shook his head.

'A lawyer there? Are they working on – ?'

'Lisa,' he said firmly. 'No.'

Two nights before, Nadine Bellouard had worked late, until after all the lawyers on her floor had left. As a partner's senior assistant, she had access to the accounts system. She searched for Citadel files, and printed the bills he'd asked her to. She put them in an envelope, and on the way home in a cab, dropped them on Tanner's front door step.

Lisa paused and looked at him and eventually nodded. 'So, this person doesn't work on the file?'

He ignored the question. 'Going into the BBK computer system leaves a trail – whoever has taken over Joe's Citadel files might notice that. But access to the billing system – no one would bother checking that.'

Lisa started flicking over pages. 'So, where do I . . . ?'

'I've highlighted them.' He turned a couple of pages and found the first relevant entry. 'Here – *Peruse draft of Campbell report*. You see the date?'

Lisa nodded.

'Then here – *Discuss report with Campbell*. Then *Discuss hydro report with Kerr*.'

'Kerr?'

'Anthony Kerr. He's Citadel's deputy general counsel in Australia. I did Google searches of Kerr-BBK and Kerr-Citadel, and came up with him.'

'So Joe was discussing this report with in-house legal at Citadel?'

He nodded, and started turning pages. 'He also had a conference call with Robert Spry.'

'Who is?'

'Spry is the global general counsel.' Tanner refilled their wine glasses, then looked at Lisa. She was running her eye down each page, reading the highlighted entries.

'Gaby's report caused quite a stir.'

He nodded. 'Did she ever mention speaking to Joe?'

She shook her head. 'A lawyer talking to a hydrogeologist about a hydro report – I get that if it's about a court case. But this is for an environmental assessment. What's – ?'

'Maybe Citadel told him to call her after they'd seen her report.'

'And say what? Threaten her?'

He shook his head. 'I don't know. I only know they had a report saying their mine would kill the river. That would make it impossible to get an approval from the government – at least for a mine of the size Citadel needed.'

'Needed?'

'They're in a joint venture with this Chinese company, North Shanxi. Investment funds buy shares in them, they raise capital, they borrow from big banks –they'll have promoted this project in the market. Citadel's probably told the market an approval for this gold mine is a sure bet. Privately, they're probably saying they've got some of our politicians on the payroll. You can bet your last dollar they wouldn't have been telling anyone they'd end up with a water report that says a river's going to be killed, or there's a risk the mine won't get approved.'

'So if it's not approved, it hurts more than Citadel?'

He smiled. 'Apart from anyone else, I doubt the Chinese like being disappointed.' He turned several pages. 'Read that.'

It was an entry for an all-day attendance for Joe Cheung, including travel time, for another BBK file for a matter involving Citadel.

'What – I'm not sure what to make of that,' she said.

'Look at the next entry.' It too said *All-Day Attendance*, as did the next two days. 'That's Joe on Tovosevu Island,' he said.

'How do you – ?'

'The dates. Joe's wife told me when he went there, within a few days. This is from a file he'd had open for years for the gold mine on Tovosevu Island.' He turned a few more pages over. He'd highlighted an entry that said *Peruse AW report*. Before it was a short telephone attendance with Anthony Kerr.

'Anne Warren report?' she said.

He nodded. 'The discussions about it start a few weeks after Joe went to the island. Not long after, Warren is killed in Port Moresby. Not Tovosevu, but still PNG.'

She shook her head. 'The AW report is something to do with Tovosevu?'

'There's a reasonable proximity between the report and Joe's trip to the island.'

'You know what Anne does? I mean, she was an ecotoxicolgist. She could be running tests – checking that mine waste isn't leaking into the environment somewhere.'

'Why would Joe need to be there for that?'

'You tell me.' She undid the clip holding up her hair. It was long and black, almost blue. 'You think all this has something to do with Joe and what's happened to him in China?'

'I don't know,' he said. 'I'm guessing this gold mine is high stakes for Citadel. A gold mine would be a much more important asset than a coal mine at the moment. He paused for a few moments. 'There's something you can do for me.'

She nodded.

'Can you find out who Campbell's and Warren's friends were?'

'I've tried with Gaby. The people I spoke to didn't know where she'd gone or why, or they wouldn't say.'

'How old is she?'

'My age. Thirty-five at most, I'd guess.'

'Not married?'

Lisa shook her head.

'Parents?'

'I don't know.'

'Was she from here?'

'I never asked.'

He nodded. 'Maybe I'll get my investigator on this.'

She looked at him for a moment. 'I want to be involved in this, Pete. This is part of my client's case – the action group's opposition to the gold mine. How do we . . . ?'

He smiled. 'We've already committed criminal offences over this, Lisa,' he said. 'We're already both involved.'

25

It was as though Dan was starting kindergarten again, Tanner thought. Back then there had been a tiny band of leg between the top of his socks and the bottom of his shorts. By the time he reached the end of primary school, he was tall and thin, a giant next to the kids in kindergarten. Now, walking through the gates of his new school, he looked like a child again, dwarfed by the stature of the older boys.

Tanner's phone rang as Dan disappeared into the throng. He put the call on speaker and pulled his car away from the school.

'You won't like this.' It was Jane Ross, his co-counsel in the Matheson case.

'Won't like what?'

'Klaudia Dabrowska's unlikely to make the committal.'

'What do you mean?'

'She's got some ear infection. Mastoiditis. She can't fly.'

'What the hell is mastoiditis?'

'I knew you'd ask,' she said. 'It's a middle-ear infection. In bad cases it can get into the small bones and cause perforation of the eardrum. You can't fly with it. They're saying she wouldn't be well enough even for a video link at the moment.'

'Who says?'

'Charles just received a letter from the DPP.'

'Do they have a medical report?'

'Not yet.'

'I'm calling Aitken,' Tanner said, and hung up.

The committal hearing was to determine whether Justin Matheson would stand trial for the murder of Elena Mancini. All a prosecutor has to establish on committal is that, based on the evidence, a properly instructed jury *could* convict the accused, not that it would. It's not a high hurdle, and many committals are done purely on police statements, with no oral evidence. In some cases, Tanner didn't want to cross-examine a witness at committal. He'd hold his fire for trial rather than giving them a practice run beforehand.

There was no doubt that Matheson was going to be committed to stand trial for the murder of Elena Mancini – the DNA alone would see to that. Tanner had decided not to cross-examine John Richter at the committal. He'd wait for the trial. He wanted to take a look at Klaudia Dabrowska, though. If Matheson was telling the truth, she was lying; he'd have to accuse her of that in front of a jury. He wanted to see how she responded to pressure, how she handled slow questioning or fast, how she reacted depending on his demeanour. He wanted to know if she'd come across as sympathetic, or as someone hiding something.

The prosecutor assigned to the Matheson case was Richard Aitken SC – one of the most experienced prosecutors in the DPP's office. Tanner and he had clashed in several cases over the years; they only spoke to each other when they had to, and the usual pleasantries were dispensed with.

'What's mastoiditis, Richard?' Tanner asked as soon as his call was put through.

'It's an infection of –'

'How long's she had it?'

'– the ear canal. Do you want to listen or talk over the top of me? We've been told it's serious. It looks like she'll need surgery.'

'Who told you?'

'Her doctor.'

'What doctor?'

Aitken sighed. 'One of the solicitors here has dealt with this, not me. The bottom line is, she can't fly.'

'My guy can't get a fair trial without her at committal.'

'Rubbish. You know you can . . .'

'Where's your medical report?'

'We're getting one. Her father's unwell too, we mentioned that –'

'Unless he's saying he was with Richter too, I don't want to cross-examine Mr Dabrowska.'

'She can't fly. Think about video link if you have to.'

'I want to see this girl.'

'So you can frighten her?'

'Has she got something to be frightened about, Rich?'

'I'm due in court, Peter. Goodbye.'

When Tanner opened his front door that night to let Lisa Ilves in, she was carrying a bottle of wine. She had her hair down, and was wearing a black dress, which ended just north of her knees.

'You didn't have to bring this,' he said, taking the wine.

'I can only have a glass,' she said, holding up her car keys.

'Say hello to Lisa, Dan,' he said when they reached the open-plan kitchen-living room.

'Hi.'

'How was school? Day one, right?'

'Yeah. Good.'

'That's the most you'll get,' Tanner said. He noticed Dan looking at Lisa's shoulder, which was uncovered. 'It's not polite to stare, Dan.'

'What is that?' the boy said.

'CO_2,' Lisa said. 'Being eliminated.'

Dan smiled. 'Cool.'

'Thanks.'

'It's about climate change, right?'

'Yes.'

'You're against it, right?'

'Of course. Aren't you?'

'Sure. We did a project on it at my old school.'

'That's a longer conversation than I've had with him for a year,' Tanner said. 'Go watch TV for half an hour, then read.'

When Dan left, Tanner offered Lisa a seat at the kitchen table. He opened the wine she'd brought and poured it into two large shiraz glasses. He sat down next to her.

'What do you have to tell me?'

'I ended up getting contact details for two colleagues of hers that sound like they were friends. She went to university with both of them, and worked with one. The guy's name is Matthew Durham. He works for the Commonwealth Department of Conservation. He's a water guy based in Canberra. The woman she worked with is called Kate McDonald. She's at KEC Group – they're a competitor of GreenDay. Anyway, the guy in Canberra was guarded. He said he didn't know where she was. I think he was lying, though.'

'Why?'

'He wanted to know precisely what I wanted to speak to her about, what project it was, why I needed her, not someone else. All that, then he says he doesn't know where she is, and doesn't have a number.'

'What did you tell him?'

'I used client privilege as a cover. I think he knows more. Just gut feeling.'

'And the woman?'

'She was suspicious at first, but warmed up. I told her about some of the other cases I'd done. Anyway, she said she thought Gaby was travelling in Europe.'

'Is she in contact with her?'

'She said she got an email a few months ago.'

'She didn't give you the address?'

'I asked. She wouldn't.'

'So now what?'

'I told her Gaby and I had worked on a case together – which is more or less true. I asked her to contact Gaby for me, and to tell her I had to talk to her about something for a case. She eventually said she'd try, when I pleaded.'

'That's progress, I guess,' he said.

She shook her head. 'Not really,' she said. 'Kate called me about an hour ago.'

'And?'

'She said she'd emailed Gaby, and Gaby said she knew what it was about, but couldn't help.'

'That's it?'

'That's it.'

Tanner took a sip of wine, and sighed. 'Well,' he said, 'at least we know she's alive.'

'Any thoughts?'

'My guess is that Citadel has made it clear to Gabriella Campbell that she and her report aren't to be seen or heard of until the Bageeyn River gold mine is approved and operational. What do you think?'

She nodded. 'You think they've bought her off?'

'Or scared her off.' Tanner picked up his wine glass and swirled the wine around. 'This Kate – what's her last name?'

'McDonald.'

He stood and left the room, and came back holding his laptop. 'You said she works for the KEC Group?' The KEC Group had a website detailing the services they offered, and a list of their offices. Head office was in Sydney, but they had two others in Western Australia, one near the Galilee basin in Queensland, and another in Newcastle near the Hunter Valley. 'There she is,' he said after a few moments. Kate McDonald was listed in the water team. There was a short biography and CV, and a small photo.

Lisa looked at him reading from Kate McDonald's profile. 'What are you going to do, Pete?'

'Make Kate say no to a face.'

26

While Tanner was in his car early the next morning, heading north on the Pacific Highway, he got a call from Charles Porter. The office of the Director of Public Prosecutions had just emailed a medical report on the condition preventing Klaudia Dabrowska from flying from London to Sydney for Justin Matheson's committal.

'She's got acute mastoiditis, as they claimed in their letter.'

'How's she being treated?'

'Oral antibiotics failed to clear up the infection. Currently intravenous antibiotics – may need surgery to drain fluids from the ear.'

'How long's this all meant to take?'

'It's not specific. "Can't fly for the foreseeable future," it says.'

'What's the doctor's name?'

'Dr Simon Anthony.'

'He's some kind of ENT specialist?'

Porter paused for a moment, and Tanner could hear him turning over a page. 'I don't think so. He's MBBS.'

'A GP? Any mention of a specialist?'

'Not in this report.'

Tanner thought for a moment. 'Write a letter to the DPP,' he said. 'Tell them we want a report from an ear specialist or we'll be taking this to court. The doctor she sees for her sniffles and pap smears isn't good enough.'

'You want me to word it like that?'

'Use your imagination.'

Tanner pulled up in front of the Newcastle office of the KEC Group at ten. He'd left home at eight, and had beaten the Friday traffic that later that day would be heading north for the weekend. The office was open plan, and as he walked into the reception area, he spotted Kate McDonald in the middle of the main room, leaning over the cubicle of another worker to talk to her.

'My name's Peter Tanner,' he said loudly to the receptionist. 'I'm here to talk to Kate McDonald. She's right behind you.'

McDonald looked up as Tanner spoke. She straightened and slowly walked over to the reception desk.

Tanner immediately handed her a card. 'I'm working on a case with Lisa Ilves. Can I take up five minutes of your time?'

McDonald looked at Tanner blankly, then at his card. 'You couldn't call?'

'I thought I'd come and see you.'

'I'm busy. I've got a flight to catch at –'

'Five minutes, Kate. Let me buy you a coffee. I've driven up from Sydney this morning.'

McDonald looked at Tanner's card as if something mysterious was written on it. 'You should've called.'

'I promise,' he said. 'No more than five minutes.'

She took him to a conference room and shut the door.

'This is new?' he said, as he took a seat at the table. 'These offices?'

'We've been here a year.'

'You live nearby?'

She nodded. 'On week days. My partner works in Sydney,' she said. 'I spend most weekends there.'

'You're heading to a work site?'

'Up north. Queensland.'

'Some big mines starting up there?' he said.

'Maybe,' she said. 'The price of coal's not great at the moment. There's a lot of community concern about CSG.'

'Should the community be concerned?'

'You're not here to ask me about coal-seam gas, are you?'

He shook his head. 'Lisa spoke to you?'

'Yes.'

'Gaby Campbell's a friend of yours? Lisa talked to you about her report? The one Citadel buried?'

'I can't talk to you about that.'

He smiled. 'Can I tell you a story?'

'Will it take more than three minutes? You said five, and it's been two.'

'What I'm going to tell you, I want you to tell your friend.'

'I can't reach her.'

'You passed on a message from her to Lisa.'

'I can't always reach her.'

'Well, when you can,' he said, 'I want you to pass something on.'

She sighed, but said nothing.

'I have a client called Joseph Cheung. He's in a jail in Shanghai. You may have read about him in the papers?'

She nodded lightly.

'He's a friend too. Gaby knows who he is.'

'I read he sought a bribe,' she said. 'Did he do it?'

Tanner shrugged. 'Joe's too polite to tell the Chinese outright they've made a mistake. I'm trying to see if I can assist with that.'

She looked at him blankly. 'How can Gaby help you?'

'Joe read her report. He talked to her about it. I don't know how or why, but I think it has something to do with him being in prison.'

'There's nothing she can do about that.'

'He's got a young family. He could be stuck there for ten years.'

She shook her head and looked at the table. 'Why are you telling me this?'

'Because I want you to tell Gabriella,' he said sharply.

'She can't help him.'

'She can tell me the truth.'

'Can't he?'

'It might be more important to hear it from her.'

'And how will that help?'

'I don't know, Kate.'

'So what's the point?'

'I don't know what I can do until I know the truth. I'll work it out from there.'

'That doesn't sound like much of a plan, Mr Tanner.'

'Did you know Anne Warren?' he said.

She glared at him. 'Gaby knew her better,' she said softly.

'Did Gaby tell you why Anne went to Tovosevu Island? Because I think Gaby knows. And I think that has something to do with Joe.'

She started to say something, then stopped herself, biting at the inside of her cheek. 'She can't,' she finally said.

'Then ask her again,' he said. 'Please? Ask her to contact us. She can call me; she can call Lisa. She can trust us. Just ask her to tell us what happened.'

She walked with him to the door.

'You know how to get a message to me,' he said.

She nodded, and said goodbye.

Two nights later, after dinner on Sunday evening, his phone buzzed with a text. *She's sorry*, the message said. *She can't help.*

27

The non-availability of Klaudia Dabrowka for Justin Matheson's committal was listed for argument on a Friday afternoon, just over two weeks before the hearing itself.

Because of the late afternoon start, there were no other lawyers in the courtroom when Tanner and Jane Ross walked in. Porter arrived a few minutes later with Matheson's parents. A video link to Silverwater Remand Centre had been set up so Matheson could follow the proceedings.

Richard Aitken entered the courtroom with only a young solicitor from the prosecutor's office. He had an annoyed look on his face that was familiar to Tanner. Aitken was so uptight, Tanner was sure one day he was going to burst. Hopefully mid-trial in front of a jury. 'This is going to be a spectacular waste of your client's money, Peter,' Aitken said as he took his seat.

'When's that ever stopped a lawyer?' Tanner knew he was unlikely to succeed with any legal argument he was about to raise. That wasn't the point; he'd learnt a long time ago to be thorough any time a witness was said to be too ill for court.

'There's a witness you want to cross-examine who's not available, Mr Tanner?' Magistrate Harry Stanley said as soon as he sat at the bench. Although the trial would be heard in front of a jury in the Supreme Court, until Matheson was actually committed to stand trial, the case remained in the Local Court criminal list, where the committal would take place. Stanley had been a magistrate for over twenty years, and it had taken its toll. He was corpulent and easily antagonised. Even in his most tranquil moods, his face retained a permanent cerise glow.

'Not any witness, your Honour. One of only two crucial witnesses.'

'I'm sure our DNA expert qualifies as crucial,' Aitken said.

'Would you like me to remind Mr Aitken to stand before he addresses you, your Honour?'

'I think he knows,' Stanley said. 'You say Ms – it's Miss Dabrowska, is that how I say it?'

'Klaudia Dabrowska.'

'She's an eye witness, more or less?'

'An alibi witness, your Honour, just not for the accused.'

'I object to that characterisation, your Honour,' Aitken said, standing this time, his hands gripping the sides of the lectern. It looked too big for him. He was a short man, five seven if he stood on his toes.

Stanley nodded, but otherwise ignored him. 'And she's unable to fly. I've been emailed a medical report with the papers.'

'We object to that report being admitted into evidence, your Honour.'

The magistrate raised his white eyebrows. 'On what grounds?'

'Lack of expertise.'

Stanley examined the report of Dr Simon Anthony. He looked at Tanner. 'Perhaps I'll deal with that argument when Mr Aitken tries to tender it. In the meantime, though, what is it you're asking me to do today? I can't order a witness in a foreign jurisdiction to attend court here.'

Tanner nodded. 'We want an order that if Miss Dabrowska isn't made available for cross-examination at the committal, her statement shouldn't be received into evidence. Secondly, if Mr Matheson is committed, we seek an order that the Crown not be entitled to call her. We won't be able to get a fair trial if we can't test her evidence at committal.'

Stanley glared at Tanner, then gave a faint smile. 'Is that all you want, Mr Tanner?' he said, sarcasm clear in his voice. 'You don't want to me to just dismiss the charges now?'

Tanner paused, and pretended to look at his notes. 'Are you considering that, your Honour?'

'I'm not,' Stanley said. 'Let's start with the second order you propose. Whether or not you can get a fair hearing without cross-examining her at committal is a question for the trial judge, isn't it?'

'We can ask you to make that order, your Honour. The Crown could seek to get it revoked if it wanted, but –'

'That's nonsense,' Stanley said, interrupting. 'Let me hear from Mr Crown about why Miss Dabrowska can't make it.'

Tanner sat down, and Aitken walked the magistrate through the pathology of mastoiditis, and how acutely Klaudia Dabrowska was suffering from it. When he'd outlined the facts about diagnosis, treatment and prognosis, he came to the report of Dr Simon Anthony.

'Mr Tanner,' Stanley said, when Aitken handed the original of the report to the court officer, 'I've read an emailed copy of this. I take it you have no objection to that. I didn't know there was going to be any issue with its admissibility.'

'I don't have any objection if your Honour doesn't rely on it.'

'What's the objection again?'

'Dr Anthony isn't qualified to give the opinions he purports to, your Honour.'

'Because he's a general practitioner?'

'Because he's not qualified to prescribe a course of treatment for a severe case of this disease, nor opine on a prognosis. Only an ENT specialist can do that.'

'Do we have his CV?'

'I'll hand that up now, your Honour,' Aitken said. 'Mr Tanner only notified us of his objection yesterday. Dr Anthony had to do this for us last night, our time. He's not used to having his qualifications challenged.'

'I'm not challenging his qualifications,' Tanner said. 'I'm highlighting them. MBBS – he's not an ear specialist.'

Stanley took off his glasses and started to chew on one end. He looked up at Tanner from the papers he was reading. 'He's been a GP in London for thirty years, Mr Tanner. Presumably he's seen a few cases of ear infection.'

Tanner shrugged. 'Presumably he has, your Honour. And when he comes across a serious case, presumably, if he values his insurance policy, he refers that patient to an ENT specialist, who's qualified to treat them.'

'Your Honour, may I assist?' Aitken said.

'I assume my friend doesn't have a degree from the Royal College of Otolaryngology,' Tanner said.

'No, I don't,' Aitken snapped.

'Maybe he wants to hand up a report from Miss Dabrowska's acupuncturist. That'd be about as much use as Dr Anthony on mastoiditis.'

'Mr Tanner,' Stanley said, 'that's disrespectful to a very experienced doctor.'

'I apologise, your Honour,' Tanner said. 'I meant my comment only to be disrespectful to the prosecutor.'

'Really, Mr Tanner?'

'This is a murder charge, your Honour. We're entitled to have this important witness here to test her, and if she can't travel to Australia, we're entitled to a proper explanation.'

'May I assist now, your Honour?' Aitken said.

'Go ahead.'

'Dr Anthony is a very experienced GP. Based on his own qualifications, training and experience, he can perfectly admissibly express the opinions he has. That's our primary position. However, another way of considering Dr Anthony's report is to read it as though he's also passing on the views of Miss Dabrowska's specialist. It mightn't be expressly stated in the report, but clearly that's what's happening.'

'Why shouldn't I read it that way, Mr Tanner?'

'Because it's not what the report says. Dr Anthony doesn't say he's spoken to someone more qualified regarding this condition.'

'The next matter I want to raise, your Honour,' Aitken continued, 'is the issue of what happens if Miss Dabrowska is at least well enough to be able to give evidence. We'll organise for that to happen via video link from the UK.'

'That's a different issue, your Honour,' Tanner said. 'It has its own problems.'

'Mr Tanner,' Stanley said, 'I'm going to admit the report into evidence. It's admissible as expert evidence. It's more a question of what weight I give it. I don't see why I shouldn't take it at face value as the opinion of a very experienced doctor. I'll admit the report, and mark it as exhibit "P1".'

'If the court pleases.'

'So, if the report's in, that makes it hard for you to argue about Miss Dabrowska being well enough to fly. So that leaves us with the video link issue.'

'Your Honour, video link would be really unsatisfactory,' Tanner said.

'Why?'

'On my instructions, Miss Dabrowska was with – if I can use that term euphemistically – my client in a room in the Richter estate when Elena Mancini suffered the injury that killed her. She told the police she was with Mr Richter. I want to test her on that.'

'You'll be able to. Just via video link.'

'The difficulties presented to a court in assessing credit when a witness is giving evidence by video link are well documented, and –'

'Mr Tanner,' Stanley interrupted, 'if this was about a jury trial, I'd be with you. It's not. It's a committal, and there'll be limits on cross-examination anyway. I can't order this witness to attend, and she's not able to fly at the moment, so video link will have to suffice. I'm with you that it'd be better if she was in a courtroom here rather than in a room in London, but that's what it's going to have to be.'

'And what if she's not well enough even for video link, your Honour?'

'I'm not ruling on a hypothetical. Let's see what happens.'

'We'll be seeking to have her statement admitted even if she's not able to give evidence, your Honour,' Aitken said. 'Any issue about that is for the presiding magistrate at the committal.'

'I agree,' Stanley said. 'The defence has other options in any event, which I'm certain a counsel of Mr Tanner's experience is well aware of. If Miss Dabrowska can't give evidence at committal and the defendant is ordered to stand trial, Mr Tanner can seek to have a voir dire hearing with her at a later date, or even during the trial if he thinks that's the best course. All of that is for the trial judge to decide, not me today.' Stanley picked up his pen and started making notes in his court book. 'Here's what I propose to do,' he said after a few moments. 'I've admitted into evidence a report of Dr Simon Anthony dated 20 February. I've considered its contents, and it's clear that the witness Klaudia Dabrowska is currently unable to fly from London to give evidence at the committal listed to commence in just over two weeks' time. What I'd ask the prosecution to do, though, is provide an updated report from Dr Anthony, say, a week out from the committal, letting the defence know if she can at least give video-link evidence. Is there any difficulty with that, Mr Crown?'

'I wouldn't expect so, your Honour.'

'Can the report be from Miss Dabrowska's ENT specialist, your Honour?'

'No, Mr Tanner,' Stanley snapped. 'I'm not even ordering a report from Dr Anthony. I can't. He's outside our jurisdiction, and you know it. I'm making a request to help you.'

'If the court pleases.'

'There's one other option, Mr Tanner,' Stanley said.

Tanner rose and nodded.

'It might be that Miss Dabrowska can't give evidence by video link when the committal is listed for hearing, but what if the medical advice is that she's likely to have recovered a short time after? I'd be sympathetic to pushing the committal back a month or so, if you were to make that application.'

Tanner shook his head. 'My client's in custody, your Honour. If he's committed for trial, he'll be lucky to get a date before the end of the year. I'm sure he doesn't want to stay in remand any longer.'

Stanley shrugged. 'I'm trying to do you a favour, Mr Tanner. You don't have to take it up.'

'I appreciate that, your Honour. I'll discuss it with my client.'

Magistrate Stanley nodded, and stood to leave the court. The barristers bowed their heads, and the court officer adjourned the hearing.

'Justin won't want it adjourned,' Bill Matheson said as soon as Aitken left the courtroom. 'We need this to be over.'

Tanner put up his hand. 'We don't have to decide that today, Bill.'

'We don't want it delayed to next year. Justin's life is on hold.'

'I know you all want this over,' Tanner said, 'but the wheels of justice turn more slowly than we'd like sometimes. If I think it's crucial to cross-examine Klaudia at committal, and we need to take up the judge's offer of a delay, then that's what we're going to do.'

William Matheson looked at Tanner for a moment, then shook his head, but said nothing more.

'Why is this girl lying, Peter?' Judith Matheson said. She looked worn down. Her son's trial was going to age her ten years.

'That's one of the things I want to ask her, Judith.'

28

Tom Cable was already in the café opposite the court complex when Tanner walked in. He was seated at a table for two and sipping on a small bottle of Coke, which he held up as a greeting. Tanner ordered a long black, then sat down opposite Cable.

'You're looking fit as usual,' Tanner said.

Cable nodded. He was mid-fifties, but had the lean physique of a professional athlete. 'I'm doing three months with no alcohol, no coffee and no red meat.'

'That's my entire diet.'

'Been in court? Anything interesting?'

'My client's charged with killing an Italian tourist. A young woman.'

Cable pursed his lips and whistled softly. 'Did he do it?'

'He says he didn't.'

'Sure. But did he?'

Tanner shrugged, and Cable shook his head.

'How's Dan?'

'Just started high school.'

Cable nodded. 'They go from twelve to grown-ups in a flash. I went in when Rob was twelve. Three years later, I come out and he's a man.'

Cable had been a thief. In the early days he'd used his agility. He scaled walls and balconies and climbed roofs the average cat burglar didn't dare too. As he matured, he developed skills in disarming security systems. As the age of security cameras expanded, he scaled back his B&E practice, and started to plan for the future – which was when he got caught.

He was arrested in a police sting, offloading goods he'd stolen from a job on the Lower North Shore. A 'fence' he worked with fingered him for a string of other robberies for a lower sentence. Cable got five at the top and three and a half at the bottom.

'How's Rob?'

Not long after getting out of prison, Cable set up a business. Given his expertise, he chose home security installation. He didn't advertise his record, his brother held the licence, and he and Cable's wife were the directors of the company. They branched into investigation work, and process serving. Rob was Tom's son, now mid-twenties, and the reason the two men knew each other.

Six years before Rob Cable had gone out drinking with his team-mates from his rugby club. Just before three am, he got into an argument with one. A punch was thrown; a jaw cracked in half. Cable pleaded self-defence, claiming his team-mate was the aggressor. Most of his team-mates sided with him, but two said Rob had thrown the first punch. The trial was before a judge without a jury. Rob was convicted, and got fifteen months non-parole. It hadn't helped him that the boy he'd fought was the son of the local mayor.

An appeal was lodged and Tanner ended up with the brief. The appellate court agreed that the preponderance of evidence was that Rob had thrown not the first, but the third punch. The trial judge had paid scant regard to this, and to Cable's evidence that he feared for his safety. The conviction was quashed. Tom Cable told Tanner he owed him a massive debt. From time to time since then, Tanner had used Cable for some investigation jobs in his cases.

'Another baby on the way,' Cable said.

'That's great.'

Cable nodded and took another sip on his Coke. 'There's something I can do for you?'

'There is.'

'Related to this trial?'

A waitress put Tanner's long black in front of him, and he waited until she left. 'I need you to break into a house.'

Cable didn't react at first. He picked up his bottle and drained the dregs. 'That's a serious request?'

'It is.'

Cable took off his sunglasses and looked directly at Tanner. 'You want me to steal something?'

'Data. From a computer. Assuming there is one.'

'Is this an office we're talking about?'

'A residence.'

'When you say "data" – why wouldn't you just steal the computer?'

'I don't want anything else stolen.'

Cable's face wasn't a picture of enthusiasm.

'It's not like it will be your first B&E.'

'It's been a while.'

'I'll pay you.'

Cable gave a humourless smile. 'I'm not risking jail for free, Pete.'

'There's a good reason for this.'

'Life or death?'

'I've got a friend in prison in China. You may have seen something about it in the papers or TV news?'

'We're talking about a computer in this country, right?'

'I'm not sending you to Shanghai.'

'There's some connection between what's on this computer, and your friend in China?'

'I don't know.'

'You don't know?'

'I need to see this person's emails, her phone records. I need to check what's on her hard drive. There may be nothing that helps. I'm trying to find someone. I'm not going to explain it all to you now.'

'You're not making much sense, Pete.'

'It's a crime, Tom – you can pass on it.'

Cable put his hand across his mouth and rubbed his chin. 'How many years will I get if I get caught? Same as your friend in China?'

'There won't be anyone at the house.'

'How do you know?'

'She spends most weekends in Sydney.'

'Where's this house?'

'Newcastle.'

'There'll be travel expenses. I'd have to go up a few days before, check the location, get my bearings, work out who the neighbours are, what their movements –'

'They'll be covered.'

Cable glared at Tanner, then sighed. 'You don't want anyone to know there's been a break in?'

'Yeah.'

'That might be hard. If she's got an alarm, bars on windows – it's not always easy leaving no trace. In the early days my main tool was a crowbar.'

'You told me you were good.'

'Not getting caught makes you good.'

'Do your best.'

'I'm no computer expert, Pete, but if she's got a computer, there might be a password to get in –'

'Someone will be on call to help with that. You'll get a number to ring if you have to.'

'Jesus. Can't this person break into the house?'

'You don't have to do this.'

Cable put his sunglasses back on. 'You must like this guy in China.'

'I don't like innocent people being convicted.'

Cable laughed, almost to himself.

PART THREE

29

Klaudia Dabrowska didn't give evidence at Justin Matheson's committal hearing. Her condition worsened, according to a further report from Dr Simon Anthony, who stated she'd need surgery to drain fluid from her right inner ear.

The DNA evidence was enough to have Matheson committed to stand trial for the murder or manslaughter of Elena Mancini. The presiding magistrate held that it alone made it open for a properly instructed jury to convict. Tanner applied to have Dabrowska's witness statement excluded, but the magistrate let it in, and ruled that any application to have her excluded from giving evidence could be made to the trial judge. Tanner knew such an application would be a lost cause.

The case was listed for a two-week hearing in the middle of October, just over six months from the conclusion of the committal.

Three nights after the committal ended, Tanner picked up his phone to dial a London number. The firm he was calling had been recommended by a member of the London criminal bar he'd met at a conference, and he'd looked briefly at their website. Their headquarters was in central London, with offices in three other cities.

He was put through to someone called Paul Matthews. Tanner introduced himself, and said he had a client who required their services.

'Do you mind if I ask you some questions, Paul? About your background.'

'Within reason.' The accent sounded educated, cool.

'I'll do my best. You're a director of IIS?'

'Yes.'

'International Investigation Services. That's quite a title.'

'We have relationships with firms across Europe, the Americas, even in Africa.'

'And you've been with IIS for how long?'

'Six years, all as a director.'

'Forgive my ignorance – you're a private investigator yourself? That's your occupation?'

'All the directors here are members of the Association of British Investigators. We're also all members of the world association.'

'Are you licensed to kill, Paul?'

'I'm not a spy, Mr Tanner. I'm a private detective.'

'My apologies. Before we go further, I need you to do a conflict search.'

'We always do conflict searches before we accept a retainer.'

'I'll give you some names. If they come up in a search, forget I called.'

Fifteen minutes later, Matthews called Tanner back with the all clear.

Tanner told him about Justin Matheson, and the night in October the previous year that ended with the death of Elena Mancini. He then filled him in on Klaudia Dabrowska. 'I want to know everything she's done since she returned to the UK,' he said. 'I want you to check the background of Dr Simon Anthony. I want to know how long Klaudia's been his patient, and how she became one. That's a start. I'll write out a list tomorrow.'

'There are some things we need to discuss first. Generally we can help you, but it will naturally have to be within the bounds of the law.'

'That's disappointing.'

Matthews paused before responding, perhaps assessing the seriousness of what Tanner had just said. 'It's non-negotiable. Do you have an address for Miss Dabrowska?'

'No. The address on her police statement is a Sydney address. Her father worked for a department store, we think, but that's all I have. Klaudia used to be attached to a modelling agency called Jade. There are still some photos of her on their website. We've got an address for Dr Anthony from his medical report.'

'Who's retaining us?'

'Make your bills out to the Sydney office of a firm called Sharrop & Prentice. Otherwise, you're to deal directly with me.'

'What's the urgency on this?'

'Justin's trial's not until October, but the witness has recently said she was too ill to fly to Sydney.'

'You don't believe that?'

'It's one of the things I want you to find out.'

'Once we receive a signed retainer, and some advance money in our retention account, we can start.'

'How much do you need?'

'The normal retainer fee for something like this would be five thousand. I can email our bank details.'

'I'll get it taken care of in the morning, our time.'

Tanner ended the call, then dialled Charles Porter's number.

'Peter – just give me a second to go outside, will you?'

'Where are you?'

'Work. A war room. We've got a trial running.'

'Apologies for interrupting.' Tanner told him about his call to Paul Matthews. 'I want to know more about Dabrowska and Dr Anthony.'

'Can you give me some details as to why? I'll need to convince the Mathesons this is really necessary before –'

'It's necessary because we say it is. We're in charge of Justin's defence, not his parents. Just tell the Mathesons I don't trust Dr Anthony, or Klaudia – either Klaudia's a liar, or Justin is. If they think she can be trusted, their son killed Elena Mancini.'

'My firm will need to formally retain – who is it you've spoken to?'

'Leave that to me. I'll deal with the investigator, you get the money to fund him.'

'Sounds like you'll get to have all the fun on this case, Peter.'

'Yeah,' Tanner said, 'and I'll be the one that gets all the blame if Justin gets convicted.'

30

Melissa Cheung was sitting at an outdoor table when he arrived at the café beside Coogee Beach, her daughter parked next to her in a stroller. She was feeding her some mush from a Tupperware container.

'The food here is better than that, I hope?' Tanner said as he leant over to kiss her. She'd been to China only a few weeks before, and he'd arranged to meet her for lunch after she'd visited her husband's parents that morning, who lived nearby.

'You don't remember having to do this with Dan?'

He shrugged. 'How are Joe's parents?'

'His mother's not well,' she said. 'What's happened to Joe is taking its toll. How are you, Pete?'

'Me? Fine.'

'When did you last have a check-up?'

He looked at her, puzzled by the question. 'Do I look sick?'

'Tired.'

'I'm not sure I've ever had a check-up.'

She shook her head. 'You're forty now?'

'Forty-one, but you can put me down as fifty.'

'You still look fit.'

'Juries are biased against fat lawyers,' he said. 'The Americans have done studies on it. It's an occupational imperative to stay in shape. How's Joe?'

A waitress came over and handed them menus, and she pretended to scan it. 'Thinner,' she said. 'He's depressed. The reality has sunk in. What his life will be for . . . however long it is. Not seeing the kids . . .' She shook her head, and he poured her a glass of water from the bottle the waitress had placed on the table.

'How did it go with the kids? Did they see him more than once?'

'Twice,' she said. 'It was awkward with Tom. He's angry. He wants to know why Joe's not coming home, why he's in prison. All normal questions.'

'Are you still telling them the same thing?'

'Joe told them a mistake had been made, that we're trying to sort it out, but it was very difficult to do that in China.'

'Joe told me he *felt* guilty,' Tanner said. 'I've been thinking about that.'

The waitress came back to the table and took their orders. Melissa ordered a salad, and Tanner ordered fish and chips. She smiled when he told the waitress what he wanted.

'What?' he asked.

'Joe used to talk about how much you ate at uni, wondering how you stayed trim.'

'Nervous energy.'

'Are you still anxious before trials?'

He nodded. 'I'm a nervous wreck.'

'I still don't understand why you do it, then?'

'I've got to make a living somehow.'

'You must like some of it?'

'Jury trials give you a rush – eventually.'

'And that makes it worth it?'

'If you win.'

'Even if the client's guilty?'

He took a sip of water and smiled at her. 'I haven't had many clients who weren't guilty, Melissa.'

'Doesn't that bother you?'

'Not consciously.'

'Subconsciously?'

'Everything I do troubles me subconsciously.'

Tanner leant forward, and looked straight at Melissa. 'Joe might be one of the few innocent clients I'll ever have. I could be a criminal lawyer for another thirty years, and I may only get a few more. I'm not abandoning him until it's over, even if he wants me to. Do you understand?'

She offered a sad smile and nodded slowly.

'Did you speak to Li when you were in Shanghai?'

'Once,' she said. 'At the hotel.'

'What's happening with Joe's case?'

'The court's been told a deal is being discussed with the prosecutor's office, and some kind of plea and recommended sentence is being explored.'

'And that is?'

'The court will give him ten years.'

He looked at her closely. 'The court *will give*?'

She sat back in her chair and looked out over the beach. 'If I tell you something, you have to promise not to repeat it. I mean to anyone.'

'Melissa,' he said, 'everything you say about Joe is confidential. You know that.'

She turned her gaze back from the beach to him. 'They've said he might be home in five years.'

Tanner narrowed his eyes. 'Who said this?'

'Joe,' she said. 'Li.'

'And who told them?'

'I don't know. The government, I think. Someone in the government.'

'I don't – and you believe this? I mean, the court is going to say ten years, but Joe will be released after five? On what basis?'

'I don't know.'

'Why will they release him then?'

'I don't know.'

'You don't know, or you won't tell me?'

'I don't *know*, Pete.'

'And you have faith in this deal? You trust the people who locked Joe up to honour it?' A secret codicil to a sentencing sounded absurd.

'What choice do we have?' Her face tightened in anger, but her eyes filled with tears. 'This is Joe's chance. Twenty years, Pete. Against five. We can't risk that. Tom will still be a boy. Otherwise . . . he misses it all.'

'How do you know you can trust these people?'

'We have to!'

Heads turned at the tables surrounding them on the footpath. The waitress was near the open doorway, and took a step towards their table, but Tanner waved her away. He reached under the table to the leather satchel he'd brought with him. He took out a document, and put it on the table. The BBK billing printout Nadine Bellouard had given him.

'Did Joe ever talk to you about a project for Citadel Resources called Bageeyn River? It's a proposed gold mine out west. Did he ever mention a hydrogeologist called Gabriella Campbell?'

Melissa shook her head. 'Pete, what is this?'

'It's a document that shows what work Joe was doing last year, up until he went to Shanghai.'

'Where did you get it?'

'It doesn't matter.'

She glared at him, then pulled her sunglasses down from the top of her head, as if she was getting ready to leave. 'Joe has a deal.'

'Do you know about this woman? She wrote a report that Citadel have buried. It said this mine would kill a river. Joe spoke to her about it. He spoke to people at Citadel about it. This woman has vanished.'

'You shouldn't have that, Peter.' She turned her face to the ocean.

'Has Joe told you any of this?'

'No.'

He trusted his instincts for when he was being lied to, but this time he couldn't tell. 'What about since his arrest?'

She took a deep breath and tears ran down the sides of her face. She picked up her bag and fished around for a tissue, but Tanner passed her a napkin. She took off her sunglasses and wiped at her eyes. 'No,' she said again.

'Joe went to a PNG island,' he said. 'You told me that. Melissa?'

She bowed her head, but nodded.

'I think he went with a woman called Anne Warren. She wrote a report about going to the island. There's a gold mine there. Has Joe said anything about this?'

She put her hand to her forehead and rubbed her brow, closed her eyes, and said nothing.

'Joe had her report. That woman is dead now. Does he know why?'

Their meals were set down in front of them, and Melissa waited until the waitress had left before speaking. She looked up at him, anger flaring in her eyes. 'No!' she cried. When she did, she startled Lily, who began crying.

Tanner leant back in his chair and was silent for a moment.

Melissa took her wallet from her bag, opened it, and took out a twenty-dollar note.

'Don't be silly,' he said. 'Have your lunch.'

She put the note on the table, put a glass of water on it, and stood up.

'I have to go, Pete,' she said. 'Lily needs a nap at home.'

He stood too. 'Melissa –'

'It's twenty years or five, Peter. They're the options we have.'

Tanner shook his head. 'What if five years goes by, and Joe's not released? What are the options then?'

She looked at him, anger on her face that dissolved to sadness. She seemed about to say something, stopped herself, then took the brake off Lily's stroller.

In a taxi back to the city, Tanner wondered if Melissa would tell Joe what he'd told her, and how he would react. And he wondered how he could help him even if he knew the truth, whatever it was.

He worked in a world of crime. Of violence, drugs, neglect and disadvantage. It was greed, though, that had made Citadel. Greed would make rivers slowly die. Joe Cheung was in a Chinese prison because of it. Only money would get him out.

Tanner took out his phone and dialled Lisa Ilves' direct line.

'Where are you calling from?'

'A taxi. I just had lunch with Joe Cheung's wife at Coogee. Listen, I'm already starving, can we meet after work?'

'I thought you said you'd just had lunch?'

'I didn't eat,' he said.

'What kind of lunch is that?'

'A tense one. Is seven okay?'

When she arrived, Tanner was sitting at one of the outdoor tables of Bambini Trust Restaurant in Elizabeth Street opposite Hyde Park, drinking a glass of wine.

He stood and kissed her cheek. 'Is this place okay?'

She nodded. 'Last time I was in the bar here I had an interesting time with two of your colleagues.'

'My colleagues?'

'Members of the bar. One of them offered me a Viagra tablet.'

'What? Offered *you* Viagra?'

'In the process of propositioning me. He said I'd love it. I forget his name. The other guy offered me some coke.'

'Coke and Viagra? You sure they weren't judges?'

'I didn't accept either offer,' she said, and opened the menu. 'What are you drinking?'

'A shiraz from the Barossa.'

'What's it like?'

'High on alcohol and fruit.'

'Sounds perfect.'

When a waiter arrived, he poured Lisa a glass of the wine, and took their food orders. 'He should've decanted it,' Tanner said when he left.

'You're not a wine snob, are you, Pete?'

'I enjoy good wine.'

'How old were you when you started drinking wine?'

'Why are you asking?'

'You drink it quickly. Like you need it.'

'I'm not an alcoholic.'

'I didn't say you were. You never let your wine just sit. You pick it up in your glass, sip, put it down, pick it straight up, repeat.'

'Probably too young,' he said, answering her question.

'How young is that?'

'My father was a vodka man, but he liked sweet ciders too. I had a few incidents with that when I was young. Thirteen, fourteen maybe.'

'Incidents?'

'Vomit all over the bathroom.'

'Did you get in trouble?'

'My parents were distracted – my father had just been charged with stealing his clients' money. It's a long story, but he went to jail for seven years. My mother . . . it was hard on her.'

She paused for a few moments, taking in what he had told her. 'I'm sorry,' she said.

'It was a long time ago. Dad's been out for nearly twenty years.'

'Do you . . . How do you and your father get along?'

Tanner picked up his wine, sipped as he thought. 'Dad doesn't talk much. When he does he's . . . direct. He didn't like being late. The only times I can remember him getting angry were if one of us made him late. It made his blood boil. I can still see his face turning red. I've never been late for court. Not once.'

'That doesn't . . . What about your mother?'

'My mother . . . What happened to Karl – it changed her. It killed her. I wouldn't say that to him. He knows it anyway.'

Lisa put her elbows on the table and rested her chin in her hands. 'You didn't answer me. How do you get on with your father now?'

'We get on okay.'

'Are you going to tell me the long story about him?'

Tanner paused for a moment, staring at his wine glass. He wanted to pick it up, felt self-conscious of her observation. 'Talking about that – it wears me out. Another time?'

Lisa nodded slowly. 'What about your siblings? Are you close to them?'

He took another sip of wine, despite her comment, then told her a little about his sister and brother, and their families.

'Why don't you like your brother's wife?' Lisa said when he stopped.

'I didn't say that.'

'I can tell.'

He paused for a few moments. 'She's a real estate agent. A pretty prominent one if you follow the housing market in the Eastern Suburbs.'

'Is that why you don't like her?'

'I have another reason.'

'Which is?'

He sat back in his chair and thought for a few moments. 'What I say may not sound completely coherent.'

'You're a barrister, Pete. I wouldn't expect it to be.'

'When my wife died. Jane . . . she didn't look very upset. I know that's hardly profound. It's . . . she never steps out of her life, into someone else's . . .' He paused for a long moment. 'Mike and Jane have three kids. Their son is Dan's age. After Karen died, she didn't ask Dan over to play with his cousin once. Not once . . . I don't know . . . is that enough to not like someone?'

Lisa nodded. 'Sure.'

'Good,' he said. 'Because I fucking hate her.'

She laughed. 'What about your brother?' she said. 'He could have arranged for Dan to play with his son?'

Tanner shook his head. 'I don't feel like we're related.'

'What's that mean?'

'He's a politician.'

Lisa picked up her glass, and was about to sip, but paused. 'Oh?' she said. 'He's *that* Tanner?' He nodded. 'You don't like his politics?'

'I'm a criminal defence lawyer, Lisa. None of us like any of their politics.

Their meals arrived and, while they ate, he told her about his meeting with Melissa Cheung.

'Does she know anything?' Lisa asked.

He cut a piece of steak and shook his head. 'I don't know.'

'Who's behind this deal he's been offered?'

'Who knows? The government. Citadel. The North Shanxi people. All of the above.'

'Do you think it can be believed?'

'I'm not in Joe's shoes.'

She nodded, and held her hand over her glass when the waiter tried to top up her wine from the bottle.

'The Bageeyn River mine,' he said, 'how long would it take to get up and running, if it's approved?'

'How long until they're extracting gold? Two to three years, I'd guess. Why are you asking?'

'Assume they get their approval some time this year. Assume your action group can't stop them. I know you don't want to assume that, but –'

'Winning will be a long shot.'

'So they construct the mine, and start producing copper and gold in two and half, maybe three years? It's a huge mine, after all?'

'Okay.'

'Do you think that – once they're up and running – there's some unwritten part of the mine plan that says Joe Cheung can go home now? Now we're certain we've scared him enough to keep his mouth shut forever?'

She looked at him for a long moment. 'You think that's what's happened?'

'I don't know,' he said. 'I'm sure he's in prison because of something to do with Campbell's report. He's told if he's a good boy, he gets out in five years. We both know that once Citadel gets its mine going, and the royalties start rolling in for the state, there's no stopping it.'

'So what now?'

'We need a copy of Campbell's report. And Anne Warren's.'

She looked at him, her head tilted. 'How are you going to do that?'

'By committing one or more major criminal offences.'

'Is that a serious answer?'

He smiled, but only for a second. 'Let's go to the bar for a drink after dinner,' he said. 'Maybe alcohol can help with a plan.'

31

Tanner's phone buzzed at three fifty-five am on Sunday morning. He fumbled for it on his bedside table, and blinked until he could see. It was Tom Cable.

'Where are you?'

'In my car. A few blocks away from her house.'

'You've been in?'

'Yeah.'

'Any trouble?'

'No. It's an old worker's cottage. It had double sash windows. I took some wood out of the meeting rail when I forced it open, but I brought some stuff to tidy it up. She'll never know.'

'And?'

'No computer. She's got wifi, it came up on my phone. Probably took her laptop to Sydney.'

'Did you check the house?'

'There was nothing. No electronic devices, no USBs, no phone bills. No copies of the reports you've mentioned. I got one thing, it might help.'

'What?'

'An old address book. Broken spine, pen marks all over the cover, pages loose inside. Looks like she's had it half her life. I checked it just in case by some miracle she's got this missing girl's address.'

'I take it she doesn't?'

'She had "Gaby" written in it, but under "C" for Campbell. I took a photo of it with my phone. It had a residential phone number, and a Sydney address.'

'That won't help.'

'Just give me a sec. Gaby's name had a circle drawn around it, and then an arrow to a new addresses, also in Sydney. Different coloured pens. I'd say for when her friend moved.'

'Okay.'

'The old address – maybe it's just the last place she rented, or maybe it's her family home? Where she lived when these girls first met?'

'What's the address?'

'Botany, 72 Maddison Road. So it's a house, not a flat.'

Tanner closed his eyes and massaged the middle of his forehead with his fingers. 'Can you find out if that's where her parents live?'

'You're not –'

'Who would you trust?'

'What?'

'Who would you trust most in the world? Gaby Campbell is a young scientist. She's had a report buried and lost her job. She's not going to throw her work away. Her employer might, the mining company might, but she'll find a way to keep what she's done.'

'Her parents?'

'Maybe.'

'Could you go see them? Talk to them?'

'I'm thinking.' If he approached Campbell's parents, why would the result be any different? He might only succeed in spooking her more. 'We'll talk on Monday,' he said. 'Go get some sleep.'

'I think you should go see them,' Cable said.

'Why?'

'Because that will be more legal than having me break into their house.'

★

Tanner walked into the restaurant at five to eleven. It was in a pedestrian laneway off George Street in the city, near the Ivy restaurant and hotel. He took a seat at the back. Nadine Bellouard arrived a few minutes later. He ordered coffee, then thanked her for coming.

'Was it any help?' she asked.

'Some.'

'What does that mean?'

'I know more than I did.'

'Is that good for Joe?'

'Not yet.'

She sighed. 'What now, then?'

'What you gave me, Nadine, it might be part of the proof of a crime. Maybe more than one.'

Her eyes widened, and she didn't speak for several moments. 'What kind of crime?' she finally said. 'Is this why Joe – ?' Her voice rose, and he held up his hand to calm her.

'There's some documents I need to see,' he said.

'I told you last time, Pete. Accessing our computer system would –'

'You know where the hardcopy files are, don't you? For the work being done for Citadel? You could find out?'

She nodded slowly.

'Can you get me a security pass?'

'A security pass?' she said too loudly. 'Our passes have our photos on them, Pete.'

'I don't want yours.'

'If you got caught, they would –'

'I won't be using it. Someone I trust will.'

She glared at him. 'You trust people who . . . break into an office and – what? Steal things?'

'I trust them more than half of the lawyers you work with. No one will steal anything.'

'Then what will they be doing?'

'This is for Joe, Nadine. Nothing gets stolen.'

She rubbed her temple like she was in a mild degree of pain. 'How are you planning to do this?'

'Late at night.'

'Our lawyers work long hours.'

He shrugged.

'It goes on a computer log. If anyone checks, it'll show whose pass was being used to enter the building at what time, and what floor they went to.'

He leant forwards and lowered his voice to a whisper. 'If nothing goes missing, no one's going to start looking at computer logs of who's been going into the firm at what time.'

She took a sip of the water that had been put in front of her with their coffees and looked away from him. He thought it better to let her process her own thoughts than keep talking, so they sat in silence until she spoke again.

'I can't think of a way I can get you a pass, Pete, even if I wanted to.'

'Someone could misplace one, surely?'

'If you lose it, you're supposed to get the old one deactivated straight away. People wear them, anyway. I don't know how I'd –'

'Do temporary passes get issued? To people who are at the firm for short periods for some reason?'

She shook her head. 'You have to jump through too many hoops to get one.'

'People must sometimes leave them on their desks, don't they?'

'I haven't been paying attention to what people do with their passes.'

'I only need to borrow one for one night, Nadine. There's a way of doing this. Just be observant for a few days.'

She shook her head. 'You've been around criminals for too long.'

'It won't be as hard as you think.'

She finished her glass of water, then stood. 'I have to go. I said I'd only be ten minutes.'

Tanner stood too. 'I meant what I said about a crime.'

She glared at him, then slowly shook her head. 'I have to go.'

*

Tom Cable was sitting in the reception area of Tanner's chambers when he arrived at work two days later. When Tanner approached, he looked up from his paper and put it back on the coffee table. Tanner motioned for him to follow him to his room.

'What's on it?' Tanner asked after Cable took a flash drive from his pocket.

Cable took a seat in front of Tanner's desk. 'Can I have a Coke first?'

'It's a small demographic of people who drink Coke at this hour.'

'So is the demographic of members of the bar who organise break and enters.'

Tanner nodded, and rang for the Coke. 'Was it hard?'

Cable shrugged. 'An element of risk. They were out, of course, but it's a semi, and the neighbours were home. No alarm, no dog. I got a small bathroom window to slide open.' He patted his stomach. 'Lucky I'm still slim.'

Tanner put the flash drive into his computer. 'What's on here?'

'Emails,' Cable said. 'I had a quick look in Word. It all just looked like the work stuff, not much else.'

'How many emails?'

'A lot. I took the inbox for the last year, the sent file and the trash.'

The emails to Gabriella Campbell from her parents in the Sent box dated back eight months. Some contained family news, some asked what she was doing. One asked if she now knew her timetable for coming home. Others were responding to emails she'd sent, mainly prompting questions about her travels.

They read through Campbell's emails in chronological order. 'This one on 3 January,' Tanner said, pointing at the screen. '"*So much gelato, I'm piling on the pounds*". Then here on February 5, "*A bit slow now, but Marco says things pick up quickly after March when the tourists start to come back and I'll be flat out.*"'

'What do you think?'

'A shop or a restaurant.' Tanner pointed to an email sent three weeks before. It said, '"*Finally did a walking tour of the volcano today. I'll tell you about it when I call tomorrow.*"'

'Volcano?'

'She's in Naples,' Tanner said, 'or maybe Sicily. There's not many places in the world you can walk around a volcano and pile on the pounds eating gelato.'

'What now? You going to send her an email?'

Tanner sat back in his chair. 'Let me think about it.' His phone rang. 'I have to take this,' he said.

Cable started to rise from his seat, but Tanner gestured for him to stay where he was.

'Nadine?'

'Use mine.'

'What?'

'Use my pass.'

Tanner looked across his desk to Tom Cable. 'The person I have in mind doesn't look like you.'

'It'll get him in the building and up the lift to my floor. Make sure he doesn't wear it face out. The guard on the security desk didn't check mine when I went in late last night. Just use it.'

'Surely you can –'

'You said a crime, Pete. I've thought about it. I'll leave it in an envelope at your reception after work. Just don't get caught. If the security guard wants to look at the pass, your guy has to turn around and leave.'

'My guy,' Tanner said, still looking at Cable, 'he's very experienced.'

'We're on level thirty-six,' she said. 'There's a set of roller cabinets on the harbour side of the building where most of the Citadel files are stored. Joe's office is – it was opposite them.'

'Nadine?'

'Yeah?'

'Thanks.'

When he ended the call, he looked at Cable. 'You own a decent suit, right?'

32

Tom Cable had broken into hundreds of homes and businesses. Not once had he been given a pass that opened the doors for him. The suit and tie were a first for a B&E too.

He walked into the atrium of the tower at eleven thirty on Friday night. That afternoon he'd walked through the foyer to get his bearings. He knew what lift to go to, and where the security cameras were. If he had to leave in a hurry, they wouldn't get a good look at his face.

When he walked past the security desk, the guard glanced at him for a moment, and Cable said, 'Hi,' without looking directly at the man, and got a, 'Hello, sir,' in reply. He used the pass to summon the lift, and again to lock in floor thirty-six.

When the lift opened, he found himself in a brightly lit foyer. There were doors on his left and right, both requiring the use of the security pass to enter the floor proper. He could see some light through the glass panel of the door on the east side of the building, but the west side was darker. He chose that side first.

When he stepped into the corridor, his stomach tightened – the lights flickered into life. He stood still and listened, heard nothing but the buzz of the lights above him, and only moved again when he realised that he'd merely triggered a sensor. He slowly started to walk around the passageway that ran between the assistants' work stations and the external offices.

Halfway around the floor was a large kitchen. He listened for human-made sound, heard none, and opened the double-door fridge. On the left side was almost a whole tray of Coke. He took one and opened it. If he came upon someone, he'd look more like he belonged with a drink in his hand.

He continued around the floor to the east side. The offices now had better views. He wondered how anyone got any work done. He reached the northern end of the floor. He had the place to himself.

He walked back and found the file storage system. He wound open the first cabinet and looked in its shelves. He'd been told that a computer code would be on the spine or front of each folder for the Citadel–Bageeyn River project. In the shelves of the second cabinet he saw what looked to be more than fifty folders labelled *CIT–BRP* on the spine, followed by some numbers. He found a folder with some correspondence and documents from January the previous year, and started rifling through it. It didn't take him long to find the report Tanner wanted – its author was Gabriella Campbell of GreenDay Environmental Consultants Pty Ltd.

There were two copies, one of which had handwritten notes on it. There were attendance notes on BBK pads in which he could see the words 'Campbell' or 'hydro report'. He opened his briefcase took out the portable scanner, and set to work. His time limit was one and a half hours.

At one am he phoned Tanner, who answered after one ring.

'All okay?'

'Nice views,' Cable said softly.

'You find anything?'

'Too much. Two copies of this Campbell report. One has notes on it. What looks like records of phone calls with her, maybe meetings. I could be here another five hours doing this.'

'What about Warren? Anything on Tovosevu?'

'I can't find any files for that.'

'That's just as important, Tom.'

'That's fine, Pete, but I can't make this thing scan any faster. How long do you want me to stay?'

'No sign of life?' Nadine Bellouard had told Tanner that security did random sweeps of floors late at night. 'What would it look like if a security guard turned up now?'

'They'd find me on my knees next to some storage cabinets, scanning documents and wearing a security pass with a face on it that is much prettier than mine.'

Tanner thought for a moment and sighed. 'Spend ten more minutes looking for anything to do with Tovosevu.'

'There's nothing marked Tovosevu or with letters like that. There's CIT–RGB, but I haven't looked in those.'

'Red Gum Basin. That'll be the CSG mine they want up there. Look for anything to do with –'

'Pete?'

'Yeah.'

'There are about a hundred folders marked that. You need to give me a priority.'

Tanner could ask him to stay longer, but that increased the risk. 'Look for Tovosevu,' Tanner said. 'Then leave in ten minutes.'

'I'll spend another hour, then go.'

'Another hour is pushing it, isn't it?'

'It is for getting caught by one of the lawyers here if they walk in, but probably not by security.'

'Why not?'

'This building uses Barnwell Security. If I get caught by one of their guards we'll probably be able to bribe my way out of it. Either the guard or up the chain of command. It will cost you a bit, that's all.'

'What?'

'Most of the security companies that look after the city office buildings are run by crooks who employ crooks, Pete. I know that for a fact. I used to come to arrangements with them quite often in another life.'

'Really?'

'Sometime you're very naive for a criminal lawyer, you know that?'

'I'll see you here at nine tomorrow.'

'I'll bring a coffee.'

'Bring three.'

'Three?'

'Yeah.'

There was a pause. 'Good for you.'

Cable arrived at Tanner's house on Saturday morning carrying a tray with three cappuccinos and a hot chocolate in one hand, and a briefcase in the other.

Lisa let him in, and when he walked into the open-plan kitchen, Tanner noticed a look on his face somewhere between weariness and suspicion. The circle of trust had been extended, and he had not been informed.

Cable put the tray down on the kitchen island, and picked up the hot chocolate. 'I got this for Dan.'

'Still in bed,' Tanner said. 'You want to take it to him?'

'I don't want to wake him,' Cable said.

'He's got cricket at ten thirty,' Tanner said. 'Mightn't be a bad idea if you did.'

Cable and Tanner looked at each other.

'I'll take it,' Lisa said, grabbing the hot chocolate and leaving the room.

Cable watched her leave, then turned back to Tanner and raised his eyebrows.

'You can trust her,' Tanner said.

'Does she know where I was last night?'

Tanner nodded. 'She's the lawyer who briefed me on this gold mine case. We're both trying to find Gaby Campbell.'

'What's with the arm?'

'A political statement. You can still trust her.'

'Talking about me?' Lisa said, entering the room.

'Dan awake?' Tanner asked.

'He's breathing.'

Tanner nodded, walked over to the bench to grab his coffee, then looked at his watch. 'Let's see what you've got.'

They sat on the L-shaped lounge, and Cable retrieved a thick pile of documents from his bag and dropped it on the coffee table.

'You're a fast scanner,' Lisa said.

Cable shrugged. 'It's what I did before I took up break and enters. I got nothing on that Tovosevu thing – I couldn't find anything with that name. I did get this, though,' he said, pointing to the top of the pile where two drafts of Gabriella Campbell's report sat. It was titled *Water Impacts on Bageeyn River and Local Aquifers from the Bageeyn River Project*. One of the copies had notes scribbled on it.

'That's Joe's handwriting,' Tanner said. 'I borrowed his lecture notes for every class we had together.'

After the reports, Cable had put all the other documents in chronological order.

'Do you want to divide this up?' Lisa asked.

Tanner shook his head. 'I know Joe's hand. I'll make a record of his notes.'

'I'd start with this,' she said, handing him a draft of Campbell's report that she'd picked up. She pointed to some handwriting on the top right corner of the front page. 'What's this word?'

'"False",' he said. 'The note says, "*Tonnage of ore required – wrong/false? = water needed = wrong/false. Aquifer drawdown – greater – years ++ rainfall – ? Recycling/evaporation rate – false/wrong; efficiency – wrong/false.*"'

He looked at her and raised his eyebrows, then started flicking over the pages of the report.

Lisa pointed to a page that at the top had 'T/A GC 22/2' in handwriting. 'Telephone attendance on Gabriella Campbell,' she said. 'I guess on 22 February last year.' Tanner nodded. 'I can't show this report to our expert, can I?' she then said.

Tanner shrugged. 'You can – but if it goes to court, you'd both have to explain to a judge how he got it.'

'So how do we use this?'

'Let's find out what it means, first.'

'Some of these notes look like hieroglyphics,' she said.

'Joe's shorthand.'

'Can you decipher it?'

'Not the Chinese symbols.'

She stared at him. 'You're kidding?'

Tanner shook his head and half-smiled. 'I told him to cut it out all the time in law school. They're not just Chinese symbols. They're hybrids of them and his own system. They make sense to Joe, not to every Mandarin speaker.'

'How will we work it out?'

He ran his hand through his hair as he thought. 'Asking Joe would be the obvious thing.'

'Assuming we can't?'

'That leaves us Gaby Campbell.'

'And the plan there is what?'

He looked down at the thick pile of papers on the table. 'Let me work out what I can from reading through this first.'

'Can I do anything in the meantime?'

Tanner walked to his kitchen table, where he'd put his satchel. He opened the bag, took out some papers, and went back to the couch. He handed her a single sheet of paper. 'It's a to-do list,' he said.

She looked at the typed notes and narrowed her eyes. '"*Citadel–North Shanxi: market information*",' she read. 'What's that mean?'

'Something I should've already done,' he said. 'I want you to find every statement Citadel and North Shanxi have made to the market about the Bageeyn River gold mine. Do the same for the coal and CSG projects up north, and in the Hunter. If there's time, move on to other proposed mines in any other countries. Look for any prospectuses they may have put out to raise capital, all that kind of thing. Focus on the gold mine first.'

'Is that all?' she asked.

'I want a schedule of their boards of directors, major shareholders, and a list of who's who in management. Do the same for a company called XinCoal.'

'Is this our case, or is this for Joe? I don't mind, but –'

'It's both, Lisa.'

'There goes the weekend.'

'It'll take you longer than that.'

'You want me to leave so I can get on with this?'

He smiled. 'I've got this pile to read. I'll call when I'm done.'

She put out her hand to Cable. 'Nice to meet you, Tom.'

He stood and took her hand. 'Nice to meet you.'

When he heard the front door close, Cable asked, 'Do you like her?'

Tanner was at the kitchen sink, putting the coffee cups in the bin. 'Sure,' he said.

'Is it serious?'

Tanner shrugged. 'We're already committing crimes together,' he said. 'Can we talk about the witnesses you found?'

Cable reached into a pocket of the jacket he'd hung over the end of the couch, and took out his notebook. 'I've got a witness from your guy's club, and I've got Richter's ex-wife's best friend.'

'Late wife.'

'What?'

'She dead. Let's talk about the witness from the club first.'

'The police interviewed the members of the club that were there that night. I looked over the statements. Some members brought guests, but not all of them were followed up. Anyway, one guy had in his statement the names of the people he took in as guests. That's how I spoke to . . . Greg McPherson is his name. He said a hostess was sitting on Matheson's lap most of the time he was there. A blonde.'

'He was sitting near them?'

'Not far.'

'Could he hear any conversation?'

'No,' Cable said. 'When I spoke to him, though, and said I was acting for Matheson, he told me something I thought might interest you.'

'Okay.'

'He goes to the Gents. He's in there taking a piss, and Richter walks in. McPherson had read about the wife's funeral only two days before. Offered his condolences. Something like "sorry about your wife," that kind of thing.'

'And?'

'And he nearly has his head shoved in the urinal.'

'What?'

'Richter got aggressive, and then threatened to kick the guy out.'

'Had this guy been drinking?'

'What do you think? He started at lunch.'

'How did he sound? Did you speak on the phone or meet him?'

'He agreed to have coffee near his work. He seemed okay.'

'Will he see me?'

'I think so.'

'Tee it up.'

'Okay.'

'And Nikki's best friend?'

Cable nodded. 'I'll get to her. You told me to try and find Richter's old girlfriend? The one he allegedly assaulted? I spoke to the list of Matheson's friends you gave me. Anyway, someone knew someone, who knew someone – I ended up with a name and a number.'

'And?'

'No go. Felicity Cairns was her married name. She was Felicity Horton when she got clocked by Richter.'

'And?'

'She's dead.'

Tanner looked at him blankly for a few moments. 'She'd only be around thirty-five. What happened?'

'She – she died of natural causes.'

Tanner glared at Cable for a long moment. 'What the hell does that mean?'

Cable looked uncomfortable. 'She died of cancer,' he said, glancing quickly at Tanner, then away. 'About three years ago.'

Tanner nodded slowly. 'You can say the word cancer around me, Tom,' he said. 'Karen's not the first person –'

'Sure,' Cable said quickly. 'I don't know. I didn't like to say it.'

Tanner tried to collect his thoughts. 'The other woman,' he said. 'Nikki's girlfriend. She still okay?'

'Amanda Weatherill is her name – she's going to be okay for you.'

'Will she – ?'

'She's happy to talk. Said she'd come in any time after work for a conference.'

Tanner nodded. 'Thanks for all this, Tom.'

'I'm free to leave?'

Tanner nodded. 'Can you pick that kid up and lift him out of bed before you go?'

Joe Cheung had spoken to Gabriella Campbell on several occasions after she'd presented her draft report for the Bageeyn River Environmental Assessment, and met with her twice.

His scribbled notes weren't entirely legible, but some names were easier to decipher than words. The same names from the bill printout kept cropping up on attendance notes for meetings and phone calls: Anthony Kerr, the deputy general-counsel of Citadel Australia, and Robert Spry, the global GC based in New York. There were several references to someone called Tom Hsu. An internet search revealed him to be North Shanxi's senior in-house lawyer, based in Hong Kong.

As he read, Tanner made notes of the date and content of every document that appeared even marginally relevant.

Good trial lawyers don't start with the law.

They start – and they finish – with the facts.

33

When Greg McPherson was shown into his room by Charles Porter, Tanner was surprised by his age. McPherson was late fifties, had grey hair, balding at the front, and a portly shape. He was in a suit that was a size too large and a size too small, depending on where you looked.

Although Matheson's trial wasn't for several months yet, Tanner had arranged for the defence team to set aside the day to meet witnesses. He liked to get them signed up to statements early, rather than leaving things to chance.

McPherson was a mortgage specialist, and a young client he'd arranged a refinance package of loans for had taken him to lunch that day to thank him. That evening, when they were still drinking, the client met up with a friend who was a member of Pantheon, and McPherson was invited along.

'I pushed the average age up a bit,' McPherson said. 'My daughters are older than the hostesses there.'

McPherson explained that he'd seen John Richter walk in just as he and his group were having their first drink. 'I recognised him,' he said. 'I was surprised to see him there, given the funeral earlier that week.'

'Rich men traditionally celebrate the death of their first wives,' Tanner said. He asked McPherson about what happened in the men's bathroom. Richter was at a handbasin when he walked in, McPherson explained.

'I went to the urinal. Then I said what I did about his wife.'

'Which was?'

'Just "sorry about your wife".'

'And his reaction?'

McPherson shook his head, and his forehead creased. 'When I turned my head he was glaring at me – like an angry stare.'

'Did you say something else?'

'I wondered if he'd misheard me. I was going to repeat myself, but he spoke.'

'And he said?'

'"What's it to you?" Or something like that.'

'You responded?'

'No. I was confused. He walked right up to me then.'

'Were you scared?'

McPherson nodded. 'He looked like he was going to punch me.'

'How close did he come?'

'Right in my face, almost forcing me backwards.'

'Pushing you?'

'He was leaning over me, looking down.'

'Okay. You spoke next, or him?'

'He told me to shut the fuck up, and asked if I was a member. I said no. Then he said that if I even looked at him again, he'd have me and the people I was with thrown out.'

'What then?'

'I left. I didn't even wash my hands.'

'Did you tell your friends about what had happened?' Jane Ross asked.

McPherson shook his head.

'Why not?'

'I was their guest. I didn't want to cause a scene.'

'How much had you had to drink?'

McPherson shrugged. 'Quite a lot,' he said, smiling weakly.

'That means different things to different people.'

'A beer and two bottles of wine at lunch. A few beers after, then two scotches at the club.'

'Did you feel drunk?'

'I was hungover the next day.'

Tanner nodded. 'Your tone of voice when you spoke to Richter – could he have mistaken it for flippancy? Sarcasm maybe?'

'I've thought about that,' he said. 'I don't think so. I'm sure I didn't sound sarcastic.'

Tanner looked at Ross and Porter. 'Anything else?'

They shook their heads.

'You okay to tell this to a court if we need you to?' Tanner asked.

McPherson nodded firmly. 'Yes.'

'You'll get a subpoena,' Tanner said. 'You won't need to be at court on day one.'

'Fine.'

'Do you have any questions?'

McPherson sighed. 'I'm not sure I'm meant to ask this?'

'Ask it anyway.'

'Your client. He's saying Richter did it?'

'Do you need us to tell you we think he's innocent?'

'I understand what your job is. It's more about Richter.'

'What about him?'

'The way he looked at me that night, when he leant over me. He really did look like he could kill someone.'

Tanner nodded his head slowly. 'Any time during the course of your evidence, Greg, you feel you can slip that in, feel free.'

Amanda Weatherill was holding a takeaway coffee cup and wearing a nervous smile when she was shown in to Tanner's room. She was blonde, pretty, and looked younger than early thirties.

At Tanner's prompting, she told them about herself. She'd done nursing when she'd left school, worked in the public hospital system, then studied physiotherapy. She'd graduated four years ago. She now worked in a rehabilitation centre, helping patients who'd suffered catastrophic injuries.

'Why the rehab centre?' Tanner asked.

'My younger brother,' she said. 'He's been a quadriplegic for a few years.'

'What happened?'

'He was at a friend's apartment building,' she said. 'There was a communal pool – Mark dived in. It was only about a metre deep. He hit his head on the bottom.'

'Did he sue anyone?'

Amanda shook her head. 'It was late at night, he'd been drinking. There was a depth sign – he didn't see it or didn't look.'

She took them through her friendship with Nikki Perovic. They'd met at a public hospital, where Amanda was a nurse. 'She broke her ankle skiing. So badly she needed surgery. I was her nurse. We became friendly, exchanged numbers. The ankle always gave her trouble. When I started physio at uni, I worked it over a lot.'

'You were close friends?'

She nodded, smiled sadly. 'Yeah.'

'Share everything close?'

She thought about it. 'Yes.'

'Okay,' Tanner said. 'Tell us what you know about Nikki and John Richter.'

'He's a control freak. Like in a – I don't know, a psycho rich boy way. He was allowed to have sex with whoever he wanted, but if she even looked at a guy, if they looked at her, he lost it.'

'"Lost it"?'

'He didn't actually have to hit her to make her, I don't know, cower, or be scared. He . . . he just looked like he was going to do something crazy. Violent, you know?'

Tanner nodded.

'He'd disappear for days, too – no explanations at all. It didn't take her long to find out what he was doing. She got some investigator. Nikki knew he had girls on the side, but she freaked when she found out how many.'

'Did she confront him?'

'After she'd made her mind up on a divorce.'

'Did she speak to you about seeing a lawyer?'

'That was mainly what we talked about, the last two or three months.'

'Did she tell you her lawyer's name, or the name of the firm?'

Amanda nodded. 'I went there with her once.'

'Why?'

'Hold her hand, I guess. That's all.'

'You didn't sit in during a conference, did you?'

She shook her head. 'The lawyer didn't want me to. Nikki said it was okay, but the lawyer . . . Sally, I think, is that right?'

Tanner nodded.

'She said it was best not.'

'Did Nikki tell you what Sally was telling her?'

'About getting a divorce?'

'About the advice she was getting.'

'Some of it. She said they had to live apart for a year, but the lawyer thought they might have been living apart . . . I don't know . . . legally, even when he was still living there.'

'Anything else?'

'She told Nikki to take photos of herself – you know, when he'd nearly strangled her.'

Tanner sat back in his chair, and looked at Jane Ross, and then Porter.

'What is it?' Amanda asked.

'Amanda,' he said, 'when we're done here, I need you to write out in note form everything Nikki told you about wanting a divorce. From the first time she mentioned it. Would you do that?'

'Sure.'

'You don't have to remember exact dates, just ballpark. You don't have to remember word for word what she said, just the gist of it, okay?'

'Sure.'

'And this is the most important part – write down everything you remember Nikki telling you that she said to her lawyer, and what her lawyer said to her. Can you do that?'

'Is this for my evidence?' she asked, smiling curiously. 'Why do you look pleased with yourself all of a sudden?'

'You've heard of legal professional privilege?'

'Your lawyer can't tell people what you've told them?'

Tanner nodded. 'Except in limited circumstances. Like you.'

'Me?'

'Nikki told you what advice she was given.'

'So?'

'She's waived privilege. That means her lawyer can tell us what Nikki told her about John.'

'Should I – should I issue a subpoena on Sally Cook for her files?' Porter asked.

'Closer to trial. You'll need an affidavit from Amanda as well, about what she's told us.'

Porter nodded and made a note.

'Now,' Tanner said. 'Charles tells me you want to tell us something about Nikki's death?'

Amanda nodded slowly, but struggled to find the words where to start. 'It's just – I can't believe she OD'd.'

'Why?'

She took in a deep breath, then spoke. 'She wasn't taking anything then. I know it.'

'How do you know?'

'We saw each other all the time,' she said. 'Unless she was away, I saw her at least once a week. She was not on heroin when she died.'

'Maybe the stress of getting divorced?'

'No,' Amanda said firmly. 'She felt good about it. She told me she had him by the balls. Not just the surveillance and photos either.'

'What else?'

'She didn't say.'

'I'm just playing devil's advocate here,' Tanner said. 'She'd been in rehab twice?'

'He got her into drugs. There's no way heroin was part of her life when she died. Not coke either. Last time I went out with them, John tried to get us all to have some coke, and Nikki wouldn't. They almost had a fight. He'd got some stash from his lawyer again, but Nikki wouldn't –'

Tanner held up his hand for her to stop. 'What lawyer?'

'Sorry?'

'What lawyer? You said John got cocaine from his lawyer.'

She nodded. 'Yeah. He had this lawyer – Tony – he got him his coke.'

Tanner looked at Jane Ross, then Charles Porter, then back to Amanda. 'You know this guy?'

She nodded. 'I think I met him three or four times, maybe. He sold coke to Jack and his friends.'

Tanner took in a deep breath. 'John Richter and Klaudia Dabrowska told the police that our client brought the coke the night Elena Mancini died.'

Amanda Weatherill shook her head. 'It would've been Jack.'

Tanner nodded. 'Does Tony have a last name?'

'Sorry,' she said. 'I don't know.'

'Would you recognise him?'

'Maybe. I mean, I only met him a few time, at nightclubs . . . once at John and Nikki's place, but, yeah, maybe.'

'You said he sold coke to John *and* his friends. You saw this?'

She shrugged. 'There was a dinner party once. This guy had the coke. A lot of it. I mean, not just for that night. People bought off him for future use.'

'Do you know where he works?'

'He's the lawyer for the company.'

Tanner paused for a moment. 'He's in-house at Citadel?'

'The first time I met him, he and John joked about dealing the coke in his office.'

'Just a second,' Tanner said. He clicked on his internet browser and went to Citadel's website. He found a section for *Our people*, then found the general counsel's office. He found who he was looking for, and enlarged the photo. He asked Amanda to look at his screen.

'That's the guy,' she said. 'Tony.'

Tanner turned his screen around further for Porter and Ross. 'Jane, Charles,' he said. 'Meet Anthony J Kerr. Deputy General Counsel, Citadel Resources, Australia. LLM, University of Queensland. More importantly for us, John Richter's coke dealer.' Tanner looked at Amanda Weatherill. 'I like you,' he said.

She smiled shyly, and blushed.

Porter leant forwards. 'Do I serve a subpoena on him?'

'Hell, no,' Tanner said. 'The prosecution knows we're coming after Richter. They don't know about his coke dealer yet. Let's keep it that way for now.'

Tanner asked Amanda to make another note, this time detailing everything she could remember of her meetings with Tony Kerr. She nodded, but he saw a momentary hesitation come over her face.

'Is that okay?'

She ran a hand through her hair. 'Will I be asked about myself?'

'Asked what?'

She paused for a long moment. 'Sometimes I did a few lines, with John and Nikki and their friends. Would I get asked that?'

'It's possible,' he said slowly. 'I'd object.'

'I wouldn't have to answer?'

'I can't guarantee that. I'd object, saying it's not relevant, but –'

'I'd lose my job,' she said. 'The rehab centre gets government grants for my salary. If I admit taking coke, I'd lose my job, I'm sure.'

Tanner sat back in his chair, and ran his hand over his mouth several times as he thought. No one else spoke.

'Let's do this for now, Amanda. Make the notes I've asked you. Then we'll talk again. Let me work out how I can protect you, okay?'

*

Later that evening, when Tanner was about to go home, his phone vibrated on his desk. The screen said *No Caller ID*, but he answered anyway.

'Peter,' the voice said. 'It's Li.'

Tanner was momentarily silenced, surprised by the call. 'Li? Is everything okay with Joe?'

'He's asked me to call you,' he said. 'We were before the court today.'

Melissa had told him that Cheung's matter was listed for the end of April. 'I was told the twenty-ninth, Li,' Tanner said. 'What were you doing in court today?'

'We indicated to the court that a contested trial of all charges will not be necessary. Joe will be agreeing to some of the allegations made against him.'

'Which allegations?'

'Peter, you know I can't tell you.'

'Was our government at this hearing? Someone from the consulate?'

'The hearing was in closed court,' Li said. 'I have advised your consulate of the outcome.'

'What are you telling me?' Tanner said loudly, anger rising inside him. 'Did Joe plead guilty today?'

'The prosecutor indicated provisional agreement to limit some allegations. A date for the taking of a formal plea will be later, at which time the sentencing will occur. I'm working towards a sentence with the prosecutor which I believe will be a favourable outcome.'

'Later? Does that mean after the Bageeyn River gold mine is approved? Does Joe get some discount for shutting up until then?'

There was a long pause before Li spoke. 'I have no idea what that means, Peter.'

'What's a "favourable outcome"? Is this the deal Melissa told me about?'

'The prosecutor will recommend ten years.'

'Well, that will be double what the Cheungs think the real deal is.'

'Again, Peter, I don't know . . .'

Tanner held the phone away from his ear and closed his eyes for a moment. Yelling at a lawyer who was eight thousand kilometres away wasn't going to help.

'Listen, there's no formal plea entered, right? Just an indication that there's likely to be? Is that correct?'

'That there *will* be a plea.'

'And Joe asked you to tell me this? That's why you've called?'

'There is another reason.'

'What?'

'He asked me to tell you that it won't be helpful to him if you continue to – and these are his words – "explore the rivers".'

Melissa had told Joe about what he'd found on the Citadel bills. About his discussions with Gabriella Campbell over her report, and his visit to Tovosevu with Anne Warren.

'Why won't it be helpful? Is that your advice?'

'I have no view on the matter, Peter. I am only passing on what I was asked to.'

'When are you back in court?'

'I would expect November or December at the latest for final sentencing. We will be informed shortly.'

'Can you let me know when a date is set?'

'If Joe instructs me to.'

Tanner wanted to yell at him again. 'Please just call me, Li, okay? Just let me know.'

After the call, Tanner made several pages of notes. When he reviewed them he shook his head, and wondered if he was more tired than he thought. Justin Matheson's murder trial commenced in October – he had a little over five months. Joe's plea might be two months after.

He listed the things he still needed. Anne Warren's report. Gabriella Campbell. Sally Cook's divorce file for Nikki Richter. Working out what to do with what he knew about Tony Kerr. Finding Klaudia Dabrowska.

Paul Matthews of International Investigation Services had so far drawn a blank on Klaudia Dabrowska. Jade Models had no address for her, and she wasn't in the telephone directory or on an electoral register. No one of that name was using any social media sites, or was listed as the owner of any property. They'd been able to find where her father had worked, and to get an address, but when they checked, he was no longer living there. They did a property ownership search on him at the same time, and came up blank.

The last thing Tanner did that night was send an email to Matthews.

Paul, he wrote, *A couple of things:*

1. *Increase the attempts with Klaudia Dabrowska. I'll get funds by EFT to you from Sharrop & Prentice.*
2. *Do you have Italian agents? I need someone found. I will pay this myself. Let me know what's needed. I'll provide some possible locations.*

Thanks, Peter Tanner.

34

Alejandro Alvares was sitting on a stool at an outdoor table for two. Dinner was at Tanner's invitation, a restaurant at Rose Bay, not far from Alvares's home in Vaucluse. Cooler weather had arrived, and the orange glow of a heater next to the table slid across the sheen of Alvares's hair as he turned to greet his host.

'Isn't it a bit cold out here for your Latin blood, Alejandro?' Tanner said as he sat down.

Alvares shrugged and motioned towards the water. 'I like to watch the *paseo* on the harbour,' he said. 'We'll go inside for dinner.'

Tanner nodded.

'Shall we order wine, or will you join me for an *aperitivo* first?'

'I'll wait.'

'There's a Bordeaux on the list I like.'

Tanner raised his eyebrows.

'You don't approve, Peter?'

'How's your nephew?' Tanner asked as Alvares signalled to a waiter.

'Tomas is doing well. Considering.'

'Considering he should be doing a sentence nearly twice as long, I should hope so.'

Alvares didn't answer him, but told the waiter they'd have a bottle of Domaine de la Romanee-Conti la Tache.

'Changed your mind?' Tanner said.

Alvares adjusted the scarf he had wrapped around his neck. It was a vivid pistachio green. Tanner didn't need to look to know it probably matched the colour of his socks. 'You told me once of your preference for Burgundies. Am I correct?'

Tanner knew the wine would cost a four-figure sum. He now regretted the smashed hairbrush. 'I hope it lives up to the hype.'

'It's not hype, Peter. It's eight centuries of history.'

'That is a long time.'

'Four years is a long time for a young man.'

Tanner leant forwards a little. 'And four more would be twice as long.'

Alvares narrowed his eyes. 'Do you need something from me, Peter?'

Tanner smiled. 'It's cold out here, Alejandro. Let's talk at our table.'

They went inside, and were led to a table by one of the windows overlooking the water. Alvares handed the waiter his scarf. A sommelier soon arrived with the bottle and showed the label to Alvares, who glanced at it before nodding. They remained silent as the cork was removed, and Alvares tasted it. 'After it's decanted,' he said to the waiter, 'you can take our orders.'

'Could you taste eight centuries of history, Alejandro?'

'It's haunting,' Alvares said. 'They way things are that close to perfection.'

'What will you have it with?'

'The scallops and chorizo to begin,' Alvares said, 'the smoked duck breast to follow.'

'Just what I was thinking.' Tanner took a sip of water, and looked at Alvares without speaking for a long moment. 'You told me your family was grateful after Tomas's appeal,' he finally said. 'I was wondering if you could do me a favour?'

Alvares smiled fractionally. 'Do you want me to pay for the wine, Peter?'

Tanner shook his head slowly. 'Only if it doesn't live up to expectations.'

Alvares raised an eyebrow. 'I believe we've paid your bill?'

Tanner smiled. 'That's not a favour, Alejandro. That's a minimum requirement.'

'Do you need money, Peter? A loan of some kind?'

'Not before you ordered the Burgundy.'

Alvares stared back, expressionless.

'No, Alejandro. I don't need a loan.'

'Perhaps we should order food now,' Alvares said. 'Then you can tell me why you're treating me to such a fine meal.'

After the waiter took their orders, Tanner tried the wine. 'You were right,' he said. 'A wine that's hard to forget.'

'Tell me what you want.'

Tanner took another sip of the wine. 'I know a man,' he began. 'He's a man who regularly purchases amounts of – let's call it a luxury consumer good. Amounts large enough for him to on-sell to friends and colleagues, and to turn a profit on those trades.' Tanner waited for Alvares to acknowledge what he said, but he simply stared back at him. 'I'm wondering whether it would be possible to find out where this man was sourcing his product from?'

Alvares sat back in his seat. Any hint of humour drained from his eyes. 'This is not a conversation we should be having.'

'I know you're a mere property developer, Alejandro. Could you find out anyway?'

'Perhaps you'd be more comfortable having this conversation with one of my staff?'

'I'm comfortable having it with you. I'm your lawyer. We can discuss anything in confidence. Could you find out?'

Alvares looked at Tanner for what seemed a long time, before letting his eyes drop to his glass, which he picked up and sipped. 'It depends,' he said, putting the glass down.

'On what?'

'It would depend first on why I am doing this, Peter.'

'You'd be doing it because I'm asking you to.'

'Then why are you asking?'

'I want someone else to supply this man with what he needs. Perhaps offer him a better price, for better quality.'

'Why?'

'To find out where and when he likes to take delivery.'

'And why do you want to know that?'

Tanner leant back in his chair as bread was delivered, and was silent until the waiter had left. His eyes never left Alvares. 'Because I want him to do the extra four years that Tomas should be doing.'

Alvares poured olive oil on his side plate and tasted the bread. 'That doesn't sound good for business.'

'Whose business?'

'Anyone's.'

'It doesn't have to harm you,' Tanner said. 'It might harm your competitors.'

Alvares chewed more bread slowly, then sipped some wine. 'I'm not at war with anyone,' he said.

'I don't want you to start one. I'm after one man only.'

'Why do you want this done?'

'I told you. Four years.'

Alvares smiled faintly. 'Why?'

'This man helped put a friend of mine in prison,' Tanner said.

'Over a product?'

Tanner shook his head. 'Something else.'

'Business shouldn't be mixed with revenge.'

'This isn't revenge, Alejandro. I'm looking for leverage.'

Alvares raised his eyebrows. 'Even so.' He sipped his wine, then dabbed at his mouth with his napkin.

'Can you do this for me? I don't expect you to risk anything. Just use the right man. Someone who knows how to stay anonymous.'

Alvares smiled. 'What is the timing on this, Peter?'

'Not immediate,' Tanner said. 'It may take a trial run to develop trust. It has to be arranged to take place at a precise day and time. I'll give you those details.'

'You know,' Alvares said, 'this is a much bigger favour than we expected.'

Tanner glared at him. 'Your family owes me,' he said. 'This is what I want done.'

35

QF1 landed at Heathrow not long after seven am, but customs and London traffic meant Tanner and Lisa didn't arrive at their Soho hotel until nearly ten. It hadn't taken long to find Gabriella Campbell – she was using the surname Lucarelli, the same name as the relatives she was staying with, and was living in a town in a region Tanner had suggested be searched. A few days after he'd asked his clerk to make airline bookings for him, Tanner got an email from Paul Matthews stating that they'd found Klaudia Dabrowska. Tanner modified his travel plans, and would make a final call on whether to attempt to talk to her after he'd met with Matthews that afternoon.

'You don't want me to come?' Lisa asked.

'Today's only about Matheson,' he said. 'Go be a tourist. You can do the whole town on one of those red buses.'

'I'm not that kind of tourist,' she said.

When Tanner walked out of the entrance to the Charlotte Street hotel, the morning grey had cleared to only a few billowy clouds, and the sun felt warm. He took his jacket off and carried it over his shoulder. He found his way to Mortimer Street and headed west until he found the building he was after.

The façade was Edwardian baroque, but when he exited the lift on the third floor, he found the space had been newly fitted out, and the reception was what he'd have expected from a boutique law practice. The young woman at the front desk was on the phone when he walked in, but smiled as he approached, and held up a finger that he assumed meant that she'd be precisely one minute. Her nails were long by any standard of decency he was aware of, and bright cherry red.

Her estimate proved correct. 'Can I help you?' she said.

'My name's Tanner,' he said. 'I have an appointment with Mr Matthews.'

She asked him to take a seat, before calling to announce his arrival. As he was reaching for an IIS brochure that lay on the coffee table, a tall, thin man appeared in front of him, smiling faintly.

'Peter,' the man said in a slow, restrained voice. 'Paul Matthews. Welcome.'

Tanner stood, took the outstretched hand, received a firm grip in exchange.

'How was your flight?'

'Long.'

'Any sleep?'

'Some on the first leg.'

Matthews gave a knowing nod. His voice was deep and echoed with authority, and his posture was ramrod straight. He was a year or two past forty, six foot four give or take a half-inch, with short black hair that was just starting to mix with some grey. He had by the barest margin enough of a chin to prevent undermining the impression of strength. He looked somewhere between a city lawyer who excelled in rugged outdoor pursuits and someone more dangerous than that.

He took Tanner into a conference room. In the middle of the table was a large computer screen and keyboard. In front of the chairs that faced the screen where two frosted glasses of water, and a yellow legal pad with a pen on it, clearly for Tanner's use.

'Can we get you a tea or coffee?' Matthews asked, motioning for Tanner to sit.

'Coffee,' Tanner said.

'We've got a new machine. Cappuccino?'

'Long black, thanks.'

Matthews walked to the corner of the room, picked up the phone that rested on a small table, and ordered coffee.

'You came through Singapore?' Matthews said as he sat.

'Dubai. I came with a colleague.'

'He's not coming?'

'She's here to talk to Gabriella Campbell. If she's willing.'

'You don't think she will be?'

Tanner shrugged. 'She's travelled a long way not to talk to anyone.'

'You've tried previously?'

'Through a friend of hers.'

'And Campbell has nothing to do concerning the trial that involves Miss Dabrowska?'

'Not directly.'

Matthews gave a smile that could be mistaken for a grimace. 'Does that mean indirectly?'

'I'm not sure.'

'You can't tell me?'

'I probably could. I just don't know.'

Matthews nodded, then turned on the computer.

'Are you ex-military or ex-police?' Tanner said.

Matthews raised an eyebrow. 'There's quite a difference,' he said. 'I was in the Royal Marines.'

'Where were you posted?'

Matthews paused. 'Parts of the Persian Empire.'

Tanner smiled. 'What did you do in – Persia?'

'I killed the enemy.'

'Who are they?'

'Anyone not on our side.'

'What was your rank?'

'Lieutenant colonel.'

'That's a high rank for someone so young, isn't it?'

'I might be older than I look.'

Tanner nodded. 'Why did you leave?'

'You're familiar with the rates of pay for the British Armed Forces, are you, Peter?'

Tanner smiled and shook his head.

'I've young children. My wife was sick of my absences, particularly considering the destinations.' There was a pause. 'Why are you asking me these questions?'

'I ask questions for a living.'

'Always such rapid fire?'

'You've obviously faced real fire many times,' Tanner said. 'You couldn't bust a friend of mine out of a Shanghai prison, could you?'

Matthews grimaced. 'Beyond my skill set, I'm afraid.'

There was a knock on the door, and Matthews stood to open it. The girl from reception walked in balancing two coffee cups and a plate of biscuits on a tray.

'So,' Tanner then said. 'Klaudia Dabrowska?'

'Yes,' Matthews said, moving his hand towards the computer.

There were a number of difficulties to overcome in locating Klaudia Dabrowska. None were more than minor hurdles on their own, but in combination they'd slowed down a positive confirmation.

Her profile remained on the Jade Models London website, but she hadn't worked since her return. 'They said she'd quit the agency,' Matthews said, 'and they didn't have any contact details.'

They'd found her father's old address from the electoral register, but she hadn't returned to live at the family home, and her father had moved since retiring. They tried to find out if she had any appointments with Dr Simon Anthony, but came up blank. In the end they found her father through his church. He'd moved homes, but not the Catholic church he'd been attending for years. They assumed she visited him, and a few weeks ago, one of their contract investigators had filmed Mr Dabrowska going to church for mass on a Sunday evening with a young woman who looked like Klaudia.

'She has a sister and brother,' Matthews said. 'The sisters are only two years apart. From further than ten yards, they could be twins. Same colouring, almost the same height and figure.'

Matthews played a video. It showed all four members of the family standing on steps outside a church. They were wearing long coats, and it was raining. Each man opened an umbrella and took one of the sisters by the arm before walking down the steps and along the footpath.

'This is just over two weeks ago,' Matthew said. 'As you can see, our weather pattern has changed considerably since then.'

Tanner looked carefully at the screen. 'Rewind it, will you?'

Matthews did as he asked, and took the film back to the steps of the church.

'She's – which one is Klaudia?'

'Let me show you more,' Matthews said.

The next scene was at a cemetery, filmed at a distance. The four stood in front of a grave. One of the girls had some flowers in her hand, and she placed them next to the headstone. The film had been edited, because it jumped forwards seven minutes, and the four were now walking off, umbrellas down as the rain had stopped, and a beam of sunlight lit up a section of the graveyard. Matthews paused the film.

'Our man walked past the grave to get to his car,' he said. 'He looked at the headstones next to her. Part curiosity, part thoroughness, I guess. Klaudia's mother was buried in the Polish section of the cemetery, and three people whose surname was "Novak" were buried next to her. He put that in his short report.'

'And?'

Matthews sat back in his chair and let out a deep breath. 'When I read his report, I did some checks on the name Novak. It was just an off chance – I wondered if that had been Marina Dabrowska's maiden name. Anyway – she's been using her mother's last name since she's come back. Klaudia Novak.'

'And you've found something under that name?'

'Klaudia's father – his name is Karol – has never owned property. We did a property search when you first retained us, and nothing came up. When we searched Novak just to check, we found a property in both their names.'

'What do you mean?'

'We found a recent purchase of an apartment that is in the joint ownership of Klaudia Novak and Karol Dabrowska.'

'Where?'

'Curzon Street, not far from Hyde Park. Mayfair.'

'That sounds expensive.'

'Three beds, two bathrooms. The last sale in the building for an identical apartment two months ago was over six million pounds.'

'Jesus.'

'He's living there. We've filmed him coming in and out a number of times, and three days ago we filmed her visiting him.'

Tanner picked up his glass of water and took two long sips. 'How do a retired salesman and an unemployed model afford a six-million-quid apartment?' he said softly, almost to himself.

'Shall we watch the last piece of film?'

He clicked the mouse again to start the video. The weather had changed. It was a sunny day, people were walking down a busy street, the pavement almost gleaming white in the sun. In the background, behind a group of pedestrians, Mr Dabrowska and one of his daughters came into view. It seemed as though the person filming was standing right in front of them, perhaps a hundred yards away, with the camera going in and out of focus until he had them in sharp outline. As they came closer, Tanner could see that father and daughter were arm in arm. He focused on Klaudia.

'Paul?' he said.

'They're going to a doctor's rooms,' Matthews said. 'This is seventy-two hours ago.'

Klaudia and her father turn slowly and walk up a flight of steps. Karol Dabrowska pushes a button, and a short moment later opens a door for his daughter, who steps inside the building first.

'I have a feeling she's not seeing anyone about an ear infection,' Tanner said, turning from the screen to look at Matthews.

'No,' Matthews said. 'She's recovered from that, it would seem.'

The footpaths outside the pubs and restaurants were thick with the post-work crowd by the time Tanner left IIS.

The buzz among the clusters of drinkers evoked a memory. He'd travelled to the UK with Karen before they were married. It was September, not long after she'd finished an exam during her specialist training. It was a sunny afternoon, and they were meeting an old friend of his who was now working in London. He had a photo at home somewhere of them at Piccadilly Circus. He was holding his jacket in the picture, and sharp light was reflected in his sunglasses.

A separate memory of his friend then flickered – of a phone call after his father had been charged, just before he'd been forced to leave his school.

'Are you okay?' his friend had asked.

'Dad says it'll be fine. Some . . . mistake.'

'Yeah, but are *you* okay?'

His words had vanished from his memory like ashes in a breeze.

The hotel bar was full when he arrived back, and rumbling with voices. He looked for Lisa, and spotted the back of her head through the French doors that led out to some tables on a terrace on the footpath. She was halfway through a cocktail of some kind.

'What are you drinking?' he asked as he took the seat next to her.

'A Bellini.' He raised an eyebrow. 'I like peaches.'

'I've had one in Harry's bar,' he said.

'Where's that?'

'Venice.'

'Should I be impressed?'

'No.'

'What took you to Venice?'

'The Australian Bar Association,' he said. 'I gave a paper on white collar crime.'

'Is white collar crime particularly rampant in Venice?'

'It's rampant everywhere,' he said.

'How did your meeting go?'

'Informative,' he said.

'They found your witness?'

'They did.'

'You're going to try to speak to her?'

He shook his head. 'I don't think so,' he said.

36

The flight from Gatwick to Catania took two and a half hours. Forty minutes after they'd collected their bags, they arrived at their hotel in Taormina.

The Grand Hotel Timeo had views of Mt Etna from its terraces, and Russian accents through its salons. It stood on the cliff at the end of the pedestrian area of the old town, high above the beaches, its back under the ruins of an ancient Greek theatre. Calabria could be seen across the water, the toenail of Italy perched faintly above the horizon.

Lisa didn't speak when the terrace doors of their room were opened, or even when the bellhop poured her a glass of prosecco from a bottle that had been waiting in an ice-bucket on the balcony. Nor when she sat and looked towards Etna, which was lightly covered in soft clouds at its peak, smoke wafting from its caldera.

'My clients can't pay for this,' she said finally, when Tanner sat next to her.

'They don't have to.'

'Very generous of you.'

'Thank the Mathesons.'

'What does Gaby Campbell have to do with Justin Matheson?'

'Citadel.'

'Do they know you're here?'

'No.'

'Would they approve of paying for a hotel like this if they did?'

'If Justin gets acquitted.'

'And if he doesn't?'

'Then I'll pay.'

It was nearly seven, and the pool below them was beginning to empty. A man was sitting on the steps at one end, two small children wrapped around him. They looked like twin girls. They had long, white curls, and he held them like prizes. Another man waded nearby, and they had a loud discussion about the excessiveness of the minimum wage in France, that ended in raucous laughter.

'I knew if I ever stayed at a hotel like this, I'd feel this way,' she said.

'What way is that?'

'That it's exquisite, but for the guests.'

'You feel superior?'

She gave him a look that hovered between quizzical and suspicious. 'Why do you ask that?'

He shrugged. 'The world is full of disagreements between groups of people who feel superior to one another for different reasons.'

'Like who?'

'Prosecutors and defence counsel, for a start.'

'I don't feel superior.'

'You don't feel superior to mining executives? Or their lawyers?'

She looked towards the sea. 'Superior is the wrong word.'

'Morally purer?'

She turned and looked at him again, a vague smile on her face. 'You don't?'

He smiled. 'I'm a criminal defence lawyer,' he said. 'I feel superior to everyone.'

She shook her head.

'Are you hungry?'

'Very.'

Buca Vincenzo was located at the end of a small laneway off Corso Umberto, the main pedestrian trail of the old town. It had a large terrace with views of the Med and of Etna.

The restaurant was full, but a young woman approached them at a brisk pace, smiling brightly. The smile dissolved when she saw Lisa. Tanner knew then that he was looking at Gabriella Campbell. She had short, dark hair, and her skin was tanned to burnt butter.

'Hi Gaby,' Lisa said. 'You look well.'

A long moment passed before Gabriella Campbell spoke. 'I've told you, I can't help you.'

'Can you show us our table?' Tanner said.

Campbell kept looking at Lisa for another moment, before turning her attention to him.

'Our table,' he repeated. 'My name's Tanner. I have a reservation.'

She didn't bother checking, just turned and walked off. She showed them to the terrace, which was lit only by strings of fairy lights and candles on the tables. She stopped at one by the edge, and then held back a chair for Lisa.

'Marco will be your waiter,' she said.

'We'd rather you were,' Tanner said.

'I'm not a waitress.'

'Did they make you sign a document?' he asked.

She didn't answer.

'We can take a look at it for you, if you like?'

'I've had a lawyer look at it.'

'Here, or in Sydney?'

'Would that matter?'

'Was it Joe Cheung?'

'I have to get back to the front.'

'We only want to discuss your report with you.'

'I can't.'

'You discussed it with Joe. We have a copy, Gaby.'

Although she was looking at him, it seemed like she was looking beyond him, back to some memory. 'Then you don't need me.'

'If Citadel has done something illegal, what they've had you sign to keep you quiet is worthless.'

Her smile was bitter. 'Do you think they'll see it that way?'

'They don't have to know. All we're asking is for you to talk privately to us.'

She closed her eyes for a moment and sighed. 'I – I just –'

'We'll be back tomorrow night if you say no.'

'We're fully booked.'

'You'll find a reservation in my name again.'

She shook her head. 'You shouldn't make threats to locals in Sicily.'

'Does that mean you're calling the carabinieri, or the mafia?'

'My cousins are more frightening than both.'

'Then let's fly them home and introduce them to the Citadel lawyers.'

For the first time, she looked at him without hostility in her eyes. 'Where are you staying?'

'The Timeo.'

'Slumming it, then?'

'I'm helping to organise a legal conference next year. I'm scouting for venues.'

'One hour.'

'Meet us for lunch.'

A man approached the table, and started talking at Campbell in frantic Italian.

'Anything else I can do for you before I get fired?' she said.

He nodded. 'What's your favourite local wine?'

37

Gabriella Campbell met them in the foyer of their hotel just after one the following day, and they took a table on the terrace overlooking the sea.

'I meant what I said last night,' Lisa said as they sat down. 'You look well.'

'I put on weight when I first got here,' she said, looking at the plate of antipasti Tanner had arranged for lunch. 'There are no single course meals at my aunt's house.'

'Is that where you live?'

She shook her head. 'I have my own flat now.'

'It's your uncle's restaurant?'

'My mother's oldest brother.'

'You've adopted his name?'

She looked towards the horizon. 'I wanted to leave Gaby Campbell behind for a while.'

'Is running a restaurant in your blood?'

'I don't run it.'

'Why are you here then, Gaby?'

'You know why.'

'I'd rather hear it from you.'

She picked up her glass of water and took a sip. 'How did you know I was here?'

'It's not hard to find someone who's not hiding.'

'Nothing will stop that gold mine,' she said, looking at Lisa.

'We can try.'

'I tried,' she said. 'Now I'm here.'

'Most people would like it here,' Tanner said.

She glared at him before responding. 'I'm a hydrogeologist. I didn't study to be a maître d' in a tourist town.'

He nodded. 'What are your plans?'

'You're not here to discuss my plans.'

'That depends on what they are.'

She sighed. 'What do you want to know about my report?'

'We know less about hydrogeology than you do.'

'So I should start at the beginning?'

'Please.'

She looked over Tanner's left shoulder, towards the volcano. 'Four or five hundred million years ago,' she said, 'there were a lot of those in what's now western New South Wales.'

'That is starting at the beginning.'

'The volcanic activity separated metals into zones in the earth's crust. They're now in handy seams for miners. Near Bageeyn River, there are seams of copper and gold.'

'Lots, I understand.'

'There's a couple of mines near Orange that have been operational for about twenty years. Citadel's exploration area is much further to the south-west. It's a bigger area, and a bigger resource.'

'And because of that they need more water?'

She nodded. 'They're seeking approval for three mines. Two underground, one open-cut. They want to dig up fifty million tonnes of ore a year. From that, they say, they'll get one and a half million ounces of gold, and maybe a hundred thousand tonnes of copper. And they want to do that for forty years.'

'Tell us about the river,' Tanner said.

'The simple version or the complex one?'

'We're lawyers.'

'I need to draw something.'

Tanner opened his satchel and gave her a pad and a pen. She lifted her sunglasses, and sat them on top of her head.

She drew three circles at the top of a page. 'These are the mines,' she said. 'What I'm drawing is a basic ore processing facility.' Lisa and Tanner nodded, and she went on: 'First, the ore is crushed.' She drew lines from the circles, down to a square which she marked *grinding plant.* She drew an arrow to another box, which she marked *flotation plant.*

'That's where the water becomes involved?'

She nodded. 'Think of it as a giant washing machine. You mix the crushed ore in the water, then add chemicals. The metals attach to the chemicals, float up in bubbles, and you scoop off the copper and gold.' She drew two more arrows, this time from the flotation plant to two more circles. In one circle she wrote *copper-gold* and in the other she wrote *tailings dam.* 'The minerals end up here,' she said, 'and the tailings water and chemical residue ends up in the dam.'

'Your report has the mine using a lot more water than Citadel says it'll need.'

'Everyone agrees the mines won't be viable without a lot of water,' she said. 'Where I disagree with Citadel is about how much water they'll need, and so how much they'll have to take from the river, and what the consequences of that will be. I also think the impacts on the surrounding aquifers will be greater than what they estimate.'

'Start with the amount of water they'll need.'

She picked up her glass, then shook her head. 'This is one of the things they went crazy at me about.'

'Why?'

'The amount of water they say they'll need for fifty million tonnes of ore per year is a big underestimate,' she said, 'but they were right when they said that isn't my area of expertise.'

'You're talking about the amount of water they've got to add to the flotation plant?'

'Citadel says it's the most efficient user of water in the world. It's complicated, and you're going to need to talk to other experts, but they say the way they crush the ore and the precise mixture of chemicals they use to separate the metals is somehow so advanced that they'll need less water than other miners would for the same amount of ore-to-metal ratio.'

'You don't believe that?'

She shook her head. 'It's not what I believe, it's what they wouldn't tell me – they wouldn't back that claim up with scientific proof. Separating metals from ore using water and chemicals isn't my area of expertise, I admit that. I know what it takes for other mines, though. I pressed them about it, and they wouldn't support their assertions – and that's all they are – with anything that made me comfortable about what they're claiming. They just kept saying, "This is the amount of water we need to run the mines, you have to accept that, and base your report on it." I kept saying these three mines are bigger than other similar mines around the world, so how are you saying you won't need more water? They wouldn't tell me.'

'This is something you spoke to Joe about?' Tanner said.

Campbell leant forwards in her chair. 'I'd met him before. He helped me with an expert report for court on a challenge to a coal mine. He made sure the report was warts and all about water impacts. My job is to assess as best I can the water loss caused by mining to rivers and aquifers. To do that I need to have some certainty as to how much water is going to be used in the process. I didn't get that. I got assertions, and a brush off.'

'Then there's the "other sources of water" issue,' Lisa said.

Campbell nodded. 'Citadel says it will get its water from several sources. Most will come from the river. To compensate, they have to buy licences from other river systems, and then not use that water, but that hardly helps the Bageeyn. They say they're eventually going to build some pipelines to various towns in the region, and use recycled effluent, and also some recycled water from the tailings dam.'

'And you didn't accept everything you were told about that?' Tanner asked.

'Maybe I shouldn't have, but I spoke to some other people about what I was being asked to assume.'

'Who?'

She shook her head. 'I didn't breach confidence. I asked general questions, without saying specifically why. This is a huge project – I wanted to get things right, not just say what suited Citadel. Rainfall overestimate and evaporation underestimate were two things I queried them on. This region is getting drier. And the evaporation rates from the tailings dam didn't seem right either.'

'Not right, or not truthful?'

'Does it matter? The result is the same – not enough water.'

'It'd matter to a judge,' Tanner said.

'Even if I accepted everything they said about water, I still think the impacts will be greater than they say they'll be, and catastrophic for the river if they're underestimating water use.'

'And the impacts on the aquifers?' Tanner said. 'The fifty versus five-hundred-year issue?'

'Whenever there's underground mining, you get subsidence,' she said. 'The earth above the longwalls drops. That causes depressurisation of the aquifers. The ones the farmers are using for their water from their bores.'

'What does that mean exactly?'

'The subsidence causes pressure loss. It creates cracks under the earth and the water level drops.'

'So you can't get water from bores anymore?'

'You have to drill deeper,' she said. 'And the risk is that water that can be used by agriculture gets mixed with saline water that can't be. And then no one can use it.'

'And Citadel and the government's expert say this is a life of mine-plus-fifty-years problem, during which they'll truck in any water a farmer needs, and you say it's a five-hundred-year problem?'

Campbell sat back in her chair, a wry smile on her face. 'Any hydro who says they know how long it'll take for the aquifer pressure to return to its pre-mining state after Citadel leaves is lying. Their estimate is way too optimistic. Three hundred years? Maybe. Five hundred? More likely. Longer than that? Just as likely. And don't tell me Citadel is going to be trucking water to farmers and fruit growers in five hundred years. They and their profits will be long gone.'

'And the loss of pressure affects the river too?'

'Sure,' Campbell said. 'There's the water coming out of the river directly, but depressurising the water underneath affects base flow as well.'

'So all up, this mine will kill the river?'

'You need riparian experts and ecologists to make that final call, but yeah, based on the amount of water it will lose, a mine of this size will eventually kill it. That river will become intermittent, and then ephemeral or worse. At about the time they're packing their bags to leave when the gold's gone.'

'You spoke to other experts?' Tanner asked.

Campbell nodded slowly. 'If you want to prevent an approval for this mine, your action group will need other experts to tell you precisely what impact the loss of water will have on the ecosystems the river supports.'

'Who did you speak to?'

'No.'

'All we want to do is –'

'I'm not dragging anyone else into this,' she said firmly. 'You can get your own experts. Just ask them how much water this river can lose without the plant life dying and the wildlife being forced away.'

'What about monitoring what happens to the river as the mining progresses? Won't Citadel have to do that?' Lisa asked.

Campbell laughed a little. 'Trust me. Things will look fine at first, or they'll say the river will recover when the mine closes. Then later they'll say, "Oops, sorry about that."'

'Can I ask a stupid question?' Tanner said.

She almost smiled. 'I can't stop you.'

'This river,' he said, 'is it worth saving?'

Gabriella Campbell looked at him like she was considering slapping him. 'That really is a stupid question.'

He shrugged. 'It's the kind a lawyer might ask.'

'You mean is a gold mine more important than a river?'

'It comes down to money in the end, Gaby,' he said.

'So I should answer your question thinking only about dollars?'

He shrugged. 'To a lot of people, that's all there is.'

'The people of Citadel?'

'We know their answer.'

'I'm not an economist. I don't know how to put a dollar value on a river.'

Tanner leant towards her. 'One day I may have to tell a court why this river is worth saving,' he said. 'I don't know the answer to that. You may think I should, but I don't. Why is it more important than all that gold?'

She smiled faintly. 'The Bageeyn isn't the Colorado, or the Snowy. It doesn't drive a turbine.' She shook her head. 'Big boats can't sail down it – it's not a transport artery. You can't value it that way.'

'Then how?'

She took a breath and sighed. 'It's not just a river. It's part of the Murrumbidgee catchment of the Murray–Darling basin. There are wetlands up and down its length. I don't know – I'd need an exercise book to write out the plants and animals that form part of its ecosystem. It's their home – if that matters to you. My father goes fishing in it. He doesn't call me when he catches something, though. He calls me when he sees a platypus.' She paused and looked at him. 'It's nature. How do you quantify that?'

'I'm sure there's an economist who can.'

'A river is a gift, isn't it?' she said. 'It's been there long before us. It's not ours or Citadel's to kill. Its custodians are half-a-dozen Aboriginal clans. Can an economist put a price on that?'

'They'd try.'

'If you need something tangible to do with the economy,' she said, 'speak to the local landowners who use the waters.'

'If this mine is approved,' Tanner said, 'the action group plans to challenge the decision. I'd like to be able to call you in our case.'

'There are other people you can use.'

'I want to prove they buried your report.'

'Just give it to the judge.'

'We stole it, Gaby. That'll be hard to explain.'

'I don't know how I can help you with that.'

'You can say there's been a cover-up.'

'I signed a document agreeing to shut up,' she said flatly. 'I took money from them to avoid being dismissed.'

'That won't protect them in court,' Tanner said.

She shook her head and looked at Lisa. 'I don't want to end up like Anne,' she said.

Lisa began to say something, but Tanner got in first. 'You don't think it was a gang robbery?'

She shook her head slowly. 'I haven't got a clue,' she said, almost under her breath.

'Why did Anne and Joe go to that island? Do you know?'

'Why don't you ask him?'

'The hospitality of the Chinese prison system has made him untalkative.'

'Anne was an ecotoxicologist,' she said. 'Why do you think she would go there?'

'A routine visit? Can you tell us otherwise?'

'Anne was killed,' she said. 'You want me to go back to Australia and call these people liars?'

'You don't have to do anything you don't want to,' Lisa said.

Campbell picked up a piece of bread on her plate, put it back without eating it. 'Look up Baia Mare Mine on the internet. Look up the Tisza River in Romania,' she said.

'If we do that,' Tanner said, 'what will we find?'

'What cyanide and heavy metals can do to a river.'

'Gaby,' Lisa said, lowering her voice to a near whisper, 'if Citadel had some accident at a gold mine in PNG it could seriously jeopardise its chances of approval for Bageeyn River. They'd be dead politically.'

'How do you keep a cyanide spill quiet?' Tanner asked.

Campbell shook her head. 'Citadel leases the whole island,' she said. 'They control who arrives and who leaves. They have security forces. They pay a lot of money to government officials at every level. They control all the communications, employ all the locals. Cyanide doesn't last long – it's the heavy metals that become the killer – but to find them you have to do testing.'

He wanted to ask her again to come home and tell her story to someone, and then to a court. He held back for the moment.

'Can I ask you a question?' Campbell said. 'Why won't Joe tell you what happened on Tovosevu?'

'Would you rather do twenty years in a Chinese prison,' he said, 'or maybe only five?'

'I don't follow.'

'Citadel has a number of joint ventures with a Chinese state-owned company called North Shanxi Resources. They're going to own thirty per cent of the Bageeyn River mine.'

He saw it dawn on her face. She rubbed at her forehead, like she was trying to remove a mark. Then she looked at her watch. 'I have to go.'

'Just five minutes?' Tanner said.

She tilted her head and looked annoyed.

'When you'd completed your report, who did you speak to?'

'I've told you, no.'

'Forget names. What kind of experts?'

'Another hydro first.'

'At GreenDay?'

She shook her head. 'I wanted to run a few things by someone else about depressurisation simulations.'

'Why?'

'You use historical modelling. You use information you can get from previous mining, and actual results from pressure-monitoring bores. You estimate likely subsidence, and you feed it into a computer model you've calibrated based on the evidence. I discussed the calibrations and the modelling I was using. I got a rough peer review of my approach.'

'Did you tell him what you were working on?'

'I chose someone discreet. I wanted my hand held a little.'

'Did Citadel find out?'

'They knew I'd spoken to ecologists. My report had some pretty firm views about impacts on ecosystems that depend on the river.'

'What happened?'

'I'd already spoken to Shields, the government's guy. Citadel said I'd breached my confidentiality deed. They said by talking to – they called them "outsiders" – I'd stolen Citadel's – I don't know, commercial information. Something like that.'

'Who said this?'

'The lawyers.'

'What lawyers?'

'They weren't handing out business cards.'

'Citadel lawyers, or external lawyers?'

'I don't know,' she said, her voice loud again, and cracking a little. 'I was panicking. I don't know.'

'Pete,' Lisa said. 'Back off.'

He looked at Lisa for a moment. Gaby Campbell was a small woman, at least half a foot shorter than Lisa. She had fight in her though, he could see that. Citadel and its lawyers must have scared it out of her, at least for a while. 'I'm sorry,' he said to Campbell. He paused for a few moments to let her compose herself. 'Do you remember any names?' he said. 'Even a Christian name?'

Campbell took a sip of water. 'The one who did most of the talking was called Tony.'

'And what did he say?'

'He said I'd breached my deed, I'd – it was wilful misconduct, I could be instantly dismissed. They made me hand over all my notes and my laptop. They said I'd end up owing them millions – all those things. I had to give a signed statement saying my report was wrong. I had to sign anther deed about confidentiality on everything that was being discussed.'

'Did you get a lawyer?'

'They offered me a deal. They said if I took it to a lawyer it would be off the table, and I'd be instantly dismissed.'

'What was the deal?' Lisa asked.

'I got to resign. They paid me six months of my GreenDay salary. If I went away they said they'd pay me another six, which they did. They bought my airfare to London.'

'Do they know you're here?'

She shrugged. 'I said I was going away. I didn't mention here.' She looked at her watch again. 'I have to go now.'

'Will you think about what I asked you?' Tanner said. 'About coming back to help stop this thing?'

She looked angry. 'You don't think I have?'

'I'm sorry,' he said.

Tanner moved to get up, but Lisa held up her hand, gesturing for him to stay seated. 'I'll walk out with you,' she said.

'There's no need.'

'It's okay,' Lisa said, picking up her phone from the table, and following Campbell out.

PART FOUR

38

Tanner sat at a table around the corner from the fireplace in a pub in the Rocks. He was three weeks out from the Matheson trial, and had cleared his diary to focus on it solely.

Right on six he saw his guest walk in. Tanner raised his arm to attract his attention. The men shook hands without a word. Mark Woods forced a smile as he sat.

'Let me get you a drink,' Tanner said. He went to the bar, and returned with two pints of Three Sheets Ale, that was brewed on the premises.

'I assume I'm not here so you can gloat?' Woods asked. He was tall and solid. His pec muscles tested the buttons of his shirt when he breathed.

'Gloat?'

Woods looked at him with a weary expression. 'Tomas Alvares?'

Tanner shook his head. 'Alvares got less than he should have.'

'No one gets more than they should, do they?' Woods was a detective in the drug squad of the State Crime Command. He'd been part of the team that worked with the drug importation unit of the Federal Police that had apprehended Tomas Alvares. He and Tanner had crossed paths in other cases.

'No one?'

Woods shrugged. 'You know I don't like traffickers.'

'Maybe we should legalise drugs?'

Woods smiled faintly. 'That would do me out of a job.'

'Only the job you have now.'

'It would do you out of work, too.'

'Other crooks would keep us busy.'

'You want everyone using? The guy driving towards you on the freeway? What about the judges you appear in front of?'

'It'd put them in a better mood.'

'You told me you had a son, didn't you? Do you want him on heroin or ice?'

'I'm more afraid of booze,' Tanner said. 'Don't you want to go after real criminals, detective?'

Woods narrowed his eyes. 'Who are they?'

'All around us.'

'Tourists?'

'The people in suits. Our corporate and political elites.'

'They're all here?'

'I carry them around in my bleeding heart.'

A bored smile appeared on Woods' face. 'What would I charge them with?'

'The disproportionate distribution of wealth.'

'That's in the books?'

Tanner smiled, and put a hand on the nearly two hundred year old wall by his side. He slapped at the convict-quarried sandstone. 'It should be,' he said. 'We owe it to the poor bastards that built places like this. We owe it to them to get the real crooks.'

Woods took a long sip of beer. 'Are we here to discuss that?'

'I'm here to provide you with work.'

'Work?'

'You think Tomas Alvares got a soft sentence? I can make it up to you.'

Woods put his beer on the table and leant back in his chair, a dubious expression on his face. 'How?'

'You want to arrest some of the elite, don't you?'

'What the fuck are you talking about, Tanner?'

'We're not talking.'

'What are we doing, then?'

'We're off the record.'

Woods snorted. 'You're an informant now?'

'If you like.'

'Not many defence lawyers are informants.'

'It's part of my strategy in another case.'

'What case?'

'One that doesn't involve you.'

'What case?' Woods said firmly.

'One in which I'm acting for an innocent man.'

'That'd be a first.'

'I can give you a name. Someone who buys in commercial quantities.'

'Who?'

'A person with a big client list. Rich people looking for highs.' Tanner took a sip from his glass. 'Interested?'

'I'm listening.'

'I can let you know when this guy is taking delivery. If you arrest him, he'll sing. This is not a man suited to prison lifestyle.'

'He's buying from Alvares?'

Tanner waved his index finger at Woods. 'C'mon, detective. What sort of defence lawyer do you think I am? Alejandro Alvares and his family are my clients. This does not involve them.'

'A rival, then?'

Tanner shook his head, nearly laughed. 'I can't give you them, detective. They are very bad boys. I'm giving you someone else.'

Woods brought his face much closer to Tanner's. 'Are you suggesting this for Alvares?' he said, a hint of menace in his tone.

Tanner shook his head slowly. 'The only work I will ever do for him is in a courtroom.'

Woods held his stare for a moment, then nodded. 'Is this personal? What's this guy done to you?'

'I've never met him.'

'Why, then?'

'I told you, it's part of a defence strategy.'

'And I don't follow that.'

'You don't have to. All you have to know is that if you arrest this man, you'll be arresting someone who will cooperate. You'll make more arrests.'

'Our aim is higher up the food chain.'

Tanner laughed. 'In between your busts of every Mr Big, a few small fish might be sweet.'

'Who does he buy from?'

'I don't know.'

'Does he?'

'You'll have to ask him.'

'Has he sold to you?'

'That's a very rude question, detective,' Tanner said slowly. 'I prefer pinot noir.'

'Then why are you drinking beer?'

'You don't look like a guy who enjoys a Burgundy.'

'You're wrong.'

'My apologies. Probably some prejudice on my part. If I look to you, though, like someone who dabbles in coke after a hard day in court, then you're wrong too.'

Woods nodded. 'Why me?'

'I owe you a favour.'

'What favour?'

'You were right about Tomas. He got unders.'

'Something else you want to tell me about that?'

Tanner shook his head. 'Best for both of us that I don't.'

'You lied for him?'

'You can't lie if you don't know what the truth is.'

'What's that mean?'

'It means I'm doing you this favour.'

'Just like that, eh?'

'For a small favour in return.'

Woods smiled and held up his glass, looking at the amber ale. 'I don't do favours.'

'If you do it the right way, it'll almost be legal.'

'What way would that be?'

'The way I tell you.'

'You're giving orders?'

'Think of it as legal advice.'

'What is it?'

'I'll tell you in a moment,' Tanner said as he stood.

'I'm still finishing this beer,' Woods said.

'I'm not getting you a beer,' Tanner said. 'I'm buying us a bottle of wine. Then I'm telling you where you're going to go exploring for minerals.'

39

Ten days before Matheson's trial, Charles Porter was served with a late witness statement by the prosecutor's office. He made arrangements for them to see their client at the remand centre urgently.

'Who's Deborah Edelman?' Tanner asked the moment Matheson was brought into the interview room.

What colour was left in Matheson's face drained from it. 'Why are you asking me?' he said.

'I can tell you're not pleased to hear her name, Justin. Who is she?'

'She worked at Stott Ackerman,' Matheson said softly.

'When?'

'About four years ago.'

'Is she someone who's likely to say nice things about you?'

'She kept calling me at all hours,' Matheson said, shaking his head. 'She came to my fucking house late one night. I had to lie to Sarah and tell her she'd turned up about work.'

'What made her do that, Justin? Your irresistible charm?'

'It only happened once,' Matheson said. 'We did a trip together to Macau and –'

Tanner held his hand up to stop him. 'I guessed you were fucking her when I got to paragraph two of the statement the prosecutor just served.'

Matheson slumped. 'Can I see it?'

'Why does she say you hit her?'

'That's a lie!'

'What's your version?'

'She was hysterical, out of control. Screaming at me, crying . . .'

'Did you touch her, Justin?'

'She ran at me, trying to hit me. I had to – I had to grab her to stop her from hitting me. She was flinging her arms, she –'

'This is in your office?'

Matheson ran a hand through his greasy hair, and drew in a long breath. 'I had to see my boss about her. She was making work impossible. He spoke to her . . . then she came into my room after.'

'And?'

'Like I told you. She attacked me.'

'Did anyone see this?'

'No. Just right at the end. A whole bunch of people came in. Deborah, she . . . she kind of collapsed . . . you know, a sobbing mess.'

'Well, at least she's alive.'

Matheson glared at Tanner, anger in his eyes. 'Fuck off, Peter.'

Tanner stared back at his client, barely stopping himself from saying something he'd regret. 'How was her "resignation" handled by Stott Ackerman?'

Matheson exhaled slowly. 'She threatened to sue them. They settled – paid her some money.'

'Did she make any allegations about you?'

Matheson closed his eyes, like he wanted to wish this part of the story away. 'She said I hurt her when she was in my office screaming at me.' He leant forwards, a pleading look on his face. 'I didn't hit her. I was only trying to stop her hitting me.'

'Anything else?'

'She said I'd pursued her, that I was harassing her, turning up at her apartment. Everything that happened, she had her lawyer reverse. How do they have a statement from her anyway? The settlement was confidential.'

Tanner shook his head. 'Confidentiality agreements don't carry much weight in criminal trials.'

'How – how can this be admissible?'

'Are you doing a law degree in here, Justin?'

'But it's not relevant.'

'Tendency evidence,' Tanner said. 'Aitken will try and get it in as evidence of you having a disposition for violence against women.'

'Nothing she said is true.'

'Justin,' Tanner said, 'you're accused of killing a young woman. The fact that another young woman you had an affair with has said you were violent is relevant, okay? That is stuff we need to know about. Are there any other incidents that you think are completely irrelevant? Have other women alleged you've hit them following an affair?'

'It wasn't an affair,' Matheson shouted. 'We'd been out to dinner with clients. She knocked on my hotel door and barged in when I opened it. I'd been drinking, you know?'

Tanner shook his head slowly. 'You and booze, Justin.'

'How can they serve this now? She wasn't part of the committal. You can object, can't you? This is unfair, they can't just –'

'They served an affidavit with the statement from a solicitor in the prosecutor's office. It says she only just came forward.'

Matheson's eyes were full of anger. 'Why would she do that? Why now?'

'We don't know.'

'Surely the judge won't let them –'

'Justin, listen to me,' Tanner said. 'Whether this witness gets to give evidence is my problem to deal with. What you have to focus on is telling us the truth. The whole fucking truth.'

The fire vanished from Matheson's face as the enormity of the upcoming trial washed over him. He was drowning, and realised he might never surface.

'Does your wife know about Deborah Edelman?'

Matheson looked up for a moment, then dropped his head again. 'No,' he said, barely audibly. 'Not everything.'

Tanner picked up his papers and stood. 'Then we're not the only ones who deserve the whole truth,' he said.

40

Just on seven thirty on the first morning of the Matheson trial, Tanner received a phone call from Jane Ross. She told him to go to the online edition of one of the newspapers, and then call her back. He did as he was told.

'Shit,' he said under his breath when he saw it. He'd expected the story to make the press, but leaving it for the first morning of the trial seemed less than polite.

'Charles says the parents are in a flap,' Ross said when he called her back. 'They're worried about whether Sarah will come to court. They want to talk to you. They're saying Justin can't get a fair trial. Pete?'

'I'll complain to the judge.'

'They want to talk to you.'

'You can handle it.'

'Thanks, but –'

'You can handle it, Jane,' he said firmly. 'This was going to come out at some stage. The article is factually accurate. He had an affair. She alleged he pushed her. She sued them, and they paid her money.'

'Yes, but it looks –'

'I know how it looks,' he said. 'Tell them I'll complain to the judge, Jane.'

'Can I tell them anything else?'

'Tell them murder trials aren't pretty.'

'You're a great help.'

'I'll make it up to you.'

Just after nine, Tanner's clerk called to tell him Charles Porter had arrived in a van that would take them to court. Despite that morning's headlines, Sarah Matheson was with him. Her blonde hair had been parted on one side, and swept back in a bun. Her face was thin, angular, and beautiful. And she looked like she would crack apart at any moment. What he was asking her to do for his client, Tanner thought, was undergo a form of torture.

'You know what to expect when we arrive?' he said once the van was under way. He was in the seat next to her. A week before, Tanner, Porter and Ross had spent an afternoon with Sarah, taking her through the witnesses, and what was likely to be their evidence.

She didn't respond, and he wondered if he'd been heard. 'Sarah?'

She was looking out the window, but then turned to face him.

'The press?'

'Look ahead, say nothing. You'll be right next to me,' she said flatly.

'Sarah experienced this at the bail hearing,' Porter said from the front passenger seat.

'This will be worse.'

'Worse than today's papers?' Sarah said. She glared at Tanner, but it was her husband that the anger in her voice was directed at. Being the wife of the accused was no easy gig.

When they arrived at the nearly two hundred year old sandstone court complex in Darlinghurst, a five minute car ride from the CBD, it was surrounded by press. They walked slowly through the throng or reporters and cameras, and ignored all questions.

Courtroom no. 3 was the largest court, and it was already full to capacity when Tanner and Jane Ross walked in. The bar table was aligned lengthways so that counsel were side-on to the judge's bench, but facing the jury who would sit in two rows in their box on the right side of the court. Prosecuting counsel were allocated seats closest to the judge, while the defence was closest to the dock where the accused would soon be brought from the cells underneath the courtroom. Behind the dock were rows of seats for the public, which Tanner called the 'stalls'. On the balcony level above were more rows of seats he called the 'dress circle'. Behind the bar table was another row of seats like the jury box, which for the Matheson case had been allocated to members of the press.

Finally, a row of seats had been reserved for those on each side of the contest. On the left of the court, some had been set aside for members of the Matheson family. On the right, nearest the jury box, were the seats reserved for members of the victim's family. Tanner had been told that Elena's parents and an elder daughter had flown out for the trial, and almost immediately he sensed their eyes on him.

As he and Jane Ross took their seats at the bar table, the court door opened again and the prosecution team walked in. Right behind them was the Richter camp. As with any criminal trial, the parties were obliged to get the major objections to evidence out of the way before the jury was empanelled. In the Matheson case, the biggest pre-trial issue was access to the files Sally Cook & Associates held on Nikki Richter. Those files had been produced to the court on subpoena, but Nikki's estate was claiming privilege. That dispute had to be decided before the trial could begin.

Joe Murphy QC usually had a seat at the table in most corporate cases where the stakes were high. Three years ago, Murphy had suffered a major heart attack at the Bar Association's annual dinner with the judiciary. The queue to give him the kiss of life was a short one.

'Peter,' Murphy said as he reached the bar table. 'Still going ahead with this nonsense?'

'Defending the accused?'

'By throwing dirt indiscriminately?'

'It's not indiscriminate, Joe. I'm aiming for your client.'

'My client is the estate of Nikki Richter.'

'Tell her widower to duck.'

Murphy snorted and took his seat. As he did, Justin Matheson was led into the courtroom and placed in the dock by two sheriffs. He was in a dark suit, white shirt and light blue tie. He'd continued to lose weight, and had dark rings under his eyes. He was still nearly as good looking as his wife.

Tanner opened a folder of documents. As he did, a woman dressed in black robes approached him from the other side of the bar table – the judge's associate. She smiled at him.

'Set to go?'

He smiled back. 'I have been for months.'

The courtroom was bubbling with chatter when the court officer knocked on the judge's door to announce his arrival on the bench. People rose at marginally different times: the lawyers first, the rest of the crowd a moment later. Those in the gallery sat after bowing to the judge, who took his seat as he bowed his head in return. When he lifted it, Tanner saw a noticeably older man than the last time he'd been in Justice Philip Knight's court. His complexion was pale, almost ghostly, and the neatly trimmed beard the judge favoured for his long face had turned from ash-grey to blinding white.

Knight had been a senior prosecutor. He favoured neither side. His rulings were unbiased, and invariably correct. Those qualities were negatives for the defence; Tanner preferred judges who favoured the accused. Jurors started with a bias towards conviction, no matter what they told themselves. They knew that criminal defendants were arrested, charged, and brought before a court for a reason.

When Justice Knight had settled in his seat, the matter of the *The Queen versus Justin William Matheson* was called. Richard Aitken announced his appearance and that of his junior for the Crown. Tanner announced his appearance with Ms Ross as counsel for the accused. The judge kept his eyes firmly to the back of the courtroom, then raised an eyebrow in the direction of Murphy.

'You're here for the privilege matter, Mr Murphy?'

Murphy rose slowly. 'I appear for the estate of the late Nikki Richter, your Honour, along with my learned junior, Mr Sloan.'

'Very well,' the judge said. 'That's first then, Mr Crown? Before we empanel the jury?'

Aitken stood and nodded. 'Mr Murphy will deal with the privilege claim, your Honour.'

'I have an application to make first, your Honour,' Murphy said, standing once more.

'I have something I want to say before you make that application, Mr Murphy,' the judge said. He looked at Tanner. 'You've seen the front page of one of the papers this morning, Mr Tanner?'

Tanner got to his feet. 'I was going to raise it with you, your Honour.'

'To make an application?'

Technically, the judge had power to postpone a trial because of adverse media coverage concerning an accused. The judge even had the power to stay a prosecution over it. In reality, it was almost impossible to prove an accused couldn't get a fair trial because of a TV story or newspaper article. The court's default position was to accept that jurors would always act in accordance with the oath they had to swear to bring impartiality to their deliberations. The article that morning concerning Deborah Edelman was prejudicial, but it wasn't going to get Matheson off the hook.

'We've debated making an application for a stay for some time this morning, your Honour,' Tanner said.

'And the result of that debate?'

'The article contains a series of untruths, and is extremely prejudicial to my client. It makes a fair trial very difficult. Mr Matheson, though, wants to get this hearing over with, and to clear his name.'

The judge looked carefully at Tanner. 'Very well,' he said. The judge delivered a cold, textbook rebuke to the assembled media about the care they had to take concerning any coverage of the trial, or concerning the accused or any witness to be called. He finished with a warning about contempt.

'Thank you for that, your Honour,' Tanner said.

Knight ignored him. 'Mr Murphy,' he said, 'you have an application?'

Murphy's application was for a suppression order of the privilege argument, prohibiting any publication about it in the media, and for it to take place in a closed court.

'The affidavit asserting waiver,' Murphy told the judge, referring to the information from Amanda Weatherill, 'contains details of alleged discussions between Miss Weatherill and the late Mrs Richter which might unnecessarily embarrass a witness in these proceedings, Mr John Richter.'

'I've read the affidavit,' the judge said.

'It would be unfair in our submission for these alleged conversations to get out into the public domain. My instructions are that if Mrs Richter said what is alleged, then what she said was false. It won't be possible, though, to refute those allegations – at least not within the confines of an application to allege that privilege has been waived. Waiver will be the issue, not the truth of the assertions, assuming they were made. The short point is that this application shouldn't have the result of unfairly embarrassing a witness when that witness can't properly defend themselves. I have some written submissions on this matter prepared, your Honour. May I hand a copy of –'

Knight held up a hand to stop him. He looked at Tanner. 'It seems to me there's some force in what Mr Murphy is putting, Mr Tanner. If these things were said to Miss Weatherill by Mrs Richter, the truth or otherwise behind them isn't central to your application. You only need to prove waiver. Do you oppose suppression?'

One thing no trial lawyer should do is fight desperately to prevent a judge from doing what they want if it costs your client nothing, especially at the start of a trial. Getting rid of the big gallery might even help Amanda Weatherill relax when it came time for her to give evidence. The more negative publicity about John Richter, though, the better for the accused.

'The public have a right to know what's happening in this case, your Honour,' Tanner said.

'You're not acting for the public, though, are you Mr Tanner?' the judge said.

'I'm sure they'd agree with me, your Honour.'

'Well, I don't. What's your view, Mr Crown?'

'Ordinarily we wouldn't support a suppression order, your Honour,' Aitken said, 'but in this case it might well be justified.'

Justice Knight nodded, and made an order suppressing the evidence of the application that was about to take place, on the basis that it could unfairly embarrass a witness in the proceedings. He also made an order clearing the court of everyone other than the parties. One of the more experienced journalists came forward and asked if the application could be delayed until they could get their counsel there to argue against the order, but the judge refused, telling the journalist he'd be prepared to hear further argument if any counsel representing one of the media companies made an appearance and sought leave.

Having been filled beyond capacity, the court now emptied but for the main participants. As it did, Tanner took the opportunity to walk over and talk to his client, who sat in the dock like an overgrown schoolboy, waiting glumly to be summoned to the headmaster's office.

'Feeling lonely?'

Matheson shrugged, and tried to bring himself to smile. 'A little.'

'If I was as nervous now as I was before my first trial,' Tanner said, 'I'd swap places with you.'

'Be my guest.'

'Shall we proceed, gentlemen?' Knight said when the court had been closed.

Tanner formally asked for Sally Cook's file to be produced, which she had already sent to the court after being served with a subpoena. The judge looked to his associate, who opened a large orange envelope containing a purple folder of documents. The associate then looked at the judge and nodded.

'Those documents have been produced, Mr Tanner.'

'I seek first access to those documents, your Honour,' Tanner said.

The judge nodded. 'Mr Murphy?'

'The estate claims privilege over all documents in Ms Cook's files, your Honour.'

'Yes,' Knight said. 'And you have a witness, Mr Tanner.'

'I do, your Honour. I thought we'd hear from Mr Aitken first, though.'

'Mr Aitken?'

'Yes. The prosecutor.'

'I know who he is, Mr Tanner.'

'You could be forgiven for not knowing it on this issue, your Honour,' Tanner said. 'I thought a prosecutor had a duty to make available evidence relevant to innocence, not just guilt. Mr Aitken doesn't seem very interested in Ms Cook's file.'

'I object to that,' Aitken said. 'Mr Tanner knows full well that the prosecution has no control over a claim for privilege by an estate. He also knows that we have no idea what's in the files of Ms Cook.'

'She's a divorce lawyer,' Tanner said. 'Her file isn't going to contain much about what a wonderful husband Mrs Richter thought she had.'

'Are you finished, Mr Tanner?' the judge said.

'Just putting my complaint on the record, your Honour.'

The judge paused for a moment, shook his head, opened up a leather-bound book he kept notes in, and put on his reading glasses. 'Let's have the witness, shall we?' he said.

41

Amanda Weatherill looked nervous when she took her oath. When she said 'I do,' it came out as a whisper. Tanner covered her family and work history before moving on to her friendship with Nikki Richter.

'You met Nikki Richter in your capacity as a nurse?'

Amanda nodded, and Tanner could see the easy questions he was feeding her – many of them leading but not objectionable as they were only introductory – were putting her at ease. 'She was a patient. She broke her ankle badly in a skiing accident.'

'You were her nurse at a hospital?'

'Yes.'

'And that's how you became friends?'

'Yes.'

'Was she married at the time?'

She shook her head. 'No. She got engaged a couple of years later.'

'To John Richter, her future husband?'

'Yes.'

'And through your friendship with Nikki, you came to know him?'

'Yes.'

'You were a bridesmaid at Nikki's wedding, I believe?'

'One of many.'

Tanner smiled. 'It wasn't a small affair?'

'No.'

Now that he had her relaxed, Tanner got straight to the details of the waiver of privilege. He wanted to make the case he needed to, but not give Murphy any more scope to cross-examine than he had to.

'You understand that the accused, Mr Matheson, has asked his lawyers to serve a subpoena on a law firm called Sally Cook & Associates?'

'Yes.'

'Were you familiar with the name of that firm before being asked to be a witness today?'

'Yes,' she said. 'They were Nikki's lawyers.'

'How do you know that?'

'She told me she was seeing a lawyer early last year, and I went there with her once.'

'To the law firm's office?'

'Yes.'

'Why?'

'Nikki asked me to go with her. Just for moral support.'

'And did you meet anyone at the law firm?'

'I met Nikki's lawyer. A lady named Sally Cook.'

'Why was Nikki seeing her?'

'I object,' Murphy said.

'Why?' the judge asked.

'It calls for hearsay?'

'But – we – Mrs Richter can't be here, obviously. So don't we have an exception to the hearsay rule, with her being unavailable?'

'We don't know the source of the knowledge behind any answer, your Honour.'

'I was about to get to that,' Tanner said.

'Continue, Mr Tanner.'

'Perhaps I should point out, your Honour, that the full name of Ms Cook's firm is Sally Cook & Assocates, Family Lawyers, so that probably rules out Mrs Richter going there because she wanted advice about a hostile takeover of Citadel Resources.'

'Continue, Mr Tanner.'

'Did Nikki tell you why she was seeking advice from Sally Cook?'

'Yes.'

'What did she tell you?'

'I object again, your Honour,' Murphy said.

'Why?'

'Again, your Honour, hearsay.'

'Can I remind Mr Murphy of something, your Honour?' Tanner said.

'If it's relevant.'

'We're not in trial.'

'I'm sorry?' the judge said, narrowing her eyes.

'The trial of Justin Matheson, your Honour. It hasn't started. This application is interlocutory.'

The judge took off his glasses. 'Yes, I see,' he said. 'And so hearsay is admissible.'

Tanner nodded.

'Mr Murphy?' the judge said, looking at him with his eyebrows raised, and putting his glasses back on.

'We consider this application to be within the trial, your Honour.'

The judge shook his head. 'No, Mr Murphy. I don't think that's right. We don't have a jury yet.'

'Well, to preserve our position, I'll have my objection noted for the record.'

'Very well,' the judge said. 'Mr Tanner?'

'I asked you what Nikki told you the reason was for her seeing Sally Cook?'

'There was more than one.'

'Let's go one by one, then. What was the first complaint Nikki made to you about her marriage?'

'She was bored. Nikki was a smart girl. She wanted to do something other than modelling, but once she was married, she couldn't.'

'She couldn't?'

'John didn't like it.'

'I see. What else did she want to do?'

'She didn't know. She thought about study, maybe doing something in PR – her own business. It never really took off. John wouldn't help her. And she . . . she had a few issues with drugs. Rehab, a relapse. That set her back.'

'I'll come back to that,' Tanner said. 'Was that unhappiness the main reason she went to her lawyer?'

Amanda shook her head. 'He was seeing other women.'

'Did she tell you how she knew that?'

'She had him followed.'

'Who by?'

'An investigator.'

'Did she tell you anything else about that?'

'She told me her lawyer advised her to do it. Sally told her.'

'Did Nikki give any other reason for wanting to divorce John?'

She nodded. 'He was violent.'

Tanner waited a few seconds to let that answer sit with the judge before continuing. 'What did she tell you about that?'

'It was more . . .' She hesitated, thinking about her answer. 'She said he was a bully. He'd – she said she felt abandoned by him the second time she'd come out of rehab. He didn't – I don't think he hit her regularly, or anything like that, it was more . . . sometimes if she was having fun, he was, she said he was menacing – she used that word. She also told me about the night she told him she wanted a divorce.'

'What did she tell you?'

'He started to strangle her. She thought – she told me she thought he was going to kill her. She said she was about to pass out. She took photos of her neck after, to show the bruising.'

'Did you see the photos?'

Amanda nodded. 'She showed them to me from the email she'd sent Sally.'

'Sally Cook?'

'She told me Sally had told her to take them.'

'Did she give any other reason for wanting a divorce, that you recall?'

She nodded. 'She said she didn't love him.'

'I guess that's a good reason.'

'She . . . by the end, she told me she really didn't like him at all.'

'Did she have any further discussions with you that involved Ms Cook?'

'She told me she'd signed a pre-nuptial agreement before she married John. She said that Sally had told her she could get a better deal for her in a divorce, provided . . . well, that's why she said Sally wanted John filmed, and it was why she told her to take photos of her injuries. She said that Sally had told her to make a complete list of everything, all the mean or worse things John had done in their marriage, introducing her to drugs she –'

'Just stop there,' Tanner said. He wanted this evidence about drugs in, but he had to control and contain it. He wanted to leave some surprises for when John Richter gave his evidence.

'What drugs are you talking about?'

'John took heroin for a while. She got hooked on it after that.'

'And did she say she'd had any discussion with Sally Cook about that?'

'Just that Sally told her to make notes about it all.'

'Okay,' Tanner said. 'Is there anything else you can recall about what Nikki said Ms Cook had told her.'

'I remember she told me that the lawyer had said you – to get a legal divorce, you have to have been separated for twelve months or more. I forget the exact term. Nikki told me Sally thought that she'd already – I'm not sure if "qualified" is the right word – but she said Sally told her they'd already been separated for more than twelve months, even though he still lived in their apartment. They weren't living like a couple, or something like that.'

'So she didn't have to wait to apply to the court for a divorce?'

'Nikki told me Sally said they could file whatever you need to right away. That's what she was planning to do just before she died.'

'When exactly did she say her lawyer had advised her this? Do you recall?'

'Not the precise day, but very close to when she died. Within days.'

'You spoke that week?'

'She rang me to invite me to a birthday party with her. She filled me in on the latest . . . the advice she'd received. She said she was going to tell me more at the party.'

'She didn't make it to the party?'

Amanda nodded.

'You need to say "yes" for the transcript.'

'She died that night.'

Tanner nodded, and pretended to look at his notes. 'Did she sound to you . . . the last time she spoke to you, or the times just before that, like someone likely to overdose?'

'I object,' Murphy said. The objection was in stereo, as Richard Aitken shouted the same words, even though he was technically not involved in the argument.

'I think I just woke Mr Aitken up, your Honour,' Tanner said.

'That question is disallowed, Mr Tanner.'

'If it pleases the court,' he said. 'That's all I have for the witness.'

The judge glared at Tanner for a moment longer than normal. 'Yes, Mr Murphy,' he said, while still looking at Tanner.

'You said that you met Ms Cook once, is that right?' Murphy's first question left his mouth before he'd fully stood.

'Yes.'

'But you didn't sit in during the conference she had with Mrs Richter.'

'No. Ms Cook said that she didn't –'

'The answer is no?'

'No.'

'And you've never heard Ms Cook give any form of advice to Mrs Richter?'

'Heard myself? No.'

'And you were never a party to Mrs Richter giving any instructions to Ms Cook concerning her marriage?'

'I wasn't present, if that's what you mean?'

'And Mrs Richter didn't show you any correspondence she'd received from Ms Cook, did she?'

'No.'

'In fact, you haven't seen any document that forms part of Mrs Richter's file with the law firm Sally Cook & Associates, have you?'

Amanda paused, just as Tanner had told her to if she needed time to think about an answer. 'I don't think that's right,' she finally said.

Tanner looked at Murphy. What he'd been expecting was another no. He couldn't let the answer hang though, or Tanner could take control in re-examination.

'Is there a reason for your hesitancy, Miss Weatherill?' Murphy asked.

'Is a photo a document? I think I've read somewhere that it is?'

Clever girl, Tanner thought.

'Leaving aside any photographs, no other documents from the legal file?'

'No.'

'Just on legal matters, Miss Weatherill, you're aware that before her wedding, Mrs Richter signed a pre-nuptial agreement with Mr Richter?'

'Yes.'

'You know what I mean by a pre-nuptial agreement?'

'I think so.'

'Among other things, it can be an agreement limiting the amount of money that one spouse might have to pay the other in the event of divorce. You understand that?'

'Yes.'

'You know that Mr Richter comes from a wealthy family?'

'Yes.'

'And you understood that Mrs Richter was attempting to obtain a financial settlement from any divorce from Mr Richter that was well in excess –'

'I object,' Tanner said.

'Yes, Mr Tanner?'

'This has nothing to do with the issue of whether there's been a waiver of privilege your Honour.'

'A relevance objection?'

'Yes.'

The judge shook his head a little as if thinking, but didn't wait for Murphy to respond. 'I'll allow this line for the moment,' he said. 'It might relate to the issue of what instructions or advice was given.'

'Do you need me to repeat my question?' Murphy asked.

Amanda shook her head. 'Nikki was only after what she thought was fair.'

'What she thought was fair? Did she mention a figure?'

'No.'

'May we take it then that she didn't tell you what advice her lawyer had given about what figure might be achievable?'

'No.'

'You mentioned in your evidence that Mrs Richter was a drug addict.'

'I think I talked about her being in rehab.'

'Well,' Murphy said, 'presumably she was in rehab because of some form of addiction, correct?'

'Yes.'

'So she was a drug addict?'

'At certain times of her life she lost her way.'

'Does that mean yes?'

'Yes.'

'And she died of a drug overdose?'

'If you say so.'

Tanner didn't mind that Amanda indicated to the court any doubts she had about that, but he didn't like the tone. Judges don't like sarcasm.

'I'm sorry, Miss Weatherill. Do you have some theory that differs from the findings of the coroner or the investigation of the New South Wales Police concerning Mrs Richter's death?'

Amanda looked at Murphy for a long moment. 'No,' she said. 'I was just very shocked at how she died.'

'You were surprised that a former drug addict might take drugs again?'

'I spoke to her most days.'

'Were you ever present when Mrs Richter took any form of illegal narcotic?'

'I object,' Tanner said. 'That question is totally unrelated to the issue your Honour has to determine.'

'What's the relevance of that?' the judge asked Murphy.

Murphy raised his eyebrows as if the answer was obvious. 'Well, your Honour,' he said, 'Mrs Richter died from a heroin overdose. Presumably she'd suffered a relapse of her addiction. I'd like to explore what this witness knew of it. If she was under the effects of a drug like heroin, in my submission she wouldn't be in a condition to be properly said to waive privilege, which on our understanding of the law would need to be an act of a sound mind, not one under the influence of a narcotic.'

Tanner was on his feet before the judge could rule. 'Your Honour, I also object to the form of the question. As it's framed now, it's asking the witness to go back years. That can't possibly be relevant.'

The judge nodded. 'I think that's right, Mr Murphy. I think you need to limit your time frame to the period from when Mrs Richter first told the witness she was intending to seek a divorce from Mr Richter.'

'Well, your Honour, in my view we shouldn't be so limited. It may be that –'

'That's my ruling, Mr Murphy.'

'If it please the court,' Murphy said.

'I wasn't aware Nikki was taking any drugs at all before she died,' Amanda said, not waiting for Murphy to repeat the question. 'To my knowledge, she hadn't taken any illegal drug for more than . . . it would have to be at least eighteen months before she died.'

'Did you ever take any illegal drugs with Mrs Richter, Miss Weatherill?'

'I object,' Tanner said quickly. 'That question shouldn't have been asked, your Honour.'

'What's the relevance of that question, Mr Murphy?' Knight said.

'Well, your Honour,' Murphy responded slowly, 'we know Mrs Richter had been a drug addict. We know she died of an overdose, at about the time she's said to have waived privilege. If Miss Weatherill also –'

'Do you have any evidence at all to support your question?'

'The witness was Mrs Richter's best friend, as she says, and –'

'That's not remotely a proper basis for your question, Mr Murphy,' the judge said angrily.

Murphy knew he had no legal standing to ask the question. If Amanda Weatherill was going to be called for the defence in order to tell the jury the things she knew about John Richter, the prosecutor was likely to drag her own past into the fray. The question wasn't about winning the privilege argument, it was about scaring her off.

'Well, if your Honour is against me,' Murphy said.

'I am,' the judge said.

'I'll proceed with something else.'

'Please do.'

'Miss Weatherill, you understand that you're giving evidence to assist the defence of Justin Matheson in the case brought against him by the State for the murder of Elena Mancini, correct?'

Amanda paused before answering. 'I've been asked to give evidence about what Nikki told me she'd told her lawyer, and what her lawyer told her.'

'Yes,' Murphy said in a tone that was heading towards condescension, 'but you understand that Mr Matheson's lawyers are seeking access to the legal files of Ms Cook, correct?'

'Yes.'

'And you understand they want to do that because they think the contents of those files might in some way help Mr Matheson?'

'Yes.'

'So you do understand that they want you here to help Mr Matheson – at least to that extent?'

'Yes.'

'You had an affair with Mr Matheson, didn't you, Miss Weatherill? A sexual affair.'

Amanda Weatherill's eyes widened. She froze for a moment, like she was wishing the question away. The pause lasted long enough for Jane Ross to write on a post-it note and put it in front of him: *WTF?*

'I object,' Tanner said. 'Again, your Honour, that question can't raise any matter of relevance to this application.'

'Well,' the judge said slowly, 'I think it can. I'll allow the question.'

Amanda Weatherill took a deep breath, and it was already obvious she was fighting off tears. 'It was a long time ago.'

Murphy paused for effect. 'How long ago, Miss Weatherill?'

'About seven years,' she said softly.

'You have to keep your voice up for the court reporters, Miss Weatherill,' the judge said. The shift in tone was obvious. She was no longer a sweet young thing.

'And how long did this affair last?'

'Not long. A few weeks.'

'I see, and after your sexual affair with Mr Matheson ended, did you continue to see him?'

'Very occasionally. Probably not – sometimes if I went out with Nikki, and a group of her friends, or with Nikki and Jack, Justin might sometimes be there. We didn't see each other privately. I mean, we didn't see each other alone.'

'Not at all?'

She paused. 'He – when my brother got injured, he rang me. After he heard about it. We had a coffee. That's all.'

'And did Mr Matheson offer your brother any financial assistance after his injury?'

'He paid for a special wheelchair.'

'A very expensive one, I understand?'

'Nikki and Jack helped . . . Nikki made Jack help make my parents' house wheelchair friendly. They paid for some additional therapy over and above what the government – Justin just bought the wheelchair.'

'You must have been very grateful for that?'

'Yes.'

'Do you recall swearing an affidavit for this application, Miss Weatherill?'

'Yes.'

'And you were obviously told by those representing Mr Matheson that on my application you'd been ordered to give all your evidence orally?'

'Yes.'

Murphy looked at the court officer, and held out a document towards him. 'I'm giving you a document now, Miss Weatherill. Is that a copy of the affidavit you swore?'

'Yes.'

'Could you take the court to the paragraph where you mention having an affair with Mr Matheson?'

She glared at Murphy. 'It doesn't.'

'Very well. Could you take us to the paragraph dealing with Mr Matheson paying for your brother's wheelchair?'

'I object, your Honour,' Tanner said. 'This is badgering. My friend knows it's not there. He can make that submission.'

'There's nothing in here about your prior relationship with Mr Matheson, Miss Weatherill?' Knight asked.

'No, your Honour.'

'I see. Yes, Mr Murphy?'

'Why not, Miss Weatherill?'

'I didn't think it was relevant.'

'Did Mr Matheson's lawyers share that view?'

She shook her head. 'I didn't tell them.'

'Why?'

'I told you. I didn't think it was relevant.'

'Is that an honest answer?'

'Yes.'

'You're asking the court to believe that Nikki Richter told you intimate things about her dealings with her lawyer, correct?'

'I'm not asking anyone to believe anything,' she said. 'I'm telling the truth.'

'You say you understand you're helping Mr Matheson with your evidence today, but you seriously thought it of no relevance that you once had a sexual affair with him, and that he financially aided your brother after a serious injury?'

'It has nothing to do with what Nikki told me.'

'Can I suggest to you it does?'

'Is that a question?'

'May I suggest to you that Mrs Richter told you none of the things you allege she told you concerning her conversations with Ms Cook.'

'She did.'

'And can I suggest that you've only come forward with this false evidence to help your friend and former lover, Mr Matheson.'

'You can suggest it,' Amanda said, regaining some composure, 'but that's not true.'

'Nothing further, your Honour,' Murphy then said.

'Is now a convenient time, your Honour?' Tanner said. It was nearly eleven thirty, and they'd been going for an hour and a half. A fifteen-minute break would give him the chance to talk to Amanda Weatherill now that her cross was over. 'I'd like a chance to take instructions on a few matters.'

The judge paused, and took his glasses off. 'Yes,' he said slowly. 'Fifteen minutes, then. We'll resume at eleven forty-five.'

42

When Amanda Weatherill entered the defence room, the tears that she'd managed to fight off in the courtroom had started to flow. The colour had drained from her face. Tanner was angry, but one look at her told him to take a breath and recalibrate.

'Why didn't you tell us?' he asked as calmly as he could, gesturing for her to sit at the small conference table.

'I – I didn't want to upset Justin's wife,' she said.

'We could have defused it. Judges have to work hard to believe people if they've lied or not been upfront –'

'I didn't lie.' Her voice was strained, cracking. She took a deep breath and closed her eyes. 'I didn't know he was married,' she said. 'I broke it off when I found out.'

Tanner nodded, and Jane Ross finally found a small pack of tissues she had buried in her document bag.

Amanda took a tissue and blew her nose. 'I didn't think it would be great for Justin either.'

'You're a pretty minor thing compared to being charged with murder.'

'Peter,' Jane said sharply.

'I didn't think anyone knew,' Amanda said.

'Did you tell Nikki?' Tanner asked.

She looked at him, then at the ground. She gave a small nod.

'She'd just married Jack. You didn't think she'd tell him?'

'She said she wouldn't. I was embarrassed . . . she said she wouldn't tell anyone.'

'And the wheelchair for your brother?'

'Justin didn't want anyone to know it was him. He didn't want to embarrass my family.'

'Nikki again?'

'I don't know.'

'Okay. I'm going to ask you some questions. I want the truth. Then you're going to have to get back in the box and tell the judge. Okay?'

She looked at him meekly, then nodded.

'You recall Mr Murphy asked you some questions about a short relationship you had with Mr Matheson about seven years ago?' Tanner asked when his re-examination began.

'Yes.'

'Where did you meet him?'

'On a boat. A party on a boat.'

'Where?'

'Here. In Sydney Harbour.'

'Whose boat was it?'

'John Richter's. Well, I don't – it may have been his father's.'

'Who else was at the party?'

'Nikki asked me.'

'Was it a large party?'

'A lot of people,' she said. 'Most I didn't know.'

'And you met Justin on board?'

'Yes.'

'What about Mr Matheson's wife?'

She shook her head. 'No.'

'Did Mr Matheson talk about his wife to you?'

'No.'

'When did you find out he was married?'

'The day before I broke it off with him. Nikki told me. It was about three weeks later.'

'Can we take it from your answer that this was the reason you ended the relationship?'

'Yes.'

'These matters aren't in your affidavit, Miss Weatherill. Why not?'

'I didn't think what happened between Justin and me had anything to do with Nikki's marriage.'

'Mr Murphy asked you about your brother's wheelchair. You recall that?'

'I'm not going to make things up about what a friend told me because of that.' She started to cry. 'I wouldn't lie for him,' she said when she'd composed herself.

'I have nothing further, your Honour,' Tanner said. He sat down and looked at the judge, who was still looking at Amanda.

'Thank you, Miss Weatherill,' Knight said. 'You're free to go.'

Tanner kept his oral submission short and to the point. The hard legal lifting was done in writing.

'Mrs Richter did what most people would do when telling a friend about what advice her lawyer had given,' Tanner began. 'She gave the substance of the advice. Get him on film. Catch him out with other women. When he hurt her, Ms Cook told her to take photos. Do all that so I can start negotiating on the pre-nup. You've already been living apart for twelve months in the eyes of the law, we can file for divorce now. The finer details may not have been there, but the substance was. And when it comes to what Mrs Richter told Miss Weatherill she'd told her lawyer – well, that was more detailed, as you'd expect it to be. She was her closest friend. She told her lawyer and her best friend the same thing – the awful details of her marriage. The cat's out of the bag, your Honour. The estate can't put it back in now. There was a clear waiver of privilege.'

The law wasn't on Murphy's side, so he went after Amanda Weatherill. He suggested she was a witness who'd say anything that would help Matheson's cause in a case where the stakes were so high. He told the judge that Nikki Richter was a liar too. She'd told her lawyer untruths about her husband, all so she could blackmail him into paying her more than she was legally due under her pre-nup.

'Does it matter if Mrs Richter was untruthful to her lawyer in the instructions she gave?' Knight asked.

'It does to Mr Richter, your Honour. It also affects the admissibility of these legal files.'

'That's a different question. We're dealing with waiver of privilege. The waiver can occur whether or not Mrs Richter's instructions to Ms Cook were truthful or not. Admissibility will be dealt with at trial, and only if Mr Tanner seeks to make use of any document from the files.'

It's rare for a lawyer to interrupt another during final address. It wasn't something Tanner did unless he thought he was on strong ground. Today was one of those days.

'I hesitate to interrupt the debate between your Honour and my friend, but I'm afraid I have to.'

Murphy pretended to be astonished, before looking back to the judge to intervene.

Knight took his glasses off and looked at Tanner. 'You have to?'

'Yes, your Honour. Because as I'm sitting here, I'm having difficulty working out who Mr Murphy is appearing for.'

The judge sucked on the tip of his glasses. 'He announced his appearance for the estate.'

'Yes. And I'm wondering what a lawyer who's acting for the estate of the late Mrs Richter is doing calling her a liar in court?'

There was a flicker in the judge's eyes, and for a moment Tanner thought he detected a wry smile. The judge swung his chair slightly and now directed his gaze at Murphy, but Tanner continued before he could speak.

'You see, your Honour, I'm assuming Mr Murphy is getting his instructions from the executor of the estate, Mr Richter.

And I guess I can understand why he – as an individual man – would want to refute the suggestion that he was a serial adulterer, abusive to his wife, and that he nearly strangled her one night before her death. What I'm struggling with, though, is how Mr Richter can give those instructions as the executor of the late Mrs Richter's estate. Because I'm pretty sure an executor has to act in the best interests of the estate. And calling the deceased a liar is not in her estate's best interests.'

'Mr Murphy?' Knight said.

'There's nothing contrary to the interests of the estate in Mr Richter instructing me that his late wife was untruthful about certain matters. His duties as an executor are to find the will, make funeral arrangements, obtain a death certificate, dispose of the assets and distribute them to beneficiaries.'

'So my friend has two clients today,' Tanner said. 'Mr Richter the aggrieved widower, and Mr Richter the executor of Mrs Richter's estate. I usually have enough trouble with one client.'

'Who are the beneficiaries under the will, Mr Murphy?'

'Mr Richter for one, your Honour.'

'Anyone else?'

Some whispering took place among the legal team behind Murphy. Murphy apologised and joined the gathering.

'Mrs Richter's parents as well, your Honour,' he said. 'And her two siblings.'

'Doesn't the trustee have to act in the best interests of beneficiaries?' Tanner said. 'I wonder if it would surprise the late Mrs Richter's parents that it was in their best interests to hear their daughter called a liar in court?'

'That's a ridiculous comment,' Murphy snapped.

'Is it, Mr Murphy?' Knight said. 'How is any of this advancing the ends of the estate? It might assist Mr Richter personally, but –'

'He's a beneficiary too, your Honour.'

'He's not the estate,' the judge snapped. There was a long pause as the judge looked to the ceiling, gathering his thoughts. 'I'm troubled by this, Mr Murphy,' he finally said.

'We can do a written note for your Honour on this issue.'

Tanner jumped to his feet. 'I hope Mr Murphy doesn't think he and whoever actually is his client can delay a murder trial so that some thesis can be done on –'

'Sit down, Mr Tanner,' Knight said. He looked at Murphy again. 'Is there anything further you want to say about why privilege was not waived?'

'No, your Honour.'

'All right. You can have until four pm to put in writing what you want on the matter that's just been discussed. You have a limit of five pages. Mr Tanner, you can have until seven to respond. The same page limit.'

'I do have a murder trial to prepare, your Honour,' Tanner said.

'You have a junior, and a large law firm instructing you – delegate. Either way, I'm ruling on this matter at ten tomorrow. If I rule there's been a waiver, we'll start empanelling a jury at two to enable some time for the parties to look at the documents. Otherwise we start at eleven.'

'Thank you, your Honour.'

'And I can let the parties know that I intend to examine the files of Ms Cook as part of my deliberations.'

'We'd resist that, your Honour,' Murphy said.

'Why?'

'Mr Tanner isn't claiming that the documents aren't privileged. He only alleges waiver. Your Honour would only need to look at the documents if you had to make a determination as to whether privilege attached to them at a prima facie level. That's not in issue.'

'I need to determine if what's in the files lines up with Miss Weatherill's evidence, Mr Murphy.'

For an instant, Murphy looked like he might press his objection, but then stopped himself. 'If the court pleases,' he said.

The judge glared at him for a long moment. 'Looking at those documents won't cause me to become prejudiced, Mr Murphy, if that's what's – '

'I wouldn't dare suggest that, your Honour,' Murphy said quickly.

The judge nodded. 'Good. Because first, based on your submissions, I'll only find untruths in the file – the untruths being any representation of fact made by Mrs Richter to her lawyer that is critical of her husband. Secondly, a jury will decide the outcome of this trial, not me. Thirdly, whatever is in the file, rest assured I'll be able to do my duty as a judge of this court. Is there anything else?' He was already leaving his chair to adjourn when Murphy said 'no'.

When the judge had left, Tanner told the rest of his team that he wanted a few minutes with his client before he was taken back to Silverwater.

When they took their seats in the interview room near the cells, Tanner looked at Matheson for a long time before speaking.

'I bet you're glad the judge cleared the court and made a suppression order, Justin?'

Matheson said nothing.

'Are there any witnesses in this case other than Klaudia, Deborah Edelman and Amanda that you've slept with? I noticed the court reporter looking at you. Anything happened with her?'

Matheson glared at him, but still didn't speak.

Tanner brought his palm down hard on the desk. 'I'm waiting for an answer, Justin!'

Matheson sat back in his chair in shock. 'I didn't think that was a serious question,' he said.

'Really? This is a serious statement: If I find out you're holding out on me again over something important, I'm walking out on you. I don't care if it's mid-fucking-trial. Is that clear?'

'We didn't think it –'

'I don't care what you think, Justin. You tell me everything. Just don't tell me you hurt Elena. Then you'll have an even bigger fucking problem than you have now.'

'I didn't touch that girl,' he said.

'Unlike Amanda. How long had you been married when you started that?'

Matheson looked angry for a moment, then breathed out, and calmed himself. 'It was a mistake,' he said. 'I didn't make one like that again until Klaudia.'

'What was Deborah? A triumph?'

Again Matheson glared, but said nothing.

'You know, Justin,' Tanner said slowly, 'we might have to call Amanda in our case. Her evidence won't be suppressed then. Not in a jury trial.'

'Do you think we'll win the application today?'

'Maybe.'

'Then can't we just use the documents in the files that –'

'Amanda can give a human dimension to what kind of man Richter is that documents alone can't. She can be like having Nikki in the courtroom for us.' Tanner paused and shook his head. 'What I'm saying, Justin, is that if I think we need to call her, you probably should have a conversation with your wife about Amanda.'

Matheson ran his hand through his hair, and shook his head. 'This will be the last straw, Peter. She will –'

'I'm not a marriage counsellor, Justin. If my judgement is to call Amanda, we call her.'

'I don't get a say?'

'Sure you do. But if we disagree, you get overruled. Getting convicted of murder might be a bigger final straw for your marriage than Amanda.'

'I thought you had to follow my instructions?'

Tanner gave a weary smile. 'Do I look like the kind of lawyer who's going to follow your instructions over my judgement? I'm giving you a heads up. We can arrange for you to see her before court. Speak to your wife.'

Matheson glared at Tanner again, went to say something, then the fight went out of his eyes, and he shook his head. 'Just – just give me twenty-four hours' notice, okay? If you think you have to call Amanda, just give me that.'

Tanner shook his head. Not quite in disgust, but heading there.

'Aren't you meant to be making me feel good about myself?' Matheson said. 'Building my confidence before I have to give evidence in my fucking murder trial?'

Tanner laughed softly, and stood up. 'We'll get to that bit, Justin,' he said. 'I'll give you twenty-four hours' notice.'

43

Tanner delegated Jane Ross to hear the judge's ruling on the privilege argument on Tuesday morning. Her call from court came through at twenty past nine. Amanda Weatherill's evidence had been accepted: the judge found that Nikki Richter had waived the privilege that attached to her communications with her lawyer Sally Cook. The defence now had access to her files.

Tanner told Ross to arrange for a paralegal to start copying the documents. 'Come straight back here,' he said.

'Pete?'

'Yeah.'

'Just on that. I know you know what you're doing. I was just wondering –'

'Spit it out, Jane.'

'Justin had a hard day yesterday.'

'You want me to be nicer to him?'

'It couldn't hurt.'

'Do you think Richard Aitken will be nice to him when he's cross-examined?'

'He's on the other side. We're Justin's team.'

'You hold his hand, Jane,' Tanner said. 'Just be careful where he puts his.'

As Tanner put his mobile down, his desk phone rang, and he punched speaker. He was told it was Richard Aitken.

'Are you looking forward to reading Sally Cook's files, Richard?'

'They're not in evidence yet.'

'My solicitor's making twelve bound sets for the jury.'

'Can we meet later this morning?'

Tanner paused. It wasn't a request he was expecting. 'I've got a murder trial starting today. I'm not sure I can.'

'Cut the crap. It won't take long.'

'What's it about?'

'It's better we do this face to face. Eleven thirty? I'll take up twenty minutes at most. I'll come to you?'

'The prosecutor's office will come to my chambers?'

'Think of it as a once-only offer.'

'Is that what you'll be bringing?'

'I'll see you at eleven thirty.'

When Ross and Porter arrived back from court, he told them about the call from Aitken.

'You think he's going to try and sell us a deal?' Ross said.

'What kind of deal?' Porter asked.

Tanner held up his hand. 'Let's just hear what he has to say.'

'Is this because we have Cook's files now?'

'Maybe. You spoke to Aitken's junior, didn't you?' Tanner said, looking at Jane Ross. 'About Klaudia being here?'

She nodded. 'He told me she arrived last Friday. You think something's up with her?'

'I don't know.'

'If he offers a deal, will you ask him why?'

'I'll fish for what I can.'

'Have you looked at the film yet?' Tanner said after Aitken had taken a seat in his room next to Ross and Porter right on eleven thirty. 'Some of those girls he was sleeping with look like hookers. And those bruises on the dead wife's neck. Your witness is all class.'

'Are you finished?' Aitken said.

'Why are you here?'

'To remind you that Elena Mancini had your client's DNA under her nails when she was found dead.'

'I can think of an innocent explanation.'

'Your client didn't offer any to police when he was questioned.'

'He was drowsy.'

'Mr Richter can explain the lawyer's files, and we're comfortable he'll be believed on that, and about the night your client killed Elena. Miss Dabrowska will be too.'

'Why are you here?'

'Discharging my obligation to try and save the state of New South Wales the time and cost of a trial.'

'What's the deal?'

Aitken paused for a moment. 'Involuntary manslaughter,' he said. 'We'll agree facts to the sentencing judge that says your client was drunk, grabbed her, had no intent to kill, was just very clumsy. With this judge, that sounds like a range of about five to seven years to me.'

'Sounds like an unfortunate accident, not a crime,' Tanner said. 'You should release him now.'

Aitken smiled tightly, and shook his head. 'Perhaps we should nominate him for some Australia Day honour too?'

'The Queen's knighted worse people.'

'We're not giving your guy a pass. Matheson got drunk, and gave everyone coke. It was no accident, grabbing this girl. He did it with negligent or reckless force. She died as a result. That's manslaughter. Nothing else flies.'

'Why?'

'Why what?'

'Why are you so worried you can't get a conviction now? Something more than the Cook files?'

'I doubt you'll even get them into evidence. They're just a smoke screen.'

'All my clients' defences are smoke screens, Richard. Is Dabrowska your problem?'

Aitken stood, and walked to the door. 'I'm going to get a conviction for at least manslaughter, Peter. Your client is taking a hell of a risk going for complete acquittal. We can do a deal on intoxication knocking out intent to kill, leaving him with manslaughter. You've been around long enough to know the judge will give him something like five to seven for that in a case like this. You might even get luckier. I think Knight's an old boy of your client's school. That might get another year or two discount.'

'He says he didn't touch the girl.'

Aitken shook his head. 'You should talk to your client about our offer. It won't be on the table once we start.'

'I'd rather talk to Klaudia.'

'I have to go,' Aitken said.

'Ask Richter how hard you have to squeeze someone's throat to leave the kind of bruises he left on Nikki. That was done with reckless force too.'

'Once we start, no deal on manslaughter,' Aitken said, leaving the room.

After they'd grabbed lunch, Tanner, Ross and Porter went to see Matheson in the holding cells at Darlinghurst Court, where his trial was due to commence in a little over an hour.

'Two things,' Tanner said when they were seated in the interview room. 'The first is good news.'

'They're dropping the charges?' Matheson said dryly.

'You're keeping your sense of humour at least.'

'I don't have much else left.'

'We have Nikki's divorce files.'

Matheson took a deep breath, then let it out slowly. 'Has anyone looked at them yet?'

'Some of them.'

'And?'

'They'll help,' Tanner said. 'We need to discuss something, though.' He relayed the conversation they'd had with the prosecutor, and the terms of the offer to accept a plea of manslaughter. 'It's not that bad a deal.'

'Maybe five years? I have a conviction for manslaughter. I see my kids once a month. I lose my career, my reputation. That's a good deal?'

'Your reputation is hanging by a thread, Justin. Let's put that aside and focus on facts. They have Klaudia. Maybe she'll come across as a sympathetic witness. They have Richter. I'll try to make him look like the prick he is, but Klaudia is going to say he's telling the truth. Believe her, believe him. Then there's the DNA. We have to sell a big conspiracy to get around what was under Elena's nails.'

Matheson looked at the ground. 'So you're saying I should take it?'

'No. I'm telling you it's not the worst offer I've ever had. I can't guarantee you five years, but this is a reasonable judge we have. If you plead to the facts the prosecutor seems willing to agree to, you might even do a touch better than five.'

'We can win, though, right? My chances are better with the files from Nikki's lawyer?'

'We can win. We can lose. That's why five to seven is something you have to think about. It leaves you with a life. Twenty plus for murder is a different ball game.'

Matheson ran his hand over his face. 'This is hard.'

'I can get Aitken to leave it on the table until tomorrow,' Tanner said. 'You should talk it through with your family.'

Matheson looked at Tanner, and a sad smile came across his face. 'Sarah and I got married young, you know?'

Tanner glanced at Ross. 'Justin, we should –'

'With Amanda . . . Sarah and I – we'd had a massive fight. It was over . . . Jesus, it was over whether we were having Christmas lunch at her parents' house or at mine. You know, "it was with your parents last year", "my grandmother won't last another year" . . . it got out of hand. I spent two nights on a friend's couch. It's why Sarah wasn't with me on the boat. I met Amanda . . . I'd been drinking all day . . .'

'We can fill in the blanks from there, Justin.'

'I liked her. I should have – I let it go on for a few weeks. She was furious when she found out.'

'Do you blame her?'

Matheson smiled bitterly. 'I was so fucking guilty about what I did, I caved over Christmas. We had it at Sarah's parents' place.'

'Justin, the offer that's been made – you have to –'

'Then with Deborah –' Matheson continued as though Tanner hadn't spoken, '– we were out of town, we had dinner, she turns up virtually naked at my hotel door –'

'We've heard the story, Justin.'

'I didn't do the things her lawyers put in her claim. You believe me, right?'

Tanner looked at his client for a long moment. 'Can I tell you something about my job, Justin?'

'Sure.'

Tanner leant back and took a deep breath, which he then let out slowly. 'My first murder case was a guilty plea,' he then said. 'My client was thirty-one years old, and had two stepchildren. He came home drunk one night, and went to bed. He soon woke up, though, because his two-year-old stepson still cried half the night. He'd been doing it for too long, according to my client. So do you know what he did, Justin?'

Matheson shook his head.

'He took the iron his wife had left out after doing some laundry, went into the boy's bedroom, and beat him to death with it.'

'Jesus Christ,' Matheson said.

'In relative terms, you're not a bad person compared to some of my clients. None of them has bought anyone a wheelchair. It doesn't matter what I believe, but I don't think you're a killer, if that's really what you want to hear.'

Matheson nodded slowly. 'Thanks,' he said, 'because I didn't do it. Tell them no to the deal.'

Tanner nodded. 'I won't be sending you a card at Christmas when we're done, though, okay?'

'I didn't think so.'

'I'm also going to get Charles to draft up a document saying we've passed on to you what the prosecutor offered, and our advice about that, but you want to push on to seek an acquittal. You're going to have to sign that document.'

Matheson smile crookedly. 'You don't trust me, Peter?'

Tanner stood to leave. 'If you were a run of the mill crim, Justin, I might,' he said. 'But you're not. You work for a global investment bank. No, I don't trust you.'

44

That afternoon, Richard Aitken told the members of the jury pool that the accused, Justin Matheson, was charged with the murder of Elena Mancini. At the end of the trial he would ask them to convict him of that offence. They would also be entitled to convict him of manslaughter if that was their verdict. He then read out a list of the prosecution's witnesses. Based on that information, he asked anyone who thought they couldn't give impartial consideration to the evidence to apply to be excused.

A woman stood, and explained that three years before, she'd sat on an insider trading case that had lasted twelve weeks.

'Enough service for two lifetimes,' Knight said, and the woman was allowed to leave.

After she'd gone, the identification numbers of those remaining were put in a box, and a court officer pulled them out, one at a time. The prosecution and the defence were each allowed three challenges to the empanelment of a juror. In New South Wales, counsel have to make a call on whether someone is likely to favour the defence or the prosecution simply by the way they look. It was hard to know whether a handsome banker like Justin Matheson, who'd been unfaithful to his wife, would be better off with women jurors than men. And what would those jurors make of John Richter? There wasn't much science to it, but Tanner decided to exercise the accused's challenges on three men.

Once the jury panel was sworn in, they were left with eight women and five men, one of whom would act as an alternate if required. They ranged in age from late twenties to early sixties.

When the jury was seated in their box, the courtroom quickly filled to capacity. Then the judge cleared his throat in a loud fashion, the murmuring died down, and the show began.

Justice Knight's opening was as Tanner expected – concise, efficient and by the book. Thirty years as a prosecutor and a decade as a Supreme Court judge meant Knight was able to deliver his comments without notes. First, he reminded the jury of the charge. It was murder, with the alternative charge of manslaughter. He told them that the accused had pleaded not guilty to both charges.

He told them next that they had each just become a judge. He would rule on the law, on what evidence was relevant, and what was not. On the law, they had to follow him; on the facts, they were in charge. They decided what witnesses could be believed. And, when it was all over, they would decide a verdict.

He then explained the role of the Crown Prosecutor, Mr Aitken, and warned the jury not to put any special weight on his arguments just because he represented the state. He then introduced Tanner, and his co-counsel, Ms Ross.

They were told they needed to elect a foreperson. It was up to them how they did that, but no matter who was chosen, they remained equals in the jury room. The foreperson would announce their verdict, and through that person any concerns or questions about evidence or procedure could be relayed to the judge.

The judge then gave the jurors the usual warnings and admonitions about not discussing the case with people outside the jury room. 'You should keep away from the internet during the course of this trial, ladies and gentlemen,' the judge said. 'You mustn't text anyone or use your phones to communicate anything about this trial. You should also keep away from – and I apologise, but I will have to read this part – Facebook,

Twitter, LinkedIn, Instagram or YouTube – or any other social networking site. I have no idea why any intelligent member of the community would want to use any of the things I have just mentioned, but if my assessment is wrong about that, then please at least stay away from the attractions of these things, whatever they may be, during the course of this trial.

'Remember your oath, ladies and gentlemen,' the judge said. 'This case has attracted publicity. It will continue to do so. That publicity will not be helpful to you in your deliberations. Put what you have read, if anything, or seen, out of your minds. Do not follow the case in the media. Your duty is to determine your verdict only on the evidence presented to this court. Newspaper articles and television stories are not evidence. Although I've already asked, if any of you feel, having considered any matter in the press or media you may have seen concerning this trial, that you can't objectively assess the evidence, please ask now to be excused. It is of fundamental importance that you are able to fulfil the oath you have sworn to be impartial.'

The judge eyed each member of the jury in turn, and none of them moved.

Finally, he outlined for them what would happen at the trial. Opening statements, the Crown witnesses and other evidence, the defence case, the closing statements, then his summation. At the end of it all were the things that mattered the most: their deliberation; their verdict.

He told them that a guilty verdict could only be reached if the prosecution proved its case beyond any reasonable doubt. The accused, on the other hand, had to prove nothing. He was presumed to be innocent.

Tanner had heard these words many times before, and no longer believed them. Jurors didn't presume anyone sitting in a criminal dock was innocent. You had to make some dent in a prosecution case to win a trial.

When Aitken was invited to open, he commenced the way all good prosecutors should in a murder trial. He told them Justin Matheson was a killer.

'In the early hours of the morning of 9 October last year,' he began, 'a struggle took place between Justin Matheson and a young woman called Elena Mancini. The result of that struggle left Elena with a fracture to the skull, and a brain haemorrhage from which she died quickly. Justin Matheson killed her.

'He may not have known that he'd killed Elena at the time. He was found semiconscious by a witness shortly after the struggle. That he killed her, though, there is no doubt.

'Mr Matheson is 191 centimetres tall, members of the jury. That's six foot three in the old scale. He weighed eighty-nine kilos. Most of that is muscle. He played fullback for his school and university rugby teams.

'Elena Mancini was 178 centimetres tall. Five-ten in the old scale. She'd always been a thin girl, her parents have told me. That's Mr and Mrs Mancini behind me, by the way. Her elder sister is seated with them. Elena was Italian, out here to study English literature at one of our universities. She weighed forty-nine kilograms. The struggle I mentioned – it wasn't a fair one.

'Elena was twenty-two years old when she died. That doesn't seem fair either, does it? Her parents are here to see that justice is now done. That's what will ultimately rest in your hands.'

Tanner sat still as Aitken spoke. Occasionaly he stole a glance at a juror to see how closely they were following the prosecutor. They were all listening intently, and provided the opening didn't go on too long, they would continue to. This was a murder trial, after all, and the stakes were high. And, with each word, they got higher still for Justin Matheson. When the trial had started, he was the accused. The prosecutor had now given him a different label: killer. It would be up to Tanner to try to shift that stain.

Aitken continued his opening, succinctly running through the facts as they were known. Justin and John Richter at Pantheon. The trip to the Richter estate. Justin Matheson bringing out the drugs. Elena, not long after, lying in a pool of her own blood.

With leave of the court, he was allowed to show a photo of her body that would later be tendered as evidence through the chief investigating police officer: Elena, lying face up on the floor, blood around her head, staining the carpet. Yellow evidence markers were placed near some blood splatter on the edge of the coffee table, and next to the main stain.

Aitken embraced all the weaknesses in his case, and made them strengths. John Richter had been out drinking a few nights after his wife's funeral. He went to his club, and two young women came back to his home. People react differently to grief. He wasn't partying – he was anaesthetising himself. He was the one who had rung the ambulance, and sought the police. He didn't try to cover things up for his friend, or for himself.

Aitken skirted deftly around any evidence that might not be admissible. Deborah Edelman was only indirectly referred to. 'Justin Matheson's family and friends might think they know him,' Aitken said. 'Maybe they only know part of him. You'll have to decide, members of the jury, if they really know what he's capable of.

'One thing we do know about the accused,' Aitken continued, 'is that he's capable of drinking a lot of alcohol.' He went on to explain to the jury that intoxication was no defence to manslaughter.

He left his strongest point for last, just as Tanner would have done if the roles were reversed.

'Elena Mancini can't tell us what happened that night. Something can though: science. You will hear evidence from a forensics expert about what was found under Elena's nails. Justin Matheson was found there. His DNA. So if Elena Mancini can't tell us who killed her, that doesn't mean we don't know. The evidence will speak for her.'

When Tanner moved to the lectern, he was holding one of the police photos of Elena Mancini lying dead on the floor of John Richter's retreat. He showed it to the jury, then slowly put the photo down on the bar table in front of him. 'A lot of lawyers would have objected to the prosecutor showing you this photo in his opening,' he began. 'They'd say it's too prejudicial to have it shown unnecessarily.'

Tanner paused and briefly scanned each member of the jury. 'There's a natural reaction, when you see a photo like that,' he continued, 'and I bet every one of you had it. "I want to find who is responsible for this." A young woman, her whole life in front of her, has been killed. Someone must be held to account for this crime.

'That was my reaction. Whoever is responsible for this act, they have to be punished. And although I can't speak for them, or feel the pain they've suffered, it's not hard to imagine that at least one of the wishes of Elena Mancini's family is that: Whoever hurt our daughter, whoever took my sister from me, they must be held to account. As a society, we have a duty to allocate responsibility, and to punish justly.'

He paused again, deliberately. Addresses to juries could not be rushed. You want them to absorb each point before moving to the next. Fast-talking lawyers persuade no one.

'That's a big responsibility. There's another one, though. Equally important, and the burden falls to you. It's the duty to allocate responsibilty to the *right* person. That's the most fundamental reason for you being here. And here also, members of the jury, is another family. They're sitting behind me. The Matheson family. Justin's mother and father, his sister and brother, and his wife, Sarah. Scattered around the courtroom are members of his wider family, his friends and colleagues. All of them share something in common with Elena's family. They want the person responsible for her killing brought to justice. He waited again for just a moment, scanning the faces of the jurors.

'My job is to tell you that Justin Matheson is not the person responsible for the death of Elena Mancini.' He paused again, hoping it would add weight to what was the defence's definitive statement.

'You may have heard, perhaps from television shows, or even from a novel, that defence lawyers prefer not to call their clients to give evidence. If you can throw enough doubt on the prosecution case, so the theory goes, don't call the accused. Well, members of the jury, you will be hearing from my client in this trial. He'll tell his story. And what he will tell you is what I have. He did not hurt Elena Mancini. He did not struggle with her. He did not throw her to the ground. He is not her killer. He,' Tanner repeated slowly, 'is not her killer.'

It was harder to decide what not to say. If Matheson was not the killer, the jury might expect him to say who was, even if the list of candidates was obviously a short one. And declaring John Richter the killer carried its own risks. The main risk was of shifting the burden. No matter what he told the jury about reasonable doubt, and no matter how strongly the judge re-inforced it, he couldn't risk them convicting Matheson because he didn't prove John Richter was the real killer. And he knew that the prosecution's subliminal message would be this: If the defence attacks our witness but doesn't prove it was him, then it has to be the accused. Tanner had thought about it on a daily basis for weeks. Saying less in opening was better. Even if that meant not mentioning the elephant in the room.

The DNA was different. You can't ignore the prosecution's best point. 'Mr Aitken, the Crown Prosecutor, made mention of the DNA evidence he intends to call. And it's true – Justin's DNA was found under Elena's nails. He also mentioned the scratch on my client's chest. We won't be disputing that either. What we will contest is how they got there. There's more than one way that could have happened. All we ask of you – all Justin asks of you – is that you don't decide how that happened until you've heard all of the evidence. I'll say it again now, though – it didn't happen during any struggle between my client and Elena Mancini.'

Tanner paused, wanting to conclude on a positive point for the defence. 'You'll be shown film, as the Crown Prosecutor told you, of my client and Mr Richter leaving the club with Elena Mancini and the witness Klaudia Dabrowska. Miss Dabrowska is apparently going to be giving evidence at this trial – so the

Crown tells us – to say she was with Mr Richter when Elena must have been killed.

'I say "apparently", because Miss Dabrowska wasn't available to give evidence at the committal hearing for my client. So when you meet her, you'll be like me – meeting her for the first time. And if she tells you she was with Mr Richter when they went back to his home, and not with Justin, you'll be meeting someone who is not telling the truth. And when you conclude she's not, you'll conclude something about my client, Justin Matheson. That he is not guilty of the crimes he's been charged with.'

45

Detective Senior Sergeant Garry Heffron had been a cop for nearly twenty-five years. Fifteen of those had been in homicide, and he'd been around the block a few times in murder trials. If you were a prosecutor, he was a good witness. He made concessions when he had to, but also held the line without losing his cool.

Aitken led him through his evidence, but didn't have to work hard. Heffron was a natural storyteller, able to break up the police investigation into easily digestible chunks for the jury. He'd been called in the early hours of 9th October the previous year by a more junior detective, and then gone to the scene. He knew where he was headed. The Richters were hardly anonymous members of Sydney society. Justin Matheson was awake but barely lucid by the time he arrived. Another detective told him Matheson had been roused when the ambulance officers arrived.

Through Heffron, all photos and video of the crime scene were admitted into evidence, and once again the jury was shown Elena's dead body. This time there was video, narrated by a police officer who walked through the rooms of the Retreat. There was a long interruption during this evidence, as Elena's mother collapsed, before being physically ill on the floor. A fifteen-minute adjournment followed. As they walked out, Tanner saw that three of the jurors were also nearly overwhelmed by emotion.

When Heffron's evidence got under way again, he told the court he'd been the senior officer at the main police interviews of Justin Matheson, John Richter, Klaudia Dabrowska, and the driver, Mario Gomez. Other detectives in the homicide squad had been delegated to interview witnesses from the Pantheon Club, the Olympus entertainment and hospitality complex, and on background matters. CCTV film of Matheson and Richter entering the club, and leaving with Elena Mancini and Klaudia Dabrowska, was shown. Some of that film was consistent with what Matheson had told police. It included Klaudia kissing Matheson in Richter's car while they waited to leave.

The video of Matheson's police interview was played. Even though it had been conducted after he'd sobered up, he looked wasted: his hair was unruly, he hadn't shaved, and he appeared exhausted. It was prejudicial, but there was nothing Tanner could do about it. The interview had been voluntary, and Matheson's then lawyer was there to hold his hand.

The upside to Matheson's police interview was its consistency with his current story. He'd drunk too much all day. Richter had offered the coke. He'd gone into a bedroom with Klaudia. They'd left Richter and Elena in the lounge room. He had sex with Klaudia, then fell asleep. When he was next conscious, and had managed to stand, he saw an ambulance officer kneeling beside Elena's body. He didn't know what the marks were on his chest, or how they got there. When it came time for Matheson to give his version of events in the defence case, Tanner was at least confident his evidence in chief would line up with his police interview.

John Richter had told the police a very different story. He said that Matheson had brought the cocaine. When Klaudia wanted to go home, Richter's story was that he'd called his driver, who then drove them to her flat. He went in, and they talked for a while. Mario then drove him home. When he arrived back at the Retreat, he found Elena lying on the floor of the lounge. Then he saw the blood. He checked her pulse by putting his fingers on her neck. He called an ambulance and with the same call sought the police. At least unlike at the committal hearing, this version of events would have to be told to the jury by Richter himself. It couldn't come in the form of a statement, and it couldn't come from the mouth of Heffron.

Heffron told the jury that he'd also been the senior officer at the interview with Klaudia Dabrowska the day following the interviews with Matheson and Richter. Her police record of interview was consistent with John Richter's. The cocaine was Matheson's. She'd talked to Richter in his study. He was upset about his wife. When she asked to go home, Richter said he'd take her. Matheson and Elena were still in the lounge when they left. She asked Elena if she wanted to go, but Matheson insisted she stay.

All through the evidence he gave concerning the police investigation, Heffron sometimes looked at Aitken, sometimes the judge if he asked a question, and at other times he directed himself to the jury. He was like a television veteran who always looked at the right camera. His voice was low, calm and polished.

Tanner couldn't let Heffron walk from the box completely unchallenged – that would look like surrender. He had to be brief, though; there was no way of winning the trial here. Too many questions, or the wrong ones, could reveal more than he wanted to. His only aim was to hint that there was more to this story than the jury had heard so far.

'How long had Mr Matheson been in custody before he was interviewed, detective?' Tanner began.

'As I told the prosecutor, we had to wait until he'd recovered from his intoxication. We applied for an extended detention warrant. It was about twelve hours.'

'Had he slept?'

'I don't know.'

'That wasn't reported to you?'

'No.'

'Mr Matheson indicated a willingness to be interviewed by you, correct?'

'That's right.'

'And, despite the varied questioning about what occurred on the night of 8 October and the morning of the ninth, he gave police a consistent history?'

'He said he didn't know what had happened to Elena.'

'His story never wavered, though, regarding anything, did it? No part of it has changed?'

'No part has changed to any significant degree. He had difficulty remembering some aspects of what he'd done the night before.'

'He had no memory of killing Elena Mancini, correct?'

'That's what he told us.'

'He's always maintained that he didn't hurt her?'

'That's his story. It's not consistent with the evidence.'

Tanner could have sought to have the last answer struck out, but decided to use it instead. 'Really? That's not quite true, is it?'

Heffron paused, immediately recognising he may have to qualify what he'd just said. 'It's not consistent with the DNA evidence, or the witness statements we took from Mr Richter, Mr Gomez, Miss –'

'Hang on, detective, you don't get to tell the story twice.'

'I object, your Honour,' Aitken said. 'The witness is merely answering the question.'

'If you're referring to the video and film, then –'

'Just a moment, detective,' the judge said. 'I think Mr Aitken is correct. You were interrupted mid-stream.'

'I was just saying that Mr Matheson's version of events to us was not consistent with all of the witness statements we took.'

'You just mentioned the film, detective, didn't you?'

'Yes, and I was –'

'That CCTV film is consistent with what Mr Matheson told you, isn't it?'

'I object, your Honour. Which part of what Mr Matheson said in his police statement is my friend suggesting?'

'All of it.'

'I can't agree with that,' Heffron said.

'It's consistent with him saying he was with Klaudia all night until he woke up, isn't it?'

'No.'

'It shows them – Mr Matheson and Miss Dabrowska – walking through the club holding hands, doesn't it?'

'Yes.'

'It shows her holding his arm, waiting outside of the Olympus complex?'

'Yes.'

'Klaudia kisses my client, doesn't she?'

'Yes.'

'They're like lovers, aren't they?'

'They're friendly, yes.'

'You know the difference between friends and lovers, don't you, detective?'

'I object.'

'How long does the kiss last, detective?'

'How long?'

'Yes, how long?'

'I haven't timed it.'

'Eleven seconds. Do you want to watch again?'

'I'll take your word for it.'

'That's a friendly kiss, detective? Eleven seconds?'

'I was being colloquial.'

'Would you mind being accurate instead? It was like a lovers' kiss?'

'Yes.'

'And that's consistent with what Mr Matheson told you – that he slept with Miss Dabrowska that night.'

'It's not what she said. It wasn't what Mr Richter said. And it's not what the driver said – about dropping Miss Dabrowska home with Mr Richter.'

'People can lie, can't they, detective?'

'Is that a serious question?'

'It's not me being colloquial. They can lie, can't they?'

Heffron half-smiled, and shook his head. 'For some people, Mr Tanner,' he said, 'a kiss is a long way from intercourse.'

'What's on the CCTV footage, detective, is consistent with Justin Matheson's evidence. Correct?'

'I object,' Aitken said, rising to his feet. 'I've given my friend plenty of licence to make submissions rather than ask proper questions, but I think he's reached his threshold.'

The judge was about to rule, but Heffron's years of experience allowed him to see an opening. 'The film is not inconsistent with it, Mr Tanner,' he said quickly. 'The DNA evidence is, and so were the scratches on his body.'

Tanner realised he'd pushed the film far enough, and Heffron was too good a witness to not bat it away. He had to move on. 'You took a statement from the driver, Mr Gomez, correct?'

'Yes.'

'How long has he worked for Mr Richter?'

'About ten years, I believe.'

'He drives for Mr Hendrik Richter too, doesn't he?'

'Sometimes, I believe.'

'Klaudia Dabrowska, you interviewed her?'

'Yes.'

'She shouldn't have even been in our country that night, let alone at the Richters' estate?'

'She didn't have a work visa, no.'

'She got deported?'

'She was cooperating with police on a murder investigation. She was allowed to leave freely.'

'She's from the UK?'

'London, yes.'

'And what else do you know about her?'

'I'm not sure what you mean?'

'Did you test her for cocaine?'

'No.'

'Why not?'

'She said she didn't have any, and –'

'Mr Matheson said she did.'

'Not until later. We didn't get to interview her until late on the tenth.'

'What about Mr Richter, was he tested?'

'No.'

'Why?'

'We had no reason not to believe him.'

'You mean, apart from all the cocaine in his house?'

'It was on the coffee table, and in your client's jacket.'

'Mr Richter had a lawyer there, didn't he? At his home?'

'Yes.'

'When did the lawyer arrive?'

'He was there when I arrived. Mr Richter said he'd rung him, but only after he'd called the ambulance and the police. That was consistent with his phone records.'

'Did you think it odd he had a lawyer there?'

'No,' Heffron said. 'They're wealthy people. Someone had just died at their home, and there were drugs on the table. It wasn't unexpected.'

'Just as a matter of interest, detective, can I ask you to look at someone in the courtroom for me?'

Heffron paused before answering. 'Sure.'

'Look at Mr Aitken and his junior at the bar table. Then go to the gallery behind them, four rows back. The man on the far left, from where you sit. Blue suit, red tie.'

'Yes, I see him.'

'Is that Mr Carrington, a lawyer from the firm Bloomberg Butler Kelly?'

'I believe that's his name.'

'And he was the lawyer at Mr Richter's retreat on the morning you attended the scene?'

'Yes.'

'And Mr Carrington specialises in white collar crime, is that right?'

'I object, your Honour,' Aitken said loudly, but Heffron answered anyway.

'I have no idea.'

'I'd ask your Honour to give the jury some instruction about what my friend just said. That question potentially has a negative connotation for Mr Richter, and it should –'

'If my friend's that excited about it, your Honour,' Tanner interrupted, 'I'm quite happy to clarify that I'm not suggesting Mr Carrington has given any advice that I know of to Mr Richter about white collar crime.'

'That's worse, your Honour,' Aitken protested.

'I can't help what area of special expertise Mr Carrington has, your Honour,' Tanner continued, 'any more than I can help it that he's sitting in court. Maybe he just likes watching criminal trials.'

'Mr Tanner!'

'All I was –'

'Mr Tanner! Resume your seat.' Knight glared at Tanner for as long as he thought it took to indicate extreme displeasure. He then turned to the jury. 'Members of the jury, you have just heard a rather terse exchange between myself and counsel, and an objection from the Crown Prosecutor concerning what he says are potential prejudicial inferences as a result of questions from Mr Tanner to Detective Heffron concerning a lawyer called Mr John Carrington. You have heard some evidence about Mr Carrington's presence at Mr Richter's home on the morning of 9 October last. Those are facts you are entitled to take into account if you think relevant to your deliberations. What you may not do is draw any adverse inference about what Mr Tanner said was Mr Carrington's area of expertise. That's not relevant, and not in evidence. Nor is it of any relevance that he's observing this trial. Now, Mr Tanner?'

Tanner knew that if he pushed, he risked aggravating the judge more, which the jury wouldn't like. He'd done the best he could with Heffron. It wasn't much, but he hadn't given him a free pass. 'Nothing further for this witness, your Honour.'

'Any re-examination, Mr Aitken?'

'Detective, was Mr Carrington present when you interviewed Mr Richter?'

'Yes.'

'Did he advise Mr Richter not to talk to you?'

'He told us his client wanted to cooperate.'

'And did he interrupt your questioning of Mr Richter at any time?'

'No.'

'When you interviewed Miss Dabrowska, detective, did she have a lawyer present?'

'No.'

'The nightclub Pantheon, and the hospitality complex Olympus – you discovered that Mr John Richter was a part owner, is that correct?'

'He owns twenty-five per cent of the shares in the company that owns the venue.'

'And the CCTV footage you told us was from cameras owned by the venue?'

'Yes.'

'Did you have any trouble obtaining film from those cameras?'

'No.'

'Did Mr Richter play any role in getting that film?'

'When we asked for it, he rang the security people there, and told them to get it to us straight away.'

'So he obviously wasn't concerned about what was on the film?'

'I object, your Honour,' Tanner said. 'The witness can't know that.'

'I reject the question.'

'Thank you, your Honour. Nothing further.'

It was three forty-five when Heffron left the box, and the judge decided to let the jury go early. He'd just begun giving them the same address he'd give every day about not watching the news or reading about the case in the papers, when Tanner felt his phone vibrate with an incoming text. He held it under the bar table to read it.

Your friend is going shopping on Tuesday morning at ten. He's buying in bulk. He likes to shop near work.

A long day in court had finished, but Tanner felt his heart rate quicken. He didn't recognise the number, but he knew who the message was from.

46

Friday began with the medical evidence. The first witness was the doctor who'd performed the post mortem at the request of the coroner.

Dr Robert Hancock told the court that the cause of Elena Mancini's death was traumatic brain injury. She had a penetrating head wound, and a skull fracture to the right side of her head, immediately above the right temple. Elena's head had been hurled at the coffee table, probably by having her body flung around, while she was also swung downwards. This led to the side of her head striking the table during rapid acceleration. Although strictly part of another scientist's expertise, Tanner had told Aitken that there would be no objection to this evidence coming through a medical examiner, as the defence wasn't challenging it. The challenge was over who did it, not how it was done.

Apart from the skull fracture and deep wound, which included a bone splinter penetrating the brain, the force involved when Elena's head hit the table caused the immediate onset of intracerebral haemorrhage. There would almost certainly have been an instant loss of consciousness, and death quickly followed.

There were some pathology tests conducted on the victim. She had a blood alcohol reading of 0.04, consistent with perhaps two glasses of champagne. There was evidence she had ingested a small amount of cocaine.

There wasn't much Tanner could do but to sit and listen to the horrors of Elena's injury and the brutal nature of her death. During the course of Hancock's evidence, Tanner noticed that three members of the jury were close to tears. And throughout his testimony the soft tears of Elena's mother could often be heard.

The mood in the courtroom didn't improve when Dr Julia Grieg, the DNA analyst called by the Crown, gave her finding on the skin cells trapped under Elena's nails. They were a match to Justin Matheson, to a probability beyond 99.99 per cent. Tanner had offered to stipulate to this, to avoid the attendance in court of the doctor, but Aitken had insisted on calling her. Tanner would have done the same thing had their roles been reversed; there was nothing like the gravity of having an expert witness in the courtroom. Aitken wanted someone to say 'ninety-nine point nine-nine' to the jury.

For the same reason, Aitken also called a mechanics expert, who part educated and part horrified the jury about the kind of force that Elena's head had struck the table with. There was evidence about the mass of her head, and of her upper body, and about momentum and time, and acceleration and force.

'What's your ultimate conclusion concerning Elena's injury?' Aitken asked.

'Only someone using their full strength could have slung her body in such a way to produce the forces involved.'

'A strong person?'

'That's highly likely.'

As the expert spoke, Tanner caught at least two jurors sneaking a look at Matheson.

The expert evidence was completed by just after three on Friday afternoon. Tanner knew why this evidence had been called first: the strategy was to get the jury thinking that it had to be Matheson; by the time Richter and Dabrowska got their turn, the jury would be predisposed to believing them.

When Aitken sat down after his DNA expert had finished, Tanner paused for a moment after the judge asked him if he had any questions. He had many, but not for this witness.

'No, your Honour,' he said.

The sense of gloom in the defence room after the judge had adjourned the trial until Monday could not have been greater. It was half-time in the changing sheds, but the team was already beaten.

'I told you this part of the trial would be difficult,' Tanner said.

No one spoke for a few moments. Then Bill Matheson broke the silence. 'That woman is always crying. It shouldn't be allowed.'

'I can't object to the victim's mother crying, Bill,' Tanner said.

'It's affecting the jury. The woman in the blue shirt has been crying too.' Bill Matheson's voice was full of anger and frustration. He'd spent most of his life in charge. The trial was something he could not control, like bleeding that couldn't be stopped.

'A 22-year-old girl had her head slammed into a coffee table,' Tanner said calmly. 'That's why her mother and some of the jurors are crying. We won't help ourselves by complaining.'

'It isn't right.'

'I said all along this trial would start next week. I know it's hard to sit through, but nothing that happened this week was a surprise.'

'We don't seem to be putting up a fight about anything,' Judith Matheson said.

Tanner looked at her. She was somewhere on the brink of both anger and tears.

'You didn't ask that last witness a single question.'

'We have to save what we have for when it counts, Judith. You don't argue with 99.99 per cent.'

'Yes, but surely –'

'Judith,' Tanner said, 'Justin got offered a deal because of what we've achieved this week. He's decided not to take it. He's put his trust in me. You're going to have to as well.'

He stood.

'I know this is tough on you. Reflect on anything you think I should have done this week. If you think something has been missed, tell Charles, and he can call me at work on Sunday and I'll discuss it with him. Okay?'

He looked at the Mathesons, neither of whom seemed satisfied, but who said no more for the time being.

47

Twenty minutes after Tanner arrived back at his chambers after court, a call came from the front desk. He'd expected to be told it was either Jane Ross or Charles Porter. 'There's a man here called Trevor Horton,' the receptionist said instead. 'He's wondering if he can have a few minutes of your time.'

'Tell him he can't,' Tanner said. There was silence on the other end of the line. He thought better of his answer. 'Find out what he wants, will you?'

Five minutes later, there was a tap on his door, and Tanner's clerk stepped into his room. 'You're going to want to see this guy.'

Trevor Horton declined any kind of drink, and sat on the edge of the seat, like he was about to get up. He was somewhere in his sixties, heavy bags under his eyes, as though he hadn't slept in years.

'You know who I am?' he asked.

Tanner nodded. 'My clerk just told me.'

Horton gazed at Tanner's bookshelf full of law reports. 'I've never been in a barrister's chambers before.'

'It's rarely good news for people who have,' Tanner said. 'Especially in my line of work.'

Horton almost smiled, but the effort was beyond him.

'I recognise you,' Tanner said.

'I've been every day,' Horton said.

'How am I doing?'

Horton shrugged. 'The prosecution's in front for now.'

Tanner's eyes drifted from Horton's face to his hands, which were holding a large yellow envelope. 'You have something that can help me?'

'Is your client guilty?'

'I don't think so.'

Horton glanced at a photo of Dan, taken on the morning of his first day at school, on a shelf behind the desk. 'Flick won a scholarship to St Mary's,' he said. 'That's what we called Felicity. We'd have never been able to afford the fees otherwise.'

'How did she meet John Richter?'

'A school dance in year twelve.'

'And they became boyfriend and girlfriend?'

'Eventually,' Horton said. 'Towards the end of uni.'

Tanner paused and waited for Horton to continue, but he stopped, like he'd become lost in some memory.

'That's about the time when John hurt her?'

'Maybe we shouldn't have taken the money?' Horton said. 'It's just . . . we thought it would set her up for life, you know?'

'Most people would have done the same thing,'

'There was no brain injury, you see. A hairline fracture. She was lucky.' He looked at Tanner for acknowledgement.

Tanner looked at the envelope again.

'My wife died when Flick was young,' Horton then said. 'Cervical cancer.' He swallowed. 'That's what killed Flick. Hereditary. Spread through her body by the time –' He stopped, and shook his head.

'I'm very sorry.'

'Flick told me in the hospice she regretted not going to the police. She was . . . I don't know how lucid she was at the time, you know?'

Tanner nodded.

'Your wife died of cancer too?'

'She did.'

Horton nodded. 'Sally Cook told me yesterday.'

'You spoke with Sally?'

Horton nodded. 'I wanted to talk to her about Nikki Richter.'

'Is that why you're here?'

'I've been thinking about it for a while. I don't – I don't want this man to get away with it.' He leant forwards, almost out of his seat, and put the envelope he was holding onto Tanner's desk.

'I think I know what's in that,' Tanner said. 'There's probably a clause binding Felicity's survivors or heirs. Just giving it to me would be a breach of –'

'I don't care,' Horton said calmly, finally sitting back in his seat.

'Have you taken any legal advice?'

'I'm not interested in that.'

'The Richters won't . . . they won't take kindly to this. They will –'

'It's too late for me to go to the police, Mr Tanner,' Horton said. 'This is the next best thing. This is what Flick would have wanted.'

Tanner nodded slowly. 'I don't know what to say.'

A sad smile came over Horton's face. 'Tell me your client is innocent.'

Tanner smiled back. 'He's not an entirely innocent man,' he said, 'but I don't think he killed Elena Mancini.'

Horton stood. 'None of us are entirely innocent,' he said. He put his hand on the envelope, and pushed it across the desk until it was right in front of Tanner. Then he stood and left the room.

Tanner opened the envelope and took out the document. He read it quickly. Then he picked up his phone and rang Jane Ross, then Charles Porter.

48

The TV crews were already at the court complex when Tanner arrived on Monday morning, twenty minutes before the trial was due to recommence. The cameras and reporters moved away from Tanner though as he walked towards the entrance, so that they could capture the arrival of John Richter, who'd been driven to court by his lawyer.

Richter and his counsel walked through the throng of press like they'd done it a million times, ignoring the questions that were shouted at them. They looked serious rather than worried. As Tanner watched them come towards him, in the background he saw the rest of the Richter family arrive in two black Mercedes. As a driver opened a door for Hendrik and then his wife, Tanner went inside.

Five minutes later, a momentary lull in the voices that washed around the room made Tanner turn and look just as John Richter walked through the doors. Someone had spoken to him about how to dress: a navy suit, white shirt, a light-blue tie; nothing flashy or aggressive. No product in the hair, just a blowdry, again to soften him. He seemed younger than thirty-six when he smiled at his family, who were sitting in the row of seats reserved for them. Richter looked at Tanner briefly as he took his seat in the witness box. His face hardened, then he turned towards the bench, and the judge's empty chair.

We're not all equal in the eyes of the law. Wealth counts. Justice may be blind, but she can smell money. Richter was the heir to a multibillion-dollar fortune. That came with obvious advantages and skewed things in his favour. In the witness box, though, the power of his riches slipped fractionally from his grasp. There, John Richter could be made more equal.

Aitken walked him through the family history. A childhood in London, his teenage years in Sydney, where he went to school, before studying commerce at university. He then had three years for Citadel in Houston and New York, two more in London, then to management in the Sydney office.

'You're the head of the new projects and acquisitions team for Asia, is that correct?'

'It is,' Richter said.

'That's a Sydney-based position? Could you explain it?'

'Sure. There's been a lot of growth in this country for us over the past decade, although that's slowed now. We're looking more towards Asia and Africa. I take control of most new projects – applications for new mines of various sorts – and I'm generally involved at a high level if we're thinking of purchasing an existing mine, or considering a takeover. We have another team leader for the Americas, and another for Europe and the Middle East.'

Aitken took him back to school, and to the friendship he formed there with Justin Matheson.

'I looked up to Justin,' Richter said. 'He was a great sportsman, but academically at the top too.' They had business discussions after university, particularly since Richter had moved back to Australia. 'He helped me with ideas I had away from mining. I have an interest in resorts, places where people could meet, relax, eat, be entertained, have fun. I love architecture too. Urban design is a passion of mine.'

Only after he'd built up his witness as intelligent and urbane did Aitken come to the days before Elena's death.

'The worst week of my life,' Richter said, referring to his wife's death and funeral. He hadn't wanted to be alone.

He'd been cooped up at home all week, and needed to get out. 'Pantheon's not a nightclub. It's more like a sophisticated retreat.'

Matheson began flirting with both Elena Mancini and Klaudia Dabrowska. 'I guess he'd had a lot to drink.'

It was Matheson's idea to go back to where he was living, Richter said. 'I didn't think it was a great idea, but I said yes in the end. Justin had been pretty supportive. I didn't want to – well, I should've said no, but I didn't.'

Richter had met Klaudia Dabrowska a few times before, when he'd been at the club on other nights.

'Can you describe her to us,' Aitken asked, 'as a person?'

'Very friendly,' Richter said. 'Quite flirtatious. She thought it was all good fun, I think. The problem was that not everyone saw it that way.'

'The problem?'

'She'd lodged two complaints about members – hands going in the wrong places, if you know what I mean. Because she complained, we followed it up.'

'What does that involve?'

'We have the manager talk to the member, and he makes a written report. If it's bad, we cancel the membership. We've only had to do that three times, though.'

'And with Miss Dabrowska?'

Richter shook his head, like he was uncomfortable giving an answer. 'Both guys we spoke to said they thought she was coming on to them,' he said. 'Some guys – they get the wrong idea just from friendliness. They're not who we want as members. Klaudia actually wanted us to give them another chance, but we cancelled their memberships. We want people to have a good time at Pantheon, but we have a zero tolerance policy for inappropriate touching of our staff.'

'Can I show you some documents? Are these the club manager's notes about Miss Dabrowska's complaints?'

'Yes, they are,' Richter said after glancing at them quickly.

'I tender those, your Honour.'

'Mr Tanner?'

'I have no idea about their relevance, your Honour.'

'Mr Crown?'

'They help explain what happened between the accused and Klaudia Dabrowska. I was about to get to that with the witness.'

'Hold the tender for the moment.'

Aitken then turned to what Richter observed between Justin Matheson and Klaudia Dabrowska.

'Klaudia was her flirtatious self,' John said. 'Sitting on Justin's lap in the club, whispering in his ear. She's meant to draw the line at flirtation, but with Justin she – on one occasion she may have crossed the line that we as owners would draw. The girls are there to serve drinks, have a chat and a laugh, that kind of thing. They're instructed to be as friendly to any women members, and we have a few. I think Justin got the wrong idea, though.'

'Tell us what happened.'

'Well . . . this is hard. In the car, Justin started to kiss Klaudia again. She told him to cool it. She hit his hand away at some point. He was really drunk by then. When we got to my place, she sort of backed away from him – especially when he brought out the cocaine.'

'What happened then?'

'I got angry,' Richter said. 'I – look, it was the end of an awful week. Justin had gone to my fridge, opened champagne . . . He'd had enough to drink. I told him to put the drugs away. He was already wasted.'

'How did he react?'

'He said he'd brought them especially to cheer me up.'

'What happened next?'

'I went to my study and shut the door. I hoped he'd just go.'

'What then – after you went to the study?'

'Klaudia walked in.'

'And?'

'We talked. She didn't want to have any coke. She said she was mad at Justin for bringing drugs given how – given how Nikki had died.'

'How long did you talk for?'

'Fifteen or twenty minutes. She ended up telling me about her visa problem. She told me how much she liked Sydney – she started to cry.'

'What did you do then?'

'I offered to help her, and said I'd take her home.'

'And did you?'

Richter nodded. 'Pretty much straight away. I'd been drinking, so I couldn't drive, and I didn't want to put her in a cab so late. I called Mario, and asked him to come back. He doesn't live far away.'

'What happened when he did?'

'I thought I'd drop Klaudia home, and deal with Justin when I got back.'

'What about Elena Mancini?'

'I asked her if she wanted to leave. I think she thought about it, but Justin was pushy about her staying, and she seemed okay with him at the time, even though he was so drunk. I said I'd get Mario to drop her home when we came back from Klaudia's . . . I really . . .' He put his head down, then shook it, before looking up again at Aitken. 'I shouldn't have left her with Justin when he was in that state.'

'You went to Miss Dabrowska's apartment?'

'Yes.'

'Where was that?'

'Near Bondi. A couple of blocks back from the beach.'

'And when you arrived at her flat?'

'I went in with her. She made coffee, and we talked for maybe twenty minutes. I said I'd try and help her get a work permit – that was about it. Then I went back home.'

'And what did you find there when you returned?'

Richter then told the jurors about the shock of finding Elena Mancini on the floor of his lounge room, a pool of blood leaking into his carpet. He checked for a pulse, and found none. Nearby, Matheson was also on the floor, breathing but not conscious. Richter rang triple 0, asked for an ambulance first, then the police. One of the ambulance officers eventually roused Matheson.

'You also called a lawyer?' Aitken asked.

'Yes.'

'Why?'

'Elena was dead in my house. I'd let Justin take drugs. I knew that was the wrong thing to do. I knew the PR damage it could do to the company. I thought – people would've expected me to call a lawyer, so I did.'

'You gave a statement to police?'

'Yes, of course.'

Aitken nodded. 'I'm afraid I'm going to have to ask you some unpleasant questions, Mr Richter,' he then said.

'I've been expecting that,' Richter replied, and forced a smile.

Aitken had two ways to go with the evidence about Nikki from Sally Cook's files. He could ignore it, and try to object to Tanner using it. The defence case, however, was that the wrong man was on trial. Attacking Richter would pass the relevance test; preventing it would be akin to depriving the accused of raising his defence. Aitken would deal with the weaker part of his case himself – that way he could contain the damage, and change the message.

'You were separated before your late wife died, Mr Richter?'

'Yes.'

'And your lawyers had received letters from a divorce lawyer acting for Mrs Richter? From Sally Cook & Associates?'

'Yes.'

'And in that correspondence, your wife indicated she wanted a divorce?'

'I was hoping that was just anger, but yes.'

'You still loved her?'

'Yes.'

'Can you tell the court . . . and forgive me for asking. Why had you separated?'

Richter shook his head, and did his best to look pained. 'We'd . . . from time to time – Look, both of us had done the wrong thing by each other a few times.'

'The wrong thing?'

'I'm sorry to be coy,' Richter said. He sighed. 'We'd both been unfaithful. I work long hours, and travel a lot. We were both lonely from time to time. People know who I am. They know I have a lot of money. Women – I let myself down a few times. Nikki did too, once when I was away. With someone I thought was a mutual friend. Out of spite I . . . well, I guess I went looking for revenge. It spiralled out of control. I wanted us to get back together, though. I really did.'

'The letters from your wife's lawyer also detailed incidents of alleged violence and bullying. In particular –'

'That's not true,' Richter said loudly. 'None of that was true.'

'Just let me finish my question, Mr Richter,' Aitken said.

'I'm sorry.'

'Did you violently attack your late wife in August last year?'

'No.'

'Did you threaten to kill her?'

'No.'

'Did you begin choking her that night with your hands around her throat?'

'No,' Richter said firmly. 'I did not.'

Tanner wondered if Aitken was going to take Richter to the photos in Sally Cook's files showing Nikki's bruised neck, but he didn't – he'd got the denial he needed. By not introducing the photos himself, Aitken could still object if Tanner tried to, saying they weren't relevant to Matheson's guilt or innocence, or simply more inflammatory than probative.

'You had a pre-nuptial agreement with Mrs Richter, did you not?' Aitken asked quickly, segueing from the injury to what he no doubt wanted to suggest was its real cause.

'Yes.'

'One that specified a financial settlement in the event of divorce, depending on the years of your marriage, whether you had children, that kind of thing?'

'Yes.'

'Without children, and if she divorced you after less than ten years of marriage, what did the agreement provide in terms of financial settlement?'

'Nikki would get five million if it was five years, a million more for each year after that, I think.'

'So seven million for seven years?'

'Not very romantic, but yes. It's pretty standard for someone in my position who's likely to inherit a big share in a major corporation.'

Aitken tendered the pre-nup, without objection from Tanner. 'Your late wife was seeking more than seven million, wasn't she?'

Richter nodded. 'She wanted an apartment worth eighteen million for a start, then a lot more.'

'How much?'

Richter paused, probably just as he'd been prepped to. 'Fifty million in cash on top of that.'

Aitken nodded slowly to let the figure sink in. 'Fifty million,' he repeated. 'And your response?'

'I think that's when I realised how angry she was.'

A few people in the gallery laughed nervously, embarrassing themselves.

'And the allegation about abuse – that came in a letter sent immediately before the letter seeking the apartment and the fifty million?'

'I believe so.'

Aitken tendered the letters, then checked his notes.

'One last thing, Mr Richter. And again I apologise, but I'm just trying to save Mr Tanner the trouble of asking you. Did you hurt Elena Mancini on the morning of 9 October last year?'

'No, I did not.'

'Did you do anything that killed her?'

'No.'

'Thank you, Mr Richter.'

It was nearly one when Aitken sat down, and the judge said he'd adjourn for lunch, and that cross-examination would start at two.

Tanner gave Porter instuctions that he and Jane were not to be disturbed in the defence room during lunch, other than to be given sandwiches and coffee. A quarter of an hour later, his phone started to vibrate. No caller ID. He answered anyway.

'I'm calling about your offer of work.' It was Mark Woods from the drug squad. 'I've decided I'll look into it tomorrow morning, as you've suggested.'

'And what I want?'

'I'll do what I can.'

'You'll let me know what you find?'

'If I can.'

'I'd like instant gratification. Time's precious.'

'I'll do what I can,' Woods said, then hung up.

'What was that about?' Ross asked when Tanner put his phone away.

Tanner stood and picked up his papers. 'I have to make a quick call.'

She motioned for him to stay put, and picked up her own folders. 'I'll see you in court.'

When she'd left, Tanner rang Lisa Ilves.

'How's the trial going?'

'It's only really about to start now.'

'Do you need something? Company tonight?'

'Meet me after court tomorrow.'

'To do what?'

'We may have something to discuss.'

'What?'

'I'm not sure yet.'

'Is that all I get?'

'I'm due in court. I'll see you Tuesday.'

49

It wasn't often that Tanner felt his job was to find the truth. Usually he had to avoid it, blur it, pour doubt on it. This case was different.

'You described Miss Dabrowska as flirtatious?' he asked Richter to begin his cross.

'To a degree.'

'And you produced her employment file to the prosecutor's office?'

'The company that owns the complex did.'

'My apologies. That file had some complaints she'd made against members who – let's use your term – may have gotten the wrong idea about Miss Dabrowska. Is that fair?'

'Yes.'

'In Miss Dabrowska's file, there's no criticism from her employer about her flirtatiousness, is there?'

'No. I think we – I think the manager may have talked to her about how guys, if they've been drinking . . . you know . . . can get the wrong idea.'

'Let me show you some film from the Olympus CCTV cameras.'

The lights were dimmed, and within seconds the court's video screen showed Justin Matheson and Klaudia Dabrowska in the main entrance of the entertainment complex. Then the kiss started. Eleven seconds went by. Tanner had it played again. He had it paused after nine seconds. Klaudia Dabrowska had her tongue down Matheson's throat.

'Is that flirting, Mr Richter?'

'That's not what I meant.'

'You said she was flirtatious, and Mr Matheson may have gotten "the wrong idea". I'll ask again, is she flirting?'

'In part. What I meant was –'

'Which part? The part where she puts her hand at the back of his head and drags it towards her, or the part where she's got her tongue in his mouth?'

'I object, your Honour,' Aitken said.

'I'll ask a different question. Which part of what we just saw was my client getting "the wrong idea"?'

Aitken rose to object again, but Richter started answering anyway. 'That's not what I meant. Justin had been drinking, and –'

'Miss Dabrowska hadn't though, had she?'

'No.'

'Did you see yourself standing to the left of Mr Matheson and Miss Dabrowska in the film we've just seen?'

'Yes.'

'You were looking at them?'

'Yeah. Well, it was quite a –'

'Tell me, Mr Richter, what idea did you get from looking at Mr Matheson and Miss Dabrowska kiss?'

'I object, your Honour.'

'I withdraw the question.'

'You said it was Mr Matheson's idea to go back to your house, correct?'

'Yes.'

'You said you didn't think it was a great idea?'

'Not with the amount Justin had to drink.'

'But you said yes.'

'Like I told Mr Aitken, I didn't think I could say no. Justin had been good to me since Nikki passed.'

'You owed him?'

'Sort of.'

'You couldn't say to him, Justin, it's late, my wife just died, it's been a rough week, see you later? You couldn't say that?'

'I could have, but I didn't.'

'You invited not only Mr Matheson to your home, but Elena Mancini and Miss Dabrowska as well.'

'Justin invited them.'

'It's your home, isn't it, Mr Richter?'

'Yes.'

'You have the right to quiet possession, not Mr Matheson?'

'I object. Your Honour –'

'You could have said no?'

'Of course.'

'So even though you say Mr Matheson wanted to keep the party going, and you didn't, the four of you ended up in your car, driven by your driver, and back at your home, correct?'

'I didn't say no to Justin. I agree with that.'

'Let's go back to the club first before we get in your car. What time did you go to Pantheon?'

'About eleven thirty.'

'And you said it was about half full?'

'Maybe two-thirds. I don't know.'

'You had some drinks?'

'Yes.'

'Okay. And at some stage did you go to the toilet?'

Richter screwed up his face, looking at Aitken, then at the judge.

'Is this relevant, Mr Tanner?' Knight asked.

'I was about to object, your Honour,' Aitken said.

'It is, your Honour. If you let me proceed for a few questions?'

'Make it relevant quickly.'

'You went to the gentlemen's room at some stage, Mr Richter?'

Richter shook his head, and smiled. 'Probably. I don't recall.'

'Well, it was pretty memorable for one of your guests. Do you recall a discussion with one of them in the men's bathroom?'

Richter paused for a few moments, making his decision: deny everything or admit something, then deny what's crucial. 'Not really.'

In criminal trials there were various pre-trial discovery obligations on both the prosecution and the defence. In New South Wales, the prosecutor had to supply the defence with a statement of the facts they intended to prove, a statement from each witness, and copies of all documents the Crown intended to tender and of any expert reports. The defence was also entitled to every document the police had given the prosecutor, and to all documents that might relate to the credibility of a witness.

The obligations on the defence were fewer. The accused had to supply an outline of the defence, and of any alibi. The defence had to serve a copy of any expert reports, but that's where its obligations ended. Tanner didn't have to give the prosecutor a list of witnesses. Which meant he hadn't had to tell Aitken about Greg McPherson.

'You don't recall someone passing on their sympathies for your wife's death?'

'I've got a vague memory, now that you mention that.'

'And when that man passed on his sympathies, did you tell him to "shut the fuck up" or use words of a similar kind?'

'No.'

'Did you physically stand over him in a threatening way and tell him that if he even looked at you again, you'd have him thrown out of the club?'

'This has nothing to do with what happened to Elena Mancini, your Honour,' Aitken said.

Knight looked at Tanner.

'My client isn't the only person proximate to Elena Mancini on the night she died, your Honour. I'm entitled to explore the frame of mind other witnesses were in. If you need me to explain that further, we might need the jury to retire for a moment while I do.'

The judge paused for a few moments to think. 'I'll let you continue for a little longer, Mr Tanner.'

Tanner turned back to Richter. 'Do you need the question repeated?'

Richter shook his head. 'I wasn't in the best mood,' he said. 'It'd been, as I said, the worst week of my life. If I was touchy –'

'When you say "if I was touchy", what do you say that means? Do you agree you threatened him?'

'No, I don't. I may have been, you know, short with him.'

'Does "short" mean you swore at him, threatened him physically, and said you'd have him thrown out of the club?'

'No.'

'So what does it mean?' Usually Tanner wouldn't ask a question that allowed an explanation. Sometimes, though, you need to give a witness some rope.

'Like I said. It was a bad week. I may have used a more aggressive tone than usual.'

'You'd agree you probably frightened Mr McPherson with your aggressive tone?'

'I don't see how he could have been frightened.'

'Have you ever been scared of something, Mr Richter?'

'Yes, of course.'

'So you agree that a person can feel scared?'

'Yes.'

'And who do you think is in the best position to assess whether Mr McPherson was fearful or not – you or him?'

'What I meant was –'

'Is Mr McPherson in the best position to say if he was feeling scared by how you spoke to him, or are you?'

'I object, your Honour. Mr Tanner is harassing the witness.'

'I'm doing no such thing, your Honour, but I'll ask another question. Let's leave Pantheon for a moment. I want to discuss your late wife.' Tanner's plan had been to cross-examine out of chronological order, to jump from topic to topic without letting Richter become settled. 'Your late wife was a fashion model when you met her?'

'Yes.'

'She didn't do any modelling after your marriage?'

'She didn't want to.'

'Forget her desires unless I ask you. She didn't, correct?'

'No.'

'She didn't work after you married?'

'She did some charity work with my mother.'

'She had no paid employment?'

'No.'

'She'd broken her ankle not long before you met her?'

'Yes.'

'She had to have three surgeries on her ankle over the next couple of years?'

'Yes.'

'She took a lot of pain killers during this time?'

'Unfortunately, yes.'

'You say unfortunately, I imagine, because she developed an addiction?'

'Yes.'

'You also discovered she began taking heroin?'

'I learnt that.'

'You didn't know at the time?'

'Not for – not until she had to go into a rehab facility.'

'Remind me – you were married when that happened?'

'Yes.'

'And you didn't know your wife was taking heroin?'

'Relevance, your Honour?'

The judge looked at Tanner.

'Mr Richter says my client took cocaine to his house. This is related to that topic.'

'I'll allow it for now,' Knight said.

'It sounds bad,' Richter said. 'I know. I – my job is crazy. If I could show you my diaries for each year. I was out of Sydney more nights than here. She hid things pretty well. I honestly didn't know until . . . she got sick, lost weight, wasn't eating. She told me, and we got her some help.'

'Did you know about the pain killers?'

'I didn't . . . at first I didn't think much about them. I thought she needed them. It was only when I found out about the heroin that I realised she had a problem with the pain meds too.'

'So she went to rehab?'

'For twelve weeks, I think.'

'And how was she when she left the clinic?'

'Better.'

'She stopped taking heroin?'

'Yes.'

'And the pain killers?'

'Yes.'

'Yet three years later she's back in the same clinic?'

'Yes.'

'Again because of heroin?'

'Yes.'

'And cocaine?'

'So we found out.'

'And this time, did you know she was taking these drugs?'

'I discovered it more quickly this time, you know, I recognised the signs.'

'So she did another twelve weeks in rehab?'

'I think it may have been a hundred and twenty days this time, and a lot of follow-up sessions when she was no longer a resident.'

'Both times before she was admitted to the rehab facility, she'd been taking drugs for many months?'

'I know I should have seen it before I did, but I honestly didn't.'

'Who supplied your late wife with heroin and cocaine, Mr Richter?'

Richter took a deep breath and sighed. 'She wouldn't tell me. I had an inkling it might have been some friends of hers, but she'd never say.'

'What gave you that inkling?'

'Just gut instinct. A feeling.'

'Gut instinct? Did you see anyone give Mrs Richter heroin or cocaine?'

'No.'

'Never?'

'No.'

'Not even when you went to nightclubs or parties together?'

'The witness has answered this, your Honour,' Aitken interjected.

'How did she pay for the drugs?'

'What do you mean?'

Tanner had been asking his questions quickly to keep Richter unsettled. He had to balance that with not going so fast that it became a blur for the jury. He took a breath now, and decided to say each word of the next series of questions more slowly. 'Where did she get the money to pay for these drugs?'

Richter shook his head. 'We had a joint bank account, Mr Tanner, I –'

'Because she wasn't working, right?'

'No, but –'

'So she wasn't earning any money?'

'As I said, we had a joint account, and –'

'So if I asked you to produce the bank records for that account for the years we're talking about when your late wife was taking so much heroin and cocaine she needed to go to rehab, they'll show her withdrawing large sums that would fit with the purchase of those very expensive drugs, would they?'

'I object, your Honour,' Aitken said. 'Mr Richter's not on trial. This whole line of questioning has gone far enough.'

'Did you subpoena any bank records, Mr Tanner?' Knight asked.

'I don't know what answers I'm going to get, your Honour.'

'No, then?'

'No, your Honour.'

The judge wrote something in his court book. 'You can proceed with the general line of questioning, but I'm not holding things up to get bank records.'

'If it please the court,' Tanner said. He turned back to Richter. 'Did your wife pay for her drugs from your joint money, Mr Richter, without you noticing?'

'I think some people gave them to her from time to time as well. So-called friends.'

'You mean they bought them for her?'

'You can put it that way if you like. I'd say –'

'Mr Richter, your late wife wasn't friendly with any cartel bosses, was she?'

Aitken objected, but Richter answered anyway. 'Of course not.'

'So anyone giving her drugs had themselves acquired them from someone else, correct?'

'I suppose.'

'Very generous, don't you think? Giving her drugs for free?'

'I wouldn't know.'

'Who were these people?'

'I told you, I don't know.'

'Your Honour, at this point the defence wants to show Mr Richter a photo of his late wife from the law firm files you granted us access to. I told the Crown about it this morning. My friend told me he was going to object. I think it's a matter that's going to take some argument.'

'I'd ask that the court be closed while we have this debate, your Honour,' Aitken said. 'If you rule in my favour but we don't go in camera, Mr Richter will have been unnecessarily embarrassed.'

'Mr Tanner?'

'I think I've already said that we think the public has a right to know everything that's going on in this case, your Honour.'

The judge shook his head. 'Not for the time being,' he said. 'Members of the jury, I'm going to ask you to go back to your room now, while the parties debate an issue of relevance and admissibility. It could take a while. If it looks like we won't get back to the evidence, I'll call you back to adjourn for the day. I'll now ask the court officers to clear the court.'

*

Once the court was cleared, the photo of Nikki Richter was put up on an easel so the judge and counsel could see. Tanner had asked Porter to get a large blow-up. It showed Nikki Richter from the top of her chest up. The bruising on her throat was obvious. Even Tanner couldn't pretend the picture wasn't prejudicial. That was the point.

'You want to suggest to the witness he did this, Mr Tanner?'

Tanner wanted to suggest to the witness that he'd killed Elena Mancini. The photo of Nikki Richter was one step on the way. 'Those bruises aren't self-inflicted, your Honour.'

'Let me hear from Mr Aitken first. It's his objection.'

'This is just character assassination, your Honour,' Aitken began. 'It's not sufficiently relevant, and it's not admissible under the tendency rule.' Aitken's reference to the tendency rule was to a rule that provides that evidence of a person's character or conduct isn't admissible to prove they have a tendency to act in a particular way unless that evidence had a significant probative value in a case. That was the contest here.

'The jury's here to decide whether Justin Matheson killed Elena Mancini. This photo has nothing to do with that. All it might do is make them prejudiced against the witness. There's no evidence of Mr Richter having a reputation as being a violent man, or being of that character.'

'There's evidence of that in Ms Cook's files, your Honour,' Tanner said.

'Any criminal convictions for violence?'

'None, your Honour. This is a man of good character. A successful businessman, well regarded in that community. Your Honour knows there was a pre-nup, that allegations were made that the witness denies, and that those allegations were made in the context of trying to better – by tens of millions of dollars – what the pre-nuptial agreement stipulated. This is a red herring to detract attention from the evidence of not just this witness, but from the evidence I've called to which there's been no challenge – like the accused's DNA being found under the victim's nails.'

The judge nodded slowly. 'Mr Tanner?'

'The key fact in issue is whether my client harmed Elena Mancini. He denies that, so whether Mr Aitken likes it or not, it's a fact in issue as to whether the prosecution's main witness is telling the truth. Elena Mancini died in Mr Richter's house. She got there in his car. He's one of two men there when he called the ambulance. Next, let's look at Ms Cook's file. It reveals that Mr Richter's wife was making allegations against him that he'd been violent during their marriage. This photo shows real injury. What's the response to the allegation? That she had it done to herself to get some more money?'

'That's precisely what Mr Richter thinks,' Aitken said.

'Really, Mr Aitken? I suppose you think battered wives all just walk into doors?'

'I resent that, your Honour, and I ask my friend to withdraw it.'

'Let's keep personal remarks out of it,' the judge snapped. 'Is that clear, Mr Tanner?'

'This evidence is highly probative,' Tanner said. 'It goes without saying it's prejudicial. So is evidence of guilt. This is a crime of violence against a woman. This photo is direct evidence of violence against another woman by a man with the means and opportunity to have killed Elena Mancini. The defence shouldn't be prevented from using it because it's embarrassing to Mr Richter. If he denies hurting his wife, he can say so.'

Knight closed his eyes. 'I'm going to rule on the use of the photo in the morning,' he said. 'Can you carry on without it for the time being, Mr Tanner, or move to another topic?'

'With respect, your Honour, I don't want to move on to another topic. I just did. This one.'

'I'm not ruling against you being able to ask Mr Richter questions about the allegations made by his late wife's lawyer. I need time to reflect on that photo. It's highly prejudicial, and I have to consider if that outweighs its probative value. It could have a dramatic impact on the jury. You can continue without it until tomorrow. We only have three-quarters of an hour to go today by the time we get everyone back.'

'The prosecution was able to show photos of Elena Mancini's dead body, surrounded by her blood, your Honour. I ought to be able to use that photo.'

'There's absolutely no analogy there, Mr Tanner, and you know it,' the judge said, his voice rising. 'Let's get the jury back and open the court. I'll rule on the photo in the morning. It can be marked for identification as "MFI 8" in the meantime.'

'You were asked about a letter your late wife's lawyers wrote to you, regarding her desire for a divorce,' Tanner began once the jury had taken their seats. 'Do you recall that?'

'Yes.'

'It contained some strong allegations about your behaviour towards her.'

'None of them were true.'

'Your wife said you assaulted her.'

'That never happened.'

'You say it was to extract a better deal on your pre-nuptial agreement?'

'That was the conclusion we all drew.'

'Who's we?'

'My family, and my lawyer.'

'So you say your late wife told lies for more money?'

'Or the lawyer told her to. I don't know.'

'You're suggesting, are you, it was all Ms Cook's idea? These allegations?'

'I don't know,' he said. 'What I know is that what was alleged wasn't true, and that it was done just before we got a letter that demanded a lot of money from my family. It looked to us like blackmail.'

'Blackmail?'

'That's how it looked.'

'You gave a eulogy at your wife's funeral, didn't you?'

'Yes.'

'Did you mention she was blackmailing you?'

'I object,' Aitken said forcefully.

'No, Mr Tanner,' the judge said loudly. 'That question is completely out of line.'

There was some murmuring in the gallery, and some deep breaths and other noises of both real and mock outrage.

'I'll withdraw it then, your Honour.'

'You're warned, Mr Tanner.'

As the judge spoke, Jane Ross handed him a post-it note: *Jury didn't like that.*

Tanner looked at her and nodded. 'Excuse me for a moment, your Honour.' He then opened a folder that was next to the lectern, and took out a yellow A4 envelope. From the envelope he took a document, looked at its front page, then placed it on top of the lectern, before looking up at John Richter.

'Do you have another question, Mr Tanner?' the judge said.

'I do, your Honour.' Then he glared at the witness some more. 'Your late wife wasn't the first woman to make an allegation of assault against you, was she?'

As soon as Tanner had asked the question, James Carrington, Richter's legal advisor, who was sitting in the gallery in front of Hendrik Richter, jumped up to speak to one of Aitken's instructing solicitors. There was a hushed conversation, following which the solicitor quickly spoke to Aitken.

'Excuse me for a moment, your Honour,' Aitken said, as his solicitor whispered in his ear.

Richter sat silently in the witness box, waiting to see if he had to answer the question.

'Yes, Mr Aitken?' the judge said impatiently.

'I object to the question,' Aitken said as his solicitor left his side. 'I apologise, your Honour, but I need a few moments to take instructions on this. It may also be that I'll have to ask for the court to be cleared again to explain my objection, so –'

The judge held up his hand, then shook his head and sighed. 'Let's go to my chambers first,' he said angrily. 'Members of the jury, I apologise for this further interruption. I'll adjourn for fifteen minutes.'

'May I have five minutes before joining you, your Honour?' Aitken asked.

The judge looked at him, nodded, then hurried off the bench.

When the lawyers walked into the judge's chambers five minutes later, he was standing.

'What's going on, Peter?' he said.

'All I did was ask a question, judge.'

'Cut it out. What do you have?'

'Another one of Mr Richter's victims, judge.'

'Judge, my objection –'

'Be quiet for a minute, Richard.' The judge looked at Tanner. 'When did you first know about this?'

'It's an allegation that's not true, I'm instructed,' Aitken said.

'Mr Aitken, please.' Knight looked at Tanner again. 'You've got a document?'

'I do.'

'It could not have been obtained lawfully, your Honour.'

'How do you know?' Tanner said.

'What do you have, Peter?'

'A deed,' Tanner said. 'The victim was paid off.'

'That's not –'

'How did you get it?' the judge asked.

'I don't think I have to disclose that, judge, with respect.'

'You might have to if you want to use it. I mightn't let you if it was illegally obtained.'

'It was given to me, judge,' Tanner said. 'I didn't steal it.'

'How did the person who gave it to you get it?'

'Your Honour,' Aitken interrupted, 'if this is a deed between a woman named Felicity Horton and Mr Richter, I'm told that it prohibits either party from –'

'She's dead,' Tanner said, cutting Aitken off.

'I'm sorry?' Knight said.

'Felicity Horton. Felicity Cairns was her married name. She died three years ago.'

There was silence in the room.

'How did you get it, Peter?' the judge asked again.

Tanner shook his head. 'If I have to use it, or when I try and tender it, then with respect, judge, I'll tell you.'

The judge raised his eyebrows.

'You've already used it,' Aitken said. 'Mr Tanner shouldn't be allowed to ask questions of this witness based on knowledge he's obtained through unlawful means.'

'I told you, Richard,' Tanner said angrily, 'the deed was *given* to me. And I already knew of the incident behind the deed before I had it.'

'How?' Knight asked.

'Through the same means I get all my useful information, your Honour. Third-hand hearsay and rumour. The question I asked this witness was not prompted by the document I was given. I was going to ask it anyway, and the information available to the defence was credible enough for me to feel comfortable as an officer of the court to ask the question I just have. If you need me to say that in open court, I will.'

The judge nodded slowly. 'If you want to use the document,' he said, 'I'll need an affidavit stating how it was obtained. You might need to call who gave it to you.'

Tanner sighed and nodded but didn't reply.

'You didn't feel the need to tell Richard about it?'

'I only got it Friday, judge. As your Honour knows, besides, I only have to give notice of a specific defence or an alibi. This is neither.'

'Professional courtesy?'

Tanner smiled. 'I'm not doing Mr Aitken's job for him.'

'What does that mean?' Aitken said.

'You've known for weeks about the Cook files. Yet neither you nor the police thought to ask this guy about prior conduct that may have been relevant.'

'He's got no priors.'

'Most killers don't.'

'Enough,' the judge said. He looked at Aitken. 'Are you still going to object?'

'Judge, I haven't seen this document. I've been given very brief instructions.'

'You take instructions from Richter's lawyers, do you, Richard?

Gee, I thought you were representing the Crown. Quick, someone ring Buckingham Palace, the Queen's being usurped.'

'Be quiet, Mr Tanner!' the judge yelled.

'What I've been told,' Aitken said, 'is that the document contains a confidentiality clause, and –'

'So what?' Tanner said. 'This is a criminal trial.'

'Let him finish.'

'The parties to the deed can only disclose its contents if compelled to do so by law. That hasn't happened if someone gave it to Mr Tanner, as he says.'

'Richter is a party to the deed,' Tanner said. 'I think me asking him questions in a murder trial qualifies as being compelled under law.'

'Mr Tanner –'

'You've got a discretion, judge. We say none of this is relevant to –'

'This is in the red-hot zone of relevant evidence, your Honour,' Tanner said. 'In the interests of justice, you are obliged to let it in.'

'Judge, if I can –'

'No, you can't.' Knight sat back in his chair and sighed. 'Here's what I'm going to do. It's three forty. I'm going to send the jury home for the day. I'll consider the photo overnight, and this issue. My inclination though, Mr Tanner, is that if you want to use this document, I'll need evidence about how it came into your possession. I want to know whether you got it lawfully.'

'This is an ambush, judge,' Aitken said.

'You should've told Richard you'd been given this document, Peter,' Knight said. 'Why didn't you tell him you intended to use it?'

Tanner stood, and motioned for Jane Ross to get up too. He walked to the door. 'It didn't suit me to do that, judge. That's not really the key question though, is it? Why isn't Richard prosecuting Mr Richter, that's what I want to know? Why's he leaving that for me to do?'

50

Tanner worked late in chambers after court. He refined his notes for finishing his cross-examination of Richter, and looked over the ones he'd made for his cross of Klaudia Dabrowska. He was getting ready to leave when his mobile rang. It was Maria, calling from his home.

'Hi. I'll be half an hour,' he said when he answered.

'The man is waiting here,' Maria said after a short pause.

He tried to think what she meant. 'What man?'

'The man. He said to me . . . he said to me you want to talk to him about your trial. He's here, waiting.'

She was making no sense. 'Maria,' he said, 'what man are you talking about?'

'He's here.'

'In the house?'

'He said you told him to wait.'

Tanner's heart started to beat faster. 'What's his name, Maria?'

'He . . . I don't know – Steve? I put him on.'

'Maria?' he said again, but she no longer had the phone to her ear. He could hear her walking through the house, then heard him say his name.

'Mr Tanner?' a man said. It sounded like a smoker's voice, deep and husky.

'Who is this?'

'We have some mutual friends.'

'What are you doing in my house?'

'Maria let me in.'

Tanner wanted to throw the phone against the wall. 'I want you to leave,' he said.

'It will be better for our friends if you talk to me.'

'You need to leave.'

Another pause. 'If you want to help your friend in China,' the man said, 'come home and talk.'

As soon as he was in a cab, Tanner called Tom Cable.

'I'm getting ready for bed, Pete,' Cable said as he answered. 'How's the trial –'

'Can you get to my house now?'

'What?'

'Can you drive to my house now, Tom?'

'Why?'

'Just do it, please. It's – Drive to my house now. Wait in your car. I'll be home before you make it. Get the plates of whoever leaves. If I text you to come in, don't walk.'

The man was sitting in Tanner's study. He was in a chair opposite the desk, looking at the back cover of a novel he'd taken from one of the bookshelves. In his other hand was a glass of water.

'Who are you?' Tanner said after he shut the door. 'Who sent you?'

The man put the book on the desk, and looked up, his face expressionless. 'Don't raise your voice,' he said. 'We don't want to wake your son. You can call me Steve.'

'I'm going to ask you once more before I call the police. Who sent you?'

'What will you tell them?'

'That I have an intruder who won't leave.'

'Maria let me in. She gave me this glass of water.' The man was in a blue suit, a white dress shirt, a white kerchief in his breast pocket. His legs were crossed. His shoes were black leather. They were handmade. He didn't look like an intruder. 'If I leave, you won't hear what I have to say about our friends.'

Tanner moved behind his desk, and sat in the chair. 'I doubt we have any friends in common.'

Steve raised his eyebrows and frowned slightly, nodding his head. 'I thought Joe Cheung was a friend of yours?'

Tanner's heart rate was still elevated, and he was not yet sure what was happening, or what to do. 'What do you want?'

Steve smiled fractionally. 'The same thing as you,' he said. 'I want what's best for Joe.'

'And what is best for Joe?'

'I've worked in countries that have the death penalty,' Steve said. 'They tell me you can be executed for some corruption offences in China?' He shook his head, looking almost sad. 'They shoot you. Five years sounds better than that, don't you think?'

Tanner felt his stomach start to churn. 'Are you threatening me? Who do you – ?'

Steve started laughing: a low laugh, almost a snigger. 'We're not threatening you.'

'Who's "we"?'

Steve shook his head slowly, a look of disapproval on his face. 'We want what's best for your other friend, too,' he said. 'I've never been to Sicily.' He lowered his eyes to examine the nails of his right hand. 'I'd like to, one day.'

'What is it that you want?'

Steve uncrossed his legs and leant forwards in his seat, then ran a hand over the stubble of his goatee beard. 'My other friends would like you to – to exercise more discretion in court tomorrow.'

Tanner shook his head and gave a forced smile. 'More discretion?'

'Asking questions about Felicity Horton – we don't think that's in the best interests of Joe and Gabriella. The misunderstanding John Richter had with this poor girl . . .' He paused as though he was searching for the right words. 'That was cleared up years ago. It's best left in the past.'

'I can't just –'

'You know, the late Mrs Richter – and I hate to speak ill of the dead – she really was trying to extort an innocent man out of a lot of money.'

Tanner took two deep breaths before speaking. 'The people who are instructing me know about the deed between Richter and Felicity Horton. So does my client. The judge knows it. I can't not use it.'

Steve shrugged, looked at his glass of water like he was examining evidence, then took another sip. 'You can find a way of losing an argument about the deed, can't you?' He paused as though waiting for a response. 'It's only right to allow Mr Richter a fair chance to give his version of events, don't you think? You want the truth, don't you?'

Tanner ran a hand across his face. 'Or what?'

'It will be better for Joe if that's what happened. How old are his kids? Younger than your boy, aren't they? Kids need a father.' He paused. 'I guess they need mothers too.' His smile almost looked real. 'That's a nice-looking woman you've been seeing. The lawyer some of my friends don't like very much? How tall is she?'

Tanner closed his eyes for a moment, trying to will the man away. 'Get out,' he said when he opened them. 'Now.'

Steve nodded slowly, and rose. He put his glass of water on the desk. 'Make a smart choice,' he said, walking to the door. 'And thank Maria for the water, will you?'

As soon as the door closed, Tanner rang Lisa Ilves. She answered on the fifth ring.

'I'm brushing my teeth.'

'You've got a number for Gaby Campbell?'

'Why?'

'Call her now. Tell her she needs to get out of Taormina for a few days. Whatever the time is there, she needs to take a break right away.'

'Pete, what are you – ?'

'Just do it, Lisa,' he said.

'What's happened? You're not making any sense. I can't just –'

'Listen to me,' he said sharply. '*They* are unhappy with her. Do you understand that? Maybe as unhappy with her as they were with Anne Warren. Just do what I ask. Tell her to leave.'

'Okay, okay,' she said, fear in her voice.

He took a breath, and focused on calming himself. 'When you're done, come around here, okay? Stay here tonight.'

As he ended the call, there was a knock on the door. He ran to the hallway. 'Who is it?'

'Me.'

Cable's hair was sticking up, like he'd just got out of bed. 'What's going on?' he said as Tanner let him in. 'Jesus, you look like you've seen a –'

'I need you to take Dan to school in the morning,' Tanner said. 'And I need you there to pick him up when he's done.'

51

The following morning, Tony Kerr took a seat at a café near the office tower where he worked. It was just after nine. He had a gift box with him, which he put on the table.

The man he was waiting for, with whom he'd had one prior meeting where a small package was exchanged, joined him five minutes later. This time he was carrying a larger package, wrapped in red paper. When their coffees came, they drank them quickly. The men talked only about the weekend sport while they sat together, the business part of their meeting having taken place at an earlier time. The weather was warm for October, but the man with the red package, who did not remove his hat or sunglasses, was wearing gloves.

He left first, taking Kerr's box from the table when he did. Kerr left not long after with the red package, only remembering to pay the bill when he was almost out the door. He returned to Citadel and went straight to his office. He opened his cupboard, then the safe that was in it, and placed the package inside.

Fifteen minutes later, his phone rang. The receptionist asked him to come to the front desk immediately, as Mr Randall needed to speak to him. Randall was his boss, the general counsel of Citadel Australia.

'What?'

'Mr Randall is here. He wants you to come now.'

Kerr had a tight feeling in his gut. He wondered why Randall hadn't called him, or come to his office. Then he reached reception, and saw five men in suits with Randall, one of whom was carrying a video camera. He knew right away they were cops. He approached the group, but didn't speak.

'Are you Anthony Kerr?'

'Yes.'

'My name is Detective Sergeant Woods, from the State Crime Command of the New South Wales Police Force drug squad. As a result of information provided by a confidential informant, we have reason to believe that you have in your possession a quantity of illegal narcotics, and that they're kept in these offices. We also have reason to believe you've been selling narcotics that you keep at these offices. We've just provided Mr Randall with a search warrant, which authorises us to search your office, including the contents of your computer. I should warn you that . . .'

The cop said more words, but Kerr didn't take them in. While the detective talked, Kerr rushed behind the reception desk, fumbled for the waste bin, and vomited.

When they reached Kerr's office, the detective directed him to enter his password into the computer, then turned the computer over to a cop who was an IT expert. Meanwhile, another officer had opened the cupboard and found the safe.

'Is this yours, sir?'

Kerr stood in the middle of the room, pale and clammy, his hands shaking.

'The company doesn't supply safes,' Randall said. He was standing in the doorway.

'It's empty,' Kerr said.

'Please open the safe, sir.'

'I've never used it . . . I'm – I have no idea what the code is.'

'Sir, open the safe now. If you don't, we'll have someone force it open, and we'll charge you with hindering police in an investigation.'

'Open the fucking safe, Tony,' Randall said.

Kerr's hand shook so much it took him three attempts to enter the correct code. When he did, he ran back to his desk. This time he vomited in his own waste bin.

52

A short time later, Justice Philip Knight was handing down a ruling in which he held that the defence could use the blown-up photo of Nikki Richter from Sally Cook's files.

While Knight was reading out his reasons to the court, Tanner felt one of the two phones he had in his pockets vibrate. He put the phone under the bar table, and looked at the message, which was from an unknown number. *Went mining. Minerals found.*

'You followed all that, Mr Tanner?' the judge said as he put away his phone.

'If it please the court.'

'Are we ready for the jury?'

'Not yet, your Honour.'

'Why not?'

'I'm waiting on an affidavit concerning the matter discussed in your Honour's chambers yesterday afternoon. I don't expect it to take long.'

'That should have been done last night, Mr Tanner.'

'Everyone on my side of the bar table is pulling their weight, your Honour. I'm asking for an hour at most.'

The judge shook his head. 'Mr Aitken?'

'I'd need some time to consider any affidavit when we have it, your Honour.'

The judge sighed heavily. 'I want that affidavit served within the half-hour, Mr Tanner. You can have fifteen minutes to consider it, Mr Crown. Don't tell me you didn't prepare an argument last night about admissibility. I'll adjourn for forty-five minutes. I'm not holding up a jury trial for any longer.'

When the judge left the bench, Jane Ross grabbed Tanner by the arm. 'We have the affidavit, Pete,' she said. 'What – ?'

'Get Porter to swear another copy with today's date,' he said.

'Pete?'

He stood. 'I need time to sort out my argument, Jane,' he said firmly. 'I want to be left alone in our room.'

Once in the defence room, Tanner responded to the text he'd received in court. *Time is of the essence for me.*

Within a minute he received a reply: *Looking.*

Twenty minutes later, another came through. *Found.*

Tanner walked to the prosecution room and knocked on the door. When it was opened he threw the affidavit towards Aitken, who was seated at the far end. 'I'll tell the associate,' he said. 'I'll see you in court in fifteen minutes.'

When court resumed, Tanner handed up an affidavit sworn by Charles Porter. It recounted a conversation he'd had with lead counsel for the accused, Peter Tanner, on the previous Friday evening, when Tanner had informed him of the details of his meeting with Trevor Horton. Annexed to the affidavit was a copy of the deed. Also handed up was a short submission admitting that Horton was in breach of the confidentiality obligations in the deed, but that the court should allow the document to be admitted into evidence anyway.

Aitken handed up a submission seeking to have the document excluded from evidence on the grounds it had been unlawfully provided to the defence, and was insufficiently relevant to the primary issue before the court concerning the guilt or otherwise of Justin Matheson.

The judge adjourned to consider a ruling, but it took him only thirty minutes. Trevor Horton was in breach of the deed's obligations of confidentiality, but that was neither a crime, nor unlawfulness of any great magnitude. The potential relevance of the deed outweighed the desirability of ensuring that what in effect was a private contract was not breached. The defence could use the document to question the witness.

When the jury came back, Tanner deferred taking up the judge's ruling to use the photo; he wanted it to be the last image they saw when he was done with Richter. He went to the deed first.

'Mr Richter, yesterday I asked you if anyone else had made an allegation of violence against you other than your late wife. There was an objection before you could answer. Do you recall that?'

'Yes.'

'And you've now heard the judge's ruling that you have to answer that question?'

'Yes.'

'Your late wife wasn't the first person to allege you'd hurt them, was she?'

Richter paused for longer than normal. 'No,' he finally said.

'Who was Felicity Horton?'

Another long pause, as though Richter was waiting for someone to save him. 'That whole thing was a setup.'

Tanner shook his head. 'I asked you who she was, Mr Richter. She was your girlfriend?'

'No.'

'Did you ever go on a date with her?'

'We went to a couple of parties together. It was more like giving her a lift.'

'She made an allegation that you caused her some form of physical harm, didn't she?'

'Not to me, she didn't.'

'Who did she make that allegation to, then?'

'My – the company's lawyers.'

'You're referring to Citadel Resources?'

'Yes.'

'What, she contacted them directly?'

'Her lawyers did.'

'Are you sure it wasn't your lawyers who contacted her family first?'

'I don't think so.'

'What injury did her lawyers allege you caused her?'

'I don't recall.'

'C'mon, Mr Richter. That's not a truthful answer, is it? What was the injury?'

'I don't recall.'

'Did your lawyers tell you to answer my question that way last night?'

'I object,' Aitken said.

'I'm not talking about the Crown Prosecutor, your Honour,' Tanner said.

'That's not an appropriate question, Mr Tanner.'

'Did Felicity Horton allege you'd fractured her skull?'

'I don't remember.'

'Did she allege that you struck her on the head with a champagne bottle?'

'That didn't happen.'

'It wasn't a trivial allegation, was it?'

'I don't remember.'

'Do you remember the amount of money paid on your behalf to Miss Horton?'

'No.'

'Does two million dollars ring a bell, Mr Richter?'

'I don't know.'

'You just told the court that you didn't hurt Miss Horton, do you remember that?' It was now past the time when he thought he had to keep up any pretence of politeness. He let his voice rise, and real anger rose with it.

'Yes.'

'You haven't forgotten that in the last two minutes?'

'I object, your –'

'Weren't you outraged?'

'I'm sorry?'

'Forget the exact sum. When you found out this woman was seeking money from you, weren't you angry?'

'I wasn't impressed.'

'Not impressed? You must have discussed it with, for example, your father?'

'I don't have a specific memory. I guess so.'

'And your lawyers?'

'I don't remember.'

'You don't remember? Who got hit on the head, Mr Richter, Felicity Horton or you?'

'I object, your –'

'Mr Tanner!' the judge cried.

'I withdraw that question. You must have told your lawyers that what Miss Horton was alleging wasn't true?'

'I would have done.'

'You don't recall being angry?'

'Like I said, I wasn't impressed. People know we have money. That can make you vulnerable to . . .'

'To what, Mr Richter?'

'People trying to take advantage.'

'To get money?'

'Yes.'

'What, like blackmail?' Tanner said, looking at the jury. 'Is this the same as with your late wife?'

'I object.'

'It was the witness's own word, your Honour,' Tanner said. 'It's what he said his late wife was doing.'

Knight shook his head. 'No, Mr Tanner.'

'Why do you think Miss Horton made this allegation?'

'I object, your Honour. The witness can't know the motivation of someone else.'

'The witness might well know –'

'I'll allow the question.'

'Do you need it repeated, Mr Richter?'

'We had a fight. A – a disagreement.'

'Over what?'

'She wanted to be a couple. I didn't.'

'Where did this disagreement take place?'

'At a party. We talked about it, I said I didn't want to, she got angry. As far as I know, she left. The next thing I know, she was making wild allegations.'

'Let me see if I understand you, Mr Richter. You won't date Miss Horton, so she says you've assaulted her and wants money? Is that it?'

'Pretty much.'

'And your father pays her money.'

'I wasn't involved in that.'

'Why pay someone money if what they're alleging is untrue?'

'She was threatening to go to the press, to go on TV.'

'Oh, you remember that part, but not the injury she alleged or what you paid her?'

'Yes.'

'So what?'

'I beg your pardon?'

'So what if she said she'd do that? You didn't hurt her, you say. How would she prove you did?'

Richter paused before answering. 'I – I don't know. That's what she was threatening.'

'Did you think she was going to get someone to hurt her and then blame you? Could it have been the same person your late wife got to nearly strangle her?'

'Your Honour –'

'I press the question.'

'It's not a proper question, Mr Tanner, and you know it!' Knight shouted.

'Do you remember signing a legal document with Miss Horton?'

'No.'

'Do you deny it?'

'I can't recall.'

'Do you deny she was paid an amount of money?'

'No.'

'You just can't recall the figure?'

'Yes.'

'I'll come back to it. You said Mr Matheson had cocaine with him the night that Elena Mancini died?'

The question disorientated Richter, and it took him a moment to refocus. 'Yes.'

'And you're aware he told police that the cocaine was yours?'

'That's not true.'

'Your late wife used cocaine from time to time?'

'Yes.'

'But not you?'

'No.'

'Did you buy it for her?'

'No.'

'Do you know anyone who sells cocaine?'

'I – not that I'm aware of.'

'Who's Anthony Kerr, Mr Richter?'

The many hours Richter had spent training for giving his testimony didn't help him. He hadn't discussed his coke habit with the prosecutor, or his own legal team. Shock froze his face for several moments. 'He's a lawyer.'

'A lawyer for Citadel?'

'Yes.'

'The company's Australian deputy general counsel?'

'Yes.'

As Tanner asked his question, he became aware of someone approaching the seats behind the prosecution team. He turned and saw a man in a suit attracting the attention of James Carrington, the lawyer from BBK who'd been assigned to hold Richter's hand.

'His office is three doors from yours, correct?'

'Yes.'

'I haven't objected yet, your Honour, but I've been wondering about relevance for the last several questions.'

'I'll get there, your Honour.'

'Soon.'

'You socialise with Mr Kerr?'

'Not really.'

'You've never had a drink with him after work?'

'Maybe a couple of times.'

'He's a member of Pantheon, isn't he? You must have seen him there?'

'A couple of times.'

'And, more than a couple of times, you bought cocaine from Mr Kerr, didn't you?'

The question seemed to slow time down. 'There's no basis for that question, your Honour,' Aitken finally said.

'Actually, your Honour, there is.'

The judge looked stunned for a moment. He knew Tanner wouldn't risk a question like that without foundation. 'We'd better talk in chambers first, Mr Tanner.'

'Are you going to tell me, Peter?' Jane Ross said to Tanner as they stood at the bar table, watching the judge disappear from the courtroom after the jury had. She grabbed his arm tightly. 'How do you know this?' she demanded.

'Let's go see the judge,' he said, moving his chair back.

Justice Knight was sitting down when the lawyers walked into his chambers. Aitken looked subdued and didn't try to lead off.

Knight removed his glasses and looked at Tanner. 'Well?'

'He was arrested over an hour ago,' he said. He looked at his watch. 'An hour and a half. They found cocaine in his office at Citadel.'

'How do you know this?'

'I was told.'

'By whom?'

Tanner shook his head. 'No, judge, with respect. I was told.'

'I've just got a text, judge,' Aitken said, almost in a whisper, 'telling me the arrest of Mr Kerr hasn't been made public yet. He's still being processed.'

'Peter?'

Tanner shrugged.

'I'll still formally object, judge,' Aitken said. It was a meek effort.

'My client says it was Richter's coke, judge. That alone is enough for me to put to this witness he bought it. Now I have a guy three doors down from him arrested for having cocaine in his office. I'm going to bash Richter over the head with that. No pun intended regarding his skills with a champagne bottle.'

Aitken looked like he was going to say something, but the judge held up his hand to stop him. 'I'll pretend I didn't hear that,' he said, looking at Tanner.

'I'm going to ask you to issue a subpoena for the arresting officer to give evidence in my case.'

The judge nodded. 'Let's go back to court.'

After the jury came back in, Tanner applied to use the blown-up photo of Nikki Richter's face and bruised neck. He'd deal with the drugs and the deed while using the image. He had the easel set up close to the dock, on an angle so both the jurors and the gallery could see it. He had the same photo put on the courtroom's flat screen television.

'You did that to your wife, didn't you?' Tanner asked.

'No, I didn't.'

'She didn't throttle herself, did she?'

'I don't – it wasn't me.'

'Were you angry when you did it, Mr Richter? About your late wife saying she was divorcing you? Did that put you in a rage?'

Aitken objected before Tanner finished his question, and the judge overruled him.

'Did you buy cocaine for your wife, Mr Richter?'

'No.'

'You bought it off Mr Kerr, didn't you?'

'No.'

'What about heroin? You paid for that?'

'No, I didn't.'

'You paid two million dollars to Felicity Horton, though, didn't you?'

'I don't remember.'

'Let me show you this document.' Tanner had a court officer hand a copy of the deed to Richter. 'Do you recognise that document?'

'No.'

'Turn to page six. Is that your signature?'

Richter looked at it for a long time. 'It looks like it.'

'Turn to page two, Mr Richter, and look at the figure I've highlighted. Do you see the figure and words for two million dollars? Does that refresh your memory?'

'I see the figure.'

'You fractured this woman's skull, didn't you?'

'I didn't do that.'

'You didn't pay her that sum for breaking her heart, did you?'

Aitken objected, but Richter answered. 'I didn't do it.'

'Did she dance with another man? Did that put you into a rage?'

'I didn't do it.'

'What about Elena Mancini, Mr Richter? What put you in a rage that night? Did she knock you back?'

'I didn't hurt her.'

'Was it an accident? Or did you mean to hurt her but not kill her, is that the truth?'

'I didn't touch her.'

'Was it the cocaine you purchased from Mr Kerr? Did that put you in a rage?'

'The coke was Justin's.'

'Who did you call, when you did it? Who came and helped clean up the mess?'

'I called the police.'

'When Justin Matheson was unconscious, did you run Elena Mancini's hands over his chest, or was that the idea of someone higher up the brains trust than you?'

'That didn't happen.'

'Who's Steve, Mr Richter?'

'What?'

'Just one more question and we're done,' Tanner said, lowering his voice. 'Did you cry at your wife's funeral, Mr Richter?'

53

In Tanner's chambers that afternoon, Charles Porter twisted the top off a beer and took a seat in front of the desk, as Tanner looked at his computer screen. 'Anything there?' he asked.

'It's on the breaking news. "*Senior in-house lawyer of multinational mining corporation arrested on suspicion of drug possession*", that kind of thing. Doesn't mention his name or Citadel yet.'

'You did, in court.'

'They've got a temporary suppression order from another judge,' Tanner said. 'It won't last long.'

'Are you going to tell us how you knew?'

'No.'

'No?' Jane Ross said.

Tanner nodded.

'What's your take now?' Porter asked, loosening his tie.

'On what?'

'Where we're at. Bill and Judith want me to call them after I leave here.'

'There's still Klaudia,' Tanner said. 'She can't save Richter's reputation, but she can rehabilitate him as a witness of truth about Elena.'

'You've avoided me so far when I've asked what the strategy is with her.'

'To get her to tell the truth,' Tanner said.

Porter put the beer on Tanner's desk. 'It'll be that easy?'

'It won't be easy, Charles,' Tanner said, 'but it will be quick.'

Porter stared at Tanner, then at Ross. 'Is there something you're not telling us? Again?'

Tanner shook his head. 'Is Sarah Matheson going to be in court tomorrow?'

Porter nodded. 'She wants to eyeball Klaudia, keep her head held high. Why?'

'She doesn't have to come,' Tanner said. 'It won't be pleasant for her, hearing me ask Klaudia about Justin.'

'You said you wanted her there.'

'Not for this witness.'

'I can tell her she doesn't have to, Peter, but I can't tell her no. Why are you asking?'

As Porter spoke, Tanner's phone rang. 'There's a man here who wants to see you,' the receptionist said. 'He won't give me –'

Tanner's heart started thumping. 'What does he look like?'

'Um. He's tall . . . He's well built. He's –'

He took a deep breath. He knew who it was. 'Tell him two minutes.' He put the phone down and looked at Porter and Jane. 'Sorry. You have to leave.'

'Who is it?' Jane asked.

He shook his head. 'I'll call you later.'

Mark Woods walked past Tanner and took a seat in front of the desk. Tanner shut the door and sat down.

Woods glared at him for a few moments, before throwing a white envelope he was holding on the desk. 'You prick,' he said. 'You fucked me.'

'You're welcome.'

'We'd barely started our interview, and you're announcing his fucking arrest in court?'

'What did you think I was going to do?'

'We're all being questioned about the leak, Tanner. I've just been grilled. The deal was you got your fucking package, and I got an arrest. That means we announce when that's happened, not you.'

'I didn't have a choice.'

'Bullshit.'

'I just gave you a guy with two kilos of coke.'

'You said the thing you wanted was for another case. "Out of the jurisdiction", you said. Not for this fucking Matheson trial.'

'What I want it for is out of the jurisdiction,' Tanner said. 'Has he made admissions?'

Woods sighed, still looking capable of a violent act. 'He said he didn't know how the coke got in the safe.'

'Has he been shown the security film from the Citadel building of him walking back to the office carrying the coke yet?'

Woods nodded. 'You can't call me,' he said.

'What?'

'You can't call me to give evidence about the arrest.'

'Why not?'

'I might get asked something that would force me to lie. I don't want to do that.'

Tanner nearly laughed. 'You're a high-ranking member of the New South Wales police force. Don't tell me you can't lie in court.'

'You're a prick.'

'I'll call someone else from your team.'

'The coke is shit, by the way.'

'You tried it?'

'Fuck off,' Woods said, but without venom. 'We got the prelim lab results. It's lignocaine and some other shit mixed with only thirty per cent coke. This guy got ripped off as well.'

'That's a shame, given what he paid. Perhaps he can sell it to his dentist.' As he spoke, his phone sounded again. 'Tell her to wait for a few minutes, will you,' he said into it. Tanner put the phone down, and glared at Woods. 'I got threatened last night.'

Woods narrowed his eyes. 'Threatened? By who?'

Tanner shook his head. 'A man came to my house. I don't know his name – he said to call him "Steve". My kid was asleep in another room.'

'What do you mean "threatened"? Over this thing I've just given you? If I get any blowback about what's in that –'

'Your name won't come up, detective.'

Woods glared at him. Tanner couldn't tell if the look was concern or contempt or both.

'Whatever it is you're doing, Tanner,' he said, 'you are way out of your depth.' He stood to leave. 'You owe me for what I did for you today.'

Tanner looked at the envelope on his desk. 'We'll see.'

Tanner held up the memory stick he'd taken from the envelope Woods had given him and showed it to Lisa Ilves. Then he put it in the back of his computer.

After the cocaine was found, Kerr was made to open all of his cabinets, including one kept locked with a key. More police arrived, and Kerr was arrested and taken to Local Area Command in the city to be questioned. Woods had his hands on some of what Tanner wanted within minutes. While the video operator recorded most parts of the execution of the warrant, he ignored Woods and his portable scanner. The IT officer meanwhile had found what he'd been told to look for.

Tanner brought up the first document. It was a copy of an email from Kerr to Randall, the Australian GC, and to Spry, the global GC. It was headed *Strictly confidential and commercial in confidence.* 'Jesus,' he said when he read it. He took a deep breath, and started to read the next document.

Lisa came around to his side of the desk and started to read. 'Do you have anyone in particular in mind? Is there a journalist – ?'

'I need to finish this trial first,' he said. 'Then we'll work out what we do.' He opened another document. 'Are you seeing this?'

Lisa put her hand on the back of his neck. 'Yeah,' she said softly.

When they'd finished reading, Tanner told Lisa to go back to his home. He rang Tom Cable.

'Lisa's on her way,' he said. 'All okay?'

'Maria's cooked paella. I'm thinking about moving in here.'

'Thanks for staying again.'

'Childcare is much less risky than B&Es.'

'How's Karl's mood?'

'I think he's gearing up for a serious father–son conference when you get home.'

'I'll be home in an hour.'

When he hung up, he dialled the mobile number of Yinshi Li. It was seven pm in Sydney, five in Shanghai. He got voicemail. He left a message that he knew would guarantee a return call.

Only minutes later, his phone rang.

'I'm not sure I understand, Peter,' Li said.

'You can manage, Li. It is very important.'

'The people you've mentioned –'

'I'll email you a complete list. I know who some of their lawyers are. I'll call them myself. If you could speak to the Chinese directors, though, I'd appreciate it. Even if you just leave a message. I don't want anything lost in translation.'

'But what . . . ?'

'Just tell them what I said in my message. Ask them if they've been fishing lately.'

'I don't understand.'

'Ask them if they've been fishing in the Tovosevu River. Tell them I have. Tell them I wasn't alone.'

It was a long time before Li spoke. 'That question might lead to a more severe sentence for my client than I have been working towards.'

Tanner wanted to laugh a kind of bitter laugh, but stopped himself. 'Then at least I know that we're asking the right people.'

When he ended the call to Li, he drafted an email. It was to Hedley Fontaine, the global CEO of Bloomberg Butler Kelly, who was based in New York. He copied in Dennis Jackson, the Australasian CEO.

In his study later that night, finishing his prep for Klaudia Dabrowska, Tanner received a call from Jackson. 'What do you mean by – ?'

'I'm in a murder trial, Dennis,' Tanner said, cutting him off. 'I don't have much time.'

'What does – ?'

'I want a meeting with the chairman of Citadel's board, and the CEO. I'm inviting some of their Chinese friends too.'

'Why would they meet with you?'

'They need educating.'

'What are you talking about?'

'Sodium cyanide. Anne Warren.'

There was a long silence. 'What – who is Anne Warren?'

'Ask your client.'

'What – ?'

'It's been a hard week, Dennis. I'll send you an email about where and when to meet. You need to tell your client that if they send someone to my home again, they will never have another mine in this country. Is that clear?'

'What the fuck are you – ?'

'Just do what I've told you, Dennis. Your client is going to want to meet me,' he said. 'The bigger question is whether they want you there.'

54

Klaudia Dabrowska was wearing a black knee-length skirt and a cream woollen top with a white shirt underneath. She looked nothing like a hostess at Pantheon.

Aitken took her slowly through her evidence. She smiled and nodded at him like he was a kindly uncle. He strayed into leading a number of times, but Tanner resisted the temptation to object – he didn't want to look like a bully. Aggression was fine with Richter, but it could backfire with Dabrowska.

Aitken spent more time than was needed on her background, no doubt hoping that the jury would grow to like her. So he had her tell the court about her Polish parents who'd emigrated to the UK, about her father, who ended up selling menswear in a large retail store, and about her mother, who first worked as a cleaner, then as a cook in a nursing home just beyond the greenbelt of London.

Dabrowska had started modelling when only fifteen, and left school once she did. Her mother died when she was nineteen, and having moved out of her parents' home, she moved back to be close to her father. She had a sister who was now twenty-seven, and a brother who was nearly thirty.

At twenty-two she decided to travel, and Australia was high on her list. She had a girlfriend who'd moved to Sydney with a boy, and she loved beaches and warm weather. She registered with the same modelling agency she'd been with in the UK. The work was intermittent, and she ran through cash quickly. One of the girls she'd met at Jade worked at Pantheon, and she was soon bolstering her income by working there a few nights a week.

She knew who John Richter was. She'd met him at the club, and was told he part-owned the complex. He was always polite and friendly, she said. She'd known Elena Mancini for five weeks before the night she died. They'd gone to a few parties together on nights off, and teamed up as hostesses from time to time.

She'd never met Justin Matheson until the night of Elena Mancini's death. He was drunk when he arrived with John Richter. 'Happy drunk,' she told the jury.

Aitken played the film of her kissing Matheson, dealing with the weakest part of her evidence head on, so Tanner wouldn't get a chance to control it.

'I'm so embarrassed,' she said. 'Elena and I had snuck a few cocktails out the back – in the kitchen. I thought he was cute, and he was funny. I was in a happy mood . . . I didn't expect him to kiss me back so hard.'

She was led through what happened at John Richter's retreat. Her evidence was consistent with Richter's, and what she'd told the police in her interview. It was Matheson who'd brought the coke out, not Richter. And when he did, Richter quickly left the room, and went to another part of the house. She decided to go with him.

'Why, Miss Dabrowksa?' Aitken asked.

'Drugs scare me,' she said. 'I had a girlfriend at school who died of an overdose. It seemed like really bad taste to bring out drugs . . . I'd read about John's wife, how she died. It didn't seem right.'

Richter had gone to his study, and they sat and talked for maybe half an hour. 'I was checking if he was okay. Then he talked a bit about the funeral, then he started asking questions about me. How long I was going to stay, that kind of thing. I mentioned my visa problem, and he said he'd try and help.

I think I yawned at some point . . . I was pretty embarrassed because he was talking about helping me, but he was nice, and said he'd take me home.'

It was a ten-minute drive to her flat. They had one cup of instant coffee, talked some more, and then he left.

'Where was Justin Matheson when you left Mr Richter's home?'

'In the lounge,' she said, 'next to Elena.'

'Did you say goodbye?'

'John checked if Elena wanted to go. I thought she was going to say yes, but Justin said no, no, and . . . she stayed.'

'Did you sleep with Justin Matheson that night, Miss Dabrowska?'

She shook her head. 'No,' she said. 'I did not.'

'You mentioned that you went to church with your father regularly after your mother died?' Tanner began his cross.

'Yes.'

'Although he went consistently before that?'

'Every Sunday.'

'Would you describe your father as devout?'

'He – yes, he is.'

'Your father – would I be right if I guessed he's a man who has fairly firm beliefs?'

'Um . . . I'm not sure what you mean. Belief about God?'

'Well, I took that as a given. My apologies. Let me give you an example. He probably doesn't think women should be priests, would that be right?'

'That would definitely be right,' she said, and there was a faint ripple of laughter in the court.

'You mentioned your sister did some modelling too?'

'Yes.'

'You look similar, do you?'

'Some people think we're twins. Sofie says I'm thinner, but that's not true.'

'Your sister's married now, you said?'

'Yes.'

'She no longer works?'

'Not at the moment.'

'She's got a young child?'

'Yes.'

'And your elder brother, he's a hotel concierge, you said?'

'Yes, in Brighton.'

'You mentioned your mother cleaned, and then became a hospital cook?'

'Yes.'

'And your father retired recently?'

'Last year.'

'When your parents emigrated, during those first few years, I imagine money was pretty tight?'

'We were a long way off rich, if that's what you mean.'

'You told us your mother died about four years ago?'

'Nearly five.'

'And that's when you went to live with your father again?'

'Yes.'

'When the crown prosecutor asked you to tell us your name, you said it was Klaudia Dabrowska, correct?'

She looked surprised. 'That is my name,' she said softly.

'And the address you gave was your father's home?'

'Yes.'

'But not where he lives now?'

A hesitation for longer than would be expected, as though she couldn't recall where she lived.

'Miss Dabrowska?'

'He mainly lives there.'

'Do we take that to mean he sometimes lives elsewhere?'

Again a hesitation. 'Yes,' she said.

'There's a property in Curzon Street. He lives there too, doesn't he?'

Aitken finally objected, citing a lack of relevance, but Tanner asked for some latitude. 'I'll get there, your Honour,' he said, and the judge allowed him to continue. 'Miss Dabrowska, the apartment at Curzon Street, it's owned by your father, isn't it? It's in the name of Karol Dabrowska. That's your father, isn't it?'

'Yes.'

'It's a property he bought quite recently, isn't it? Only four months ago?'

'I don't know.'

'You don't know? Aren't you on the title too?'

'I don't know what my father's done.'

'Your mother's maiden name was Novak, wasn't it?'

She nodded almost imperceptibly.

'Yes?' Tanner said, for the first time raising his voice.

'Yes.'

'And you now sometimes call yourself Klaudia Novak?'

'Yes.'

'Why?'

'Because . . . a journalist tried to talk to me about this case. I thought it might be easier –'

'What was their name?'

'I don't know.'

'Were they from television, or a newspaper?'

'I don't know.'

'Were they from the UK or from here?'

'I don't –'

'Male or female?'

'A man.'

'The Curzon Street property was bought four months ago – does that sound right?'

'I don't know.'

'Is there a mortgage?'

'I don't know.'

'Because we can't find any indication of a mortgage on the title, Miss Dabrowska. Does that surprise you?'

'I don't –'

'Would it surprise you that another apartment of the same size in the same building sold last year for over six million pounds?'

'I – it's an expensive area,' she said faintly, but the earth was opening beneath her.

'Could you and your father afford to pay six million pounds for an apartment, Miss Dabrowska?'

'I don't know,' she said loudly.

'You must have discussed buying this property with your father? Surely you asked him, "Hey, Dad, where'd you get the money from?"'

'He doesn't like to discuss money,' she said.

'Did someone buy the apartment for you?'

'I don't know.'

'You didn't give evidence at my client's committal hearing, did you?'

'No.'

'You were so ill you couldn't even give evidence by video link?'

'I had an ear infection. I was in a lot of pain for three months. I had to have an operation.'

'And your treating doctor was Dr Anthony? Your general practitioner?'

'Yes.'

'Who recommended Dr Anthony to you?'

'I don't – I can't remember.'

'But it must have been an ear specialist who performed the surgery on you?'

'Yes.'

'Was that Dr Alastair Vaughan?'

She froze. When she failed to answer, Aitken objected, but the judge allowed the question when Tanner assured him the topic would soon show itself as relevant.

'Dr Alastair Vaughan, Miss Dabrowksa? Did he operate on your ear?' He said the last four words as though each was a sentence itself.

She kept looking at Tanner, and then, for a moment, shifted her gaze to Justin Matheson.

'The answer is "no", isn't it, Miss Dabrowska?'

'No,' she finally said.

'You know who I'm talking about, though, don't you? You know Dr Alastair Vaughan.'

'Yes,' she said softly.

'What's Dr Vaughan's specialty, Miss Dabrowska? You know, don't you?'

She nodded, but didn't answer.

'You have to answer in words, Miss Dabrowska. You're under an oath. You have to say "yes".'

'Yes,' she said, as faintly as she could, as though the softness of her voice might mean it wasn't a real answer.

'He's an obstetrician, isn't he?'

She nodded again.

'Miss Dabrowska?'

'Yes.'

'Your obstetrician, isn't he?'

She nodded, and said something, which might have been 'Yes'. Her head was down now, and she was crying.

Tanner didn't hesitate for her tears. It had to be finished. 'He delivered your child, didn't he, Miss Dabrowska. Just over three months ago?'

She sobbed violently for a few moments, and Aitken rose to ask for a short adjournment.

'I'm going to give her a moment to compose herself first,' the judge said.

Everyone waited, and Klaudia Dabrowska cried. It was the only sound in the courtroom for a minute – a minute that seemed like ten. Tissues were provided, water poured.

As Tanner waited, a note was passed to him by Jane Ross, who in turn had received it from Porter. *Sarah wants to know what's going on?* He looked over to the dock, and saw his client looking at him. He'd looked calm all trial, even on the first few days when the evidence had all been against him. He now wore a look that was equal measures shock and anger. Tanner didn't care how Matheson looked, but he could only imagine the look on Sarah Matheson's face.

'I'm right, aren't I?' he continued at the first sign the witness would be able to talk.

'Yes.'

'And at the time of the committal hearing, you were nearly six months pregnant, is that correct?'

'Yes.'

'I need you to consider this question very carefully, Miss Dabrowksa,' Tanner then said slowly. 'If Justin Matheson was to do a blood test, and that blood was to be compared to your child's, would that identify him as the father?'

There was no immediate answer. Matheson stood in the dock and yelled, 'No!' as if commanding Dabrowska not to answer. Then he looked over at Tanner, anger and fear in his eyes. 'No!'

At the same time, from behind, Tanner heard a scream. It was Sarah Matheson, doubled over, crying. Judith Matheson tried to grab her, but she pushed her away. She managed to stand. She looked at Tanner like she might kill him, then at her husband. Her face collapsed again, and a man in the row behind her, one of Matheson's friends, rushed around to grab her and lead her out of court. In the confusion, no one noticed for a few moments that Dabrowska had relapsed into a fit of tears, this time crying more uncontrollably than before. Opposite her, Matheson sat down again, his head bowed, his hands covering his face.

'We might have to break this time, Mr Tanner,' the judge said.

'Yes!' Klaudia Dabrowska cried before Tanner could respond. 'Yes.'

Tanner looked at the judge, who nodded at him almost imperceptibly.

'It's nearly over, Miss Dabrowska,' he said. 'You had intercourse with Mr Matheson on the night Elena Mancini died, didn't you?'

'Yes,' she said clearly, even though she was sobbing.

'And some weeks later, you discovered you were pregnant?'

'Yes.'

'And Mr Matheson is the baby's father?'

'Yes.'

'And ... the cocaine that night. It was John Richter's, wasn't it?'

There was no answer this time, so Tanner repeated himself more loudly. He hadn't finished the sentence when she spat the answer. 'Yes.'

'And you weren't driven home with Mr Richter, were you?'

'No.'

'How did you get home?'

'I don't – two men took me. Then someone came to my house.'

'Who?'

'I don't know.'

'You don't know his name?'

'No ... he said his name was Steve.'

'Did he tell you a last name?'

'No.'

'When did Steve speak to you?'

'After the other men took me home,' she said, now controlling the tears, starting to detach herself from where she was, and her pain.

'How much later?'

'I don't – it was daytime. Morning.'

'Did he tell you to tell the police that the cocaine was Mr Matheson's?'

She shook her head. 'He told me Justin had killed Elena.'

'Did you believe him?'

She took in a deep breath, and looked at the ceiling, and closed her eyes. Massive tears ran down either side of her face. 'I don't – I didn't know.'

'What else did he say?'

'He said Justin was going to say that the cocaine was mine. That Justin had wealthy parents, tha– he said if Justin was believed, I could go to jail for years.'

'What did this man tell you then?'

'He told me . . . he told me to say the drugs were Justin's. That John –' she shook her head, and smiled through tears, '– that John would back me up.'

'What else did he say?'

'He . . . he said Justin had – there'd been a struggle, Justin was drunk, Elena's head had hit the table –'

'But Mr Matheson was with you, not Elena Mancini. He was in a bedroom with you, wasn't he?'

'I know that,' she screamed, and her chin crumpled and shook, and she started to cry again. 'He said he must have gotten up . . . that he –' She started to cry again, and Tanner was forced to wait.

Aitken stood to ask for a break, but his heart was no longer in it, and the judge waved the objection away.

'They said I would go to jail if I didn't say what they told me to. They said they would help me. If – if I just said the drugs were Justin's, and that I went home with John . . . they told me it would be best to say I wasn't with Justin – that way Justin couldn't blame the drugs on me. I didn't know what to do. Elena was dead . . . they said they'd help me, help my family . . . I just – He went out and came with a – they had a statement for me.'

'Who did?'

'The man . . . Steve . . . he talked to me, told me what to say, then he left. He came back later. He had something typed. He made me read it and read it and read it. Then they said I had to go to the police the next day. And that's what I told the police.'

'You don't really think Mr Matheson hurt Elena Mancini, do you, Miss Dabrowska?'

Aitken objected, but the judge said she could answer. She made herself stop sobbing for a few moments. She shook her head. 'Justin was with me,' she said faintly. 'Justin was with me.'

Tanner paused. It was almost done. 'The apartment in London. Who bought it?'

'I don't know.'

'You must have some idea?'

'When – when I got back to London, I had some numbers to call. I rang when I knew I was pregnant. I met a man.'

'What man?'

'He never said his name. Not once.'

'And?'

'And he asked me to have an abortion.' There was a new wave of anger and tears. 'He said they would pay me.'

'Who?'

'Who do you think?'

'I don't know, Miss Dabrowska. You have to tell us.'

'I don't know.'

'You said you wouldn't have an abortion?'

'Yes, I said that!'

'And then?'

'Then . . . later they told me what to say about my ear.'

'Who is "they"?'

'There were two of them. Only one spoke whenever we met.'

'And the apartment?'

'I told them they had to help my family. That's what they promised. They said it would be property, not money. They said Dad could leave his share to my brother and sister if he wanted.'

'And this was so you wouldn't say the baby was Mr Matheson's, and so you would say to this court what they told you to?'

'Yes.'

Tanner paused, then looked at the judge. 'There's more I could ask, your Honour, but that can be someone else's job.'

Aitken asked Klaudia Dabrowska one question in re-examination – whether she'd told the police the truth when interviewed, or whether she'd now told the truth to the jury. She said she'd told the jury the truth, and he let it go. When he sat down, Tanner said he'd apply for a directed verdict in the morning. The judge asked Aitken to formulate the Crown's position by no later than three that afternoon, and to convey it to Tanner. He then adjourned the court.

*

When Tanner, Porter and Jane Ross walked into the interview room to wait for Matheson to be brought to them, Ross slammed the door behind them.

'Why didn't you fucking tell us?'

'Because you would have said we had to tell the client.'

'And why would that be wrong, Pete?'

'Because he might have stopped me. Because he might have pleaded guilty to something he didn't do.'

'Shouldn't that be up to him?'

Tanner shrugged. 'No.'

'But you –' She stopped when the door opened. Justin Matheson was brought in by a sheriff's officer, and looked like he might take a swing at all of them.

'Before you say anything, Justin,' Tanner said, 'Charles and Jane didn't know.'

'You found out through that investigator?' Matheson said. He stood, facing Tanner directly.

'Yes.'

'The fucking investigator my parents paid for?'

'Yes.'

'And you didn't tell me?'

'I didn't tell you.'

The muscles in Matheson's jaw bulged, and his right fist was clentched. 'Do you – do you know what you've done? My wife had to fucking sit through that. My fucking parents – do you know what you've done?'

'I've got you off a murder charge, Justin. That's what I've done.'

'You arrogant fuck. How could you not tell me?'

Tanner picked up a folder from the table. 'I'm going to apply for a directed verdict in the morning, Justin. That's where the judge tells the jury they have to find you not guilty. I'm going to prepare for it now. If the prosecutor tells me it won't be opposed, I'll send Jane up this afternoon to apply for unconditional bail. I imagine you'll get it.'

He stood still, watching Matheson, knowing he had to walk past him to get out the door.

'Answer the fucking question!' Matheson yelled. 'How could you not tell me?'

Tanner said nothing.

'Can you answer me? Why make Sarah go through that, you arsehole?'

'I didn't fuck Amanda Weatherill or Deborah Edelman,' Tanner said calmly. 'You did. And you had coke with your mate Jack Richter the night a young woman got her brains smashed in while you fucked someone else and got them pregnant. *You* made Sarah go through that, not me. I didn't hire myself to defend you. No part of my role is to worry about your marriage. You hired me to get you an acquittal. I've done my job. Now unclench your fucking fist, and get out of my way.'

Matheson glared at Tanner for a little longer, but the anger left his eyes.

Tanner brushed past him and left the room.

55

In any criminal trial, a duty falls on the judge to direct an acquittal if the prosecution hasn't led evidence that could sustain a guilty verdict at the close of its case.

When Tanner sat down from making such a submission to Justice Philip Knight, Richard Aitken rose and told the judge that the application was not opposed. The Crown had called John Richter to give evidence, and it had called Klaudia Dabrowska: they couldn't both be telling the truth. Having made further inquiries with Miss Dabrowska yesterday, the Crown no longer had confidence in its prosecution.

The judge accepted the arguments of the defence, for the reasons it proffered. He asked the court officer to get the jury back in.

'Members of the jury,' he began, 'having heard argument this morning, I have reached the conclusion that the evidence as it stands could not establish the ingredients of the offences with which the accused is charged. I am now going to ask you to return a verdict of not guilty. As a matter of law, you must follow my ruling.' He paused to check that they'd understood him.

'Madam Forewoman, do you, in accordance with my direction, find the accused Justin William Matheson, not guilty of the murder of Elena Mancini? Please stand and respond.'

The forewoman rose from her seat. 'Yes, your Honour,' she said. 'Not guilty.'

'And in accordance with my direction, do you find the accused not guilty of the manslaughter of Elena Mancini?'

'Yes. Not guilty.'

The judge discharged the jury from further service, with the thanks of the court. His associate took her pen, and on the back of the indictments for murder and manslaughter wrote the words *not guilty*, and then the date and time. She handed it to the judge to initial and date himself.

The judge then looked over at Matheson in the dock. 'You're free to go, Mr Matheson,' he said. He adjourned the court, and the show was over.

Justin Matheson left with his parents without speaking to Tanner or the other lawyers. He'd hired a media spokesman, who was waiting for him in the foyer of the court to address the press.

'It's customary to thank your legal team if you get an acquittal,' Tanner said to Jane Ross, still sitting in his seat at the bar table as the court emptied. 'Do you think that's happening out there at the moment?'

'No.'

'Have you seen Sarah Matheson? The least we can do is recommend Sally Cook to her, isn't it?'

Jane shook her head. 'Jesus, Pete.'

As she spoke, Charles Porter poked his head inside the court door, and then walked over to where they were sitting. He pulled over what had been Aitken's chair, and sat. 'The Mathesons have told me they want to make a complaint to the bar.'

Tanner shrugged. 'I don't think you'll find many lawyers being sanctioned for failing to tell their client they'd become a father again.'

'You should have told us, Peter.'

'You would have told him.'

Porter nodded. 'I'll try and talk them out of it.'

'Thanks. And I appreciate your assistance throughout this case, even if you did say at the beginning I wasn't your first choice.'

'I said the clients wanted someone else.'

'Justin would still be unaware of the birth of his third child if you'd retained their first choice.'

'I'll put it to him that way when I ask them to forget about the complaint,' Porter said.

When he returned to his chambers, colleagues drifted into Tanner's room to congratulate him, wanting to talk about the trial. He got rid of them quickly, and took a cab home.

When he heard the front door open at about four, Tanner walked out of his study and saw Dan heading into his room. Tom Cable walked in just after the boy, followed by Karl.

'Dan all right?' Tanner asked his father.

The old man glared at him, shook his head, then walked past him to the back of the house.

The boy had thrown his bag in a corner, tie already on the ground, and laptop on. He looked up when Tanner walked in. He sat in his big red chair, legs stretched out, crossed at the ankles. They looked longer than last time Tanner had noticed them. 'Hi,' the boy said casually, as though his father was there every afternoon when he got home from school. 'You won?'

'Yeah.'

'I thought so.'

'Why?'

'You look like you won.'

'What's that mean?'

'You've got that look.'

'What look is that?'

'Not like you won Wimbledon or anything, but . . . like you beat someone at something.'

'I guess I did.'

'Did the other guy kill her?' Dan said, sounding too casual for Tanner's liking. 'The rich guy?'

'I think that's likely.'

'Has he been arrested?'

'One day.'

'Will they get him for murder?'

'I don't know. Maybe it was an accident.'

Dan nodded.

'What are you looking at?'

Dan shook his head, and looked back at the screen. 'I'm in the school's system, Dad. I'm looking at my assignment.'

'You want something to eat?'

'Sure.'

Tanner turned to go to the kitchen.

'You told me once that not all rich people are bad,' Dan said.

'I did?'

'I don't remember why, but you told me that.'

'I was wrong.'

Dan looked up from the screen, a crooked smile on his face. 'Seriously?'

'Yes.'

'Was your client happy?'

'Not really.'

'I didn't think so,' Dan said.

'Why?'

'Tom had the radio on this morning. A man said something about him having a baby with a witness.' He looked up, and Tanner nodded. 'His wife's going to be angry, right?'

'She's more likely to be . . . vengeful.'

Dan nodded, then paused, like he was thinking about something, or wondering if he should say it. 'I remember Mum once was vengeful with you.'

Tanner looked at him, partly amazed at the segue, and yet not surprised at all. 'Not like this.'

'You forgot to get me from preschool. You said you thought Granddad was. When you got home, I remember her yelling.'

'You can remember that?'

'That's the only time I can remember her yelling at you.'

'She was very forgiving.'

'I bet.'

Tanner paused, not sure what to say next.
'Are you happy?' Dan said.
'What?'
'About the trial. You don't look happy.'
'I though you said I looked like I won.'
'Yeah, but you don't look happy.'
'Why wouldn't I be?'
The boy raised his eyebrows. 'You tell me.'

56

'It felt like you were avoiding me,' Lisa said. They were sitting on the steps that led down to the backyard at the rear of Tanner's house. It was dark, but still warm. Winter had ended, spring had been skipped. 'At least until you called on Monday night.'

'I was.'

'Why?'

'Short temper. Unremitting anxiety.'

'Is this during every trial, or just this one?'

'Most.'

'That's not healthy.'

He nodded. 'This is a litigator's life. Anxiety, trial. Anxiety, trial. Anxiety, trial. Retirement. Near immediate death follows.'

'Maybe you should try something else?'

'No.'

She narrowed her eyes. 'Is that because you feel so good now that you've won?'

'Now that I've won,' he said, picking up a piece of pizza from a box, 'I feel hungry.'

'Can we talk about Anne Warren's report now?' Lisa asked after the others had gone to bed. They were sitting on a couch, finishing a bottle of wine.

'Is tomorrow okay?' he said. 'I need to decompress tonight.'

'I'd like to tell my client.'

Tanner put his glass on the coffee table and sat up straight to look at her. 'We didn't get it legally, Lisa. We lose control once we go beyond –'

'She's the president of the Bageeyn Action Group, Pete. She won't –'

'We have to decide what we're going to do with it before we share it.'

Lisa picked up her wine. 'We have to get it out there, Pete. We can try to challenge the water and ecology evidence all we like if the mine gets approved, but Warren could blow them out of the water before it gets a green light.'

'There will still be a gold mine, Lisa. It just won't be Citadel.'

'Hey,' she said, her tone sharp, 'what happened to fighting the fights we can win? We can only defeat one enemy at a time. At the moment it's Citadel. We can't wait for long, Pete.'

'We're not going to change the world with one report.'

'Don't talk to me like I'm a child.'

'You told me when I first met you that these people were criminals, Lisa,' he said. 'Now I know.'

'And that's why I don't understand why we're not talking to the police right now. It's why I don't understand why we haven't already given Anne's and Gaby's reports to –'

'There's another thing,' he said. 'Joe's sentencing – it's next month. We have to sit on Warren until after that.'

'Why?'

'Why?' he said more loudly than he intended. 'There's a state-owned Chinese company involved in this, not just Citadel. We can't do anything that might make things worse for him. Leaking this report might get him more jail time. It might – We have to wait until he's been sentenced. That's non-negotiable, Lisa. We have to.'

She looked at him for a few moments, and then nodded. 'We can't wait longer than that, Pete. I've got an obligation to my client. So do you.'

He nodded slowly. 'It's only a month.'

She took a sip of wine, and looked up at the ceiling. 'I want to screw these bastards,' she said. 'Don't you?'

He leant back and tried to smile. 'How badly do you want to do that?'

'What do you mean?'

'You're a class action specialist, aren't you?'

She nodded.

'Can you help me with a pleading for one?'

She raised her head. 'A pleading?'

He picked up his glass and took a sip. 'Something that looks like it could be filed here, or in the States – or even in Europe,' he said. 'Anywhere there's a representative actions scheme.'

'What are we alleging?'

'Catastrophic pollution. Unlawful killing. Fraud leading to the loss of investors' money and shareholders' equity.'

She raised an eyebrow. 'Sounds intriguing.'

'I'll do you a note setting out a series of facts tomorrow. Some we can prove. Others we can't. All of them true.'

57

Tanner scheduled the meeting for three pm, in a conference room at the Grand Hyatt in Shanghai. He'd been told Citadel's and North Shanxi's lawyers would be there, but not their Chinese directors.

The day before, Tanner had contacted Dennis Jackson to find out where he was staying. By nine on the day of the meeting, Tanner had couriered to him two large folders of documents. The document behind tab one in the first folder was the report by Anne Warren on the spill into the Tovosevu River from the tailings dam of Citadel's gold mine on the island. Tab two contained a report from Gabriella Campbell on the probable water impacts of the proposed gold mine near Bageeyn River. The documents that followed were confidential Citadel internal documents concerning both reports.

Behind tab twenty-eight were newspaper clippings reporting the death of Elena Mancini, and the trial and acquittal of Justin Matheson. Tab twenty-nine contained press reports about Anne Warren's death, and tab thirty covered the overdose of Nikki Richter.

The last document was a draft class action proceeding, which nominated unnamed investors and shareholders as plaintiffs. The defendants were Citadel Resources, North Shanxi, their various directors, Hendrik Richter, John Richter and the one thousand three hundred and twenty-seven partners of the law firm Bloomberg Butler Kelly.

Lisa Ilves had divided the draft claim into various chapters. The first listed the pending applications that Citadel and North Shanxi had, in joint venture or separately, for mining project approvals around the globe. These included Bageeyn River, the Upper Hunter Valley, and proposed CSG mines in northern New South Wales and Queensland. The next chapter outlined all of the public statements the companies had issued concerning the projects, and what they meant for their financial futures.

The third chapter of the pleading was headed in bold 'Cover-Up And Non-Disclosure Of Cyanide Spill At Tovosevu Gold Mine'. Lisa used Warren's report to outline the spill, and the damage done to the river. The section ended with an allegation linking Citadel with Warren's death.

The fourth chapter was headed 'Bageeyn River Project'. It detailed the burying of Campbell's report, and the corrupting of other experts in order to deceive various government departments in the process of seeking project approval for a gold mine.

The fifth chapter pleaded a conspiracy to have Joseph Cheung arrested and charged with a corruption offence on false grounds. It alleged that the arrest of Cheung, and the charges against him, had been made in order to ensure his silence regarding the matters pertaining to both the reports of Campbell and Warren.

It was then alleged that Elena Mancini had been murdered by John Richter, and that Nikki Richter had been murdered by or on behalf of John and Hendrik Richter. It was alleged that partners of the firm Bloomberg Butler Kelly had aided and abetted the other defendants in the criminal activities pleaded.

The penultimate chapter of the pleading contained a hypothetical damages claim. Each of the events particularised in the preceding chapters commencing with the Tovosevu cyanide spill were assumed to have caused all mine project applications to be rejected. This in turn caused a loss of future profits, and a decrease in Citadel's share price, and that of its joint-venture partner. The hypothetical class of plaintiffs were entitled to damages likely to be measured in the billions as a result of the consequences of the actions of the companies, its executives and directors.

As a footnote to the pleading, a warning was put that as the allegations were founded on dishonesty, fraud, and other acts of a criminal nature – as distinct from negligence – the pleaded events would be excluded from any insurance policies held by the directors and officers of the companies, who were also named as defendants.

When Tanner walked into the meeting room, he found one end of the table had been left vacant. At the head of the far end, Hedley Fontaine, global CEO of BBK, sat next to Andre Visser, Hendrik Richter's long-serving lieutenant. Next to Visser was Robert Spry, Citadel's global general counsel, and opposite him was BBK's Australian CEO, Dennis Jackson. There were six other lawyers seated at the table. Four of them were from two large American firms, who were acting for North Shanxi and XinCoal. The other two were lawyers for the same companies from Chinese firms. Lastly, sitting in a chair in the far corner of the room, but not at the conference table, was Yinshi Li.

'You're not joining us, Mr Li?' Tanner said when he sat down.

Li stood, and almost bowed. 'Thank you for the documents, Mr Tanner,' he said. 'I have not read them.'

Tanner smiled. 'There's plenty of room at my end of the table, Li.'

Li shook his head and walked to the door. 'For this meeting,' he said softly, 'it will be best if I'm not here.'

'How did you get these documents?' It was Hedley Fontaine who began. He had a commanding voice: deep, with a hint of gravel. He'd kept his suit jacket on, and his tie was perfectly knotted. Like most men who end up CEOs, Tanner thought, he looked like he'd had a father with a very big study, and a very small heart.

'I'm not telling you, Hedley,' Tanner said.

'You've committed a number of criminal offences already,' Fontaine said. 'I'm only asking once more. How did you get them?'

'As criminals go, I'm the lightweight in the room.'

'You've been involved in the theft of property which is owned by my client and my law firm, Mr Tanner. We intend to have you prosecuted for that.'

'If you think that will help your client, then you're the dumbest guy in the room.'

'My client will sue you, Mr Tanner, and so will my firm. We will be unrelenting.'

'I'm sure the families of Anne Warren and Nikki Richter wish your client had only sued them.'

'You can entertain yourself with these ludicrous fantasies if you want. You won't have anything soon.'

Tanner turned his gaze from Fontaine to Visser, noticing that he was looking across the table, but not at the North Shanxi lawyer opposite him. He was looking beyond him, beyond the wall of the room. Into the near future, or the long gone past.

'I'm not feeling like being entertained,' Tanner said. 'I don't want to dance.'

Fontaine narrowed his eyes. 'You don't want to dance?' he said with mock incredulity.

'I'm not dancing with you, Hedley,' Tanner said slowly. 'I'm not dancing with your client, or with the law firms of these other gentlemen. I'm not here to negotiate.'

'When I said my client will –'

'John Richter killed Elena Mancini. Who knows about his wife? Anne Warren wasn't killed in a robbery. Your client had her bashed to death, and then burnt. You act for the worst of the worst, Hedley. I've acted for unlucky fools and dead-beats. I've appeared for some – some very, very sick bastards. People who don't deserve life. I've still done my best for them. I've never known where I would draw the line. I know now. I'd draw the line at Citadel.'

'You don't have anything but illegally obtained –'

'No elected government is going to grant a mine approval to a company that just flushed a few hundred thousand litres of cyanide down a river and tried to hide it. And the name

Richter – that's not a vote winner either. Here's the future for your client. Think Richter, think killer. Think Citadel, think cyanide. It doesn't matter how I got these reports. When people start to lose money because of your client, they won't be looking to blame me. If you were the smartest guy in the room, you'd stop the bullshit. You'd work out what your strength is, and then play to it. I'm going to say it again because I like it – Think Richter, think killer. Think Citadel, think cyanide.'

Fontaine stared at Tanner as a broad, false smile appeared on his face, like an animator had drawn it. 'We won't just sue you, Mr Tanner. We will be calling in investigators, the Chinese police, the FBI –'

'If I was one of your client's partners, Hedley,' Tanner said, 'if I was North Shanxi – I'd run a million miles from Citadel right now. I'd be blaming it for the shit everyone's in.'

'You're not listening to me. We –'

'Shut up,' Andre Visser said.

It was the first time Tanner had heard him speak. He was not making a request. He was giving a command.

Visser looked at Tanner for the first time. 'I've read the material you sent us, Mr Tanner,' he then said. 'Thank you for the courtesy.'

'My pleasure.'

'I have two questions for you,' he said slowly. 'What do you want? And what are you offering for it?'

Tanner looked at Visser and smiled, before scanning the rest of the men in the room. 'Now I know who the smartest guy in the room is,' Tanner said. 'Shall we send everyone else home?'

'What do you want, Mr Tanner?'

'I want you to speak to your Chinese partners.'

'And what do you want me to tell them?'

'I want them to speak to the government. And I want the government to speak to its prosecutors.'

'And?'

'And I want Joe Cheung here, with his passport, before the flight to Sydney leaves tomorrow night.'

Visser raised his eyebrows just a fraction. A look of vague amusement came over his face. 'Is that all?'

Tanner shook his head. 'He bought his wife a watch before you arranged to have him deprived of his liberty. I'd like that too.'

Visser took in a deep breath, and sighed. A look that simultaneously conveyed respect and contempt came over his face. 'What are you offering us?'

Tanner smiled, and shook his head. 'I haven't finished telling you what I want, Andre,' he said. 'When I'm done, I'll tell you what I'm offering.'

58

'We just got back from the playground,' Melissa Cheung said after kissing Tanner on the cheek. 'Joe's out the back.'

He followed her inside and out to the kitchen. He could see Cheung playing with his youngest child on the lawn, pretending to mow it with a plastic mower.

'Who mowed the lawn when Joe was away?' he asked.

'The same guy who did it before he left,' she said. 'Joe's dad.'

The sliding doors opened, and Cheung walked in, but the child stayed outside to complete her mowing.

'Summer's here,' Cheung said, wiping his brow.

Melissa put a plate of biscuits on the table.

Tanner picked one up and looked at it. 'Tim Tams,' he said. He looked at Cheung. 'Did they have these in Qingpu?'

Cheung smiled faintly and shook his head.

'I meant to ask you last time,' Tanner said, looking at Melissa's hand as she poured some tea. 'Did you get the watch back?'

'No.'

'Did BBK give you a gold one as a retirement gift?'

'They've put my money in our account,' he said. 'We can live without the watch.'

'You've signed all the documents?' Tanner asked.

Both of them nodded.

'I hope not being allowed to say the word "cyanide" for the rest of your lives won't cause a problem?'

Cheung sighed. 'My memoir about my year in a Chinese prison could've been a bestseller.'

Cheung had not been released by the night following the meeting at the Grand Hyatt. There was a bureaucracy to get through, so it took three weeks. The prosecutor's office released a press statement when he was freed, which came out by prior agreement with government officials from both sides only after Cheung's flight back to Australia had landed in Sydney. *Due to a change of witness testimony, the charges of corruption against Australian citizen Joseph Cheung will no longer be pursued*, the statement said. No further explanation was given. Cheung's Chinese lawyer, Yinshi Li, had no comment to make, other than he was pleased that his client would now be reunited with his family.

BBK put out its own statement, welcoming the news, and saying Mr Cheung would be taking a leave of absence while he recovered from his ordeal. The Australian Government was only able to say that it had been provided with no information from Chinese authorities beyond that contained in the press statement issued by the prosecutors, and that it would be seeking an apology on Mr Cheung's behalf if he requested such assistance. Compensation wasn't necessary – Tanner had seen to that during the meeting.

'Have you thought more about what you'll do?'

Cheung shook his head slowly. 'I don't want to go straight back to the law. I need to – this will sound strange – maybe it's because I was confined for a year, but I feel like I need to do something physical.'

Tanner nodded. 'You could join Dennis Jackson's cycling group.'

Cheung smiled. 'I don't think so.'

'I'm planning on running him over soon anyway.'

As he spoke, there was a cry from outside. Lily had started mowing the brick pavers under the pergola, and had fallen over and banged her head. Melissa ran out to inspect the damage.

'I still want to know what you did, Peter,' Cheung said.

'I told you,' Tanner said. 'I pleaded with the Chinese that corruption in relation to the grant of mining approvals in Australia was compulsory. I said your actions were based on cultural misunderstanding.'

'I'd like to know, Pete. For my own piece of mind.'

'I agreed to keep my mouth shut, Joe. It'll cost me if I don't.'

'I'm only asking you to tell me.'

'You weren't an exclusion.'

'I got Gabriella sacked,' Cheung said. He looked out through the glass, at his wife comforting their child. 'And I got Anne Warren killed.'

'That's crazy talk –'

'I told Citadel Gaby had gone outside GreenDay. Anne sent her report to me. I told them they had to disclose what had happened as part of their new applications for mines. I warned them that Anne would disclose it herself if they waited much longer. She was dead soon after.'

Tanner leant forwards. 'I'm the lawyer who's entitled to assume my clients are killers, Joe.'

Cheung shook his head. 'I should have spoken out myself.'

'You would have,' Tanner said. 'That's why they had you arrested.'

'I let them go ahead on Bageeyn River with Gaby Campbell's report buried in my files,' Cheung said, a sad smile on his face. 'Do you know when it occurred to me that was the wrong thing to do?'

'Joe, you can't –'

'Do you?' he said, his voice louder. 'It was when I was in prison, Pete. That's when I realised I was guilty. Not of what they were saying I'd done. Of something worse.'

'Joe –'

'Everything okay?' Melissa returned, Lily in her arms, the tears now quelled.

'Joe was thanking me again,' Tanner said. 'I told him he has to stop it. Besides, I've been paid.'

'Paid?' she said.

He nodded.

'By who?'

'I sent a bill to BBK.'

'Is that the truth?'

'It covered disbursements. It was part of my private discussions with Visser.'

'Are you surprised? That they paid?'

Tanner shook his head and looked at Joe Cheung. 'The really guilty should have to pay, don't you think?'

59

'Why did you insist on here?' Lisa asked when she sat down. They were at a café in Queens Park that stood on one side of the various fields that hosted soccer games and cricket matches.

'I'm working at home today,' Tanner said.

She nodded, but didn't smile. She hadn't kissed him hello. 'You didn't return my calls last week.'

'You got my texts?'

'I'm not a sixteen-year-old girl,' she said sharply.

'I'm sorry,' he said. 'I had some issues to work through with Joe. His partnership exit, what releases he had to sign, that kind of thing.'

Her expression stayed blank. 'Are you going to tell me what's happening?'

Tanner leant back while the waitress put down his coffee. Then he met Lisa's eyes. 'We can't use Anne Warren's report,' he said. 'And we can't use Gaby Campbell's.'

Her face showed not so much surprise, as expected loss. He thought that she must have feared he'd say those words. 'What are you talking about?'

'They're going to scale back the gold mine. They're cutting production each year until they work out how to use less water. They won't kill the river.'

She pushed her cup out of the way and leant forwards. 'They poured cyanide and heavy metals down a river. We can't just let them –'

'They've cleaned a lot of that up. They're going to stop using cyanides.'

'Are you their spokesman now?'

'I understand you're going to be upset. You have to –'

'You *understand*?' Her voice cracked a little as it rose. 'Those reports weren't just going to stop Bageeyn River, they can stop all their mines.'

'Someone else will dig that gold up if it's not them.'

She shook her head, and her mouth contracted in anger. 'We can stop *this* company.' The café was nearly full, and the people at the tables near them stopped talking and looked over.

'You can't,' he said.

She glared at him for a few moments. Tears welled in her eyes.

'I had to give those reports up,' he said. 'They were what I had. To get Joe, I had to give them up.'

'You used me.'

'We weren't in court, Lisa. There is no winner and loser. I settled with these people. We reached a compromise. I got Joe. They got their reports. I had to give something.'

'Fuck you,' she said, and as she spoke two slow tears were replaced by many more. 'You can't stop me, Peter. You can't shut my clients up. You can't . . .' She put a hand to her mouth, and used the other hand to shield her eyes.

'You can't do that, Lisa,' he said when she'd almost stopped crying.

'I can do what I want.'

'Listen to me,' he said. 'The deal I made is not one that can be broken.'

She sneered at him. 'What? They're going to kill us, Pete?'

He shook his head. 'They came to my home, Lisa. You know them. This is not a deal that you break. Not with these people.'

They sat in silence.

'I helped you,' she finally said. There was more grief in her tone than anger. 'With Anne. Finding Gaby. All of that was to stop them. That was our deal.'

He wanted to take her hand, but dared not try. 'I'm a criminal lawyer, Lisa. My job was to save Joe, not a river. I'm sorry about how that sounds.'

'What about your duty to my client?'

'Did you expect me to leave him in prison?'

'There may have been a way to –'

'There was no other way,' he said. 'This was the way. Did you want me to leave him there? These are not people you make unhappy.'

'I wanted you to tell me the truth,' she said. He voice was louder again. 'You didn't trust me with that.' She closed her eyes and shook her head, then threw the strap of her satchel over her shoulder and stood.

'I'm sorry,' he said.

She pushed her chair behind her to leave.

'Look in the playground before you go,' he said.

'What?'

'Look in the playground, Lisa.'

She stared at him, then left.

Lisa walked out of the café by the door that faced the street. When she got to her car, she took out her keys and unlocked it, put her hand on the door handle, and then stopped. She turned her head, and looked back towards the park. A child's playground was in front of her.

In the corner of the playground a man was pushing a small, black-haired child on a swing. He was looking in her direction.

She'd never seen him before, but she knew who he was.

ACKNOWLEDGEMENTS

First, thanks to Tara Wynne, my agent at Curtis Brown Australia, who worked with me on a very long first draft.

My colleague David Staehli SC read a slightly shorter draft. Any mistakes in this book concerning criminal procedure, the architecture of the criminal mind, or the admissibility of evidence are his.

Sincere thanks to the team at Simon & Schuster Australia, especially Fiona Henderson, Roberta Ivers, Larissa Edwards and to my editor Kylie Mason – this novel benefited greatly from her judgement and the attention she gave it.

Finally, thanks to my wife Trish for her limitless support and encouragement with another book.

Richard Beasley

If you enjoyed Peter Tanner in *Cyanide Games*,
you'll love *The Burden of Lies*,
coming to a bookstore near you in December 2017.